The Sunday Spy

ALSO BY WILLIAM HOOD

Mole

Spy Wednesday

Cry Spy

The Sunday Spy

WILLIAM HOOD

A Novel

W. W. Norton & Company
New York London

PRINTED IN THE UNITED STATES OF AMERICA

First Edition

The activities described in this book are entirely imaginary. No character is derived from any living person, and there are no hidden clues or sly puns that might allow a canny reader to match any imagined character to a living person. For better or otherwise, there is no element of American intelligence that much resembles "the Firm."

The text of this book is composed in New Caledonia with the display set in Helvetica.
Composition by Crane Typesetting Service, Inc.
Manufacturing by Courier Companies, Inc.
Book design by Jack Meserole.

Library of Congress Cataloging-in-Publication Data
Hood, William, 1920–
The Sunday spy : a novel / William Hood.
p. cm.
ISBN 0-393-03937-4
I. Title.
PS3558.O545S86 1996
813′.54—dc20 95-38609

W. W. Norton & Company, Inc., 500 Fifth Avenue, New York, N.Y. 10110
http://web.wwnorton.com
W. W. Norton & Company, Ltd., 10 Coptic Street, London WC1A 1PU

1 2 3 4 5 6 7 8 9 0

for John Bross and Edward Grainger

As always, with special thanks to Mary Carr

Go search for people who are hurt by fate or nature . . . those suffering from an inferiority complex, craving power and influence but defeated by unfavorable circumstances. . . . In cooperation with us, all of these find a peculiar compensation—a sort of secret compensation. . . . The sense of belonging to an influential, powerful organization will give them a feeling of superiority over the handsome and prosperous people around them. . . .

—Attributed to General Pavel Sudoplatov, KGB
(Nikolai Khokhlov, *In the Name of the Conscience;*
New York: David McKay Company, 1959)

The

Sunday

Spy

1

NEW YORK, AUGUST 1991

"How on earth did you come upon this place?" The diplomat peered peevishly along the dimly lighted bar, and into the empty restaurant at the rear. He paused to scowl at a collection of framed book jackets interspersed with scattered photographs of race horses and baseball players on the wall beside the booths.

"I tried to think of something convenient for you, close to the U.N., but far enough away so you're not likely to be bothered by anyone you know . . ." Charlotte Mills's voice trailed off as she noticed his grim expression.

The diplomat eased himself into the booth. "Until you telephoned, I didn't even know the Department had assigned you to New York, and the U.N. mission."

"I've been here ever since I got back from Moscow . . ."

The diplomat cocked his head slightly and said, "As pleased as I am to see you again, Miss Mills—it is Charlotte, isn't it?—this might have been more convenient and looked less like an assignation if you'd just dropped by the eleventh floor and told the secretary you'd like to say hello."

"I knew this would be a terrible nuisance for you, but I didn't know what to do . . ."

He raised his eyebrows, acknowledging her remark. "I don't mean to seem impolite, but I've had the very devil of a day, and I've got to get the shuttle back to Washington in time for a working dinner tonight." He managed a tight smile. "In truth, I can't imagine what prompted you to telephone me at the hotel . . ."

"I telephoned you because I'm being blackmailed," she said, her soft voice breaking.

"You're *what*?"

The diplomat turned to glare at the waitress brushing against the corner of the booth. "You want menus?" she asked.

"I should think *not*," the diplomat said. "Just an aperitif." He looked more closely at Charlotte, wondering how much she might already have had to drink. "Unless you'd prefer something more solid, a sandwich?"

"Just a drink," she said. "Stoli on the rocks . . ."

"A dry sherry," the diplomat said. "Tio Pepe if you have it."

The waitress sniffed and turned away.

"I *hated* to bother you," Charlotte said. "If I weren't desperate, I'd never have had the courage to telephone . . ." Her eyes watered as she rummaged in her handbag for a handkerchief.

"Until two minutes ago I thought I'd heard just about every problem the distaff help can conceivably get themselves into," he said. "This is a new experience, but I can assure you that you've got my undivided attention."

"It's just that when I saw your name on the visitor list, I remembered how much you knew about the Russians, and how kind you were to me in Moscow."

The diplomat made a dismissive gesture and glanced at the barman and waitress huddled near the cash register.

"I've got myself in terrible, terrible trouble," she said, dabbing at her eyes with a lipstick-stained handkerchief. "I don't know where to turn . . ."

"The sooner you can give me some notion of what this is all about, the more time we'll have to deal with it."

Now Charlotte glanced anxiously around the bar. Looking flushed and sticky, she had let her linen jacket fall in a heap beside her on the banquette.

"Did I hear you correctly?" he said, lowering his voice to a whisper.

Charlotte nodded. "I think so."

"Why on earth would anyone want to *blackmail* you?"

The waitress lingered for a moment before sliding both glasses in front of the diplomat. "I think I'll just leave the drinks here, you can sort them out yourselves."

"Thank you," he said.

"You want to run a tab, or pay me now?"

"Later, if you please . . ." He turned to Charlotte. "Now, tell me about it."

Charlotte watched as the waitress made her way back to the cash register. "You remember when we were in Moscow together?"

"Not quite *together*," he said quickly. "As I recall it, you were one of the embassy secretaries helping to shepherd the delegation I was with when we were visiting Gorbachev in the early days."

Charlotte nodded. "I was the senior administrative assistant."

He remembered her as a plain, muffin-faced woman. She was still plain, but now seemed badly worn as well. Her jacket was not clean, her mouse-brown hair was messy, and such makeup as she had applied did not hide the circles under her eyes. The diplomat took a sip of sherry. He lowered his eyes and glanced quickly at his watch. "Now, what about this trouble you say you're in?"

Charlotte leaned forward, elbows on the table, her fingers pressed against her brow. "About the time you were in Moscow, I got involved with this Russian," she said. "We began seeing one another. Right off, on our first date at the museum, he warned me that the embassy would send me home if I told the security people I had found a Russian friend." She dabbed at her eyes before saying, "You remember, we were all supposed to file a memorandum on any locals we met?"

"That's cold-war stuff," he said. "You wouldn't have been sent home unless the fellow was known to our security people as a bad hat. Who is he?"

"An actor. At least he said he was an actor at MosFilm and maybe some other place. But I never saw him act or anything."

"What's his name?"

She took a deep breath before saying, "That doesn't matter now. Despite all the promises, I've never heard a word from him since . . ." Her voice trailed off.

"Since when?" the diplomat asked.

"Since a few weeks after we'd been seeing each other—that was when he told me he'd been arrested for consorting with a foreigner and that the security people had pictures of us together. He even showed me the photographs. They had everything, mostly things I don't even want to remember. He said the police tried to make him believe that I was a spy, and that they were going to charge me with corrupting a Russian citizen."

"Really, Miss Mills . . ."

"He said if I'd agree to meet his lawyer and a security man, we might be able to talk them out of pressing charges. Dumbo me, I believed him. He took me to what he said was the lawyer's apartment. Along with the lawyer, if he really was a lawyer, there were *three* security guys. The lawyer and Yuri argued a little, but in the end the security people said the only way I could avoid a scandal would be if I cooperated. If I didn't, Yuri would go to jail, and they would send the photographs to everyone—the embassy, the newspapers, and even my family, just to prove I was a spy and to keep anyone else from trying what I did."

"Come on, Charlotte, they stopped that stuff years ago . . ."

"That's what you think. I know different." Tears ran down her face. "Maybe the people you know believe that, and today maybe even Yeltsin does. But I know different. Those terrible people live in their own world. They don't care a damn about anything else."

The diplomat shook his head. "I find this very hard to believe."

"When they said they'd send the pictures to my mother, to the rest of the family, I knew for sure that the whole thing was a fake and that I'd been set up. They had my sister's address in Detroit, and toward the end, even showed me a picture of my mother coming out of our house in Bethesda . . ."

"Charlotte, for God's sake. I really can't believe this . . ."

"It's true, every word." She buried her face in her handkerchief.

The diplomat glanced around the bar as if he were worried that someone might mistake their meeting for a romantic tryst gone wrong. No one was watching.

"Didn't you tell anyone—the security office, your section chief, anyone?"

"No."

"In heaven's name, why not? We'd have had you out of Moscow overnight, and no one would ever have known what happened."

Charlotte stuffed the soggy handkerchief back into her handbag. "They said they would send the pictures the minute I told anyone in the embassy."

"If you had told someone, the ambassador would have raised hell with the Foreign Office and promised a stiff retaliation if the photos were ever leaked. The new Russian administration understands the old days are over."

"Not the people they sicced on me. They were terrible to me. They said that if I told any of our people, they'd know, and they'd mail the photographs before the embassy could take any action with the Foreign Office. Once the pictures were sent, they said, there wouldn't be anything the Foreign Office could do about it."

"But they wouldn't have known you had reported to anyone until the embassy raised a rumpus."

Charlotte shook her head. "That's exactly what I thought, but they told me different and proved it. They showed me Xerox copies of reports right out of our office, with all our security markings and everything—Top Secret, LIMDIS, EXDIS, everything. They said they were getting the documents through official channels. They said they'd let Yuri and me go if I gave them some independent samples of the stuff they were getting officially. All they wanted was confirmation that the papers the embassy was passing to them were the straight stuff, and they wanted me to help explain it all. I couldn't believe this, but I wasn't sure and I was terrified for Yuri and me."

"They could *not* have been getting any such papers," he said. "Surely you know that."

"By the time they finished threatening me, I didn't know what to believe . . ."

"So, you gave them documents?"

Charlotte nodded. "In my head I knew once I started, they'd never let me go, and of course that was the one thing I was right about. But I was half crazy with worry about Yuri."

"And you're still passing them documents?"

Charlotte Mills began to sob.

"Why in heaven's name did you wait so long before telling someone about this?"

"I just couldn't risk them sending anything to my mother. It would have killed her. Now it's different. My mother, God bless her soul, died six weeks ago, right in Washington. They don't know they've lost control because now I don't care a damn what happens to me. I know plenty, and I'll do anything I can to pay them back for what they've done to me."

"Lord Almighty . . ." The diplomat tugged a handkerchief from his pocket and passed it across the table. "Just what is it you expect me to do?"

"I'm going to hurt them any way I can," she said, dabbing at her eyes. "But even so, I can't just tell this story to *anybody*."

The diplomat shook his head. "The correct thing to do is disclose everything to our security people," he said slowly. He waited before saying, "But if you do that, and if the Russians find out that you've confessed as you say they will, I'm afraid you still have to face the fact they will leak the photographs. They'll realize that it will be too late to stop you, but they also know that all the publicity will help convince the next fellow that they really mean what they say."

Charlotte pulled herself closer to the table. "I've got complete notes on everything I did for them, and everything about all of them, and I'm going to hurt them no matter what."

The diplomat frowned and pursed his lips. "What makes you think they'll find out if you talk to security?"

"I don't know, but I can tell you that in Moscow they had every sensitive briefing document our delegation used in the meetings with Yeltsin and his people. I *know* that for a fact—they showed me the papers. You should see the list of stuff they're asking for now on our aid policy, about loans, and what we're saying to the British and Germans about it."

"Just what is it you think I can do?"

"You've got to tell someone high enough up so no one else will have to know about it," Charlotte said. "You're important, you must know someone who's in a position to do something about it quietly." She took a sip of vodka. "I'm not stupid, I have a good memory and I'm a very good secretary. I made complete notes on everything they ever said, and everything they asked me about since 1989. I only want two things. I want to hurt them just as much as I can, and I want to swap my notes and everything to protect my pension. All someone has to do is transfer me to a job where I can work enough more years to qualify for early retirement." She picked up her glass with both hands and drained it.

The diplomat remained silent, his attention fixed on a tobacco-crusted tin ashtray. With a disgusted gesture, he pushed the ashtray to the far corner of the table, and took a sip of sherry. He stared at the photographs on the wall for a few moments before saying slowly, "Now that I think about it, there just may be someone in Washington I might be able to discuss this with . . ."

"Tell him that I'll do anything I can to make things right . . ."

"The trouble is," he said, "I'm going to be out of the country for at least three weeks . . ."

"Tell them they can trust me, that I can pass false documents, tell them lies, anything. They must have some use for people who will do *anything*."

"Even when I get back, I may not be able to see this man right away . . ." He leaned closer to Charlotte. "When are you supposed to see them again?"

"It's once a month, in the reference room at the Forty-second Street library. I've got almost a month before the next meeting."

"Have you told anyone at all about this?"

"No one," she said. "There's no one I dared talk to."

"Did you tell anyone you were meeting me?"

"Of course I didn't," she said. "No one even knows that I know you."

"You've got to promise me two things."

Charlotte nodded. "Anything . . ."

"First, you absolutely must not say a word to anyone about our talk or about your problem until I get back. Promise?"

"I promise . . ."

"Second, from this moment on, you're not to give your contact any information at all—no documents, no oral reports. Nothing. As of right now, you're back on our side, and you're completely under our orders."

Charlotte's broad face brightened with relief. "Like I said, I promise absolutely."

The diplomat looked at his watch. "I really have to go—my driver is waiting and it's hell to get to La Guardia this time of day." He smiled and raised his glass to Charlotte. "There," he said. "Now that you've got it off your chest, the world should look a little better."

She nodded. "I'll never forget this . . ."

"It's only three weeks, but you've got to take care of yourself. Weren't you one of those wellness people, out running around in your BVDs at all hours?"

"Jogging," she said with a slight smile. "I try to keep at it, but lately I just haven't been able to do anything."

"Along with keeping your promises, you've got to perk up, start taking care of yourself, maybe even start jogging again. They say it's good for the psyche too."

"I promise . . ."

"Now, you've got to go," the diplomat said. He pushed his drink aside. "You leave before me. I'll take care of the waitress."

As Charlotte Mills fumbled for her jacket, the diplomat reached across the table and took her hand. "Chin up," he said.

"I knew you would help . . ." She squeezed his hand. "Forever grateful, forever." She pulled on the jacket, and walked quickly to the door.

The diplomat counted his change and computed the tip at precisely twice the tax.

As he left the restaurant, he remembered that Charlotte had forgotten to return his handkerchief. It was one of two dozen he had ordered, the linen so fine his shirtmaker promised he would be able to read his morning newspaper through it.

The handkerchief was gone, but the diplomat could not imagine sacrificing it in a more worthy cause.

2

KEY WEST, AUGUST 1991

From the window Broom watched the courier move slowly along the quiet street.

He walked deliberately, pausing to read the numbers and stepping carefully along the broken pavement of the narrow cement sidewalk. He stopped to peer through the ragged hibiscus hedge in front of the shabby white house, and after checking the hand-painted number on the cement gate post, he pushed the gate open and stepped onto the porch.

It was exactly nine-twenty, the specified time, and of course on neither the hour nor the half-hour. The statue of Iron Felix Dzerzhinsky had been decapitated and dragged from the square in front of the Lubyanka. Western journalists had been escorted into the old Moscow Center offices for a sanitized glimpse of a few archives and the museum, but some things had not changed. It was as if the recent management were convinced that the new offices at Yasenevo would collapse if tradition were broken and an agent were to be met on the hour or half-hour.

"Don't bother with the *parole*," Broom said. "You look authentic enough."

The courier ignored the comment and stepped through the doorway. He glanced into the narrow living room before reciting the prescribed greeting. "I'm a friend of Bruce. He said I should look you up when I got to Key West."

Broom sighed, and said, "Tell Bruce I've missed him."

"It's a real pain in the ass meeting here," the courier said, staring toward the open kitchen beyond the dining table. "To come all this way to meet here, a house fifteen feet from the neighbors and on a narrow street, easy to be blocked. Why couldn't you come to Miami? Make an easy meet in one of the joints on Miami Beach South?"

Broom ignored the question.

The courier sniffed irritably as his eyes adjusted to the light. He had studied the recognition photographs in the file, but Broom looked younger than he had expected. Many case men neglected to update the filed mug shots, and in most of the courier's blind meets the intended contacts looked older, sometimes almost suspiciously older, than the file photographs. Broom was the first to seem younger.

"If you feel you have to run for it, head for the cemetery, just down the street. The fence is quite low." Broom smiled, realizing that it irritated the courier to have missed the chance to spend a few days on special funds while dipping into the high life in a more modish resort than Key West. "It's one of the few cemeteries in the country like this, all the graves above ground. In the big hurricane, they say the sea washed over the tombs, and the coffins floated out and along the street." Broom gestured toward the fence, barely visible on the far side of the narrow street. "But not to worry, there'll be no need to run."

The courier tugged at the collar of his lisle sport shirt. It was a subtle lavender and went well with his pleated linen trousers and blue blazer. He glanced at the overhead fan. "Is it always this hot?"

"It's always this hot all summer long."

"I have letters and bring personal greetings from Vadim Ivanovich Koltsov." He pulled a copy of *Time* magazine from the side pocket of his jacket and passed it across the coffee table. "As always, on page twelve."

The microdots would be imprinted near the binding. The miniature microscopic reading device was concealed in a table cigarette lighter, on the shelf by the heavy wooden easel. There was no one in Moscow, certainly no one from the old days, that Broom could imagine would think to write a personal letter. They would have long since been retired, or sent to some barren, bureaucratic pasture to finish their careers pruning old files, while contemplating writing their memoirs. Broom had never encountered Vadim Koltsov, and could not remember ever having heard his name.

"I know the microdots are a nuisance," the courier said. "We have what the smart-ass Americans call state-of-the-art communications, but because you've been out so long, and there's no time for training right now, the chief agreed to go along with the old system."

Broom nodded, leaving it to the courier to decide whether the gesture was polite or merely tolerant.

The courier's glance held for a moment on the double glass doors leading to a narrow deck, a few feet from the neighboring frame house. "What's a joint like this sell for down here?"

"Maybe two hundred fifty thousand." After noting the courier's surprise, Broom added, "Perhaps even more these days. This is a much more chic part of town than some visitors might imagine."

Broom knew the courier would have studied the briefing notes, and guessed that he had assumed that even in the off-season, Key West would be a cross between the newly stylish South Miami Beach and St. Tropez. Or maybe even Pompeii. Clearly, he had not expected so small an area, or such a jumble of apparently shabby frame houses.

"What the hell do you *do* here?"

"Sometimes I rent rooms—bed and breakfast in winter, in the tourist season. But that can be a bother if I have to travel." This came with a smile, acknowledging that the courier knew about Broom's occasional need to travel. "I also teach sailing, small craft handling, and even cruising, especially for women. It's fashionable these days, all mixed up with the new feminism."

The courier's eyes brightened. "Young women?"

"No, as a rule not very young."

"Too bad . . ."

"And, of course, I paint." It would have been gratifying to mention to the courier, to anyone in fact, the letter just received from an important New York gallery, praising the work and promising a show in early spring. But it would have been pointless to mention it to this philistine. Broom gave him another appraising glance. Perhaps not a philistine. Just a self-centered, Russian yuppie, enthusiastically proud to be shaking off a discredited culture and convinced he had made a faultless transition to the new. Still, to give him his due, he was steps ahead of the comrades of even a few years ago.

As if he had perceived Broom's reaction, the courier got to his feet and stepped to the nearest painting. He stood silently studying the vivid colors and bold, impressionist forms that a few years ago he would surely have thought too crude even to fit Broom's cover as an eccentric amateur artist. "Cézanne?" he asked without turning from the picture.

"If you're suggesting it's a knockoff, it would be more nearly a Matisse," Broom muttered.

"Please, I meant no offense. This is new to me."

He had studied the file, and knew Broom was the grandchild of a general, one of the most respected operatives of the old service, and that Broom was the sole member of the family to have escaped Stalin's fury. It was only by special permission of the unlamented Leonid Ilyich Brezhnev that Broom had been allowed to settle in a climate that did not tax a chronic bronchial weakness.

Broom tossed the magazine into a soft wicker basket that slumped sideways with the pressure of newspapers and art journals beside a canvas director's chair. There would be time enough to recover the microdots. There was no one at Yasenevo, the offices that Broom had never seen, who might write anything of interest, least of all the operations chief of the new service.

"A drink?"

The courier nodded and dropped into one of the canvas sling chairs. As he hitched up his trousers to protect the crease, Broom saw that he wore no socks, a fashionable affectation that would have been more effective had his legs been tanned.

The courier peered toward the bottles ranged along the counter separating the room from the open kitchen. "White wine, a Chardonnay? Otherwise a margarita—if not too much trouble."

Broom remembered the old days when agents were briefed never to drink vodka in public.

"With a side of chips, or cheese, please," the courier added, as if ordering french fries with his Big Mac. "It's to be a robbery," he said softly as he got up to follow Broom to the counter that separated the kitchen from the living room. "I was instructed to tell you that first, and to emphasize it."

Broom closed the refrigerator door and twisted the plastic tray to spill ice cubes into a drum-shaped ice bucket.

"I told them never to send anyone here," Broom said without looking at the courier. "I said if anyone ever contacted me here I would leave this area and only communicate by letter through Walter." Broom took a bottle of wine from the refrigerator.

As he had been instructed to do, the courier ignored the threat. "This business is *absolutely* urgent," he said, "and it took time to get here." He took a sip of the wine and held the glass to the light. "California, heavier than the French, but respectable in its own way." He took another sip and, as if he were making an even weightier observation, said, "This Key West—it's at the very end of the country. I had to rent a car in Miami, no public transportation to here except by plane." He took another sip of wine and glanced approvingly at his new, tasseled loafers. "There'd be no way to shake a surveillance if anything happened. I don't know why the Center insisted I come here in all this heat, unless it was to see that you are all right and fit. You are fit, aren't you?"

Broom poured more wine and blinked rapidly. "So it must be something vital—something that slipped past Vadim Koltsov—to require you to risk precious cover just to come here at this late date. What is it? Has Vadim Ivanovich perceived a new problem? More chaos at Dom Dva, House Number Two?" Broom's grandfather had been arrested in the building at 2 Dzerzhinsky Square and probably put to death in the cellar. "What kind of panic can be afoot in these days of guided tours and the peddling of old dossiers to anyone with a fistful of dollars and a book contract?"

Irritated, the courier cut himself a thick slice of cheese and took a deep swallow of wine.

"Are you suggesting that the comrades—change that to *our colleagues*—at Yasenevo have left some stone unturned?" Broom continued, "That someone has failed to make all the necessary preparations for the new service?"

"That's why I'm here now," the courier said. "To tell you that you and one other, also from the old 'S' Directorate, the Eighth Department, and a long time abroad, have been taken into the SVRR—the Sluzba Vneshney Razvedki Rossisukoy Federatsii."

"The Russian Foreign Intelligence Service, I *am* flattered," Broom said, "but I'm not going to turn bandit at this late date. There are others for that work."

"You misunderstand, the target is to *die* in the robbery—a mugging, a gun wound or a knife. You will choose."

"Just what else is it that the new service has to do these days?"

The courier emptied his glass and leaned forward. "You may not think so, sitting on your ass in this sweltering playground, but these are serious times. Our country—Russia—is going through a transition, a desperate transition. Abroad, the old enemies pretend to help, but gloat and wait for us to fail. At home, the self-serving bastards left over from the old days pretend loyalty, but try to sabotage every initiative. More than ever the leadership needs time to make repairs, to find the new way. Now, as never before, they need information. The apparat had rusted under the old crowd, but we're moving again. New sources, and now, once again, clandestine well-wishers, it's like the early days, before our time . . ."

"Then what do you need of me, a tired specialist? My time has long passed."

"It has not," the courier said, his voice stiff with anger. "Our service is one of the few organs in the country that still functions as well—maybe better now—than before the changes. We've done away with the worst of the old apparat, but we've got to protect the best of what's left of it. Some old sources have lost their footing, but can be reestablished—money is available. Others, the foreign well-wishers, who welcome the changes at home, are more active than ever. But they must be protected from the renegades and mercenaries out to serve themselves."

"And does Koltsov think I have a role in this?"

"He does, of course he does. You and one or two others can help protect old friends—sources whose reports are more precious now than ever."

They talked until the courier had finished the bottle. "The details are all there," he said, pointing at the copy of *Time* in the basket. "Five microdots, the operational plan, letters, and the message from Koltsov as well." He was clearly irritated that the magazine had been tossed aside so casually.

"I will not accept your reconnaissance, Moscow knows that—or used to know it."

"It's a big city, high crimes, these things happen every night . . ."

"I will decide on that," Broom interrupted.

The courier remained silent.

Broom remembered four, maybe five years earlier. For some forgotten security reason, a young woman, a secretary perhaps, had been sent to Broom with messages. Before the girl left, she admitted having read the briefing file. "But you're not like that at all," she said. "The file said 'surly . . . sometimes the manner of a dilettante . . . ultra-cautious of cover . . . difficult to work with.' But that's not you at all," the woman had gushed.

"This is an urgent matter. There's almost no time," the courier said. "You must get started quickly—you've got to be done with it in ten days' maximum. That's a direct order from the Center." He had disliked Broom from the time he had read the file. Broom was a typical *oplaka*, a big hat, a lieutenant colonel, but on special service, above all the rules, and always trading on the grandfather's reputation. The courier would have liked another bottle of wine, but he got up and moved toward the door.

He opened the gate in the waist-high fence and turned to wave an American farewell to Broom in the doorway. The shaft of light reflected in the shock of Broom's ash-blond hair reminded the courier of an ancient helmet he had seen in the Hermitage in St. Petersburg.

As he crossed the narrow street and began to hurry alongside the fence bordering the cemetery, he turned for a last glimpse of the narrow house. Seven, maybe ten jobs in fifteen years, he thought. All those years of luxury because of the grandfather and the time in the camps. He shrugged, murmuring in Russian, and then repeated himself in English—"A rotten specialist. They can call it what they want, but it's just plain murder."

3

NEW YORK, SEPTEMBER 1991

Andy Mitgang liked to leave his office in time to reach his East 85th Street apartment by seven. There was rarely even one letter a week he could call personal among the bills and junk mail that crowded the box he shared with his roommate, but Andy always took time to sort through the envelopes before changing into his running gear.

Although his speed was more than adequate, Andy was not an athlete, certainly not a competitive runner. He ran two miles a day, four days a week, because he considered it to be good for him and because it was cheaper than working out in a health club. Depending on his mood, and lately this was pretty much determined by his boss, Thelma S. ("call me T.S.") McGruder, Andy always tried to average a consistent seven minutes a mile. This, he believed, was enough to keep the cholesterol moving through his arteries, and to help maintain a reasonable emotional balance.

As he crossed Fifth Avenue at 84th Street and headed for the reservoir, Andy's mind was on his boss. What did it really say about a woman who preferred to be called "T.S." rather than Ms. McGruder, or even Thelma? It said, he told himself once again, that she saw herself as the classic drill sergeant, brutal to the platoon, but confident that the cruelty she enjoyed so much was for the recruits' own good and that in some future crisis they would respect and love her for having conditioned them to the rigors of survival. In fact, Andy reassured himself, T.S. McGruder was a desiccated old bitch who had been shunted from the creative side of one of the largest public relations firms in New York to a dead-end administrative job as an archivist and librarian, and who took out her frustration by attempting to terrorize the one trainee assigned to her office. Andy consigned T.S. to purgatory and glanced apprehensively at his watch. It was just after eight, too late really to be running in Central Park even in September.

As he hurried up the broad steps to the cinder track that circled the reservoir, he noticed with pleasure that the thick black clouds scudding across the park had shrouded the topmost floors of the Fifth Avenue apartment buildings and were denying the rich inhabitants their view of the lesser mortals condemned to exist at lower altitudes. It was darker than Andy liked, and he moved out at a slower pace than usual. He would stick to the reservoir until he was warm. There was no point in risking an injury on the uncertain footing of the bridle path below. At the half-mile mark, he was sweating freely as he moved from the reservoir onto the bridle path and began slowly to increase his pace.

He was still running easily as he passed along the gradient at West 91st Street. Glancing back over his shoulder, Andy could see that he was quite alone. He muttered an imprecation about sunshine athletes, and doused a flicker of anxiety by reminding himself that although the Central Park felons liked the dark, they rarely troubled to work in dismal weather. Not entirely convinced by his own logic, Andy pushed up the pace until he could distinguish three figures, at least a hundred yards ahead, and running easily in the dark. As he would later tell the police, two runners were nearly abreast and the third, a hundred or so feet behind.

He was running faster now and breathing more heavily, his glasses lightly fogged.

Later, Andy could not remember whether it was a sound or some slight change in the pattern of the runners ahead that caused him to look up from the path at the moment the leading figure seemed to stumble, and fling his arms forward as if to fend off an unseen obstacle. The runner's left leg stiffened as if the knee had locked, and he lurched sideways before pitching, face forward, onto the dirt path.

The closest runner, within a stride of the fallen man, took a few uncertain steps forward before slowing sufficiently to wheel about and drop to his knees beside the fallen figure.

Mitgang cursed beneath his laboring breath. Bridle path or not, he knew it was foolish to run flat-out in the near darkness.

There was an incoherent scream, and then, more clearly, a high-pitched shout from the kneeling runner. "There's an accident . . . someone call for help . . ." The kneeling figure looked up, and with both arms spread in appeal, screamed again. "An ambulance, for God's sake, we're going to need an ambulance . . ."

The third figure, now only a few yards from the fallen runner, shouted, "Coming, coming . . ."

Mitgang broke his stride as he approached the two runners huddled over the fallen body. As he stopped, a thin black man in a dark, one-piece running suit, his hands covered in light cotton gloves, rose unsteadily to his feet. "She's hurt bad, it's her head," the black man said, his breath coming in heavy gulps. "When she fell . . . a stone or something . . . her head's a mess . . ."

"Jesus Christ," the second runner said. "I don't even dare to turn her over . . ."

For a moment, Mitgang stared at the fallen body. "We've got to move her a little," he said. "Just enough to help her breathing . . ." He bent to ease the fallen woman's face from the dirt, and then turned suddenly away, his stomach churning. Her long hair tied in a loose bun, secured beneath a baseball cap, had fallen loose. Her eye hung from the socket, and blood oozed around the bits of flesh still covering the shattered bone around her temple.

"I'll get help," the black man said, his voice shrill. "The precinct house, right here in the park, on the 85th Street transverse." Before Mitgang could speak, the man brushed the loose dirt from his immaculate running suit and sprinted away, along the path toward 85th Street.

"We need help here," Mitgang shouted. "There's been an accident." In the distance another cluster of runners approached.

"A flashlight, has anyone got a flashlight?" Mitgang called, waving his arms. "There's an accident here, we need light . . ."

A heavyset young man, his long hair gathered in a ponytail, dropped to his knees beside the body. He slipped his left hand gently under the woman's shoulder. With his right hand, he cradled her head. He lifted the woman's left shoulder and eased her head back from the dirt. He leaned closer to see the wound more clearly. Then, his mouth sagging with surprise, he turned to Mitgang. "Shee-it, man," he drawled softly. "That's no accident, your friend's been fucking shot. Twice, right in the fucking head." With a widening grin he looked up at the gathering group of runners. "It's the O.K. Corral, right here in the park . . . God *damn*."

He got slowly to his feet and then stooped and attempted to wipe the blood from his hands on the ragged grass along the border of the path. He straightened up and began to jog in place, lifting his knees high and stamping his feet. "Somebody better go check for the cops and the meat wagon," he said. "We don't watch out, we've all got cramps by the time they get here." He pulled a crumpled plaid handkerchief from the pocket of his blue shorts and made another attempt to get the blood off his hands.

4

LONDON, JULY 1993

"A dry sherry, and two Tanqueray martinis, in and out," Roger Folsom said, glancing with mock anxiety across the table at Alan Trosper. "You haven't dropped any of your bad habits, have you?"

"In and out?" Trosper was as puzzled as the waiter.

"Put ice in the glass, and add the vermouth." The waiter nodded. "Dump the vermouth and slosh in the gin." With a wink Folsom dismissed the irritated waiter and turned to Emily Trosper.

The dark paneled walls, high ceiling, and abundance of starchy waiters and service staff at Simpson's usually had a quieting effect on visitors. But Roger Folsom had never bothered to mask his brimming self-confidence with the air of diffidence affected by some case men. He was not quite six feet tall, but bulky enough to occupy the entire side of the booth facing Trosper and Emily.

"I never developed a taste for sherry," he said to Emily. "Even in Spain I didn't like it. After a while, I found I could drink the brandy they concoct if I put enough soda and ice in it."

"Spirits put me straight to sleep, but I rather like sherry," Emily said with a polite smile. She wore her dark auburn hair pulled up in a French twist and sat erect, barely brushing the back of the booth. Her simple black dress was cut to reveal the graceful line of her shoulders.

Folsom leaned toward Trosper. "Have you heard why I left the Firm?" It was as if he were a salesman breaking the ice by asking a prospective customer if he had heard the latest joke.

Trosper realized it was folly to have hoped the business babble could even be postponed until after dinner. He shook his head.

"Damn it," Folsom said. He turned to Emily. "In fifteen years, I've never known Alan to give a straight, affirmative answer to the simplest question. I don't know how you can put up with it."

"I remind him that he's not sparring with an agent," Emily said, with a canny glance at Trosper.

"I've never got in trouble by admitting I don't know something," Trosper said. "It's when I try to act well informed that people seem to leave out the important parts of the story they're about to tell me."

Folsom groaned. "Let's begin again. Had you *heard* about my leaving the Firm?"

"I heard that you left a couple of years ago, just after you struck it rich."

When Roger Folsom telephoned to say he was passing through London, and wanted to meet Emily, Trosper suggested they have dinner at Simpson's in the Strand. In the years since he had resigned from Research Estimates, Inc., Trosper had distanced himself from his friends who remained in the non-official cover intelligence organization. Since his marriage and settling in Emily's native London to do research for his book on fighting ships, visits by former colleagues had waned. Folsom's telephone call was a surprise.

"Why do you recommend Simpson's to visitors?" Emily asked. "It's not the best restaurant in town, and it certainly isn't a bargain."

"Because I've never known a visitor who didn't think it was what a posh London restaurant is supposed to be."

"And Roger Folsom? Will he expect to see Alec Guinness dawdling over a glass of port with his favorite novelist? Or is he another one of your old crowd?"

"Red Roger joined the Firm four or five years after me," Trosper said. "He had a good reputation as a case man, but they let him go a while back."

"*Red* Roger?"

"Just his hair, Emily," Trosper said patiently. "Not his politics."

"*Let* go?" Emily said. "Is that dainty for getting the sack?"

"He always was a sort of loose cannon," Trosper admitted, "and there was some scandal."

Folsom picked up his glass, and stared speculatively at the remaining drops of his drink. "There's something I'd like to talk to you about . . ."

Against the odds, Trosper tried to change the subject. "A strong man's crossroads? Another martini?"

Folsom stirred from his reverie. "Not at all, I've pretty much cut out the booze. California does that to you." His red hair, flecked with white, had faded, but his normally light complexion was freckled by the perpetual California sun.

"If you weren't being polite just now, you may not have heard that I left under a cloud."

"I never knew any of the details," Trosper said.

Folsom waited for a moment, both elbows on the table, his fingers flexing like a pianist about to strike the opening notes in a complex concerto. "It's all because of that bastard Volin—Viktor Feodorovich Volin, the kind of creep that gives the racket a bad name."

Trosper shook his head. "Never heard of him. Is he one of the new boys, or an old Moscow Center survivor?"

"Both," Folsom said. "Volin actually telephoned our Munich office, in July, '91, claiming he was an illegal. He was playing hard to get, and trying to work out a deal by dangling names of some Moscow heavies as bait—guys who were short-listed as key players in the takeover everyone was expecting."

"*Hard* to get?" Trosper said. "I've had the impression that you guys have trouble making your way into the office through the lines of . . ." He paused. "What do you call defectors these days—volunteers?"

"There's always room at the top," Folsom admitted. "Volin was no dope, he'd dangle a bit of bait, insist on commitments in advance, and threaten to peddle himself for some of the big money the Germans are tossing around if we didn't meet his demands. This was a month *before* the August dustup when the junta, the gang that couldn't coup straight, grabbed Gorbachev, and announced that they were running things. The key players were exactly the people Volin claimed access to—all the right names—Kryuchkov, the guy Gorbachev had chosen as KGB chief, Pavlov, the prime minister, Marshal Akhromeyev, Gorbachev's military man, the whole crowd . . ."

Trosper laughed. "That coup had more advance publicity than last year's Super Bowl. The press had been chewing on it for weeks."

"Which was all the more reason the White House was scared witless at the prospect of an old-fashioned Russian blood bath with half the world's atomic weapons and chemical warfare gadgets up for grabs." Folsom stopped short. "You haven't been away so long that you can't remember what happens when the squeeze is really on . . ."

"Oh, yes." Trosper smiled. "I remember occasional moments of pressure . . ."

"*Pressure?*" Folsom snorted. "The heat was blistering the paint right off the buildings—the Agency, the Firm, State, the Pentagon. But trade was lousy. Nobody knew whether Gorbachev would last another twenty-four hours, or what Yeltsin had on his mind. Aside from that, Duff Whyte was in the hospital with a heart attack and all but incommunicado."

"I remember . . ."

"*So*, Bob Dwyer was Acting Controller. When the crowd Volin claimed to know put Gorbachev under house arrest, Dwyer grabbed on to Volin as if he had a new version of the Rosetta stone under his arm." Folsom glanced anxiously at Emily. At best, talking shop in front of wives was a tricky business. But Emily's huge brown eyes, half-masked by the reading glasses she affected, showed no trace of the telltale glaze that in others usually preceded a demand for a change of subject.

"Five days after the coup, Gorbachev was back in the Kremlin, still dithering, and Kryuchkov was locked in his own KGB jail. By this time Washington had cooled off, and Dan Webster had pretty well proved that Volin was just a clever illegal agent who had made good use of his time in Prague while staging for his mission in the States. He'd studied the Western press, and was crafty enough to have elicited some bits and pieces from his Russian handlers. For all his smarts, Volin was an outsider who had less access to what was going on than some of the CNN TV people. All he had was one real zinger, and he swapped it for asylum and resettlement help—not as easy a deal as it was when defectors made out like lottery winners."

Folsom drained his martini and for a moment munched noisily on a bit of the remaining ice. "Volin was to have only one job in the States—he'd been prepped to handle a State Department secretary, Charlotte Mills." Folsom pursed his lips and shook his head slowly, sadly. "While she was working at the embassy in Moscow, she'd been photographed in what you might call a romantic interlude with a stud, a guy working for some of the Second Chief Directorate hands who were still doing business as usual for the old Moscow Center. Volin's disclosure was heavy stuff—Mills had access to absolutely everything pertaining to our chatter with Gorbachev right on through to Yeltsin. If it hadn't been for Volin, she might still be at it. As it was, when she left Moscow, she wound up in a job just about as sensitive at our mission to the U.N. in New York."

"With the country falling apart around them, how can the Russians find time for things like that?" Emily asked, her voice more surprised than indignant.

"This began in the Gorbachev era, so it was still business as usual when she was set up," Folsom said. "Nowadays, the service is more up-to-date—less rough stuff, and they're happy to pay market prices for value received. They're not much worried about Western military intervention, but they damned well need all the economic and political poop they can get, and they're willing to go way out on a limb for really good stuff."

"Doesn't anyone ever refuse to cooperate?" Emily asked. "I'm always surprised when I hear one of you speak so casually about recruiting someone to be a spy."

"She didn't just *agree* to be a spy," Folsom said. "She was blackmailed by the oldest trick in history . . ." He glanced across the table for support.

Trosper nodded. "It's an even money bet that right now, somebody, somewhere, is setting up just such a stunt."

Folsom brightened. "Mills was a drab little thing, but she was decent and hard-working until they ran that guy against her." He glanced at Emily. "A gigolo, who claimed to be an actor. She had a few good weeks before they showed her the photographs."

Emily's face flushed. "Even so, how much trouble should a few pictures of a woman—whatever age—in bed with some hunk cause anyone these days?"

"The poor woman had probably never even heard of the things that bum had her doing." Folsom's face colored, and he turned away from Emily to toy with his empty glass.

Twenty years in the racket, and Red Roger could still blush.

"Besides, the bastard probably used drugs to get at her," Folsom added gallantly.

"Couldn't she have told someone about it?" Emily asked.

"Of course—she'd have been out of Moscow the next day, and the ambassador would tell the Foreign Office to knock off the Stalinist crap and rein in their goons if they expected any further cooperation from Washington." Folsom paused while the waiter served thin slices of pale smoked salmon. "As it was, she didn't ever report it."

"Couldn't she have tried to fight back in some other way?" Emily asked.

"That's the big catch in blackmail," Trosper said. "Victims with enough spunk will always be looking for a chance to hit back at the bastards who are tormenting them."

"Sure," Folsom said, "and that's why the smarter punks always sweeten the pot with money. For more people than you think, there's nothing like a tax-free income." He shrugged. "To her credit, Charlotte Mills never touched a penny. She just stuck it in a separate bank account."

"Didn't anyone notice anything?" Trosper asked.

“Mills was a solitary soul, and no one even realized she’d begun boozing. Not that it mattered. By the time Volin’s information hit the fan, she’d been dead for a couple of weeks—shot in a Central Park mugging that went haywire—case closed.” Folsom shook his head. “At first, the security geniuses didn’t quite believe Volin. But he had a set of negatives of the original pictures, just to remind Mills in case she got restive. Then they found a wad of Xerox copies of LIMDIS cables tucked in the office safe she used, and uncovered an account in which she’d been depositing eight hundred bucks a month ever since she left Moscow. That was exactly the salary Volin said she was getting.”

Folsom took a final bite of the salmon before saying, “As it was, Mills’s apartment was ransacked and burglarized a day or so after her death. It was probably done by one of the Moscow hard boys trying to make sure she hadn’t left any compromising stuff in the apartment.”

They were finishing the beef when Emily asked, “Didn’t that poor woman have any friends, someone who might have noticed what was happening to her?”

“Senior secretaries are supposed to be experienced enough to take care of themselves,” Trosper said. “Not that that’s any excuse for failing to keep an eye on the staff in a place as stressed as Moscow was in those days.”

“Douglas Hardwick was the ambassador heading the delegation in Moscow, and he sure as hell was surprised when he was told about it,” Folsom said.

“Is Hardwick the fellow we used to call ‘Lord Douglas’?” Trosper asked.

“That’s the guy, Douglas Huntington Hardwick, a striped-pants, old school diplomat, who spent most of his time impressing everyone with his fluent Russian,” Folsom said. “Handsome Harry Slocombe was his number two, and trying to keep the negotiations on track. He’s been someone’s deputy for so long all he can worry about is getting his own embassy.”

“Harry is a bit stately,” Trosper laughed, “but he’s been around since Brezhnev and his gang were in short pants.”

"Shouldn't someone have noticed that a secretary had fallen head over heels for some fancy man?"

Folsom glanced uneasily at Emily. "It isn't that poor woman I want to talk about. It's *me* I've got to get Alan interested in."

Trosper knew when he had lost. "Let's go back to the flat for coffee," he said.

5

LONDON

Folsom swirled the brandy in his glass and took a deep reflective puff of his cigar. In the soft light of the study, his flushed face seemed darker. "Aside from what Volin had on Mills—who was killed before he even could get to the States—he didn't know much of a damn about anything. As an illegal, he'd always been kept at arm's length, all he had to peddle were bits and pieces he had come across in Prague where he'd spent a year or so working up his cover."

Trosper leaned back in his chair. "You must know this is none of my business."

Folsom seemed surprised. "Look, I know you're retired, but with Duff Whyte as Controller, you . . ."

Trosper interrupted. "Damn it, I didn't retire, and I wish to hell people would stop assuming that I did." He pushed his coffee aside and got up. At the drinks table he poured himself an ample Glenlivet. So much for his resolve not to drink after dinner. He hesitated a moment and splashed a jigger of water into the whiskey. "Four years ago, I quit. I didn't retire. I quit because I'd had enough."

"But since Duff Whyte took over, I heard you'd taken on two or three jobs, big ones." Folsom spoke rapidly, hiding his embarrassment.

“Everyone knows that.” He knocked the ash off his cigar and began to fish for a match.

“Just so long as you know I’m really out of it.” Trosper would not explain that when he left the Firm he was stale, tired of the secret world, of conspiracy and everything that went with it. But every time he thought he had finally shaken the old life, it came back and seized him. And with it came the old habits, like sitting up half the night drinking malt whiskey and talking shop.

“Sure Alan, if you say so.” Folsom took a sip of brandy. “It’s just that the three of us—the Troika—were really screwed by Volin and Bob Dwyer.”

“The Troika?”

“That’s what the idiots on the investigation panel dubbed us—it’s probably the only Russian word they knew.” Folsom’s light blue eyes blinked rapidly. “It’s like Volin, all he had to peddle was Mills and some bits and pieces on Prague.”

“Even these days, I’d have thought that blowing the Mills case was enough to qualify anyone for resettlement.”

“Up to a point, but Volin had some bizarre notions carried over from the old days. All he had going for him were Mills, a couple of languages, and a knack for cultivating women—not the most obvious talents to build a résumé on.” With a gentle, tap, Folsom knocked the ash from his cigar. “In fact, he was just a pretentious blowhard, whinging about money and demanding special treatment.”

“So how did you get mixed up in it?”

“When the creep realized that he was due for resettlement, he *incidentally* recollected that he had one more piece of exciting intelligence.” Folsom nodded several times as if to underline the irony. “Once upon a time it seems he heard two of his trainers talking about an important agent a pal of theirs was handling—and in the Firm, yet.”

Trosper shrugged. It was the sort of tease that any agent who had run out of gas might be tempted to concoct. “I suppose he had a few details?”

“Of course. The agent—the alleged agent—was one of our senior operations people. His—maybe her—usual beat was Europe, and the last name began with an F.”

"That's all?"

"Not quite. Volin supplied a few dates and cities where the agent was supposedly met."

Trosper took a sip of whiskey. "This is all very interesting, Roger, but why are you telling me?"

Folsom made a gentling gesture with his hand, an orchestra conductor softening a strident brass section. "A few hours after the report hit Dwyer's desk, Volin was back in the safe house, and the whole thing classified Top Secret, with a maximum hold-down codeword attached to it." Folsom paused before saying, "In fact, it was supposed to be so damned sensitive that even His Nibs, Thomas Augustus Castle, wasn't allowed in on it."

"Are you sure?" Trosper had always assumed that Castle, the Controller's assistant for Special Operations, would figure in any case touching on the Firm's security.

"Hell yes, I'm sure—after two weeks of their stupid questioning, and trying to remember where I was five years ago at four o'clock on a Sunday afternoon in the middle of May, I bulled my way into Dwyer's office and told him I damned well wanted to see Castle, and have him tell me face-to-face what the hell he thought was going on." Folsom slammed his fist against the arm of his chair. "That's when Dwyer told me that Castle had been kept out of the investigation because he might be too close to the former management to be objective."

Trosper remained silent.

"Dwyer said that he'd established the panel—three outsiders, as he put it—because he was determined to get to the bottom of the case urgently and without getting hung up with any of the sick-think crap that he thought had caused the Firm so much trouble a few years ago."

Trosper took a sip of his drink and rolled the heavy whiskey over his tongue. Sick-think was a pejorative used by some of the Firm's bright young men and liaison specialists to describe what they considered to be Castle's skepticism and security strictures. In turn, Castle referred to these operatives as "flat-earthers" who were convinced—history notwithstanding—that no one in Moscow or elsewhere on earth was conceivably wily enough to put anything over on them.

"It was a month before the panel was satisfied there were only three people in the shop who could possibly fit the evidence—if that's what it was—that Volin was peddling."

Folsom got up, walked to the window, and pushed the heavy portiere aside to look out into the street. He turned back to Trosper and said, "Alex Findley, Lotte Friesler, and me."

He dropped the curtain and stepped slowly back to Trosper. "As soon as Dwyer was convinced that we were the only people who fitted the profile the panel had contrived, our clearances were lifted, the interrogation began, and I spent more time on the cooker than I want to remember."

"What about corroborating data?"

Folsom sniffed. "Damn all, as far as I could figure out." He drained his glass. "So when Dwyer couldn't prove a case against any of us, he came up with a Scotch verdict. As he put it, I might not be guilty of anything, but I couldn't be proved innocent either. And so he said he had no choice but to be safe rather than sorry."

Trosper had no reason to believe that Folsom and the others were anything less than competent and loyal employees, but he knew that just as secret intelligence has its discrete perquisites, it is also bound by its own disciplines. Accepting the perks meant abiding by the rules. When Research Estimates, Inc., was founded, the Controller was granted authority to dismiss any employee without giving the reason, or even honoring the customary rights of redress. Trosper had no brief for Dwyer's judgment, but as Acting Controller he had the authority to dismiss employees he could not trust. Fair is fair, except in war, in love, and in the racket.

Much as he might sympathize with innocent victims, Trosper accepted the fact that secret intelligence could be a dangerous and messy business. But as far as he knew, nobody had ever been forced to join it.

With a gesture begging Trosper's permission, Folsom stepped to the bar. He poured another brandy. "After a few words on what a great out-placement shop we had, Dwyer told me I was fired." Folsom grimaced. "That's a level of preventive medicine that would have a doctor amputate your leg because you're going skiing and might break it."

"I'm sorry this happened," Trosper said, "and it certainly doesn't do Dwyer any credit, but why are you telling me about it *now*?"

Folsom lowered his head and flexed his shoulders, a boxer shaking off a heavy blow. "Because it wasn't right. It hurt the Firm and it damned well hurt the three of us." Folsom dropped his cigar into the narrow crystal ashtray. "Maybe I've been away too long, but in the old days we used to be sure we carried our wounded off the field."

Trosper shot to his feet, stepped beside Folsom, and gently pushed him back into the chair. "I'm sorry, old friend, I just wasn't thinking." He took Folsom's glass from the table, handed it to him, and dropped back into his own chair. "I'm the one who's been out of things longer than I realized."

Folsom hesitated. "It's okay . . ."

"What about money?" Trosper asked quickly.

"Alex and I qualified for retirement, but Lotte came up short. All she got was a year or so severance pay."

"What have you been up to since then?"

Folsom brightened. "About the time the Firm was putting all its eggs into the electronic memory box, I was sent off to give the computer wonks some notion how a field man would maneuver an inside agent to break through the computer security systems." He picked up his dead cigar, lighted it, and took a few quick puffs. "Within a week I'd found a second home. It was like joining the racket all over again. A couple of years later one of the computer guys hit me for some dough. I plopped every penny I could scrape together into his company. By the time Dwyer handed me my walking papers, we'd tripled our investment, and I've been making a bundle ever since."

"I still don't see where I come in?"

"I've got a proposition for you," Folsom said. "It's right down your alley." He raised his glass in a mock salute.

Emily was still reading when Trosper eased the bedroom door open. "It's after one," he said. "I thought you'd be asleep."

She thrust her glasses back into her hair and put the book on the night table. "I liked Red Roger, all of his enthusiasm and wanting to put things right . . ."

"He never was one to walk past a closed door," Trosper muttered as he hung his tie on the rack.

"So what about that poor woman?"

Trosper sat on the side of the bed and ran his hand along her high cheekbone. "You heard what he said—she'd been dead a month before the security people were satisfied that Volin was telling the truth, and that she had been an agent, blackmailed or otherwise."

"What she must have gone through, and then to die in a mugging."

Trosper kissed her lightly.

"What does Roger want you to do about it?"

"He's a realist, sweetheart, there's nothing can be done about it . . ."

"Then what did he want?"

Trosper bent to untie his shoes. He fitted the three-piece trees and flicked bits of dust from the heels. "Roger had a nutty notion about my investigating what he calls the Troika crowd. Now that Duff Whyte is back at his desk, Roger wants me to get his permission to go through the files, talk to the people, and sort out Volin's story about the penetration." Trosper began to unbutton his shirt. "Roger said it wouldn't cost the Firm a bean. He would give me a fee, pay all my expenses, and wouldn't even insist on seeing my final report."

"That's wonderful, darling . . ."

Trosper's face sagged. It had been a long night. "Sad as it may seem, it's out of the question. With everything that's going on these days, Duff Whyte would think I've blown a gasket if I went to him with a proposal like that . . ."

"You mean you're not going to do anything about what they did to that poor woman, and your friends?"

"That poor woman, as you keep putting it, has been dead for some two years now. What Roger wants me to investigate is the allegation that either he or one of two others is a traitor. That's something for the Firm, maybe even the FBI, to figure out." He tossed his shirt over the back of the chair beside the bed. "There's not a thing anyone can do for Charlotte Mills."

“That’s really rotten,” Emily said as she abruptly turned on her side, her back to Trosper. “Even in the grave she hasn’t got anyone who gives a damn . . .”

For a moment Trosper wondered just how many people dead or alive he could give a damn about. Then he touched Emily’s shoulder. “If it makes you feel any better, I do plan to write Duff. Roger said that Lotte Friesler, a woman I never did like very much, is flat broke.”

“And when we go to the States next month, you’ll see Duff?”

“I shouldn’t be surprised.”

6

CASCO BAY, MAINE

Alan Trosper eased the sloop slowly along the lee of Cliff Island, savoring the last hour of the two-week cruise. He would skirt Ram Island to take a lingering look at Portland Head Light and then head back across the harbor for the short run to the marina and mooring.

It was the kind of early fall day that invariably kindled comment on Indian summer. But as Trosper remembered it, Indian summer came only after the first frost, and for the purists only in November, and on a full moon. Indian summer or not, the golden afternoon air, clear and cool and crisp, was a sure and welcome attestation of autumn. Emily had gone ashore at Camden for the weekend with a distant cousin and, as she reluctantly admitted, “for repairs.” As Trosper suspected, after nearly two weeks on the thirty-four-foot boat, her interest in having her hair done was at least as compelling as the opportunity to see the relative, an English expatriate recently retired from the U.N. in New York.

Trosper looked forward to a hotel room, an abundance of showering, and an hour with the *New York Times*. Then a quiet dinner in Portland and a long night, spread-eagled in the luxury of a hotel bed three times as wide as the bunks on the *Krushia*. He flicked the VHF switch, and paused to take a last fond look at the trim little craft, knowing that his call would acknowledge the end of sailing for the year. He shrugged and activated the microphone. "Handy Boat dock, this is *Krushia*. Over."

It was like Tim Preble to have named his boat for Krushia, the prettiest girl in Podvolochiska, and much admired from afar by two of her Polish schoolmates who were later to be numbered among the most competent of the early defectors from Stalin's intelligence service. It was also like Tim to have insisted that Trosper and Emily use the *Krushia* for their cruise along the Maine coast.

The VHF squawked. "*Krushia*, this is Linda, Handy Boat dock person. Your mooring is clear." Trosper acknowledged the message, but before he could sign off, Linda called again. "*Krushia*, you have telephone messages in the office. Please be sure to pick them up before you leave."

He eased the boat onto a tighter course. Only Tim Preble and Duff Whyte knew that Alan and Emily Trosper had been cruising for two weeks.

Two message slips. A telephone call from Emily Trosper in Camden. "A Mr. Château called just after you left. He asks you to call him at the Sonesta Hotel in Portland as soon as you land. He says it's pressing." The second message, taken by the boatyard, was more concise. "Call Thomas Shatow, Sonesta Hotel, Portland." Trosper knew no Thomas Château, or even Thomas Shatow. But he did know Thomas Augustus Castle well enough to suspect that even in Portland, the head of the Firm's Special Operations Staff would be too security conscious to use his own name in leaving a telephone message for a former colleague.

"*Shrimp Wiggle*," Castle exclaimed, as he attempted to adjust his heavy body to the uncompromising right angle of the wooden booth.

Trosper glanced suspiciously around the small diner, uncertain whether Castle was speaking in tongues or referring to the bill of fare. He decided to buy time. "This your first visit to Maine?"

Castle adjusted his gold-framed half-glasses and brought his long slim fingers together in a temple as he fixed his attention on the plastic-covered menu. "Summer camp," he said without looking up. "Three seasons at Camp Abenaki, and I still can't start a fire with anything less than a box of matches and a carafe of kerosene."

They were wedged opposite one another in one of a row of booths facing the counter and stools that ranged along the length of the chromium-and-plastic Miss Longfellow Diner. The long counter was dotted with plates of doughnuts, assorted cakes, and a variety of pies, each on its own pedestal and protected by a clear plastic dome. A sign above the pass-through to the kitchen proclaimed, "Open 24 Hours Daily. 'Closed Xmas.' The Best Food In Town." The random use of quotation marks by American sign painters had always baffled Trosper.

Castle shifted his attention from the menu to a laminated wine card jammed between a bottle of catsup and a generous sugar bowl with a hinged metal cover. "And Bacchus wept," he said, staring at the card. "We'd best concentrate on the food and perhaps a beer."

Trosper nodded glumly. After two weeks of seafood, he had set his heart on dinner at Hugo's, a perfect martini, a fresh salad, meat, cheese, and whatever bottle of wine Johnny Robinson, the owner, might recommend. "Are you merely passing through, or are you here just to see me?" he asked.

"Shrimp Wiggle," Castle repeated, pointing to the menu. "There aren't many places, even in Maine, where you can get a good one these days. It's special here on Friday, I recommend it."

"So that's it, just passing through?"

"For openers, a bowl of clam chowder?" Castle looked up from the menu, focusing on Trosper. "And then the shrimp—small local shrimp, rather a delicacy if they're done properly?" His flannel blazer had been cut for a lesser Castle, and was stressed dangerously tight across the chest and upper arms. A gold collar button peeped from beneath the white collar and a club tie that Trosper failed to recognize.

"Maybe they can rustle up some Blueberry Slump for dessert," Trosper said.

Castle looked up, surprised. "I've been fishing in Canada. When the Controller got your letter, he asked me to talk with you before you went back to the U.K."

Trosper nodded. He would let his host begin the shop talk when he was ready.

Castle took a final forkful of the small shrimp and glanced speculatively at Trosper. "Dwyer left a lot of loose ends, considering he was only Acting Controller," he said. "Since Duff's been back there's not been any time for the Troika or for anything that his staff seems to think is history."

"I remember Darcy Odlum saying there's no statute of limitations in counterespionage," Trosper said. He was not sure that Odlum, the man Harry Truman had chosen to establish the Firm, had ever mentioned anything about statute of limitation, but the observation was valid and it was something Odlum might well have said.

Castle dipped a small piece of grainy Tuscan toast into the remaining white sauce and, without looking up, said, "To be sure—and Allen Dulles used to say that he'd never read a file, no matter how old, without learning something new." Castle popped the bread into his mouth with a delicate gesture. "The unadorned truth is that with everything else that's going on, we can't spring anyone competent enough to sort out the Troika mess."

Trosper doubted that Castle had ever uttered the *unadorned* truth. "What is it exactly that you might want me to do?" he said reluctantly.

"Red Roger could only have given you part of the story," Castle said. "By the time Duff got back, Volin had been put back into the hands of the resettlement people. As soon as Duff found the time to look into it and ask me to resolve things, our three friends had been out for months. If Volin was actually on to something, obviously Duff has to get to the bottom of it. If our three colleagues were treated unfairly, he wants to put things right." Castle pushed his empty plate aside and reached for the menu.

"What did you get out of the files?"

"Some dessert?" Castle asked. "A meal like that calls for dessert." He looked up from the menu. "I barely glanced at the files."

Listening to Castle was like looking through a child's kaleidoscope. "Just what is it that you and Duff have in mind?"

"All you have to do is study the files, rake over the data, backwards and forwards. Maybe talk to a couple of people. Then come up with some recommendations for action," Castle said. "Two weeks, maybe three at the outside."

Trosper sighed. "I suppose Emily wouldn't mind a little more time over here," he said uneasily.

"Then it's a deal?"

Trosper nodded.

Castle continued to study the menu. "There is one other thing," he murmured without looking up. "Though it's not necessarily cause and effect."

Trosper closed his eyes and bowed his head, waiting for the blow to fall.

"A week, maybe ten days after I called for the Troika files, Volin walked out of the apartment we had for him. We haven't had a trace of him since January '92."

Trosper forced himself to look up and open his eyes. "Is this where I am supposed to grin and say 'snookered again'?"

"As I said, it may not have been cause and effect."

Despite himself, Trosper began to laugh.

Castle smiled. "What in the name of heaven is Blueberry Slump?"

"What's that tie you're wearing?" Trosper asked. It was green, with small red figures, like potted plants.

Castle glanced down at his chest. "Sometimes irreverently described as 'a pansy rampant on a bed of thorns,' it belongs to one of the British military intelligence outfits. They presented it to me after an all-skate we had a few years ago."

7

WASHINGTON, D.C.

"I've got the big picture, just tell me what you found, and what's to be done about it." Duff Whyte, still thin from his illness, shifted uneasily in his high-backed leather chair. Despite his gray flannel suit, double-twist poplin shirt, and heavy foulard tie, there was the usual hint of the American West about Whyte. Even seated, the Controller's every movement suggested a self-reliance that Trosper, because of his childhood devotion to cowboy films, would always associate with the open prairie.

"What you have," Trosper began, "is hours of recorded lie-detector testings on the three alleged suspects, security background files, and upwards of four hundred pages of typed transcripts of the oral interrogations."

Castle sat, Gabriel-like, to the right of the Controller's old-fashioned desk, and appeared immersed in the complex geometrical doodle he was sketching on a memo pad.

"What about their conclusions?" Whyte asked.

"The panel decided that the allegation couldn't be proved," Trosper said, "and that although none of the three was necessarily guilty, none could be proved innocent."

"Your view?" It was Castle's first question, and he did not look up from his pad to utter it.

"The panel wasn't qualified," Trosper said. "I'd guess Dwyer was more concerned that there would be no leaks or gossip within the Firm than he was about picking the strongest team. Neither Logan, a reports officer, nor Wasserman, from the I.G. Staff, had any operations experience. Bill Murphy was from the security office, but his only experience was in background investigations."

Castle nodded agreement.

"They established," Trosper continued, "that each of our three *suspects* had been in, or could easily have got to, the areas cited by

Volin—Paris, Munich, Geneva, Mexico City—at about the times he specified."

"At least, our villain had orthodox taste in venues," Whyte sniffed.

"Unfortunately the panel ignored the fact that at any given time, there were certain to be dozens of other American officials kicking around in the same watering holes," Trosper said. "State, Commerce, Agriculture, the Pentagon, even Treasury has people abroad, any one of whom might have been mistaken by Volin's alleged source." He waited before adding, "Along with that, the panel neglected to study the work history of the trio and to identify any sensitive data known to them and subsequently found to have been compromised."

Trosper turned from Whyte to Castle. He recognized Castle's complex doodling as a bit of business usually employed to rattle an agent or a briefing officer engaged in a rehearsed and too slick presentation, and was irritated to find himself responding to it. He glanced at Whyte, who, with a dismissive wave of his hand in Castle's direction, motioned Trosper to continue.

"Because no real effort was made to collect collateral data before the questioning began, the panel had too few questions for each suspect. This meant that they fired their best ammunition in the first few hours of questioning. After that, the interrogations degenerated into mindless repetition of identical questions and even simpler denials. 'You're a traitor.' 'No I'm not.' 'Yes you are.' 'Prove it.' "

Trosper caught a flicker of reaction from Castle.

"Obviously it wasn't quite that bad, but it went on for hours."

Whyte glanced expectantly at Castle, but the chief of Special Operations remained buried in his notepad.

"Someone should have reminded them that if an interrogator needs the answers to four questions, he'd better wrap them in twenty others whose answers he already knows," Trosper said. "That's the only way to keep a running check on any games a suspect might be playing."

"So, what do you recommend?" Whyte asked with an impatient gesture.

"There's no evidence that the three were guilty of anything," Trosper said. "I suggest that you have someone interview each of them and go over the few questions I've attached to my report. If this doesn't show anything, and if there's no evidence from other sources, I recommend that you restore all three to full benefits."

"But no return to duty?" Whyte asked.

Trosper shrugged. "Folsom is well fixed. A personal letter telling him that the slate is wiped clean would probably take care of things as far as he is concerned."

"Alex Findley, what about him?" Whyte glanced impatiently at Castle.

"Once you've been outside for a while things begin to look different," Trosper said. "I'm not sure that Findley would want to come back. But you can always make an offer."

Castle stirred. "Friesler?" he asked softly.

"From what Folsom told me, I'm sure Lotte Friesler will expect to be reinstated the moment she's cleared," Trosper said.

With a faint sigh, Castle picked up his notepad, jammed the top onto his thick fountain pen, and stuffed the pen into his breast pocket. He turned his full attention to Whyte and said, "I think it's time for you to put Alan more fully into the picture."

Trosper leaned back in his chair, stared at the ceiling as if making an appeal to heaven, and then bent forward toward Whyte. "I really dislike being blindsided by my own team," he said.

"It's not that at all," Whyte said quietly. "I wanted your opinion before you saw the new evidence."

"We got this yesterday," Castle added with uncustomary haste. He pulled two folded sheets of typewriter paper from the leather folder on his lap. "This is Xerox," he said with a trace of apology. "The original was addressed to a letter drop we used in the Tomahawk case and was mailed from a post office in New York." He looked across the desk to Whyte for support.

"You know about Tomahawk, Alan?" Whyte asked. "Pyotr Skoblin—a senior colonel, with two tours at the Soviet mission to the U.N. in New York. He was promoted to general after his return to Moscow. A year or so later he was arrested and allegedly executed a couple of months after Yeltsin took over." Whyte raised his eyebrows and shrugged to underline the coming irony. "Moscow Center hard-liners gave a long account of the case to the Russian press and on the sly slipped a couple of Western writers a few more details. All of this, I presume, to make sure that Yeltsin and those who follow realize just how much they must depend on a strong intelligence and security service."

Trosper nodded. Skoblin's arrest and execution had complete coverage in the spy-hungry British press.

"What's more," Castle laughed, "the American press thought it was a CIA case."

"Has the moment arrived when I'm supposed to ask just what this has to do with me and my . . . ah . . . *brief* assignment to review the Troika files?"

"You'll want to study the letter, but the obvious connection is that the author, who claims to be a Moscow Center illegal, offers to play ball if I agree to handle him more competently than the Firm did the investigation of the Troika." Whyte smiled grimly. "Aside from that, you'll remember that 'Troika' was an informal usage, known only by the security panel, two secretaries, and our three former colleagues."

"You'll also want to keep in mind," Castle said, "that when Moscow spilled most of the details of the Tomahawk operation, there was no mention of the letter drop. That suggests the writer has access to data I consider sensitive." Castle unfolded the letter and appeared to be making a final check of the contents before letting it out of his grasp. "What's more, the knowing reference to the way Troika was investigated, and the fact Tomahawk was Skoblin's cover name, could only have come from a source within the Firm."

Duff Whyte inhaled sharply and leaned across the desk toward Castle. "From a *source* inside the Firm, Tom? Why not a one-time-lucky audio operation? Or a bit of paper that went astray, perhaps left in a pants pocket and pinched by a hotel maid? What about a bit of indiscreet chatter on some monitored telephone? Such things have happened to every goddamned service in history." Whyte's face was flushed. "Thanks to the Department of State's nice-Nelly approach to security, the Russian embassy is perched on the best spot in Washington to eavesdrop on ninety percent of the government's telephone calls without a single Russian tech even leaving the building!

With facilities like that, I'm surprised Moscow even bothers with any damned agents at all."

For once Castle seemed off balance. "Of course, Duff, but . . ."

"We've been over this before," Whyte said, his voice rising. "Every pissant security lapse isn't necessarily a signal that there's a penetration agent a few feet down the hall from my office." In frustration, Whyte thumped his open hand on the desk. "Just once I'd like to feel sure that I'm not the only one around here who can balance plausible suspicion and raging paranoia . . ."

"That's precisely what you pay me to do," Castle said. "If you think I can't make allowances for coincidence, plain bad luck, and momentary lapses in judgment, then . . ."

Trosper raised his hand and snapped his fingers twice. It was one of the signals used by the Special Forces long-range scout teams trained to operate too deeply within enemy territory to risk even a whisper.

Whyte turned from Castle to glare at Trosper.

"If you two don't knock it off, you'll have me feeling like a twelve-year-old watching a family shoot-out . . ."

There was a moment of quiet before Castle said, "I was out of order. *Je m'excuse*, Duff."

"Too much on my plate," Whyte apologized.

"Before I tiptoe out," Trosper said, "there's one question." For the first time he had the undivided attention of both men. "Do we know how Moscow learned Tomahawk's pseudonym? I know it sometimes happens, but is it possible that an agent as important as Tomahawk ever got to know the codename the Firm assigned to him?"

"Paranoia notwithstanding," Castle said slowly, "there's no reason at all to believe Skoblin ever learned that our in-house name for him was Tomahawk."

As he reached for the letter, Trosper reflected on his half-finished manuscript on fighting ships. He reminded himself of Emily's interest in remaining briefly in the Washington area, and of the comfortable apartment Whyte had arranged for them to use. He knew that if he asked even one more question, he would be stepping into a maze that could only lead to the further involvement he had promised himself to avoid.

He waited in silence, the office a *tableau vivant*. Finally, admitting defeat, he turned to Castle. "Two more questions—are the Troika comment, the letter drop, and the compromised codename the only bona fides your volunteer had to offer?"

"Not half," Castle said quickly.

"Second, am I supposed to assume that there must be more to all this than the likelihood that the defector Volin has assumed a new identity and has come back to us for a second helping?"

Castle shook his head. "Just read the document, and check the Winesap file."

As he folded the letter and stuffed it into his breast pocket, Trosper glanced at Whyte, who had begun to leaf through a sheaf of cables, and turned to Castle, who was unable to suppress a slight smile. "Snookered once, snookered again," Trosper muttered.

Whyte looked up. "That reminds me," he said. "Young Widgery has been cooling his heels in New York. On the chance you can use a caddy, he'll be working with you for the present."

"Who Widgery?" Trosper asked impatiently.

Castle stirred. " 'Tis Widgery who brought us Winesap," he said softly. "Miss Pinchot will have the Winesap file on your desk by the time you get back."

8 WASHINGTON, D.C.

The typing was ragged, and the margins were close to the edges and bottom of the pages. The "e" had shouldered itself a bit above the other characters, and the capital "T" and "N" were slightly askew. It would be easy enough for the Magicians to identify the typewriter and country of origin. With luck, and if the machine was old enough, a microscopic measurement of the wear on the most common letters in the various tables of frequency—in English, e-t-a-o-n-i-r-s-h—might even indicate the language that had most frequently been punched through the keyboard. But this was a technical problem, and something for the experts.

He took a sip of the tepid coffee and reminded himself to make sure the Controller's secretary brought him tea instead of the anemic coffee that was one of the lesser amenities of the Controller's mess. He turned again to the text. The date, typed in the upper right corner, was in European style, "10.IX.93," and no effort was wasted in the blunt salutation.

Dear Sir:

My present circumstances mandate that I have a proposal of interest to you. I am in the U.S. illegally, sent here after much training and preparation to represent certain clandestine interests of the new Moscow Center, the SVR as you know it.

Because of present international situation, and ostensible détente in intelligence strife, my chiefs informed me that my work has been suspended. My record and accomplishment is such that I am offered the possibility of returning to Moscow for assignment, or to remain here until I will be reactivated in future. But if I am staying here I will *not* be paid until I will be reactivated.

After three years hard training and perfecting cover, I prefer not to work in Russia at present. I choose to remain here and develope available business opportunitys. For this I need financial support originally promised by the Center.

My proposal is following: For $300,000 in cash I will disclose one very important Moscow Center activity that will positively not be set aside for considerations of present policy of good relations. The affaire is too important to Moscow and is very serious from your security points of view.

I understand you get many propositions like this. But my offer is authentic. To prove I have special knowledge, I *give* the following.

a. I am sending this letter to an address well known to you. It also known in Moscow, and was used by one of your men. You called him Tomahawk.

b. As second prove, I recommend that you have a trusted person check up on the traitor Gholam. For detail you must look in your active sources list.

c. Because I risk my life in dealings with you, I insist that you Mr. Whyte take personal interest in my offer and that you insist it be handled more professionally than your bureau showed in the TROIKA investigation.

This will convince you that I am valid collaborator. Because my business opportunitys are ephemeral, and to be dealt with quick, I must know soon if you are interested in my proposal. You must contact me by putting and advertisement on PERSONALS page of BLOOD 'N GUTS magazine in *next issue*. Address advertisement to SINON and give me address where I can write one of your best men.

SINON

Clipped to the last page of the letter was a note from Miss Pinchot to Castle. "*Blood 'N Guts* is one of the smallest of the several guerrilla/soldier-of-fortune/survivalist magazines. It lives up to its title in every respect, and is filled with allegedly first-person accounts of guerrilla activity, tips on counter-terrorist tactics, dirty fighting, etc. There is also advice on how to survive when 'they'—never very clearly identified, presumably the readers supply their own demons—try to take over and redblooded chaps must use desperate measures to survive. I suspect that most of the readers are fantasists, although the magazine is also sold in Army PX's here and abroad. Oddly enough, the material is consistently well written."

Trosper read Sinon's letter again, more slowly. The written English was clumsy, but effective enough to be rated by the language staff at the Fort as "operationally fluent, adequate for field use." Trosper's familiarity with three foreign languages had irrevocably corrupted his ability to spell in English, but as he continued to read he underlined numerous misspellings, errors in syntax, and mistakes that a non-native speaker might make when reaching too far for a synonym. Or, as he reminded himself, errors that might be made by a person pretending not to write fluent English. The erratic use of the definite article was characteristic of native Russian or Polish speakers using English.

The letter had been mailed from New York in an envelope addressed to Mrs. Jane Noldy Womack, 73 Blossom Path, Baltimore, Maryland 21210, and was prepared exactly as specified in the Tomahawk communications plan. "Mrs. Womack" was the nonexistent sister of Ms. Bertha Noldy, a retired, regular-army master sergeant, who had been recruited by the support staff to serve as a letter drop. As far as the Baltimore postman might know, "Mrs. Womack" lived with her sister, Sergeant Noldy. Had the local postman been suborned to keep a mail-cover on Mrs. Womack, he would have reported that she received one personal letter and *Time* magazine every week, and the *Reader's Digest* monthly. Although she also received the usual lashings of junk mail—magazine subscriptions were a sure way of inspiring enough advertising mail to add verisimilitude to an otherwise fallow letter drop—the only regular personal correspondence Mrs. Womack received was the weekly envelope with a Cleveland postmark, and an occasional letter from Europe.

Had the postman been more determined, he would have reported that although the magazines, advertising mail, and the weekly personal letter were addressed to Mrs. Jane Womack, the occasional personal letters mailed from abroad were invariably addressed to "Mrs. Jane *Noldy* Womack." The postman would not have known, and could not have learned, that when he delivered a letter addressed to Mrs. Jane *Noldy* Womack, retired Sergeant Noldy would telephone an unlisted number in Washington and drive immediately to a safe apartment on Connecticut Avenue. There she would deliver the unopened letter to an affable young man she knew as Bert Johnson.

Like a book collector whose eye is drawn to a shabby but vaguely promising volume on the bottom shelf in a thrift shop, Trosper never opened a case file without a rush of anticipation. Although he had read hundreds of such files, he had never shaken the feeling of discovery as, page by page, he studied the development, and sometimes the unraveling, of operations.

He shoved aside the stiff plastic folders labeled *Support* and *Production*. This necessary but static material would be studied later. It was the operations section of the file that he wanted, the jumble of dispatches, cables, meeting reports, tri-annual summaries, and memoranda that pieced together a narrative of the operation, day by day, meeting by meeting, crisis by crisis. This was the real stuff of espionage, and no matter how hurriedly, brilliantly, badly, pretentiously, or dimly written they might be, these files would forever fascinate Trosper.

The first cable requested a name search on "Subject," and gave the skimpy biographical data that "Treadwell," a case man assigned to the Firm's Vienna cover office, had elicited during a chess game in a Vienna coffee house. "Subject" was an Iranian, employed as a clerk in the Iranian embassy in Vienna. About thirty years old, he described himself as married, and a career functionary of the Iranian foreign office. Subject had apparently welcomed Treadwell's hospitality, and, as he wished to practice his English, would be pleased to meet him again. He presented himself as a staunch democrat and freely stated his deep dislike of certain fundamentalist members of the Iranian staff.

As a further security safeguard, the subject's name was transmitted in a separate cable which was not included in the case file.

At this point Trosper picked up the two sealed envelopes that Castle's administrative assistant had delivered to his desk. He broke one of the seals, glanced at the enclosed card, "James Russell Widgery," signed the card, scrawled his name along the envelope flap, and used a wide strip of cellophane tape to cover his signature and seal the envelope as well. The card in the second envelope read "Gholam Alizadeh, born 6 May 1964, Tabriz, Iran." Trosper sniffed as he repeated the sealing process. "Treadwell and Winesap" sounded more like a Boston law firm than a case man and his Iranian agent.

After cables giving additional biographical data, and brief sketches of the personnel in the Iranian embassy, the Vienna office chief asked headquarters authorization for Treadwell to recruit the Iranian. The approach was approved and a few weeks later, the codename WINESAP was enciphered and buried in the Firm's active sources register.

Trosper flipped through the pages of the tri-annual progress reports. But these polished documents were not what interested him. It was the informal MRs, the meeting reports on which the summaries were based, that he sought out. However many hundreds of case files Trosper had read, the number of MRs he had studied would amplify the total by a factor of at least ten. It was the unvarnished aspect of these informal accounts, written immediately after each contact with an agent, when the case men were flushed with achievement, irritated by failure, or bored with routine, that gave Trosper the necessary, intimate, and grassroots picture of the operation. Or should have done.

But Widgery's MRs were as crisp and impersonal as a wad of traffic tickets. Aside from a fitful carelessness with infinitives, the style was conventional, graduate-student prose. There were no apt descriptions, no flashes of emotion, and none of the casual insights that sometimes illuminated even the dreariest case files. At times Widgery seemed to be holding Winesap at arms' length, handling him as if he were a nominally competent servant who warranted no more intimacy than to be called by his given name.

The meetings with Winesap produced a scant minimum of routine information, but revealed a pattern of suspicion that one after another of the Iranian staff were important figures, clandestinely servicing terrorists transiting Vienna. After weeks of investigation, interest in each of these potential targets appeared to trail off as Winesap focused on a different person.

Trosper reached for another cookie. The stale oatmeal confections were giving him heartburn, but he continued to read. If the Winesap operation had not been tied to Sinon's offer of cooperation, he would have dismissed it as marginal, more useful for providing a young operative his first experience in handling an agent than it might ever be for any of the scraps of intelligence it produced. Perhaps at that time in Vienna, Walt Hamel had been willing to let Widgery cut his teeth on this tame activity before taking on something more productive.

He turned to a Top Secret, Limited Access précis of the Tomahawk operation. Trosper remembered Tomahawk, a Soviet general with important diplomatic and political assignments, as one of the most significant of the Firm's agent operations to have been uncovered by Moscow Center in a decade or more. Unless, as seemed most unlikely, Sinon had learned the precise details of Tomahawk's communication arrangements by a fluke, he must be presumed to have had access to some of the most highly classified counterintelligence data in Moscow. But if Sinon was in a senior enough position to learn of, and then actually address a letter to Duff Whyte through Tomahawk's Top Secret letter drop, why would he have troubled to cite Winesap's humdrum activity as an earnest of his access to Moscow Center secrets? And why would such an allegedly senior officer have knowledge, *any* knowledge, of an Iranian double agent as insignificant as Winesap seemed to be?

Nor was there any explanation for Tomahawk's compromised codename. In internal correspondence, agents were referred to by codename—most often nouns picked in rota from a random list held at headquarters, with care taken to avoid any inadvertent pun, or possible association which, if the codename were compromised, might provide a clue to the agent's identity. Codenames were restricted to internal use within the Firm and, when assigned to an agent, were as closely guarded as the agent's true identity. In contrast, worknames were selected for use in open communications. These were usually common given names, appropriate to the area and language in which they were used—"Tell Harry that Max called."

Taken at face value, Sinon's letter with its four bits of evidence appeared to substantiate the defector Volin's allegation that the Firm was penetrated. But the expressions "at face value" and "at first glance" were anathema. If he were lecturing at the Fort, Trosper would remind the plebes that at face value almost any forty-year-old actress in Hollywood could be made up to play a ravishing ingenue.

Sinon's reference to "the traitor Gholam" was puzzling. If Sinon was well enough informed to know that Gholam Alizadeh was a double agent being run against the Firm, why would he refer to him only by his given name and make no reference to his family name? Did he assume that Gholam was a pseudonym known by the Firm? Or did he assume Gholam was a family name? One thing was certain. Gholam Alizadeh was one of the Firm's marginal agents in Vienna, and the only person in the central agent index with a name even remotely resembling "Gholam."

Sinon's use of the Tomahawk pseudonym and communications plan, his pointed reference to "the traitor Gholam," and his casually correct evaluation of the amateurish Troika investigation were certainly not to be taken at face value. They were to be studied and tracked back to their origins. In his precise script, Trosper penciled the four points on the lined yellow pad beside his work folder.

As he turned back to the Winesap file, Trosper added another note to the yellow pad. "What can Winesap, who sometimes comes across as intelligent and always as sly, possibly think he is doing to warrant wages of four hundred dollars a month?" Then with a slight smile in deference to the problem of balancing plausible suspicion and paranoia, he made note of another possible source for Sinon's data.

This done, he took a bite of the last cookie, and continued to read.

9

WASHINGTON, D.C.

Trosper glanced respectfully at the wall of photographs showing the Firm's Assistant Controller/Personnel in various degrees of proximity to Washington's great and near-great. "Your collection is coming along nicely," he said.

"It's the most benign of my vanities," Frederick P. Tuttle said with a wink. "What with everyone else around here hiding under a bushel, I see no reason why the employees should have the idea that we're *all* a bunch of faceless nonentities."

Trosper smiled politely. "Of course."

"Besides," Tuttle said with a gesture toward the signed photographs on the opposite wall, "some of these have accumulated a certain value."

Trosper turned to the wall, and his grin broadened. Three presidents, two secretaries of state, four national security advisers, a platoon of general officers, a pod of admirals, and more ambassadors and cabinet officers than Trosper could identify. "To be sure," he said.

"Now that you've attempted to make your point," Tuttle said, laughing, "is there something of a more professional nature I can do for you?" He sat behind a desk which if provided with a net might have served as a tournament Ping-Pong table.

"I'd like to see one of your files, something on James Russell Widgery."

"Back with us these days, are you, Alan?"

"In a narrow sense . . ."

"Supervising Mr. Widgery, planning to show him some of the ropes, I presume?"

"We may be doing some work together."

"Personnel files are still restricted to the employee's senior supervisor," Tuttle said as he pressed a button on the panel at the side of his desk.

"Maybe you could just read some of the best bits aloud . . ."

"Widgery, James," Tuttle whispered into the intercom. "While you're waiting, you might want to look at the photograph of Henry the K at the U.N., and the one of Eisenhower on the tee at Burning Tree. The lean gent with the most regular features is young Widgery's pa."

Trosper got up and walked to the photographs. Widgery senior appeared to be comfortably over six feet tall, with close-cropped hair, and a sense of confidence clearly to be seen in the black-and-white photographs.

Tuttle took his time with the personnel file, more time than Trosper thought necessary. He looked up at last. "The usual undergraduate work at Williams, capped with a master's in modern history at Princeton. In the upper ten percent of all our usual pre-employment tests, and, predictably, a better than average training record at the Fort. Long on tradecraft theory, good paperwork. He had fourteen months in Vienna, and is high average for the new boys these days."

"How come he only had fourteen months in Vienna?" The average first field assignment usually ran for at least two years.

Tuttle flipped back through the file. "He developed a little something on his thyroid—not an unusual sort of complaint these days—and we didn't want him operated on in a local hospital, anesthesia and all that."

"But he never went back?"

"While still in hospital, he was picked for the intensive course in Arab studies at Columbia. Because of a complication after the operation, he missed the course. We decided to keep him in New York until another course begins. He's handling a couple of things for us up there." Tuttle shrugged impatiently.

"No shortcomings at all, not the least idiosyncrasy?"

Tuttle frowned and thumbed back through several pages in the file. He glanced up at Trosper and pursed his lips. "I'd have to say he's a bit short on the interpersonal side, impatient with routine activity." Tuttle riffled through a few more pages of the file. "He impressed one of his bosses as being abrupt, not to say abrasive, with colleagues—even, I must say, with supervisors."

"That sounds like the same old blarney," Trosper said. "Isn't it about time to come up with a new litmus, something that will uncover contradictory qualities in the same person—like attention to detail *and* imagination? Maybe even a true-or-false form that will expose what we used to call a nose for news? You could label it an abiding curiosity about what's happening on the other side of the mountain?"

"Good grief, Alan . . ."

"What about testing the ability to see the world through another man's eyes, and to think with the other fellow's heart?"

"Out of bed on the wrong side this morning, is that it?" Tuttle tossed his reading glasses onto the desk and tilted back in his swivel chair. "It was 1919 before the old Army War Office realized that in the war to end all wars, it had had no way of telling which officers were most likely to succeed in combat. During the first few days in the trenches some of the best-trained chest-thumpers froze, while some of the mildest-mannered clerks came on like bloody samurai. What's more, a glance in the rearview mirror showed the same story in the Civil War—that fellow Chamberlain from Maine, for example. World War II, Korea, Vietnam, the Gulf, and all that's happened since have produced a ton of studies, the result of which is zip. Nothing."

"It's not quite the same thing . . ."

"Exactly," Tuttle said. "The Firm can test for a good level of general education, an upper-percentile IQ, the ability to reason, language-learning aptitude, stable personality, and performance under stress. After that it's up to you operators to figure out if the best and the brightest will ever learn to see in the dark."

Trosper got up. "Brightest and best," he murmured. "I take it that this son of the morning has passed on all counts?"

Tuttle smiled. "As I said, he's high average."

10 NEW YORK

"Hi guys, I'm Amanda, your wait-person. I'll be taking care of you today."

Trosper lowered his menu and found himself smiling.

"Something to drink while you're making your decisions?" Amanda wore a blue button-down shirt and a red-and-blue-striped, Brigade of Guards bow tie. Her black harem trousers bloused over the tops of scuffed running shoes.

James Russell Widgery glanced up at Amanda. "Tomato juice. Crushed, not canned. No ice."

Trosper waited, expecting to hear "shaken, not stirred." Perhaps the younger generation had outgrown Ian Fleming.

Widgery favored Amanda with a confident smile and put the menu aside. He was lean, clean-shaven, and the remnants of a late summer tan played perfectly against his dark blond hair. A glance at Amanda's rapt expression confirmed Trosper's opinion that although time had yet to leave any message on Widgery's face, he was spectacularly handsome.

"Orange juice," Trosper said.

Although he usually declined spirits before an operational meeting, Trosper resented the possibility that anyone Widgery's age might suspect he had avoided ordering a martini because it would make a poor impression. Not that wait-person Amanda could have filled such a request even if she hadn't fainted dead away on receiving it. "You've eaten here, what can you recommend?" Trosper said with a grim glance at the white enameled walls and stainless-steel trim that made Annie's Cloud Nine Buttery look more like an operating room than a restaurant.

"I always have the same thing—cool carrot soup, a tofu crepe, and a half-bottle of Edelkraehe."

"Red or white?" Trosper asked hopefully.

"It's water," Widgery murmured. "From Liechtenstein."

"I'll have it all the same."

Amanda began to write.

Widgery took a deep breath. "I'd better confess right now that I'm totally in the dark. All I know is that Dick Todd, my division chief, telephoned me at home this morning and said I was to choose a restaurant where it would be easy for a man to identify me and to introduce himself. He also said I was to be at your disposal until I was told otherwise."

"They say half the fun is in the anticipation," Trosper murmured.

Even more than many of his East Coast peers, Widgery directed a part of his speech through his nose. Years of having to repeat himself at prep school and college had taught him to tilt his head slightly backward as he spoke. This extended his range of audibility, but also risked giving the not entirely erroneous impression that Widgery was talking down to his interlocutors.

Trosper lowered his spoon, still half-filled with what he had decided was cold porridge soup, laced with slivers of raw carrot. "Tell me, how come the FBI isn't handling Winesap?"

Widgery touched a napkin to his lips. "A month or so after I had to leave Vienna, Winesap—whose English is pretty good—was transferred to the Iranian mission here. About that time, Vienna was on the verge of dropping Winesap—no product, as the boss saw it. When the Firm told the FBI that we had a marginal source coming here, they read our file, and suggested that since I was already here, I might as well continue to handle him."

"But they get all of your reports?"

"Of course, and if Winesap ever comes up with anything, I expect the Bureau will want to take him over."

Widgery lapsed into silence as Amanda approached the table. She placed the plate in front of Widgery and lingered long enough to make a delicate adjustment in its position. As Widgery murmured his thanks, a smile broke like a perfect wave across his impeccable features. Amanda blushed, shoved Trosper's plate across the table, and hurried away.

"I'll be able to digest lunch better if you can give me at least a clue as to what is going on," Widgery said.

"It's simple enough," Trosper said. "I've read the Winesap file, and I'd like to get a more nearly firsthand impression of your agent."

"Oh . . . uh, I see." Flustered, Widgery reached for the stemmed glass of Edelkraehe. He took a sip, and rolled the water over his tongue. Then, like a wine taster admiring a vintage color, or a restaurant guest who has found a trace of lipstick on the rim, he raised the glass and for a moment held it to the light. The image flickered as he caught Trosper's amused expression. "But may I at least know why?" he blurted.

"Winesap has come up in another connection, a matter important enough for me to want a personal impression of the man," Trosper said. "Since he's accredited to the U.N., and you're meeting him in a safe house, it shouldn't be much of a problem for me to slip into the back room and listen for a while."

"If you think it's worth the time, but frankly, I've spent hours with this guy, and covered it *completely* in my reports," Widgery said.

"I'd have thought that almost any special interest could be answered from reading the file, or talking to me, and without any . . . er . . . intrusive, back-room monitoring . . ."

"To put it more simply," Trosper flared, "I found the reporting on Winesap superficial, unfocused, and quite useless for my purposes."

Widgery flinched and lowered his head. "For months now, I've been busting my ass trying to make something out of this creep, and now in the first few minutes of talking to someone I never thought I'd catch sight of, much less meet, I find I've been doing everything wrong." He was no longer talking through his nose.

Trosper recognized the *cri de coeur* and throttled his exasperation. So much for forgetting that Widgery was scarcely out of the Firm's romper room when he recruited Winesap. Trosper forced down another bit of the crepe and said, "Let's start over again . . ."

Widgery occupied himself with the soup.

"First, except for the food, I think this is a good place to meet—we're the only two men in the joint, and if one of us was followed, the tail would be as conspicuous as a bald ballerina."

Widgery brightened.

"Second, I might have told you at the outset that I'm involved in a sensitive case—a case that may involve half a dozen other matters, some of them quite touchy. Aside from Mr. Todd, no one in your division is aware that I'm here. What's more, even Todd doesn't know *why* I'm here." Trosper took a final morsel of the tofu crepe. "To make the cheese more binding, you're not to mention this to anyone whomsoever without my express permission."

"But Mr. Todd is my division chief . . ."

Trosper pushed his plate slightly to one side. "Is it possible to get bread in this place?"

Widgery, his face still flushed, beckoned to Amanda. "Some of your house bread, please."

"Just write your routine report on the Winesap meeting without any reference to my being in the back room. If Dick Todd has any problems, he knows who to talk to." Trosper smiled at Widgery. "Now, if I may see the questions you've prepared for the meeting."

"I didn't think I needed any written notes," Widgery muttered, his discomfort returning in a rush of color. "All I have is some follow-up stuff from the last meeting, and a query from the FBI."

"What is that?"

Widgery appeared to have composed himself and was again talking through his slightly upturned nostrils. "An absolutely routine question on the official community."

Amanda put a plate of tissue-thin sliced bread and a saucer of olive oil with garlic cloves on the table. Widgery picked up a slice of the bread and dipped it into the olive oil.

Trosper had never tasted a Communion wafer, but he suspected that Annie's Cloud Nine house bread had the same flavor and consistency. But Widgery was right about one thing. The oil and garlic did wonders for the bread.

It was one of the undistinguished small apartment buildings in the lower thirties on the east side of Manhattan. The safe apartment was on the ground floor—a desirable feature that made it unnecessary to chance using the small elevator and risk sharing it with strangers, who in the absence of other distractions would have the opportunity to study and remember, or possibly recognize a fellow passenger.

"The gear is in the back room," Widgery said. "My friend is due here at five forty-five. Meanwhile, I'm going to test the audio and recording system."

Trosper waited until Widgery had adjusted the earphones and tested and set the volume on the tape recorder before saying, "Why are we here?"

Widgery looked up angrily. "I'm here to meet Winesap," he said. "You've already told me why you're here. But if you're testing my cover, I'll confess right now that I should have told you that I'm documented with the same name I used in Vienna, Peter Lynch. Now I'm a businessman from Boston. Rather than pay for hotel rooms, my firm keeps this apartment, and I stay here when I'm in town. Argo Electronics is in Boston, the apartment is on a two-year lease . . ."

"All right," Trosper said with a grin, "you've passed." There was much to be said for operating in the benign atmosphere of one's own backyard, but it did tend to erode the security disciplines necessary to work effectively in less forgiving climates.

"All the documentation is backed up," Widgery continued, his face flushed. "But in the event a team of hard boys from the Iranian mission and a TV-Tehran spot-news outfit break the door down, what's *your* cover?"

"I'm Paul Doughty, a nautical equipment salesman and golf-playing pal of your father in Boston." Trosper's smile broadened. He was an enthusiastic supporter of doing things by the book. The ability to improvise quickly was a necessary skill for anyone in the racket, but Trosper had always found that case men with the best knowledge of conventional tradecraft were also the best at improvising.

He adjusted the feather-light earphones in time to hear Widgery ask, "How much time do we have?" Trosper nodded; first things always first.

"Not too long, my wife worries if I am late."

There was a rustling sound as Winesap moved to cross his legs or change position in the upholstered chair. Trosper wondered if Winesap adjusted his posture every time he answered a question or only when the question required a defensive answer.

"I had to see that dummy Karem Nabavi. At the office, all day he does nothing, just oversees the housekeeping, watches his helper Bazargan fix that the roof doesn't leak, and the toilets work. Nabavi is just a janitor with a diplomatic pass. Then, at about five o'clock he wants to give a few orders, ask some questions, just to impress everyone how good a revolutionary worker he is."

Winesap's responses to Widgery's probing for details on the mission staff were grudging, those of a man speaking impatiently and from superior knowledge. His accent was light, his English adequate.

Finally, Widgery asked, "What do you have for me?"

There was another rustle of cloth against the upholstered chair. "That bum Hassan is still selling tax-free whiskey to some bar he knows."

"This is not exactly what a newspaper would call a big news day," Widgery said. "I find it impossible to believe there's nothing going on in the mission except a bit of illegal whiskey peddling."

"Look," Winesap said. "I got to be careful around that place. I can't just walk into offices and ask questions like some big diplomat from third floor. I have to be careful. No one trust anyone there. It's like the old days, just after the takeover, no one knows who to trust. You can't believe security police have just stopped work can you?"

"That's exactly the sort of thing I've been trying to find out," Widgery said sharply.

There was a long pause. If Widgery was not fussing with his notes, but remaining silent long enough to force Winesap to continue talking, he was on the right path. Another few seconds and there was the now familiar rustle.

"What you expect from me, anyway? I always try hard but it's not easy. Diplomats look down on me, my wife makes trouble at home. I do my best . . ."

There was another long wait before Widgery said, "What I expect is one thing, what I *want* is another. Do you understand?"

In the silence that followed, Trosper imagined Winesap shaking his head, and acting the simple but honest man, struggling to do his best in a complex world.

Even before Widgery had fixed the date of the next meeting and sent Winesap on his way, Trosper had recognized the man as a museum-quality example of a low-level agent who had no intention of reporting on anything that might conceivably jeopardize his tranquil existence. Unless the local FBI had a different reading on Winesap, the link between Sinon's apparent access to highly restricted data and his casual reference to Winesap as an agent of the Firm and traitor would remain baffling.

11

NEW YORK

Trosper took a deep breath and braced himself. In contrast to the informality and clutter of the secret intelligence outposts in which he had spent much of his working life, the New York field office of the FBI was as taut and businesslike as a bank. The empty in-trays at the corner of each desk offered a mute but scarcely subtle suggestion that not so much as a moment's backlog was to be tolerated in the daily activity. He would have welcomed at least a trace of the jumble of shabby files, worn city directories, tattered telephone books, and torn street maps that marked the workplaces he knew best. But the desks of the FBI agents sharing space in the squad room were immaculate and the work files as neat and uniform as the volumes of an encyclopedia.

In the elevator to Grogan's office, Widgery had glanced anxiously at their escort, and edged closer to Trosper. "I get the impression," he whispered, "that all the Bureau guys are overworked, but Grogan's fair and has always seemed to play straight with me. If there's any problem at all, I think it's just because he doesn't have a very high regard for us, and he's always worried about protecting his turf."

As they threaded their way across the squad room toward Grogan's office, Trosper wondered if it was Dr. Spock's guidance that rendered the new generation so dismally neat, or whether the desk discipline echoed back to Director Hoover's day when legend had it FBI agents were not allowed to have more than one file and two pencils in sight at any time. Widgery broke the reverie with a final bit of advice. "His name is Elmer, but don't *ever* call him that. He prefers Mike—it fits his image better."

"It's your nickel," E. M. Grogan said with enough of a smile to bring the requisite few moments of persiflage to term.

The chief of CI/Section P was five-ten, weighed about a hundred and sixty pounds, and exuded a let's-get-on-with-it approach to life and its problems. If Grogan was like the other Bureau men Trosper had met, he probably worked out three times a week at the New York Athletic Club. Aside from a few photographs and three plaques attesting to his ability with a handgun, Grogan's office was strict government issue. It could as well have been in the Bureau of Indian Affairs as the FBI. The executive class-three desk and the chair behind it were as precise a measure of Grogan's rank as the bronzed oak leaves on the shoulders of an infantry major. With Grogan's next promotion would come a larger desk, a more impressive chair, and a chromium tray with a handsome metal carafe. Never in the years he had frequented government offices had Trosper seen any liquid poured from one of these emblems.

"I'm not sure what you've been told," Trosper said, "but I understand Mr. Whyte or Thomas Castle spoke to your director in Washington yesterday."

"It was Castle," Grogan said.

"It concerns Widgery's friend, Gholam Alizadeh, functionary at the Iranian mission here."

"So I was told," said Grogan with a glance at Widgery.

"A few days ago," Trosper said, "the Firm received an anonymous letter that, along with other data, made it clear that Alizadeh's relationship with us was known to Moscow."

"To Moscow, not *Tehran*?" Grogan's spurt of interest was not feigned.

Trosper nodded and said, "Our tipster presented himself as a former Moscow Center agent, allegedly being recalled from the United States by the new crowd, the SVR. He's looking for a deal, and enough money to establish himself in private business. Along with a few bits of substantiating data—all of it ostensibly and plausibly of Moscow Center origin—he tossed in the Alizadeh allegation for good measure. He didn't explain why he had access to both Russian and Iranian information, but he was sure enough of himself to tell us we'd find Alizadeh in our active source registry."

"And enter at stage center, Thomas Augustus Castle—counterespionage, penetration, deception, and epistemology?" Grogan suggested with a slight smile.

"You've met?"

Grogan took a deep breath. "Ooooh, yeees," he said. "Castle spoke at one of our training seminars at Quantico. Fascinating, but almost incomprehensible until afterwards, when he joined us for a couple of hoots. The bourbon may have helped." Grogan leaned back in his chair. "At this point, I'd better tell you what I told Widge some time ago. We've never been much impressed with Alizadeh. And, to be blunt on a very busy day, the material Widge has passed to us is about at the level of the intelligence bouncing around on the street in front of the Iranian offices—we don't even have to bend over to pick up that sort of stuff."

Widgery tilted his head and was about to speak when Trosper intervened. "In the course of your other activity, has your shop ever spotted anything of concern about Alizadeh? Any connection with the usual terrorist suspects, with the old Moscow Center staff, or the SVR?"

Grogan frowned. "Up front, I can tell you that we've never noticed any particular contact between Alizadeh and any of the hard boys—Iranians, Algerians, Iraqis, the wrong kind of Egyptian, or with anyone in whom we have any special interest. Certainly, nothing with the Russians."

"What about his personal life, social activity, finances, girlfriends?" Trosper waited a moment before saying, "Any suspicious activity on Alizadeh's part—countersurveillance maneuvering, using a pay phone at odd times of day? Odd incoming calls? *Any* of the usual stuff?"

Grogan stiffened. "If you're asking if the Bureau has one of your agents under surveillance, the answer is no. And you can quote me."

Trosper waved his hand impatiently, brushing aside Grogan's obvious irritation. "Not at all . . ."

"But to confirm your suspicions, I'll confess that sometimes we put an eye and an ear on the little birds that one of your crowd promises us are as innocent as newborn chicks," Grogan said with a barely audible chuckle. "Every once in a while we do just that, maybe even a little more than usual for someone like Alizadeh because, after all, he's family—*your* family—in a manner of speaking." He eased himself closer to the desk. "But there hasn't been so much as a whisper. Until a few minutes ago, if you'd asked me, I'd have said

Alizadeh was running clean, and there are damned few in his part of the world I'd say that about."

Grogan glanced at Widgery and turned back to Trosper. "I probably shouldn't admit this either, but since you've come all the way from Washington to discuss this, I might as well tell you that for a few weeks now one of my men has had someone in casual contact with Alizadeh. Not that we planned it, he just bumped up against us. From what he's gathered, your man is just about as advertised, a loyal Iranian clerk, good family man—wife and son—and as our mayor would surely say, a credit to his race, creed, and color." Grogan pulled the bottom drawer of his desk open, propped his feet against it, and leaned back in his chair. "The only thing wrong, if anything is wrong, is that Alizadeh is so *very* clean that anyone with a really suspicious turn of mind might think he's blowing smoke."

"Look," Widgery said. "My man, as you call him, may be a bit tricky, but he's not blowing smoke. He may not be much of an observer, but he's too dumb to lie convincingly over a long period of time."

Grogan stared at the ceiling for a moment before leaning forward to fix his attention on Widgery. "Dumb?" he questioned. "When I was still on the street I always figured I had to know someone pretty well before I could be sure he was any dumber than I am. If Alizadeh is so damn dumb, how come he and his wife are regulars at the opera? Tickets don't come cheap on his wages, and a taste for Western fine arts is not likely to sit well with the neighborhood ayatollah. How come he has a library card, and uses it every couple of weeks? How come the family lives in a better apartment than any of the other clerks? How come they don't hang out with any other clerks at about their level in life?" Grogan kicked the drawer closed and hunched over his desk. "*Dumb* is when you don't take time to get to know anything about your agent except the chicken feed he tells you to write down."

"Alizadeh lives well because he's a double agent, and they probably cosset him," Widgery said loudly. "We know that now, we didn't know it a while ago . . ."

"Easy does it," Trosper interjected. He turned to Grogan.

"In this connection, I also want to mention Viktor Feodorovich Volin . . ."

"The Russian who handed you the Mills woman?"

Trosper nodded. "Yes, and as you probably know, he levanted out of our resettlement program a while ago, presumably so anxious to get on with exploiting the free enterprise system that he didn't take time to say goodbye."

"There was a notice circulated, but I've heard nothing since," Grogan said. "I gather all he had to offer was the Mills woman?"

"Not quite," Trosper said. "Along with the usual bits and pieces he picked up while in training, he also let on that he had heard gossip about a penetration of the Firm."

Grogan whistled sharply. "Well, well, well . . ."

"This came out while Bob Dwyer was Acting Controller. He investigated the allegation, but there was nothing conclusive. By the time Duff Whyte got back and could put the heat on, Volin decamped. I mention Volin in this context only because if the anonymous letter is a scam, it's the sort of a swindle he might try to contrive."

"These days, a fellow has to stand in line to come up with a dodge involving old Moscow Center activity," Grogan said. "The alleys are full of these guys, most of them phony." Grogan leaned back, his hands clasped behind his head. "But say what you want to, Volin had the Mills woman dead to rights. It's only a pity he didn't get here while she was still on her feet."

"I wanted to ask you about her death," Trosper said.

"Ostensibly quite straightforward," Grogan said.

"*Only* ostensibly?"

For a moment Grogan seemed to be measuring Trosper. "The wrong time of day for an armed mugging, the wrong place, too much traffic, and no reason for the suspect to think that Mills would be carrying enough in her running clothes to make the effort worthwhile." He waited before saying, "Dumb as they are, and even coked to their ears, most street creeps have *some* smarts."

"What about the weapon?"

"Two rounds from a 22-caliber, semiautomatic pistol, the shots perfectly placed," Grogan said. "Not your everyday gun, and not the work of a street punk who's never been on a target range."

"Witnesses, collateral evidence?"

Grogan leaned forward, holding his chin in his hand. "We went over the area inch by inch, and questioned all but one of the apparent witnesses. Their stories are confirmed, and their background checks are all negative."

"The missing witness?"

Grogan blinked in surprise. "That's what it gets down to. The one we can't locate was closest to Mills when it went down. A thin, black male, expensive running threads and a visored cap, like those flimsy things bike racers wear. As best we can reconstruct it, this guy was within a few yards of Mills—maybe even closer. He was first to touch the body, and the first to run for help—as he said, to call for an ambulance from the precinct substation right there in the park. But he didn't go to the police, he didn't call for an ambulance, and he ain't been seen since."

"Was there any suggestion of a sexual assault gone wrong—maybe an attempt to drag her into the bushes?"

Grogan smiled and shook his head. "Highly unlikely, wrong time of day, too many witnesses in the vicinity . . ."

"Was the pistol close enough to leave powder burns?"

A flicker of irritation crossed Grogan's face. "You know, we're getting into NYPD business here," he said. "I'm CI, the Mills murder is a violent crime. The only reason I'm involved is the allegation against Mills, and the apparent proofs of her espionage."

"I understand," Trosper said, "but . . ."

"And the only reason the Bureau has any responsibility at all for the case, and that it's not the exclusive property of the NYPD, is that the victim was a State Department—that is federal—employee, and assigned to our U.N. mission, and the whole goddamned U.N., the jelly-bellies from the State Department, and even Mayor Loud-Mouth were screaming about *our*—the *Bureau*, mind you—having lost control of the streets." Grogan shook his head in disgust. "The fact remains that along with the protection of the NYPD, Mills also was entitled to some measure of federal protection, even though she didn't have diplomatic immunity."

"Or even immunity from getting shot dead in Central Park,"

Widgery muttered. In the spartan atmosphere of Grogan's office, Widgery's nasal delivery was strident as a cornet.

Trosper waved him to silence, and asked, "No collateral evidence on the ground?"

Grogan shook his head. "We found the empty cartridge shells, but the area had been too much tramped over to hope for any footprints of interest."

"Prints on the shells?"

Grogan blinked; not everyone knew that spent cartridge shells were excellent sources of fingerprints. He shook his head. "The empties are damned small, and both had been stepped on. Ballistics thought that maybe the ammo had been wiped clean, or handled with gloves—there was almost no trace of the lubricant they come coated with."

"How far afield did your search go in the park?"

Grogan leaned back and folded his arms across his chest. "If we'd done the whole damned park, we'd have found enough weapons to outfit a Special Forces battalion—of course, it would have taken the entire New York office a month to do it."

"I mean did you go a hundred, two hundred yards from the scene?"

"With the local precinct, our people covered all of the escape routes the suspect could have taken from the scene," Grogan said, his face flushed. "This means we checked every place he might have ditched the weapon, his gloves, his cap, bloodstained clothing, or anything else that might have linked him to the crime. To do this, the uniforms and our guys sorted out every goddamned trash can for three blocks around the scene, examined the sewer inlets, and waded around under every bridge the guy might have crossed." He stopped, took a deep breath, and said, "Digging in garbage cans is standard cop practice, but it's not what my guys call a day at Disneyland."

"I gather the NYPD still carries the murder as a mugging by persons unknown," Trosper said. "Is this your reading?"

Grogan shook his head. "It never was *my* opinion. As far as I'm concerned, Mills was murdered by a professional hit man for reasons unknown."

"Reasons unknown?"

"At the time we were checking this out, we didn't know Mills was an agent," Grogan said. "When this surfaced, it added a whole new dimension to our investigation. Unless it actually was an attempted mugging, I would have to guess she was hit by her Russian pals." Grogan tilted way back in his chair. "From what I've learned, she could only have been a damned valuable source for Moscow."

Trosper smiled. "Which suggests that the most plausible reason for them to have killed her would be to protect an even better source?"

"Amen," said Grogan.

Trosper turned to Widgery. "Jim, will you call for our car?"

"We don't have a car," Widgery said sourly. "But I take your point." He got up and moved toward the door.

"Hey, Widge," Grogan called as he stepped around the desk. "No hard feelings, huh?" He took Widgery by the shoulder and shook him as if he were ruffling a puppy's fur. "I've got a hundred open files, and only half the staff I need just to stay even. Sometimes things just pop out." As they shook hands, Grogan held on to Widgery's shoulder. "There are some things we've all got to learn—I'll square it with your boss."

"Okay, okay," Widgery said. "It's a deal."

As the door closed, Grogan turned to Trosper. "I'm sorry I blew off . . . Widge is all right. It's probably just because he's here without a boss, someone to keep him on his toes." He dropped into the chair behind the desk, and laughed. "I'll try to *cosset* him a little the next time he comes over . . ."

"It won't do any harm . . ."

Grogan gazed speculatively at Trosper before saying quietly, "There was one thing, perhaps a bit of evidence. Maybe it's nothing, but you never know." He leaned back in his chair, laced his fingers, thrust his arms straight forward and turned his palms outward. Then, in a series of deft twists, he cracked one after another of his knuckles. With a satisfied grin, he dropped his arms and pulled his chair closer to the desk. "One of my bright young men turned over a trash can, about three hundred yards from where Mills died, but *not* on the route the black guy started on when he cut out for the precinct.

There was the usual swill—you know we dump the cans onto a plastic sheet, and then sort through the crap one item at a time."

"Not, as you say, a day at the beach even in cool weather," Trosper said.

"It comes with the territory, and the elbow-length, heavy gloves in case we hit a contaminated needle," Grogan said. "In the middle of all the usual mess, my man found a piece of what seemed to be a latex face mask. What's more, he had the brains to take it over to Brooks, the big theatrical costume outfit in midtown. Sure enough, it seems to be from a professional latex mask, the sort of thing they use in movies, and usually custom-made." Grogan waited for Trosper's reaction.

Trosper nodded obediently.

"It was a part of a Negro mask, like the whole thing had been torn up, and in the dark this piece got dropped and later maybe one of the street sweepers or someone tossed it in the trash."

"A male mask?"

"As far as we could tell . . ."

"I'll be damned . . ."

"But there's nothing to link it to the murder except the probability that the job was done by a pro, not some dumb-ass street junkie—a *trained* professional, someone who really planned the hit." Grogan was silent for a moment. "Take, for example, the fact that the trash can was so far away from the shooting, and in exactly the opposite direction from which the missing *black* witness left the crime scene. If it was a planned hit, it just might be that the suspect figured to start out in one direction, and then changed course at about the time he tore off and destroyed the mask."

"And you see no connection with the people who had blackmailed her?"

Grogan shook his head. "Even if they had known that their man Volin had done a bunk, and would sooner or later peddle Mills, why would they mess around with a high-risk stunt and hit her? She was already down the drain. From what I know about the case, Mills was recruited just before Moscow Center called time-out and established their new-look service, the SVR, a bright and shiny troop of Boy Scouts if ever there was one. If Mills was arrested and confessed to having been blackmailed, and if any of our cookie-pushers got up the courage to complain, all Moscow had to say was that it happened in the bad old days, and that—Scout's honor—everything's different now."

"Which brings us back to the probability that Mills knew something Moscow was afraid she would spill under interrogation," Trosper said.

"That's certainly my view," said Grogan.

"Did you talk to any of Mills's supervisors here at the U.S. mission to the U.N.?"

"Oh, yes," Grogan said. "For what it was worth, I talked to them all—right after the shooting, and then when we learned about the espionage allegations, I did it all over again. Everyone seemed to like Mills, although a couple of her pals thought she had a drinking problem. Aside from that, the consensus was that she was a solitary woman, shy, and not blessed with men friends of any variety."

"What about the people she worked with in Moscow?"

"The Washington office handled that—and as their records show, no one had the slightest notion that there was anything out of order about Mills. She was a competent, hard-working, senior secretary, a bit shy, and a nice person. I talked to Ambassador Hardwick, who was head of the delegation she was posted with in Moscow. He had a high opinion of her, and didn't believe she could have been blackmailed into espionage." Grogan laughed. "Hardwick is a dandified sort of ambassador, but a nice guy. Nothing like Slocombe, his deputy at the time, and a really pompous featherhead. Slocombe nearly had a fit when the Washington guys asked if he could identify the stud in the photographs Volin had supplied."

Trosper smiled. "I've never met Hardwick, but I know Slocombe from way back, and I plan to have a chat."

"Aside from the boozing that seems to have started after she was blackmailed, Mills had a clean sheet," Grogan said.

As they shook hands, Trosper said, "The way our anonymous tipster came on, there could be a considerable domestic angle in running down Volin's allegation, not to mention the Mills case. If it turns out that way, would you like a piece of it? Maybe get yourself sprung for a few days to come along on a joint project?"

Grogan began to laugh. "That's an idea—even if they wanted to, my outfit couldn't just turn over legal jurisdiction to something called Research Estimates, Incorporated." He waited before saying, "But who'd be in charge?"

"That's the sort of thing I let other people worry about," Trosper said. "Besides, maybe your people might like to have someone keep an eye on what I'm up to . . ."

"Now that might be," Grogan said slowly. "As you just saw, I could use a breather. Maybe a little R and R with the wild bunch could be worked out."

"It'll be up to Washington, but I'll mention it to our people," Trosper said.

At the door, he paused to glance at a framed black-and-white photograph on the wall near Grogan's desk. It was slightly out of focus, and grainy for an 8 × 10 enlargement. A blond woman held a black poodle-like dog to her breast as the dog strained to lick her face. The joy of the woman in the dog and the dog's devotion were plain to be seen. It was a remarkable photograph, an unpretentious moment of truth and a work of pure art. Trosper studied the photograph before turning to say goodbye.

"My wife really loved that pooch," Grogan said.

12 NEW YORK

"Mr. Slocombe is expecting me," Trosper said. "Mr. Harrison Slocombe."

The receptionist at the U.S. mission to the United Nations nodded and ran her finger down a list on the desk beside the telephone. "I'll just call Mr. Slocombe's assistant to escort you," she said.

Trosper stepped out of the elevator, surrendered his coat, and settled down in one of the club chairs in the reception area. Had he been betting, he would have wagered that Slocombe would underline his view of their relative positions in life by inflicting a fifteen-minute wait. It was, however, nineteen minutes before the secretary beckoned Trosper into an office two doors to the left of the ambassador's suite. All these years so close to the summit, and still a bridesmaid, Trosper reflected.

"Alan, my dear old boy." Slocombe thrust himself up and leaned across the desk to shake hands. The gesture was not wasted. Had Minister Counselor Slocombe accepted Trosper as an equal in his protocol-encrusted life, he would have stepped from behind the desk to greet him.

"It's been a while," Slocombe said as he waved Trosper to a chair in front of the desk. He was well over six feet tall. A severe gray suit, stiff collar, spittlesfield tie, and a waistcoat adorned with a gold watch chain gave Slocombe's spare figure the aspect of an elegant vicar, or an overdressed undertaker.

"Where were we last—Berlin? All those tiresome negotiations, trying to swap some wretched Russian for one of your sordid villains?"

"Something like that," Trosper murmured.

"You're looking fit, I'll say that for Research Estimates. Have your own trainers, do you?" Slocombe's prominent cheekbones, beaked nose, deep forehead, and limp hair combed straight across his head never failed to give Trosper the impression he was confronting a naked skull.

Slocombe shot his cuffs, fumbled in his waistcoat for a thin gold watch, and released the chain. "I've been running twenty minutes late all day," he said, propping the watch upright on the desk. "I'm here for a few days to get things on the track for the opening of the General Assembly. It's simply hell not working with one's own staff."

"I'm sure it must be."

"I'll admit I've no idea what echoes of the late cold war bring you to Gotham and to the U.N.—it seems to me that I'd heard you were *en poste* in London?"

Trosper had no interest in explaining his employment status. "I want to ask you about Charlotte Mills . . ."

Slocombe knitted his heavy eyebrows in apparent concentration. "*The* Charlotte Mills? The one who got herself shot in Central Park?"

Trosper nodded.

"That superannuated little *tramp* and damnable spy." Slocombe shook his head in disgust.

"Surely not a tramp . . ."

"*Not* a tramp?" Slocombe said, his voice rising. "Those ghastly photographs would turn your stomach." He paused as if striving for a temperate expression. "Perhaps not *your* stomach. That sort of thing may be common coin in the world you scuffle around in, but *I've* never seen anything like the pictures. Our security people actually looked me up in Washington to brief me on what she had sold to the Russians, and then the FBI insisted I check the photos on the chance I might be able to identify the lout they had caught in the act. Imagine those cretins forcing me to study those photographs!"

Trosper imagined it very clearly and the scene delighted him.

"What's more, I can't understand why a forty-year-old woman would pose for anything like that."

"Charlotte Mills wasn't posing, she was betrayed by a man, an expert at that sort of maneuver."

"Whatever excuse she came up with, it was damned decent of someone in Moscow, in the local community I suppose, to let us know what one of our staff had got up to in her off hours," Slocombe said.

"It wasn't anyone in the *local community*, as you put it, who had the photographs, it was the operative sent from Moscow to handle Mills in this country who gave us the photographs when he defected."

"It's just too damned bad she died before they caught her," Slocombe said. "She would have deserved just what she got."

"As may be," said Trosper. "When we passed the defector's report to the FBI and your security people, they found ample evidence to bear out the story."

"Then she never made a confession?"

"Unfortunately she never had the opportunity . . ."

"The security people were keen to know what I knew about her in Moscow. As it happened, I scarcely knew the woman, but if I can believe what they told me, along with her pornographic stardom there was no doubt that your Miss Mills was a mercenary little spy."

"I'm not sure that money entered into it . . ."

"I never believed much of it anyway," Slocombe said. "The Russians I've come to know would scarcely need any advice from *une telle dévergondée*."

"Quite true, Harry. They've never been much interested in advice, but they do like to read our documents—top-secret cables, dispatches, position papers."

"That's not true at all—they *do* appreciate advice, it's just that they're particular about who they get it from."

"Perhaps, Harry, but along with everything else the SVR has in common with the old Moscow Center outfit, it's an absolute fact that they'd rather have a fistful of documents than some self-styled pundit whispering in their ear."

"Each to his own," Slocombe said with another, more portentous, glance at his watch.

"Had you known Charlotte Mills very long before the unpleasantness?"

Slocombe leaned back in his chair and formed a cathedral with his long fingers. "Good Lord, it's difficult to remember, one gets around so much in this work. Speaking bluntly, she was one of those drab little people one gets so accustomed to seeing in the background that one forgets specifics. But we must have rubbed shoulders—*so to speak*, Alan, so to speak—somewhere or other before her unhappy excursion to Moscow."

"She was your secretary in Moscow?"

"Certainly not. She was pool property, available to anyone who needed secretarial help. In practice, that meant that Ambassador Hardwick—Ting—made the most use of her services."

"The security people and the FBI got detailed statements from the ambassador at the time, but none of it was very useful or particularly perceptive."

Slocombe shrugged. "What can I say?"

"But you were her supervisor?"

Slocombe thought for a moment. "As I recall it, there were ten or twelve people, including two or three clericals, in our delegation.

I was second to Ting. On form, he would have been Mills's chief. Actually, Ting must have known her a lot better than I ever did, he's always been a great one for keeping in touch with the troops, bucking up their morale and such."

"From what the defector told us," Trosper said, "Mills met their agent, a man she knew as Yuri Krotov, a few days after arriving in Moscow. He also reported that she was confronted and recruited four or five weeks after their affair began."

"I really have no idea," Slocombe said. "I suppose the security files would have the details."

"I've read the file, but I'm not sure how Mills might have met a Russian quite so early in her assignment in Moscow."

"I'm afraid I still can't help you," Slocombe said impatiently.

"Were there any receptions, big parties to which the clerical staff might have been invited?"

"I suppose so, the Russians are rather good about that sort of thing when they put their mind to it, although they usually make a very intelligent distinction between proper diplomats and the *functionaries*, as they call them." Slocombe pursed his lips. "That, alas, is more than I can say for our service. These days, it's almost impossible to distinguish between our clerical and administrative staffs and the high table, so to speak."

"Would your hosts have done something special for your delegation?"

Slocombe paused. "Now that you mention it, I think we may well have been invited to an informal reception the day after Ting arrived. I got to Moscow with the advance party, and seem to remember suggesting that to get things off on the right foot, our hosts might want to do something for Ting when he got there. As I remember it now, we were invited to a reception for some Soviet film people who had won awards of some kind."

"Would Mills have gone?"

"I'm sure little Miss Hot Pants would have leaped at the opportunity. The clerical staff have very little social life, and most of them are quite incapable of organizing anything at their own level." He paused reflectively. "I suppose if she did go, she might even have been in Ting's car. The embassy was so damned chintzy with its transport we often had to share cars and drivers. That's the sort of economy that makes us look like a bunch of yokels to our foreign colleagues."

"It's too much to suppose you might have known who she met, or talked with, there?"

"I'm afraid I still remember the woman as an old maid, and rather a wallflower, but this may be an assumption on my part. The film and theater set in Moscow are pretty much the cream—perhaps I should say champagne—of their society, and always add a bit of zip to any gathering. Some of them are damned attractive, socially *and* intellectually. I remember that even Ting—because of his ability in the language, he never was stuck in that cold-war time warp that your crowd still inhabits—was delighted by the reception we got. My guess is that if any of the Russians talked to Mills, she'd have been damned impressed."

"Did you ever hear of a Yuri Krotov?"

Slocombe shook his head. "Afraid not."

"Are you sure?"

Slocombe smiled. "Look, through the years I've got to know a lot of Russians, and quite a few Yuris. But out of context I can't recall any Yuri Krotkin."

"Yuri *Krotov*," Trosper said patiently. "He's allegedly an actor, associated with one of their film organizations."

"Why would I have known him?"

"Judging from what the defector said, Krotov was the man who drugged and seduced her . . ."

"Sorry," Slocombe said, shaking his head.

"Would you know if Miss Mills had hung out with the marines, the embassy guards at all?"

"Really, Alan, I've no idea, but I'm sure our security people questioned them at the time." Slocombe leaned forward across the desk. "Isn't all this fuss about Miss Mills getting to be rather old hat? I mean Gorbachev is history, the tramp is dead, and the Department has probably already published the documents she sold. Nowadays, we can scarcely close a negotiation before the Department publishes our papers as fodder for the current Ph.D. crop and their illiterate theses."

A light flashed on Slocombe's telephone. "The meeting will be in the ambassador's office at five-thirty," Slocombe said crisply as he dropped the phone into its cradle. "Let's face it, Alan, the cold war's been dead for years, and even your bunch has had to admit that your meal ticket, the dread Moscow Center, wasn't half so fearsome as you've been telling the congressional wise men all these years. What's your sudden interest in this?"

"It touches, or may do, on something that's just come alive," Trosper said. "As you know, we've cleared my speaking to you with your people in Washington."

"Exactly, old boy," Slocombe said. "These days you couldn't have got past the guard downstairs without clearance from on high." Slocombe got up and stepped around the desk. "Are you still sailing at all? I heard you were representing *Poshcraft*—really, Alan?"

"That was a brief episode, but I've not been sailing much either. How about you?"

"I've just picked up my new Cheoy Lee—thirty-eight feet, absolutely gorgeous, and I'm out on Chesapeake Bay every weekend that I'm not working—summer and winter."

"Cripes, that's a bloody ship," Trosper said.

"It's as much as I can handle—most weekends I'm all alone. I find a few hours' solitude on the water helps to clear the mind."

"I always find that you diplomats take good care of yourselves . . ."

"And the best of us take care to marry a woman who can afford to indulge us," Slocombe said with a tight smile.

As they shook hands, Slocombe asked, "Is there some sudden urgency about all this interest in history?"

"I'm beginning to think so," Trosper said.

13

SAVANNAH

The trim two-story building sat fifty feet back from the brick sidewalk that ran along the quiet street. A freshly painted, waist-high picket fence framed the neatly cut lawn, and a thick bank of rose bushes ranged in front of the tall, six-over-six windows that faced the street. From the sidewalk, the building looked more like a discreet medical center, occupied by a group of successful suburban doctors, than the office of ONAN Publications.

Trosper lifted the latch and closed the gate carefully behind him. As he approached the varnished door, the late afternoon sun caught the small brass numerals at the side. There was no indication of who or what might occupy the premises, and no response when Trosper tried the heavy door. He drew back to check the number again. Six hundred seventeen—at least the address was correct. He found the bell and pressed three brief rings. The door latch released and Trosper stepped across a small hallway and into the reception room.

Two comfortable wicker chairs, a chintz-covered sofa, and a coffee table were the only furnishings in the softly lighted room. Copies of *Time*, the *Economist*, and the *Wall Street Journal* were neatly arranged on the coffee table. A small grated window opened onto what appeared to be a receptionist's room, but the desk was unoccupied.

The only address listed for the editorial and advertising departments of *Blood 'N Guts* was a letter box in the Savannah, Georgia, area. No telephone numbers were given, and Trosper's efforts to call showed clearly that if ONAN Publications or its flagship magazine *Blood 'N Guts* had telephones, the numbers were unlisted. When his express letter to the magazine stating that Mr. Paul Doughty would be in Savannah and had urgent business to discuss with the advertising department was not answered, Trosper asked Castle to have one of his operatives uncover the telephone number and whereabouts of the magazine's editorial offices.

"Mr. Doughty? Is it Mr. Paul Doughty?" The inner door of the reception room had swung open. "I'm Abigail Slotter, Mr. O'Hara's assistant."

She was short, plump, and past sixty. Her gray hair was in a pompadour and her gray-blue dress fit too subtly to have been bought in any women's department.

Trosper dropped the *Economist* on the coffee table. "Paul Doughty," he said as they shook hands. "I'm glad to have found you at last."

"Mr. O'Hara is out of town, but y'all come right on in with me."

She led Trosper along a carpeted hallway, and through a cluttered editorial room, with three computer stations. "You've caught us just at the moment we've put our upcoming issue to bed," she said. "We've only got a caretaker staff today. If you'd been here yesterday, you'd have found all three of us with our sleeves rolled up and in our usual closing frenzy. No matter how hard Mr. O'Hara tries to do things in advance, the twelve hours before closing is always Chaos Castle."

She stopped at a half-glass door marked Terrence O'Hara, Publisher/Editor. Beneath this, but in equally large print, was inscribed Abigail Slotter, Assistant. She held the door open for Trosper. "That's why Terry—Mr. O'Hara always insists that we call him Terry, so we're all on a first-name basis hereabouts—always gives the staff two days off, just to catch our breath once an issue is locked in."

She motioned Trosper to a chair and took her place behind one of the two desks that, placed side by side, dominated the office. On the wall to the left of the desk were framed blowups of what Trosper assumed were the more lurid *Blood 'N Guts* covers. A poster-size photograph of Terry O'Hara dominated the opposing wall, his epauletted, khaki shirt open wide enough to show a hint of chest hair, and the sleeves carefully rolled to expose well-developed biceps.

"Now, Mr. Doughty, perhaps some tea while you tell me what we can do for you?" Without waiting for an answer Abigail Slotter turned to an intercom, flipped a button, and said, "Kathy-Jo, it will be tea for two this afternoon, dear."

Trosper poured a few drops of milk into his cup. "I've had quite a time finding you people. Are all of your phones unlisted?"

Abigail Slotter smiled. "We used to be in the phone book, and listed in the business directory, but we found that too many of our subscribers liked to drop in for a chat with Terry. He always made himself available—some of them had driven hundreds of miles—but the visits turned out to be very time-consuming." She took a sip of tea. "It was a little dangerous too, they were forever bringing along their guns and survival gear—canisters of nausea gas, fragmentation grenades, miniature chain saws and such—for Terry to admire." Her smile broadened. "It's rather a relief to see that you're not armed." She pushed her glasses up onto her forehead. "You *aren't* armed, are you?"

Trosper opened his jacket. "Clean as a whistle, what you see is what I am."

"And what brings you here?"

"It's nothing of any great importance. If I could have found your advertising department I'd have handled things by telephone. All I want is to place a notice in the personals column of *Blood 'N Guts*."

Abigail Slotter peered more closely at Trosper. "That shouldn't be much of a problem," she said slowly, "though we do have to insist that our content rules be complied with. I'm afraid we get rather more than our share of what you might call the fantasy fruitcakes . . ."

Trosper could not help laughing. "Fantasy fruitcakes?"

"You'd be surprised, Mr. Doughty, how many people want to advertise themselves as available for really *odd* jobs—the sort of thing that involves putting a hit on someone's inconvenient but rich old auntie, or perhaps taking out an overinsured helpmeet . . ."

"I see . . ."

"Then there's the nut trade, the weirdos who've bought so much mail-order commando equipment that they think they're ready to hire out as freelance warriors, instantly available for any little old guerrilla movement or militia that might like to have them." Abigail paused to drop a slice of lemon into her teacup. "That sort of advertising is against the rules." She studied Trosper more closely. "You're not on the lam from some bin, are you, Mr. Doughty?"

"Bin?"

"As in *loony* bin?"

Trosper laughed again. "It's the first time anyone ever asked, but the answer is no."

"I didn't think so, you're not the type," she said. "The real nutters either run to fat, or are bone thin, with the complexion of a maggot." She adjusted her glasses. "But you look fit. Six feet, and a dab more. Fifty years and maybe a few months. Pushing two hundred pounds I'd guess, but you'd better keep an eye on it." She smiled brightly. "What I can't figure is your getup. I haven't seen shoes like yours since my husband died. He used to have them made in some little shop in Boston that he started with while he was still in Cambridge."

Trosper put down his teacup and took a bite of cucumber sandwich. "I realize it's very late, but I really need to place this notice in the personals column of your next issue." He pushed a typewritten paper across the desk.

Abigail picked up the paper and began to read aloud. "Sinon, please call Mr. Peach soonest at . . ." She stopped before reading the telephone number. "Is this a legitimate telephone number? I might want to call it."

Trosper nodded. "Go right ahead, call now if you wish." He didn't like the cover name Peach and had meant to have the support staff use a more common name, but there hadn't been time.

"Sinon?"

"That's what the fellow I'm trying to reach calls himself." Trosper thought for a moment and added, "He's offering some unusual military memorabilia . . . Mr. Peach is a collector . . . museum-quality pieces."

Abigail pushed the notice to one side and picked out a thick volume from the bookcase behind her desk. She flipped through the pages, pushed her glasses up, and read for a moment. She smiled, and slipped the book back into the bookcase. "We have to check these things—obscene anagrams, bad puns, scatology, codewords for kiddie porn. There's no end to what some of Terry's readers try to put over on us."

"Then you'll accept our notice?"

Abigail smiled. "Yes, of course. I've enjoyed meeting you, but you really might have done all this by mail."

"Which brings me to my second problem," Trosper said softly. "It is essential that this notice appear in your upcoming issue."

Abigail shook her head. "Oh, Lordy, I'm afraid that's just not going to be possible. We've just closed and we print tomorrow."

"This is really important . . ."

"I'm just as sorry as I can be, but there's nothing I can do—even our printer is up north in Dayton."

"It's such a small notice—couldn't it just be squeezed in, boldface?"

"I do wish I could help you, but for the life of me, I can't see . . ."

"In the circumstances, I'm sure Mr. Peach would be willing to make some special arrangement," Trosper said.

Abigail pushed her glasses up and leaned forward. "What sort of arrangement?"

"He might authorize my picking up the cost of any replating, or whatever might be involved . . ."

"Like about how much?"

"Will two hundred cover it?"

"No, but five hundred should do the trick . . ."

Trosper nodded agreement.

"Now just sit still for a moment, Mr. . . . your name is Paul, isn't it? Do you mind if I call you Paul? I'm Abigail. Terry prefers first names, and I've come to think he's right." She picked up the telephone and began to dial.

Trosper got up, stretched his legs, and walked around examining the framed magazine covers on the wall. As he returned to his seat, he glanced over Terry's desk. Aside from a telephone, desk calendar, a leather-cornered, spotless rose-colored blotter, and an expensive pen set, Terry O'Hara's desk was clear. Abigail's desk was cluttered with manuscripts, galleys, photographs, and news clippings. As he lowered himself into a chair, Trosper picked up his empty teacup and leaned across to put it on O'Hara's desk. He was close enough to glimpse the leather-bound desk calendar. Chaos Castle indeed.

Abigail slid the phone back onto its cradle. "It's done. The printer fussed some, but your notice will run in the current issue. We're such a small customer they slip us in any slot they can find. So we never know exactly when they will wrap and mail."

"That's great," Trosper said with evident relief. "I'd have been face down in the soup if Mr. Peach had missed this opportunity." As he got up from the chair, he asked, "Shall I make out a check, or will you send a bill?"

"A check now will be easiest," Abigail said. Trosper pulled a checkbook from his briefcase. "ONAN Publications?"

Abigail nodded.

Trosper began to write, stopped, and said, "Damnation, I knew there was something else."

Abigail looked up expectantly.

"Mr. Peach asked me to get a list of your subscribers—the sort of thing you make available to mail-order advertising firms."

"Is your Mr. Peach in advertising?"

"Not at all, but he does send brochures and want-lists to anyone he thinks might have military memorabilia of interest. I'm sure many of your readers are both veterans and collectors."

"We do have such lists, but for legitimate advertising firms only, I'm afraid. We mustn't let our subscribers' names fall into the hands of our competitors, you know."

"Mr. Peach understands that, and would of course protect your privacy."

Abigail thought for a moment. "It will come out to three hundred dollars, plus copying costs. I'll have to mail it to you."

Trosper made the second check out to Abigail Slotter personally.

"Look, Paul, if you're staying over, please come and have dinner with me. My cook loves having guests, and she'll fix us a real Savannah meal. Authentic southern cooking is something you just don't get very often these days, particularly eating out."

From the doorway, Trosper waved to reassure the taxi driver. "Thank you very much, Abigail. I really enjoyed myself. I've never had chicken with dumplings that way, or such a good pecan pie. But I'm afraid I overdid that delicious Bordeaux . . ."

"There's never too much wine if it comes out of the right bottles."

Abigail cocked her head to one side, and pushed up her glasses. "There's just one more thing, Paul."

"Yes?"

"Would you tell your Mr. Peach that if he ever has any use for a . . . mature . . . volunteer, I'm available? I've read a lot about what you people call 'the racket' and it sounds like much more fun than creating all that fantasy pulp for my crowd."

"The 'racket'?"

"You shouldn't try to kid a kidder, Paul—if that's your name. And you should check on 'Sinon' before you try to fool an old southern lady."

"Check on *Sinon*?"

"See Woolley's *Mythology*, one of the books I use to check on pseudonyms. The original Sinon was the young double agent the Trojans sent across to help convince the Greeks that their hollow horse really was a gift."

"I'll be damned . . ."

"You'll remember about Mr. Peach . . ."

"You can count on that . . ."

"Y'all come on back when you've got a few more years on you," she said affectionately.

"At this rate it won't be long," Trosper said as he bent to kiss Abigail lightly on the cheek. "And if you want to make Terry the Tiger O'Hara really convincing, maybe you should see that his desk is dusted, and his calendar kept up-to-date—July twenty indeed. It would never do for your readers to find out who really edits *Blood 'N Guts*—and probably does most of the writing as well . . ."

14 SAN FRANCISCO

Trosper glanced uneasily across the table. Grogan had finished a glass of prune juice, and was cheerfully tucking into a large helping of low-fat yogurt, with dry, extra-thin, multigrain toast and a pot of decaffeinated coffee. Trosper avoided a shudder and dipped a bit of English muffin into the remaining traces of egg on his plate. Breakfast was a favorite meal, and the opportunity of eating it in hotels was an occasion to escape from the tyranny of no-cholesterol cereals and skim milk. Free from marital disciplines, he could order eggs and bacon, burned brittle.

No matter whether he flew against the sun or chased it westward, Trosper knew that jet lag murdered one night's sleep. Had Grogan been less cheerful, and contrived to look less tanned and fit, Trosper would not have been so grumpy. Not only was Grogan eating a clinically correct breakfast, but he looked as if he enjoyed it.

"Did you run this morning?"

"Not really," Grogan said. "Just enough to work out the kinks."

"Let's walk from here," Trosper said, "I never can get any sense of a place when I go straight from an airport to a hotel, and then to a meeting in a taxi."

Fresh, with no trace of jet lag, Grogan nodded.

Trosper had not been in San Francisco since the flower children had outgrown Haight-Ashbury. But the Union Street area was a far cry from the Haight, and marked by carefully restored buildings, attractive shops, and promising restaurants.

The shop was in a corner building of unfinished stone, freshly painted white. Three granite steps led up from the sidewalk to a brightly varnished oak door with a heavy, beveled-glass panel. Beneath the glass, a shimmering brass plaque proclaimed "The Studio." In the bow window at the left of the steps a burnished leather attaché case floated on a thick blanket of oxford gray velour. To the side, and barely visible in the half-light, Trosper glimpsed a dark leather carryall, with heavy brass fittings. Propped casually in front of the bag was an onyx tablet inscribed, "Leather For the Connoisseur" and signed, "Billy Hopwood, Artist in Residence."

Trosper pushed the door open and held it for Grogan. From across the showroom, a thin young man rose from behind a cobbler's bench. His knee-length tunic was cut from gray tweed as loosely woven as burlap. His sandals, fashioned from well-worn automobile tires, were secured with leather thongs. It was a style, Trosper remembered, adapted from the Khmers Rouges and affected for a few months by admiring American graduate students in the seventies. His hair was loosely combed back and gathered in a pigtail secured by a leather thong tied in a bow.

"If he's just founded a religion," Grogan whispered, "he shouldn't count on my joining."

The young man stepped from behind his bench. "Look about, and ask questions if you see anything of interest," he said. "I do the work and answer all the questions too."

"Is Mr. Findley here, Alex Findley?" Trosper said.

"Upstairs," the young man said with a gesture toward a stairway at the back of the shop. "He likes it up there—sorting papers is one of his biggies." He paused as he stared openly at Trosper. "I'm Billy, should I tell Alex who's here?"

"I'm Alan Trosper, I think Alex is expecting . . ."

"Michael Grogan, Federal Bureau of Investigation."

Billy's jaw dropped. He stumbled back a step, clutching at his throat with both hands. Trosper had only a vague memory of the film, but thought he recognized Fay Wray reacting to her first sight of King Kong.

Grogan's face colored and he stepped closer to Billy. He flipped open his ID card with the badge, and thrust it toward the youth.

Billy's eyebrows shot up and he turned toward the stairway. "Hey, Alex, it's a bust!" he shouted. "It's the Feds—flush the stash."

From the stairway, Trosper heard the scrape of a chair across a bare floor, and then, in a pleasant baritone, "Shut up, you silly bastard . . ."

"It's some of your old crowd, all the way from the *Fuehrer Bunker*, the seat of power . . ." Billy's voice rose with each word.

A door slammed. From the top of the stairs came another suggestion. "Shut up, and stop acting the twit."

Grogan turned to Trosper.

Trosper shrugged.

"If that's you, Alan, come on up . . ."

As they moved toward the stairway, Billy shouted again: "Make sure they read you your rights . . ."

They chatted until Alex Findley said, "What in creation brings you . . . brings you both . . . all the way out to Lotusland?" Without waiting for a response, Alex bent over the small espresso machine on the corner of his desk. "Everyone out here is bonkers over coffee," he said with a smile. "The beans have to come from the crop on the south side of some place in Central America, where the sun doesn't hit the plants before ten twenty-two, or vice versa. Or whichever is more expensive . . ."

Findley's open collar shirt, light cashmere sweater, and gray flannels were well chosen to show off his trim, five-foot-ten build. As the biographic section of his personnel file showed, Alex had completed three years in an English public school when his father, an American businessman, brought the family back from Britain to Berkeley. By the time Alex finished high school and had been accepted in the Russian studies program at Columbia, all that remained of his early schooling was, as he put it in his application to the Firm, "Greek, Latin, ancient history, the rudiments of restaurant French, and an occasional English turn of phrase."

"It's something dear to your heart," Trosper said with a smile. "Duff Whyte asked me to look into the charges made by ex-comrade Viktor Feodorovich Volin. Because of the domestic aspect, Duff and the Bureau agreed that Mike should come along."

Alex busied himself serving the coffee. "In these circumstances, I suppose I should say the entire episode seems like very old history. But it doesn't. Now that you've brought it up, it feels as if it all happened yesterday afternoon."

"We've read the interrogation reports," Trosper said.

"It was a really stupid performance," Alex said. "The team Dwyer had doing the questioning weren't necessarily so dumb, it's just that they were in over their heads. One of the guys had worked in the attorney general's office in Dwyer's home state before he joined the Firm. Most of his work must have been against criminals, like the fellow who's had a dozen beers and gets into an argument with his no-good brother-in-law, and shoots him. That's a crime of passion—the perpetrator didn't really mean to do it, wouldn't have done it if he'd been sober, and feels guilty as hell."

"Exactly," Trosper said. "Lift a spy, you find a guy with a built-in alibi, no sense of guilt, and who's at least as smart as the fellow asking the questions."

Grogan, who had obviously expected the worst, brightened.

"Dwyer's team was hopeless," Findley said. "In three days I knew that all they had was an allegation and a vague notion where some of the hanky-panky had taken place. It was only after Lotte and I got together that it became clear that Volin was their primary, probably their only source."

"They never questioned you as a group, did they?" Grogan asked.

"That's about the only mistake they didn't make," Alex said. "They began by trying to keep us apart—separate buildings, different times for meetings so there'd be no chance we'd bump into one another in the parking lot. But after a couple of days their security broke down, and the interrogation had become so thick-witted, we each realized what was going on, and who else was involved. The only thing I never did determine was how Volin convinced them that it was the Firm, and not the Agency or some other outfit that had been scuppered." He began again to fuss with the coffee machine as he said, "When it was all over, we were supposed to sign oaths swearing that we would never discuss the questioning with anyone, ever." He glanced at Grogan. "I refused to sign."

As Findley poured another round of coffee, he began to smile. "There was another thing about me that bothered them . . ." He dropped a sugar cube into his cup. "About midway in the interrogation, the ex-D.A. said that along with everything else wrong, they'd found me to be promiscuous. When I asked how come, the D.A. said that even for a bachelor I had too many girls. For a while I thought my memory had failed. 'At one time?' I asked. 'No, no,' the little guy said. 'Too many live-ins.' "

Trosper began to laugh. Findley's social life had been the envy of his contemporaries.

"More live-ins than normal was the charge," Findley said.

"I've always wondered about *normal*," Grogan said. "Did they define it?"

"No, but they had figured out that my various relationships came to term on an average of eleven months, give or take a few days."

"Could this have been because of some very unfortunate shortcoming of yours?" Trosper asked politely.

"Certainly not," Findley said. "But toward the end, when it became obvious they really had their teeth in this part of my problem, I decided to take the Firm off the hook for having harbored a libertine like me. So I told them that Darcy Odlum . . ." Findley turned to Grogan: "Odlum was our first Controller, the man who hired me." Grogan smiled politely. "So, I told them that Odlum had asked me much the same question—why did I have to keep house with so *many* different girls?"

Trosper began to smile. "And?"

" 'Noblesse oblige' was the best I could think of at the time." Findley tilted back in his chair. "And that was the last of me with the Special Investigations Group—rotten amateurs, the lot."

They talked for an hour. Trosper had exhausted his questions, and Grogan had clarified other points, when Alex said, "What brings all this up at this late date?"

Trosper flipped his notebook shut. "You have to understand that Duff's been pretty busy since getting back from hospital. He knew what had happened to you people, but as he told me the other day, this is the first chance he had to look into it."

"It's none of my business," Alex said, "but have you guys talked to Lotte Friesler?"

"Not yet . . ."

"She's a damned difficult dame," Findley said, "but she had a lot of depth on the U.S.S.R. and Russia. I was a journeyman case jockey, and there's a dozen other guys . . ." He thought for a moment. "Let's make that three or four guys Duff could replace me with and never lose a step. But Lotte's worked on the Soviet Union since she signed on. When Dwyer kicked her out, she walked away with a lot of the tribal memory." He collected the coffee cups and put them on the table behind his desk. "As I remember it, Lotte was even in on the Tomahawk case of late lamented memory. If they'd paid more attention to her, that one might have come out differently."

"Did she have anything to do with Volin?" Trosper asked.

"I really don't remember, but I'd guess she might have been brought in when he first came over. She was very valuable in any early evaluation of a defector's product, and might well have been in on his early questioning." Findley shook his head slowly. "One thing's certain, when I talked to her during our interrogations, she seemed to have a slightly better opinion of Volin than any of the others who worked with him."

As they walked out through the shop, Trosper lingered behind, studying the leather work. Billy Hopwood looked up from his workbench and watched Trosper for a moment before saying, "Y'all hurry on back now."

"You do good work," Trosper said. "I've always liked fine leather work."

"And that's a pretty good-looking pair of shoes you're sporting," Billy said. "You make 'em yourself?"

"I wish I could," Trosper said, "the way prices are going."

"Billy's my nephew," Findley said as they stood by the door. "When I told my sister I planned to settle down here, she asked me to keep an eye on him." Findley glanced approvingly around the shop. "Actually, we're beginning to show a little profit—he's really very good." He pushed the heavy door open. "Have you guys got to Volin yet? He's the one who should have the answers, and there's no way the dumb bastards Dwyer put on the case could have wrung him out."

"That's part of the problem," Trosper said with a glance at Grogan. "It seems comrade Volin did a bunk about the time Castle decided to take a real look at things."

"Cause and effect?" Findley asked, his eyebrows raised in wry concern.

"That's a good question," Trosper admitted, "but I wish people would stop asking it."

15

WASHINGTON, D.C.

Widgery sat at the far end of the narrow office Duff Whyte had made available for Trosper. Two days after the young man's arrival from New York, a new desk had replaced the tacky metal table Trosper had scrounged from a nearby office. On the following morning, an immaculate, low-backed executive chair was substituted for the varnished oak relic that Whyte's administrative assistant had provided.

As he closed the daily briefing file and tossed it into his out-tray, Widgery looked up and caught Trosper's expression. "I didn't ask for any of this stuff," he said with an embarrassed gesture at his desk. "Hattie Barton—I'd met her at Doug MacRae's the night I got back—said she had some stuff she wanted to get out of the warehouse, and asked if I could use it."

Trosper reminded himself never to underestimate the impact of a handsome face. Hard-hearted Hattie, the deputy chief of administration for supply, was notorious for her grim reluctance to repair, much less replace, any bit of office furniture or equipment whose original function could still be discerned. In her eyes, the supply budget was best spent for the price-be-damned gear uniquely designed for secret operations. For Hattie to issue a piece of new office furniture to any employee other than one of the senior officers she knew to have been with the Firm since its inception was to surrender to a foe determined to destroy civilization as she knew it.

"*Mes compliments, quand même,*" Trosper muttered as he continued to scan the *Blood 'N Guts* subscription lists. Thirty-two hundred subscriptions seemed a modest circulation, but there were also newsstand sales which, according to Abigail Slotter, more than doubled the readership. He understood the interest fantasists might have in the magazine, but could not fathom why it had enough appeal to active-duty military personnel to warrant the Department of Defense ordering eight hundred copies a month for sale in PXs from Seoul to Heidelberg.

"Now that Abigail has finally forwarded the subscriber list, I'm afraid there's no alternative," Trosper said, "but for you to name-search every one of the subscribers on the *Blood 'N Guts* list . . ."

Widgery blinked. "What can one hope to find in a list like that—a few dozen Walter Mitty types and a platoon of would-be storm troopers?" he asked politely.

"If I knew what I expected to find," Trosper said, "I'd do the search myself."

Widgery's plangent plea was partially offset by an insistent buzz from Trosper's telephone.

"Alyce Pinchot here."

The assumption of Thomas Augustus Castle's executive assistant that the mention of her name obviated all the customary telephonic courtesies irritated Trosper, and he was pleased to respect the security stricture against answering telephones by name. "Yes," he said.

"Mr. Trosper?"

"Yes . . ." Ms. Pinchot's telephone manners were, he remembered, a not very subtle means of pulling rank.

"There are more than three thousand names on this damned list," Widgery bawled from across the office.

"Start in the middle of the alphabet, and then work back to the A's . . ." Trosper spoke loudly, without moving away from the intercom. "It could seem less tedious that way . . ."

"What's that?" Ms. Pinchot demanded.

"Alan Trosper here . . ."

There was a satisfying pause before Ms. Pinchot said, "Mr. Castle is on his way to the Controller's office. They would like you to join their meeting."

"They're not even alphabetized," Widgery moaned.

"Just remember some of the computer magic they teach you at the Fort," Trosper said, still speaking directly across the telephone. "Use a scanner to create a file and then run the sort command." For all his apparent confidence, Trosper knew he had reached far beyond the scope of his computer knowledge.

"The meeting is right now . . ." Ms. Pinchot's throaty contralto had soared up the scale to a shrill soprano.

"Of course," said Trosper, gloating.

Duff Whyte waved a letter-size sheet of paper. "Sinon's come through, he telephoned from Vienna. The nervy little creep announced that we're to meet him in Prague. Here's the transcript of the call."

Castle looked up from his sketch and nodded his greeting.

Trosper took a copy of the transcript. Again, Sinon had wasted no time on pleasantries in the prepared message he had obviously read into the telephone. "Mr. Peach, tell Mr. Whyte that for good reasons, I will meet his man in Prague. He is to stay at Hotel Pǎríž and be documented as Sam Anderson. On arriving he will ask for mail. My letter addressed to Mr. Anderson will inform your man when and where he is to find me. He must be prepared to meet me on very short notice and have $300,000—in dollar and Swiss franc—to be paid me when he is satisfied my information is correct and important. Your man is to arrive at Hotel Pǎríž on November 3 and stay there until date specified in my letter. There can be no changes in my plan. I positively will not disclose my information until I have valuta."

Trosper read the transcript again before looking up.

"What about it?" Whyte asked.

"I've got a linguist comparing the telephone voice with our tapes of Volin's interrogations," Castle said. "But I'm sure it was Volin on the phone."

"So why meet in Prague?" Whyte asked irritably.

"Given the forty years that Moscow Center had its hands and feet in the trough in Czechoslovakia, we can only assume they're pretty well nourished," Castle said, his attention still apparently directed to his sketch.

"Damn it, Tom, it's been the Czech Republic for two years now," Whyte said.

"The Red Army is gone, but the Russian embassy is right where it's always been," Castle said. "The only real difference is that the *rezidency* is larger than it was four years ago, with a very senior colonel—Gretsky the last I knew—in command. You can bet that *most* of the in-place penetrations Moscow Center squirreled away in the past twenty years are in good order, and keeping busy." He paused to hold his sketch at arm's length. "Even if the new Czech security team is lucky, it could take a generation to peel the secret collaborators out of the police, the security services, the foreign office, the government at large, and the press."

Whyte grimaced. "Tell me more . . ."

Trosper ignored the irony. "You can be sure that the old agents, retired and otherwise, are kept as breeding stock—establishing replacements for themselves by selling peacetime spying as an avocation that provides a low-risk, tax-free second income."

Trosper glanced at Castle, and said, "More to the point, Sinon's message suggests he's already waffling . . ."

Whyte glanced again at the letter. "How so?"

"First, he says we're to give him the money *after* we're satisfied the information is important and correct. Then, at the end, he gets all iron-assed and says he won't spill any beans *until* he has the 'valuta.' He can't have it both ways."

Whyte sniffed. "For a fellow who's been telling us how much he knew about the old Moscow Center—and the Firm—this guy comes on pretty naive."

Castle nodded. "If Sinon is Volin, he knows Prague very well."

"I don't give a damn how much of a hurry Sinon or Volin may be in," Whyte exclaimed. "I'm not about to stand on my head just because someone drops me a note saying I'm to document my best operative as Sam Anderson, give him a wheelbarrow full of assorted currency, and have him in Prague in a few hours. It's been years since I've seen a proposition as bald as this. The hoariest trick in the repertoire is to make sure the mark doesn't have time to get his act together."

"Isn't this exactly what we've been waiting for?" Trosper asked.

"Not to snap at a gift herring, but I've had two weeks to bone up on everything we have that's pertinent. I can have someone briefed and ready to go in forty-eight hours."

"There's a big tourist crush in the republic these days," Castle said softly. "Plenty of cover."

"I'm quite aware of that," Whyte said. "But even if Prague's become the Paris of Eastern Europe, and I could send an entire team, I can't even imagine what kind of unevaluated data I'd consider paying that kind of money for."

"If you send someone to talk to Sinon, maybe get a notion of what he has," Trosper said, "you could remind him that we're the only game in town. If he goes to the Agency or the FBI, they'll hotfoot it straight to us and the ex-comrade will be back on square one. Neither the British nor any of the NATO services would consider much of a payment without referring it to us."

Whyte tossed the letter aside.

"Does that mean it's no go?" Castle asked.

"Just a minute," Trosper interceded, tapping on the corner of Whyte's desk. "We've got no choice, this isn't just some passerby whispering that the Firm is penetrated. Sinon—whoever he may be—wrote to *you* personally through a high-security drop that was blown in an important operation. He exposed a double agent Iran or Moscow is running against us, and he's casually referred to the Troika. The baby's well and truly right on our doorstep."

Whyte tilted back in his chair, laced his fingers behind his head, and stared at the ceiling.

"If I were to pick the worst place in Eastern Europe for us to make a meeting with an unknown man, I'd choose Romania," Castle said as he jammed the top onto his gold pen and slipped it into his pocket. "The fact Sinon didn't choose Bucharest is another indication he's our old friend Volin. We have no choice but to run it out."

"What exactly does the Firm have in Prague, or nearby, right now?" Trosper asked.

"Damn all," Whyte said. "We've never had an office or even a resident staffer there. By the time the Soviet occupation began to wind down, we'd already cut back on active work. All we had left were two separate nets, maybe half a dozen or so agents, all targeted on the Russians. When things began really to lighten up, I sent Steve Marsh in to have a look. He talked to both head agents, and one or two of the people down the line. As I recall it, one net was damned nearly hermetic, tight as a lightbulb. Was that Dahlia?"

Castle nodded.

"Steve thought the other chain was moribund. Probably penetrated and run by the STB in the old days and then abandoned when some of the internal security thugs found they had more important things to do, like running for cover."

"That was Tulip," Castle said softly.

"So what does that leave us?" Trosper persisted.

"Nothing," Whyte said flatly. "Given our budget, Czecho is a very low priority."

Castle twisted sideways, and with an effort tugged a red foulard handkerchief tied to form a sack from his trousers' pocket. Whyte and Trosper watched in silence as Castle untied the handkerchief and spread an assortment of what looked like paper-wrapped saltwater taffy on his leather portfolio. Castle glanced up at Whyte. "My diet counselor put me on to these—only eighteen calories each."

Trosper leaned closer to read the label—No-Kal Kandee-Klusters.

"Once you get used to them, they're really not too bad," Castle said wistfully. "Try one, Duff. The cantaloupe have no flavor at all, but the peppermint are quite tasty."

"I'll keep one for later," Whyte said gravely.

Castle turned to Trosper. "The idea is to take away your appetite—they're a mixture of wheat germ with a pemmican binder and artificial flavor . . ."

Trosper chose blindly and said, "What about commo to and from Prague?"

Whyte shook his head. "There's the telephone—with all of Eastern Europe listening in—the open mail, and express mail of some sort." He glanced at Castle. "And I suppose we could mount a courier from Vienna. But even in the fullness of our peaceful new world, that's not the way I'm going to run a quarter-million-dollar caper involving the Firm's security."

"We're still way ahead of ourselves," Castle said. "Before we close the file . . ." He paused to make sure he had Whyte's attention. "Or . . . start making reservations at the Paříž, I'd like to be sure we have consensus on *why* Sinon wants to meet us in Prague."

Whyte shrugged. "Sinon is probably worried about a *coup de main*, and afraid that if he were to meet us in any of the NATO areas, Alan might try one of his famous stunts, and lift him."

"Maybe Sinon has, or thinks he has, facilities there that we know nothing about, and can't hope to cope with," said Trosper.

Castle selected a Kandee-Kluster and opened the waxed paper wrapping. He popped the peppermint drop into his mouth and folded the paper wrapping into a perfectly proportioned square. He studied the square until, like a scientist deciding to reduce the size of a computer chip, he repeated the folding process to form an even smaller square. Then, satisfied he had Whyte's full attention, he said, "Or, all of the above, plus the possibility that a little bird told him we haven't *any* facilities in the neighborhood?"

16

SALZBURG

"It's rather nice when you think about it," said Emily as she pushed the hinged window open and leaned out to peer down the Getreidegasse. She closed the window and turned to face Trosper. "I mean, to be staying across the street, a few doors from where Mozart lived, and at a place he must have passed hundreds of times."

Trosper grunted a neutral response. He had always liked the Goldnerhirsch Hotel and the baroque aspect of the old city of Salzburg. But he was jet-lagged from the trip to Munich, and tired after the train ride to Salzburg. He would have welcomed a few moments to concentrate on his meeting with Lotte Friesler and to still the anxiety he always experienced before any operational activity.

"Turn the other way, look up the street, northeast, about eighty miles, a little southeast of Linz, and you'll see the forgotten Austria," he said sourly.

Emily stepped back into the room and gazed quizzically at Trosper.

"Mauthausen," he said. "One of the early concentration camps, built shortly after the Anschluss. There were nearly forty thousand prisoners there, with corpses piled up between the barracks when the camp was overrun in 1945."

Emily's face flushed. "If I ever knew, I'd forgotten," she said with a hint of apology.

Trosper pulled a 3 × 5 card from his pocket and glanced at the cryptic notes he had made for his talk with Lotte. It was no use. He was too preoccupied to concentrate, and increasingly uneasy about having agreed to meet Sinon in Prague. He had belatedly begun to question having agreed that Emily accompany him.

"You might take Emily along," Duff Whyte had said expansively, when Trosper first refused to make the Prague rendezvous. "She'll enjoy the trip."

"Americans named Sam aren't likely to visit far-off places without at least a token representation of their loved ones," Castle added with a benevolent grin. "Emily will lend what Felix calls 'some of the old verisimilitude' to your cover."

Trosper shrugged. Felix Waldman could document a chorus girl as the Queen of England in less time than it might take most operatives to obtain a driver's license.

"It won't cost any more for Felix to rig you and Emily as tourists than it would to cobble up a valid business cover for you," Whyte said. "Besides, Emily deserves a treat after that diet of hardtack you subjected her to on your cruise."

"It's not cover I'm concerned about," Trosper said. "It's the blank pages in the file that bother me." He pushed himself back in his chair and crossed his legs. There were times when he regretted having stopped smoking a pipe. Like the ebb and flow of Kim

Philby's stutter, a bit of creative fumbling with the paraphernalia of pipe smoking had occasionally provided even Allen Dulles with a useful pause in the conversation. "Send one of your hip young guys," Trosper said. "Someone Sinon should recognize as not having the authority to carry heavy money, let alone make any big decisions without consultation. Once he's gotten a line on Sinon we can regroup."

"There isn't time for anyone else to read in, and get to Prague on schedule," Whyte said. "Aside from Steve Marsh—who's out of the country—I haven't got anyone who's even been on vacation in Prague in the last three years." He leaned forward, putting both elbows on the desk. "We also have to remember that as of now the only means we have of contacting Sinon is through that stupid magazine. If we don't make the Prague *Treff*, we'll have to wait for Sinon to drop us a line. Considering what might be at stake, I'm not prepared to linger."

"But there *is* something to be said for convincing Sinon that he's not in any position to call all the shots," Castle murmured. "If we let him think he's got us by the nose, he'll be just that much harder to bring down to size. If Alan gets to Prague on time and in the right alias, we'll have complied with Sinon's every directive."

No matter what the issue, Trosper realized, Castle always placed himself slightly to one side, never quite agreeing with any proposition. Even his choice of words had an operational spin—in this instance, to serve as a goad for Whyte. The National Security Council issued directives, the director of Central Intelligence issued directives, and so did Duff Whyte. But agents and sources answered questions and took orders—they did not hand directives to the Controller.

"Damn it, Alan, that's why I want you to take this job," Whyte said. "You know the case, and you're not going to jump if Sinon snaps his fingers."

The goad had worked, but Trosper decided to wait for the next maneuver.

"What's more, Alan," Castle said, "you're obviously the man to stop off in Salzburg and interview Lotte Friesler. She's not likely to respond to any youngster, no matter how hip he might be."

If he were to pick a motto for his nonexistent personal escutcheon,

Trosper mused, it would be *Numquam Postea*. Never again would he assume it was possible to unsnarl one thread of a secret operation, or to deal with the single aspect of a complex case, without becoming enmeshed in a tangle of related issues. He turned to Castle. "Do you remember telling me that all I had to do was study a few files, rake over the data, and come up with recommendations? Two to three weeks at the outside? That was a month ago. Since then I've read myself nearly blind, been in New York, Savannah, and San Francisco. And now, after a detour in Salzburg, all that's expected is a stunt in Prague, a city I've never visited."

"Not for nothing do they call it the secret world." Castle spoke almost in a whisper.

"I'd *like* you to take the job," Whyte said softly.

Trosper got up, and walked past Whyte's desk to the window at the side to stare through the mesh drapery into the enclosed courtyard. It was a move he had often seen others make, and it always reminded him of the unconscious way experienced agents glance around a room before they get down to business. It was as if they thought they might actually spot a clue as to the backup that might be hiding behind a closed door. The custom of breaking the tempo of a meeting by suddenly rising to gaze out a window, pretending to check for a stakeout or some other peril on the street below, was a quirk that Trosper associated with experienced case men. It served to break tension, and to offer a few moments more for thought before making a decision. Neither Castle nor Whyte seemed to have noticed it as out of place.

Trosper turned away from the window. "I'll want a caddy who can double as a courier," he said as he stepped back to his chair.

"Widgery?" Whyte asked.

Trosper nodded. "He'll need documents, but if the FBI agrees, Grogan can probably get by with a tourist passport."

"Why Grogan?" Castle asked.

"If there's anything to this, we may be taking legal evidence. If someone has to testify, or go into court, Grogan will be in a position to do it. I plan to read about it in London and not to make my TV debut on the witness stand at a treason trial." This was only partially true, but if Emily should insist on going along, Trosper liked the idea of having Grogan present.

• • •

Emily turned away from Trosper and crossed the room to a dressing table. "Say what you want to about the war, I like this place. Every bit of the furnishing is authentic . . . Tyrolean, I guess you would call it." She dabbed at her makeup with a paper tissue. "What's she like, Lotte Friesler?"

Trosper looked up from his notes. "She came to us from one of the Pentagon outfits, fifteen years or so ago. Nominally, as a reports officer, one of the experts who deal with product. Her habit of pushing subordinates around was probably a reaction to her own dissatisfaction at not having started out in operations."

"If operations are such a big thing, why didn't she insist on a transfer?" Emily said without turning.

It was almost time to leave. Trosper pulled on his jacket. "She signed on just before the curve, a year or so before the Firm—for better or worse—actually began to encourage women to take operational assignments."

"Why didn't she change when it did become possible?"

"I suppose she was pretty well established in reports by then, and had begun to develop a reputation as a Soviet expert." Trosper sniffed. "More likely, when she got right down to it, she didn't have enough confidence in herself to make the switch."

Emily sat before the mirror for a few more moments before saying softly, "You know, when I asked about Lotte I didn't expect an analysis of her as a secret operative. I wanted to know something about her as a person, as a woman. Is she married? Children? Does she have lovers? A mother she's close to? Is she pretty, plain, striking, perhaps a *jolie laide*? Or is she *really* just a creature of your precious racket?"

Trosper winced. "I'm sorry, sweetheart. I shouldn't have jumped at you about Mauthausen, it's not your fault the Austrians are such master opportunists that some of the press seems to assume that Austria was on the Allied side during the war." He stuffed his notes into his breast pocket. "Talking about Lotte that way was just a flashback to the days when my first thought about anyone was how they might be fitted into the racket. It's a habit I thought I'd kicked . . ." He shook his head. "As far as I know, Lotte was never married, never had children." He offered a conciliatory smile. "I'm quite sure about a mother, but now that I think about it, I can't recall any gossip about boyfriends."

Trosper's habit of bracing himself before an operation was less grand than that prescribed in the training courses as the final review of objectives and sorting out of priorities. He needed time to quiet himself and to still the anxiety he had come to recognize as a form of stage fright. Much as he enjoyed Emily's company, he was not accustomed to have anyone with him when he was traveling on operational business. He was even less in the habit of answering questions.

"Mike Grogan and James Russell Widgery will be coming by any minute," he said. "I've booked a table for you all downstairs." He pulled on his trench coat, and bent to kiss Emily's cheek. "If you must have the truth," he said so softly it was as if he were speaking to himself, "I never liked Lotte very much."

17

SALZBURG

That afternoon, when Trosper telephoned Lotte, she had been blunt. "No, I do not want to come into town for dinner with you," she said. "I eat early. If you like, you can come here after dinner. I'm in the Gaisbergstrasse, not all that far from the Hirsch, but you'll want a taxi. Get a pencil, I'll give you directions." Lotte's cool response had not moved Trosper to ask if Grogan might come along.

Now, as he hitched up the collar of his trench coat against the light, near-freezing rain, Trosper was reminded that his first and most lasting impression of Salzburg, and the entire Salzkammergut for that matter, was its miserable weather. He must have glimpsed the sun there on some occasion, but as he paid the cab driver, and hurried along the shrub-lined walk to the low, two-story building, he could not remember any such day.

There would be four small apartments, he guessed, in the building that according to the mock-Gothic lettering above the door had been constructed in "Anno Domini MCMXLII," the high tide of Hitler's empire. But unless the construction had begun early in the year, Trosper reminded himself, only a well-connected Nazi would have been in a position to obtain building materials in Austria. For by December 1942 the tide had turned, and a quarter of a million German troops were trapped at Stalingrad. Salzburg was an odd locale for Lotte to have chosen as a retirement hideaway. The city was choked with visitors during the music festival and throughout the lingering tourist season. Lonely in winter, expensive in any season, Salzburg's baroque charm was not enough to erase an aspect too reminiscent of the area's past. He rang Lotte's bell.

"The call—and from you of all people—was a complete surprise," she said. "I've been led to believe that you wouldn't use a telephone to order up a taxi."

In Trosper's view, Lotte had rarely been *led* to believe anything. "It's the devil's own device," he said as they shook hands. She had the grip of a tennis professional, was shorter than he remembered, and, perhaps because she was so thin, seemed younger.

In the moments it took for his eyes to adjust to the light, the room appeared to have a sort of eclectic coherence. But as Trosper peeled off his soggy coat, his vision cleared. The merciless, white painted walls exposed every facet of the hotchpotch of chunky, peasant-style chairs and stools that clashed with the occasional pale, smoothly turned, Swedish modern pieces, the kind that Trosper always assumed belonged in an office, preferably not his own. At the far end of the room, a potbellied fireplace bulged from the wall. A leather sling chair was at one side, and a roomy, chintz-upholstered bergère at the other. Between the two, a Swedish teak-framed sofa rested on spindly legs. Behind the sofa, a handsomely carved peasant *Treuhe* lay like an ornate wooden coffin. Bookshelves, tightly packed with German, French, and English volumes, ranged along the far wall. At the other side of the room, and beneath a chest-high picture window, four squat, carved chairs ringed a massive dining table. Along the back wall a narrow table sagged under trim stacks of magazines and journals. Two expensive speakers, a high-tech tuner, record player, and cassette deck were wedged beneath the table. Aside from the books and audio gear, there was nothing in the room that suggested Lotte's presence.

Trosper surrendered his trench coat and dripping hat. Lotte moved to hang them in the narrow hallway, and bent over the radio to lower the volume. "I didn't think it was possible to tire of Mozart, but after all these months here I'm not so sure," she said, turning to face Trosper. "A drink? Something to make it easier for you to segue into business—this *is* business, isn't it?"

"A glass of wine, something local if you have it."

"Come off it, Alan. Have some scotch." Lotte knelt to lift the cover of the *Treuhe*. "This is the only piece of real furniture I've bought here, and may be the only time a two-hundred-year-old blanket chest has ever served as a liquor cabinet." She freed a half-filled bottle of bourbon, checked the label, and thrust it aside in favor of an even larger vessel of vodka. "Third time lucky," she said, as she brought an unopened bottle of scotch to the light. "There's no cognac left, I'm afraid, but I'm not so broke I can't provide a little whiskey." She poured a generous drink and gestured toward the kitchen. "Ice? Water?"

"A little ice and some *Sprudel* if it's handy, please."

"No thanks to that charlatan Dwyer, but I've managed to hang on to my reserve commission," she explained as she added the soda water to Trosper's drink. "I'm still only *Major* Friesler, but I do get to stock up on essentials at the PX when I do my active duty in Heidelberg." She handed Trosper the glass and poured vodka for herself.

As he watched Lotte move about the apartment, Trosper realized that although he had for years recognized her as a familiar figure, and had accepted her reputation as a part of tribal lore, it was not until Emily's rebuke that he had ever given any thought to her as an individual with a personal life that existed in a dimension beyond her work. Even his reading of Lotte's personnel file, with its detailed curriculum vitae, had focused on her role in the Firm and security history. Now, all he recalled of her background was that she was one of two children born late in the life of their parents, both tenured professors at a midwestern university. She had taken a degree in history and modern languages—Russian and German—at that university, and a graduate degree at the University of Chicago.

He wondered if he had always sensed there was a missing aspect to Lotte, a part of her personality he had never recognized. She was about five-five, and slim as a photographer's model. But for Trosper *slim* was a word that had pleasant, feminine associations, akin to slender, willowy, and even lissome. Now, as he watched Lotte add wood to the fireplace, he realized she was not so much slim as wiry. Her black hair showed no touch of gray. She wore it pulled straight back and drawn close to her head as if to accentuate her prominent nose. He wondered idly whether her brunette coloring, pointed up by the pale lipstick she affected, was perpetually tanned by the sun, or merely makeup. For a moment Trosper felt a twinge of pity. He had known Lotte as a work-obsessed woman, a person whose life seemed rimmed by her profession and its ramifications. Her abrupt banishment from the racket could only have been punishment indeed.

For all this, Lotte was also known as a bitch on wheels, relentlessly demanding of any subordinate she deemed less than dedicated. Incidents akin to cruelty marked her treatment of younger women. But she knew her job, her memory was famous, and unlike many of the analysts whose work kept them behind a desk, she had acquired a measure of operational judgment.

Drink in hand, Lotte poked at the embers and added a stick of wood to the fireplace as carefully as if the fire were an art form. After a moment of prudent consideration, and a final, thoughtful thrust, she laid the poker aside.

Lotte dropped into the leather sling chair, crossed her legs, and took a sip of vodka. "I take it this is business?"

Trosper was silent, his attention wandering.

"Speak up, Alan," she said sharply. "Is this business?"

"Duff Whyte asked me to talk to you."

Lotte took another swallow of vodka, raised both eyebrows and smiled skeptically. "And about time . . ."

"I've spoken to Roger Folsom and Alex Findley in San Francisco."

"Red Roger telephoned me from Vienna, he said he'd had dinner with you in London."

"Duff wants to . . ." He paused, groping for an expression innocuous enough not to rile Lotte. "Duff wants to *rationalize* . . ." He winced and stifled a curse at the half-forgotten slang that had slipped out. "That is, I mean, to *resolve* the Troika business."

Lotte cocked her head and pursed her lips ironically before saying, "As I recall it, *rationalize* was one of our junk phrases, a bit of cynical cant, meaning either to resolve quickly or to kick under the rug. Which is it he has in mind?"

"Duff wouldn't have sent me here if all he wanted was to deep-six one of Dwyer's legacies, and I wouldn't have got involved if that was all he was after."

"Then what *is* it you're here for?"

"I already have Roger Folsom's views of the interrogation, and Findley's as well as . . ."

"Interrogation my backside," Lotte interrupted. "Pure Disney World. By the time they had been at it for a few hours they were completely lost. After two sessions, it was perfectly clear that the interrogation team thought their source had *overheard*—that's the word—some gossip by a couple of Moscow Center hot shots about an important agent in the Firm. In another hour or so it was transparently obvious to me that their source was none other than that seedy charmer, Volin. Before they were through, I had a wilder notion . . ." Her voice trailed off as she peered intently at Trosper.

He waited before saying, "What notion was that, Lotte?"

"That Comrade Sleaze, Volin if you prefer, had made no such charge . . ."

"But Volin did make the allegation," Trosper said.

"You disappoint me," Lotte sniffed. "You've been around too long to buy junk like that. Even before Volin was brought to the States, I'd read every word of his early questioning in Munich. What's more, I sat in on two of the initial debriefings when he first arrived in Washington. Never once did he even hint that he had any serious security poop beyond what he dumped on Charlotte Mills. She was Volin's only claim to fame—until he was selected and trained to handle her, he was nothing but a low-level swan, a gigolo. A bastard trained to prey on women."

"All right," Trosper said. "You're all three in agreement about the quality of the investigation. What about the charge?"

"You mean, am I actually a Moscow Center agent?"

"I mean, what do *you* make of Volin's allegations?"

"I think he was mishandled by his debriefers," Lotte said dryly.

"You've all three made that point . . ."

Lotte shook her head in anger. "When Dwyer learned that I'd been 'allowed' to participate in the questioning, he let it be known that Volin was such a prize he could only be handled by men, certainly not a 'susceptible' woman."

She paused, apparently aware she was speaking too rapidly to mask her emotion, and took another sip of vodka. "After all," she said, nodding her head several times to underline her next observation, "he was a trained stud, like some damned dog used to service timid bitches. Dwyer's assumption was that I couldn't spend half an hour in Volin's presence without tearing off my clothes. So I sent Ed Meachum to represent my office, and just listened to the tapes."

"It's not the worst way to monitor an interrogation," Trosper said softly.

"Baloney!" said Lotte. "The only good thing about monitoring a debriefing and not being able to jump in is that you don't have to look your best—if you remember that old joke."

"What makes you think Volin didn't make the allegation about the penetration of the Firm?"

"As I said, he never mentioned it in the early debriefings when he was trying hard to impress us, even when the interrogators asked about any other operations he might know about," she said.

"You're not suggesting that he simply forgot to mention it?"

"Not at all, not foxy Volin . . ."

"I scarcely have to remind *you*, Lotte, that defectors have been known to withhold data for later use, just to ensure they're kept on the payroll . . ."

"Really, Alan!" She took a sip of vodka. "It was only after he made the first, rather general allegation, and was brought back for further interrogation, that things changed. Two or three times when the interrogators were reading from prepared questions, they made references to a 'high-level' hostile penetration, but never once did they refer to this fantastic agent as being in the Firm."

"So?"

"Then, overnight, from one day to the next, they suddenly began acting as if it were a simple matter of fact that the source was a well-placed member of the Firm."

Trosper shrugged. He had read the file carefully, but had not noticed this instant transition in the transcript covering Volin's first disclosure of the allegation.

"At one point I was so fed up," Lotte said, "I actually suggested to the dope who was questioning me that maybe their source—I knew perfectly well it was Volin, but I never admitted it to the interrogators—was having a little fun with the guys who were questioning him. Volin damned well knew what a storm he'd stir up if he referred to an important agent and then solemnly allowed it to be drawn out of him that although he didn't actually know, he'd always *assumed* that the agent was in the Firm."

Lotte got up to stir the fire. "If there was anything at all to the gossip Volin allegedly heard, there was no reason to assume it necessarily involved the Firm," she said. "You know how important it is for an interrogator not to lead a source. My guess is that late in the game and after Volin had so conveniently remembered his allegation, one of the interrogators jumped up and shouted, '*You mean in the Firm?*' That would have been more than enough to convince Volin—who was not stupid—that he'd struck pay dirt. Maybe when he said it, he was so panicked at the thought we were about to let him go, to resettle him somewhere, that he decided on the spot that there'd be a lot more interest if he said the source *was* in the Firm."

"What about the meeting places that the source specified?" Trosper asked. "He was quite specific about the dates and places."

"If he hadn't thought the thing through, he probably just pulled the approximate dates and places of the alleged meetings out of his hat . . ." Lotte grimaced. "Thanks to those damned computers being able to relate everything to everything else, he hit on places where in the whole bloody Firm only one of the three of us might conceivably have been meeting someone from Moscow—no matter that half a hundred other Americans might have been in the same areas at the same moment."

Lotte got up. "Another drink?" She walked back to the *Treuhe*.

"A half," Trosper said. "Just a half . . ."

Lotte slipped back into the sling chair. "Dates and places," she said heavily. "You can bet that I've given that some thought. The places were specific, the dates, as best I could understand it, were only approximate, but always on Sunday, or a holiday. At least that's the most I could gather that they had on me. First, Ferney-Voltaire, a skip and a jump from Geneva. No doubt about it. I'd been sent out on TDY to handle the documents being filched by Jeep, a nutty little Bulgarian secretary Bill Torrey had recruited. She was having an affair with Ivan Borosov, one of their senior trade delegates, a regular at all the U.N. trade conferences. Because he worked late—usually on a couch with Jeep in the ambassador's office—and was so senior, he had the keys and combinations to the vault room and the master safe. He was also bone lazy—in a week Jeep had the combinations, the keys, and the job of locking up. About that time, Jeep realized she wasn't the only secretary Ivancho was fooling around with and she needed a shoulder to cry on. Torrey had me take her over. We pretty well looted the office by the time Borosov went back to Sofia."

Lotte took a sip of her drink. "That was my first good field operation. I liked it, and I did a damned good job with Jeep." She smiled ironically. "Of course, it meant that I could nip over to Ferney-Voltaire any Sunday—to meet with my Moscow control." She shook her head in disgust. "At least that's the way Dwyer's bright boys saw it."

Trosper nodded. "What about the other places?"

Lotte leaned back and crossed her legs. "Let's see. There was Christmas weekend in Mexico City, in 1987. I was en route for a couple of weeks' vacation in Cuernavaca, but stopped for the holiday with my old roommate from Chicago. She's married to a TV news guy stationed in Mexico City. I was there three days—long enough to meet everyone in the *rezidentura*. Very suspicious." She put her glass aside, and rolled her eyes. "Apparently my big mistake was that

I didn't check in with our office in Mexico City. I didn't have any friends there, and you know as well as I do that we're under specific instructions not to pay office calls unless we're on the Firm's business. But with my luck, this was one of the times that the *alleged* agent had an *alleged* meeting in Mexico. No matter what my record was, Dwyer's Gestapo considered this very suspicious."

Lotte got up and poked gently at the fire. "A year later, I was in Brussels for five weeks helping back up the debriefing of Slipper, a really hot Syrian." She fixed her eyes on Trosper. "Easter weekend—I could easily have got to Ghent for the *Treff* their source seems to have reported." Again she shook her head. "Of course there were probably five hundred other Americans on vacation or duty in and around Brussels at the time—NATO, the embassy, the consulate, not to mention those next door in Luxembourg. For that matter, Germany isn't all that much of a drive from downtown Brussels."

Trosper finished his drink. "Enough, I do get your point . . ."

Lotte's eyes watered. "They couldn't lay a glove on me, Alan, not one of the bastards. Not a glove, not one bit of proof, not a scrap of derogatory . . ."

Trosper got up.

"Duff and Castle can't expect me to prove a negative . . ."

"I know that . . ."

"I'm good at what I do. I've got ten, maybe fifteen years left to work. I wouldn't say this to anyone but you, because you already know—I'm one of the best. And I've done nothing wrong."

"Whatever happens, it will take a little while, Lotte . . ."

"I want a job, *my job* back," she said. "There's no one else can do what I can do, no one who's had my experience . . ."

"Everything's changed, Lotte. It changed faster than you think."

"Exactly what's changed, Alan? Do you really think the new crowd running Russia is about to strike out one of its own eyes, the one eye that has a clear vision of what's going on in the world? If there ever was a time when Moscow needs to know what's going on in Washington, in Bonn, in Tokyo and London, it's right now when Russia's all but flat on its back and desperate for any aid it can get . . ."

"Lotte, for God's sake . . ."

"Do you think their military are just going to stack arms? Most of their science is twenty years behind the rest of us. Is it likely they'll give up stealing the technology they need to keep up with the rest of the world?"

"You're kicking at an open door, Lotte . . ."

"They've got a new name, but it's the same old racket, just slimmed down, and rid of some of the fat and the ideological crap they've been carrying all these years."

"You're preaching to the choir, Lotte . . ."

"I'm not going to rot here for the rest of my life. Duff has to know that he hasn't got the only racket in town. You talk about things changing, and you're right. There are plenty of foreign services that could use an advisor, someone in the back room who can help them figure out what's going on in Washington, how to get along with the Agency, and how to deal with some of the other rackets. Most of them would rather have me than some of those Moscow goons who are circulating their résumés."

"That's foolish, Lotte . . ."

"There's the whole Near East—I know for a fact that I could bring a lot to the table in half a dozen places."

"That's not for you, and you know it."

"Before that happens, I'll go to Senator Mewley," she said. "That's a promise, you can tell Duff."

"That's just dumb, Lotte."

"Alan, I'm broke. There's not a damned thing I can do about it . . ."

Trosper pulled on his coat. "Give us a little time, Lotte. It shouldn't be long." As she opened the door, Trosper took her hand.

"Just tell them I want my job back . . . any job, I just don't give a damn."

18

PRAGUE

Trosper glanced up from the street map and muttered, "I guess no one's perfect . . ."

"Trouble?" Emily smiled as she continued to admire the church at the bottom of Karlovo Square.

"This may be a better area than somewhere in the Mala Strana, across the Moldau," Trosper said, as he stared across the grassy center of Karlovo Square toward the dead drop area. "But I'd have picked a spot with tourists elbow to elbow rather than the biggest park in Prague with only a handful of dog-walkers, and lines of sight stretching three city blocks." They had strolled from the subway, stopping occasionally to check a building or street sign against their guidebook and, not incidentally, to allow Trosper a better chance to glimpse any possible surveillance. Not that it mattered. With no support other than Grogan and Widgery, neither of whom were to come within two hundred yards of the drop, it would be a simple decision—go or no go.

"In a way, I suppose this site is fitting," Trosper said, looking up from the guidebook. "On the north that Gothic relic went from being a town hall to a criminal court and prison." Book in hand, he turned south. "That baroque joint, known as the Faust House, is where Rudolf II underwrote the research to turn lead into gold."

It was dusk before their flight had reached the bleak airport and dark before they arrived at the Paříž Hotel, an art-nouveau building tucked discreetly on the street winding beside the baroque Smetna Concert Hall near the Republiky Square. The massive, dark wood concierge's desk crowded the small reception area. "A letter, Mr. Anderson," the reception clerk had said, puffing his rounded cheeks like an anxious rabbit. "It was delivered yesterday."

Trosper glanced up, but continued to fill in the registration form—Mr. and Mrs. Sam Anderson, Cambridge, MA, USA. Tourism. Five days. He jammed the ballpoint pen back into the holder and took the letter. As they waited for the elevator, Trosper turned to Emily and spoke loudly enough for the clerk to hear. "For once, Jan has come through. He said he'd have the letter here, and by God here it is."

Emily stopped unpacking to watch Trosper as he studied the letter. "Everything in order?" she asked.

Trosper shook his head. Not the slightest cover text. Even the boy who brought their bags to the room could have recognized the letter for what it was. The envelope was addressed to Mr. S. Anderson, with "Arrivée" and the date scrawled at the corner of the envelope. Cheap stationery, one blank sheet folded over a second sheet with a message and carefully drawn sketch of the dead drop area. The crisp type was proof enough that the letter was not written on the machine Sinon had used for his earlier correspondence.

Trosper scowled as he studied the text. Sinon, that prince among operatives, had not troubled with any cover message. "Mr. Anderson, For security, I have left instructions in a drop. You must empty the cache between 0930 and 1000 hours tomorrow morning, not later. It is essential you keep this skedule and be prepared to meet me after you study the material I will leave for you. Please to come alone. Sinon."

He dropped the empty envelope into the wastebasket and began to orient Sinon's sketch of the dead drop on the street map given him when he picked up the cooked passports in Washington. For his own purposes Sinon had done one thing right. He had picked a site that Trosper could not possibly reconnoiter before the deadline.

As he prepared to brief Grogan and Widgery, Trosper began to mark a tentative route on the map, and made notes for visual signals—coat collar up, collar down, gloves on, gloves off, blow on fingers. If there was no indication of more than a single watcher along the route or at the drop, it would at least indicate that Sinon was, as claimed, operating on his own. In the absence of any other apparent problem, Trosper would risk emptying the drop. If there was any sign of a more sophisticated stakeout, he would assume it to be proof that

Sinon was not operating on his own, or that his maneuvering had attracted professional attention. In this circumstance, Trosper would not approach the drop.

Trosper cinched up the belt of his trench coat and mumbled a complaint. Although he was convinced that at least half the English-speaking, male tourists in Europe wore trench coats, he was also certain that there was not a policeman, security officer, or counterintelligence operative on the continent who would waste a second glance at these travelers, let alone assume any one of them to be involved in any operational hanky-panky. But from the moment Trosper slipped into a trench coat, he felt as if he were wearing a sandwich board proclaiming "Agent on Secret Mission." Silently he damned Le Queux, Sapper, Hitchcock, Hollywood, Ambler, and Ian Fleming. But maybe not Fleming. James Bond, who rarely bothered to adopt a pseudonym, live a cover, mask his movements, or speak a word of a foreign language, had one operational virtue. Trosper could not recall Bond wearing a trench coat.

As they crossed into the park, Trosper remembered the reversible topcoats from his college days and wondered why manufacturers had stopped making them. Perhaps the waterproofed gabardine on one side and tweed on the other made the coats too bulky for city wear. Whatever the reason for the coat's demise, it was a pity. It was one of the least compromising operational gimmicks, and Trosper had worn his to shreds. A few seconds in a telephone booth or public toilet was time enough to turn the coat inside out, to exchange a cap for a rolled felt hat, and to pull on a pair of clear cheaters. This quick change scarcely qualified as a disguise, but could offer enough camouflage to permit an agent to risk continuing a surveillance, or perhaps even help to shake off an inexperienced follower.

He glanced at Emily. Her soft felt hat and tweed coat were inconspicuous, but could not cloak her height. Despite low-heeled walking shoes, Emily was tall enough to attract an extra flicker of attention. They crossed into the park. Trosper glanced over his shoulder. Even at two hundred yards, with an affected limp, and on the opposite sidewalk, Grogan was clearly a tourist. No matter, Trosper told himself, if there was to be a problem it would come at the drop site. The most Grogan could hope to do would be to identify any observer and, if the worst happened, to alert the police to the violence being perpetrated against a fellow tourist. Widgery was to remain far behind Grogan, and to move closer only as Trosper approached the drop. If anything hit the fan, Trosper said firmly, Widgery's only role would be as handyman, an operational gofer. No heroics *whatsoever*, Grogan added with heavy emphasis.

Trosper had always avoided the use of uninvolved bystanders as operational props, or even to provide protective coloration. Admonitions tumbled through his mind. "It ain't the Boy Scouts," was one of Odlum's laconic observations. "If they haven't got shoulder pads and a helmet, they'd better stay the hell in the bleachers," was Nobby Tilson's advice.

Now, as his glance settled on the lone figure near the entrance to Karlovo Square, Trosper cursed his decision to have Emily accompany him to the drop site. The public obsequies of the former Moscow Center and the notions of an intelligence détente were but smoke, fanned by newspaper and TV intelligence experts. How long would it be before some compromised Moscow operation would remind the press that though organizations and players might change, the need to uncover what one's adversaries and even allies wished to conceal would not diminish, and that the racket would go on much as it always had.

The sole figure on the far side of the crowded Ječná thoroughfare moved slowly across the four lanes of traffic. His shabby raincoat and nondescript black Austrian hat were adequate, but the man's *aspect*, the most important factor in passing unnoticed, was hopeless. Once on the sidewalk, he seemed preoccupied, his pace fitful. He lacked the skill to loiter. An easy make, amateur hour.

Trosper glanced back to catch Grogan's eye, and raised himself slightly on the balls of his feet before turning slowly in the direction of the man in the shabby raincoat. Grogan followed Trosper's glance. He studied the man for a moment and then turned up the collar of his topcoat to acknowledge Trosper's signal.

So far so good. Trosper bent over Emily's shoulder as if interested in what she was studying in the guidebook.

Grogan pulled off his gloves and blew on his fingers. Widgery, who had closed to within a hundred yards of Grogan, abruptly thrust both hands into his pockets and then, as if worried that Grogan might not have noticed this confirmation of his signal, nodded twice.

"I'm pooped, let's find a place to sit for a minute," Trosper said as he took Emily's arm. Surprised, Emily turned as if to protest. "It will be easier to study the book sitting down," he said softly as he guided Emily toward the double row of benches a hundred yards ahead, at the bottom of the park.

In the distance, Grogan pulled on his gloves, confirming that he too had identified only one watcher. So far, so good.

Shabby Raincoat, or Sinon, if it was Sinon, slowed his pace as he moved along, roughly parallel to Trosper. If it was Sinon, he remained too far away to compare against the memory of the Volin mug shots Trosper had studied in Washington. Call him Sinon, and the hell with it.

Trosper bent toward Emily, and as he appeared to study the guidebook map, peered once more along Spalena Street at the side of the square. If anything comes down, he realized, the first sign will be a very businesslike car, possibly two cars. One along past Grogan, the other down the busy Ječná Boulevard. With all the real estate in Prague, Sinon had chosen a drop exposed to surveillance from every direction at ground level, and from any of the apartment houses, offices, and churches lining the square. Even the Karlovo Square was not a square, it was an oblong park, maybe three hundred yards long, the largest in Prague.

With an impatient movement, Trosper took the guidebook from Emily, and began thumbing the pages. Then, after another quick glance around, he pulled off his gloves. Enough already. He would empty the drop.

In the distance, Grogan turned down his coat collar. A signal to Widgery. Grogan moved slowly toward Trosper.

With his right hand, Trosper groped under the edge of the bench. Nothing.

He leaned slightly to the side and ran his fingers along the second slat in the bench. A Ping-Pong ball taped or tied to the wooden slat? Not possible. He worked the object loose. Without looking at it,

Trosper recognized it as a 35-mm film canister, wrapped in plastic or a condom and thumbtacked to the bench. He eased the packet into his coat pocket and turned to Emily.

"We might go along now, and take a look at the St. Cyril and Metodej Church," he said. "It's where the Czech parachutists who killed Heydrich took refuge when they were betrayed," Trosper mumbled, making conversation to mask his increasing anxiety from Emily. "Heydrich was a real swine, but one of the brighter lights in Hitler's inner circle. The poor Czechs knew they were trapped but they fought off the SS for hours. In the end they committed suicide. The guy who sold them stood outside with the Gestapo and watched."

Trosper got quickly to his feet. "If anyone asks, that's where we're headed . . ." He reached down and pulled Emily gently to her feet.

"Are you all right?" she asked. "You jumped up as if you'd just realized you've been sitting on wet paint."

Trosper managed a smile. "Just remember, you're Mrs. Sam Anderson, from Boston," he said. "Don't say anything a tourist wouldn't say, and demand to speak to the American embassy."

"For God's sake, Alan, those days are over . . ."

"My name is Sam . . ."

They turned up the graveled sidewalk and stepped out of the park. At the corner of his vision, and at least two hundred yards away, Trosper could see Sinon. If it was the master operative, he had given up all pretense of cover and was staring directly up the street beyond Trosper. After a moment's hesitation, the man turned and hurried along the tree-lined avenue.

The tires on the black Skoda protested as the driver gunned it around the corner. Trosper pulled Emily aside as the driver braked and the car slued to a stop on the frost-covered paving stones at the curb beside them.

Two men lurched from the doors as a second shabby Skoda braked to a halt, its bumper flush against the first car. The first man—black alpine hat, dark brown leather coat, heavy black shoes with thick, cleated soles—sprang directly in front of Trosper. The second—tweed cap, dark green raincoat, and heavy shoes—stepped to

Trosper's side. He touched his cap and said, "You are coming with us, please."

"Don't be so damned silly," Trosper said.

A stocky woman in a black beret and ankle-high shoes stumbled from the front seat of the second Skoda and approached Emily.

"Who the hell are you people?" Trosper said loudly, twisting his arm away from Leather Coat.

"*Verějná bezpečnost*—police," Tweed Cap said quietly. "There's a problem. You're to come with us, please."

"There's no goddamned problem at all," said Trosper loudly. He could see Grogan walking slowly toward the Jěcná street at the top of the park.

"Missus, you come now," Stocky Beret said, as she took Emily's arm.

Emily's face flushed as she shook off the woman. "Sam, who are these people . . ."

Tweed Cap turned to Emily and bowed slightly. "The police. There's a small problem, some questions. You must come with us now . . ."

From across the street, a handful of pedestrians gathered to stare. Along the sidewalk a hundred feet away, two young men and a blond girl, smoking and chattering, fell silent and edged closer. Czech students, Trosper assumed.

"You have identification?" Trosper said loudly. "Some slight token of authority?" Over Tweed Cap's shoulder, he could see Widgery start to run along the sidewalk toward Grogan.

Tweed Cap pulled a folded identification card with a silver badge pinned to it from his pocket. "You will come now. No more problem, please."

"I don't know what the hell your problem is, but my wife has nothing to do with it," Trosper said, his voice harsh with anger. "She will not go with you."

"No difficulties, mister. Sergeant Hlinka will be with Madame at all times." He shoved Trosper toward the car. In the distance, Trosper saw Grogan grab Widgery's arm and spin him to a halt.

"This is stupid nonsense," Emily said, the color draining from her face. "And I will protest at the embassy the minute I can get to a phone . . ." She attempted to pull free of Sergeant Hlinka.

"My wife will come with me," Trosper said firmly.

"Mister, there is not room in the car for everyone," Tweed Cap said with a hint of apology. "Sergeant Hlinka and her driver will come behind." He turned angrily to confront the three students who had moved closer, and barked something in Czech. The shortest student, a girl in a New York Yankee baseball cap, shouted back. The three moved closer to Trosper.

Tweed Cap waved his open ID document and badge toward the trio and grasped Trosper's elbow. "Get in the car now, before real trouble."

The tall student, in a worn green fatigue jacket, raised his arms and beckoned to the gathering crowd across the street. He shouted in Czech. All Trosper understood was "*Státni bezpečnost*!"—the STB, the former Soviet-controlled, Czech security service. Tweed Cap, his face flushed, shouted "*Veřejná bezpečnost*," which Trosper recognized as the current name for the Czech police. Still grasping Trosper's elbow, the policeman shoved him toward the open door of the lead car. "Get in the car *now*!"

Trosper tore his arm free and turned to Emily. "You'd best go along with the sergeant until we can sort this out." He clasped her hand and led her toward the rear car. At the curb, she paused long enough to straighten her coat and to adjust her hat. Dignity restored, she kissed Trosper lightly on the cheek, signaled Sergeant Hlinka to open the door more widely, and slipped gracefully into the back seat of the Skoda.

Trosper wedged himself into the other sedan. He pulled off both gloves and stuffed them on top of the film canister in his trench-coat pocket. The Skoda lurched as it pulled from the curb, and Trosper twisted around to be sure the second sedan was following.

The Skoda tires spun on the wet pavement as the driver skidded into a sharp right turn. Trosper checked again to be sure the second car had made the turn. It had.

Trosper leaned back and took off his hat, which was brushing against the upholstered top of the small sedan. The Skoda picked up speed. Steamer coats, he said to himself. The reversible topcoats were known as steamer coats, and thought to be just the thing for the changing weather in the days when the gentry crossed the Atlantic by ship.

In moments of crisis it was Trosper's habit to fix on something entirely irrelevant. The students, all smoking as they walked along beside the park . . . The New York Yankee baseball cap . . . Steamer coats . . .

Was it luck, prudence, or had Sinon been warned to leave the area before the police arrived? No matter, there would be time enough to sort it out.

He loosened the belt on his trench coat and twisted around to glance through the rear window. The black sedan with Emily still followed close behind.

19

PRAGUE

The man behind the desk motioned Trosper to the wooden armchair. He studied Trosper for a moment and said, "Zitkin, Chief Inspector Zitkin."

Trosper sat down. He had not unbuttoned his trench coat since he had been hustled past the uniformed policeman inside the door of what seemed to be a shabby office building.

"Your passport . . ."

Trosper pulled his passport from his breast pocket and pushed it across the desk. He glanced around the office. It was standard Central European issue. A bulky, old-fashioned intercom and telephone occupied much of the left side of the large wooden desk. Scarred in- and out-trays were stacked on the right side. Aside from a calendar, a detailed city street map, and a large map of the former

Czechoslovakia, with a bright red line marking the border between the Czech Republic and Slovakia, the walls were bare. Trosper sat in the wooden armchair directly in front of the desk. Two slightly smaller chairs stood at either side and a bit behind Trosper.

"You will be more comfortable if you take off your coat," Zitkin said softly. He pulled a pair of half-frame reading glasses from a collection of pencils in a pewter tankard on his desk. Close-cropped gray hair, brown eyes, the upper half-inch of his left ear missing, tanned complexion, muscular build, brown tweed jacket, dark blue shirt, red knit tie. The impression of self-confidence was so strong it seemed to be a deliberate effect.

"I must demand to see my wife and that she be released immediately thereafter," Trosper said.

"Madame will have coffee with Sergeant Hlinka," Zitkin said without looking up from the desk. He began to thumb the pages of the passport. "She will leave when you do." He reached to flip a switch on the intercom. "Syrovy!"

The heavy door swung open and a man—rugged features, dark blond hair, and about thirty-five years old—stepped into the office. Tweed Cap, Trosper realized, looked ten years younger indoors. Syrovy said something in Czech.

"Take Mister's coat." Zitkin spoke with a slight accent.

"It's all right," Trosper said. "I'm not going to be here that long."

"Please take off your coat," Zitkin said with a faint smile. "Regulations do not permit me to sit in my office with a man who may be carrying a weapon."

"I can assure you I am not armed . . ."

"Syrovy," Zitkin barked. "Help this man with his coat." Syrovy stepped smartly behind Trosper's chair.

Trosper shrugged, got to his feet, and handed his hat to Syrovy.

"Your coat, please Mister," said Syrovy.

Trosper unbuttoned his trench coat and dropped it over the back of the chair. He opened his jacket to show he wore no shoulder holster, and patted his side pockets.

Zitkin said something in Czech, and Syrovy pulled Trosper's trench coat from the chair.

Trosper ignored Syrovy, and sat down. "I must protest the entirely unwarranted treatment my wife and I are being subjected to. I demand to be allowed to call my embassy."

"In time," Zitkin said. He looked up from the passport and appeared to be studying Trosper.

"I demand to know on what grounds you have brought me here." Trosper's voice was firm, but not harsh or emotional. There was no point in provoking a policeman, probably a security service officer, in his own office.

Syrovy dropped Trosper's gloves onto the desk and fished more deeply into the trench-coat pocket. The condom was still tightly wrapped around the plastic 35-mm film container. Syrovy tossed it twice in his hand before gently placing it on the blotter in front of Zitkin.

"*Zo-zo,*" Zitkin said as he poked at the package with a long yellow pencil. "This is yours, ah . . ." He paused to check the passport again. "This is yours, Mr. *Anderson*?" He raised his eyebrows, glanced again at the passport, and said, "You *are* Mr. Sam Anderson?"

"I am Sam Anderson, and that is my passport," Trosper said. "What's more, I demand to be allowed to call my embassy."

"This is a peculiar little package, Mr. Anderson. Is it also yours?"

"I found it on the bench, when my wife and I sat down," Trosper said.

"It was in your pocket, Mr. Anderson. We both just saw Lieutenant Syrovy take it out."

"In the course of all that hugger-mugger with your men, I must have dropped it into my pocket."

"For safekeeping, I suppose you might say?"

"A reflex," Trosper said. "I assumed we were about to be robbed and I wanted to free my hands."

"Not bad," Zitkin said as he continued to toy with the package. "But *hugger-mugger*? I have not heard that word." He said it again. "Hooger-mooger?"

"It's an old usage, but these days usually means a sort of disorderly melee," said Trosper, now ruefully weighing the probability that Sinon had addressed whatever message might be in the canister to Sam Anderson by name.

Zitkin turned to Syrovy and said something in Czech. Syrovy hurried out of the office.

"So, I am correct in saying that you claim this . . . uh . . . peculiar little package does not belong to you?"

"You are."

"Things like this remind me of the old days," Zitkin said with a sigh. He picked up the canister, and flicked the intercom open. "Pika!"

The door opened and a heavyset, older man stepped in. Zitkin spoke in Czech as he handed the canister to the man, who smiled and hurried out. "For photographing," Zitkin explained. "Everything exactly according to our rules."

Trosper affected to be waiting expectantly.

"Your device takes me back," Zitkin said, his heavy-lidded eyes fixed on Trosper. "Early 1942, during the German occupation, I was a kid. Before the Heydrich affair, no one suspected a twelve-year-old, and I was useful as a courier. After the team from London assassinated Heydrich, we had terrible losses. I came within seconds of being taken." He swallowed heavily. "You know about Heydrich?"

"Reinhard Heydrich—the one the Germans gave the title Protector of Bohemia and Moravia? Everyone knows about him. Your people got him early on, and the Germans burned a village—Lidice. It's covered in every history of the war." If Sinon had addressed the message in the canister to Sam Anderson by name, as Trosper now considered likely, his only defense would be to stop answering questions and to keep insisting on seeing some American authority. Unless Sinon's message had implicated Trosper in a violation of Czech law, no serious charge could be brought.

"History or not, no one remembers what swine the Germans were," Zitkin said slowly, his eyes fixed on Trosper. "They killed every man in the village, and then burned it and plowed the ruins flat to destroy every trace. One hundred seventy-three men were shot, as many, maybe more of the women died in Ravensbruck." Zitkin's fist tapped lightly on the desk. "No one was in any way connected with the parachutists. Everyone was totally innocent."

Trosper was baffled. Was Zitkin playing both roles, good cop, bad cop, or were these apparent confidences merely part of a softening-up routine? "Are you from Lidice?"

"No, no," Zitkin shrugged. "From Lizaky, smaller than Lidice, but also destroyed because the parachutists used a transmitter from there." Zitkin's fist continued to tap gently on the desk. "All these memories just because of this one peculiar package." He squinted at Trosper over the rim of his half-glasses. "Before they were through avenging Heydrich, the Germans had murdered two thousand people, maybe more." He waited before saying, "There are times when I feel I've outlived my own death."

Trosper hoped his bewilderment did not show.

"General Moravec took care of me after the war, but I'm afraid he overvalued my work. It was boys' play until Heydrich. There were no problems until right at the end when I got hit—too sure of myself. Later, when Moravec came back from London, he insisted I have some education, even got me into university. A fine man. A brilliant officer." Zitkin looked up to squint speculatively at Trosper. "You know of him?"

Trosper shook his head. He remembered reading Moravec's modest account of his intelligence life, and in other circumstances would have liked to discuss it with Zitkin.

"After the war, after the Soviet occupation, he was invited to the States?" It was half statement, half question.

Trosper shrugged and shook his head.

Zitkin continued to study Trosper. "After Heydrich, it was a while before anything started again. By the time our group had re-formed, I was too confident, and got shot at . . ." He touched his mutilated ear. "A near thing . . . it couldn't have been closer, but it had its uses." He closed the passport and pushed himself back from the desk. "It convinced me that I'm not half so smart as I thought, and not nearly so brave. The way things developed, it probably saved my life."

The door opened and Pika handed the canister to Zitkin. As he walked slowly out of the office, Pika spoke in Czech, over his shoulder. Zitkin grunted a response as he picked up a metal letter opener and appeared ready to cut the canister free of the condom. "Do you understand what I'm saying, Mister . . . ah . . . Anderson?" he asked, staring intently across the desk.

Trosper nodded. "I've always thought that experience is a great teacher, but very, very expensive."

"There's a problem about *confidence* too," Zitkin said. "Too much confidence makes for wasted heroes." He reached for the intercom. "Syrovy!"

The door swung open and Syrovy came in carrying a stenographic notebook.

"Make a note that you are witnessing the opening of this concealment device in the presence of Mr. Anderson, and give date and time," Zitkin directed. "Make it ultra-legal, with a copy for the American ambassador." Zitkin waited before adding with an ironic flourish, "Maybe one for the White House in Washington too . . ." He freed the canister and glanced up at Trosper, who managed a confident smile. Zitkin popped the canister open, examined it closely, looked again at Trosper, and tapped the canister loudly on his desk. "Make a note that the device is empty," Zitkin said stiffly. "And check the bloody thing so that you can testify to my statement."

Trosper made an effort to conceal his surprise.

Syrovy ran his finger around the inside of the canister. "Empty . . ."

"Get your statement typed up, and ready for Mr. Anderson's signature," Zitkin said as Syrovy headed for the door.

Zitkin leaned forward, putting both elbows on the desk. "A lot of trouble for nothing," he said. "Do you agree, Mr. Anderson?"

"I think you're the best judge of that," Trosper said.

"There's something you must understand, Mr. Anderson." Zitkin took a deep breath and exhaled heavily. "The Czech Republic is an independent country, free of the Germans, free of what was the U.S.S.R., and now, stupidly if I may say so, of Slovakia as well. After what we've gone through since '48—I myself spent most of my career with criminal investigations, never with security matters as I do now—we will not tolerate secret intelligence activity within our borders, no matter who the sponsor may be. Do you understand me, Mr. Anderson?"

"I understand what you're saying, but I fail to know why you are lecturing me . . ."

"I think you *do* know, Mr. Anderson," Zitkin said sharply. "My experience with General Moravec taught me a few things that stood me well during the Russian time. But, thanks God, those days are over. Now, I have no wish to interfere with your work, Mr. Anderson, as long as you do not do it here in the Czech Republic."

Trosper raised his eyebrows and shrugged.

"For that reason, I must insist that you and your wife, and your . . . ah . . . *friends* leave the Republic within thirty-six hours—there are planes tomorrow, mid-afternoon."

"My wife and I would have preferred to remain here long enough to see some of this city we have read so much about," Trosper said. "But in the circumstances, I'm sure she will be quite ready to leave."

"You will understand that we do not expect you or your friends to be back here for at least a year?"

"That would be a most unlikely possibility." Trosper got up and reached for his trench coat. "My wife and I will be on a plane tomorrow afternoon." In the past, he had always been able to leave one step ahead of the sheriff. This was the first time he had ever been apprehended, and declared persona non grata. For all of Zitkin's tact and informality, it nettled.

"Sergeant Hlinka will drive you back to your hotel . . ."

Trosper pulled on his coat and reached for his hat.

Zitkin got up from his desk. "As I have heard you Anglo-Saxons say, no hard feelings, eh, Mr. Anderson?"

"Speak for yourself," Trosper said, as he managed a slight smile and a wink.

20

PRAGUE

"It's for you, sweetheart," Emily called, her hand cupped over the telephone. "It sounds fearfully official." She had just finished dressing and sat on the side of the bed. "It's only nine-fifteen—you haven't been naughty already, have you?"

"Very funny . . ." Trosper was not in the best of humor as he stepped out of the bathroom, shaving brush in hand. He balanced the brush on the table beside the telephone and reached to take the receiver from Emily. The cord flicked across the brush, toppling it off the table and onto an open book on the floor beside the bed. He muttered an imprecation, and took the phone. "Anderson here."

"Ya, here Zitkin, Mister Anderson. Good morning."

Surprised, Trosper spoke loudly, and with a transparently specious geniality. "And a very good morning to you, Inspector Zitkin." He glanced across the room at the rain slashing against the windows, and attempted to wipe the shaving cream off the book with a corner of the bedsheet.

Emily began to giggle.

"Breakfast?" Trosper said, staring angrily at Emily. "Breakfast? No, I haven't had breakfast yet . . ."

"I usually have my *parek*—my second breakfast, *Gabelfruehstuck* the Austrians call it—at about ten. Would your lady be offended if you came to have some snacks with me?"

"A moment, please . . ." Trosper turned to Emily and said hesitatingly, "I've just been invited out for some snacks . . . ?"

"It's a man's world," Emily grumbled. "Go right ahead." She smiled too sweetly and said, "Should I pack the things you'll need, shaving stuff, the Bible?"

"Where exactly is the cafe, Inspector?"

• • •

"Some visitors think it's a habit left over from the old days, when we were supposed to be Austrians," Zitkin said. "That's not true, I think the Austrians got it from us. We Czechs are the hard workers. We rise very early here, get to work early. Our *parek*—a pair of sausage, coffee, and a roll make a good pause." He stopped to take a bite of the *Krapfen*. "Me, I prefer a bit of pastry." He took a sip of coffee. "Do you have such habits in the States?"

Trosper shook his head. "Unfortunately not, but sometimes a cup of coffee at one's desk." The U medvidku was pleasant, but like most cafes, it was fogged with cigarette smoke.

Zitkin leaned back in his chair and, without pretense, studied Trosper for a few moments. Then, scarcely moving his head, he glanced around the crowded room before pulling himself forward until he could rest both elbows on the polished tabletop. "I have something for you, Mr. Anderson. I must presume it's important—you've traveled so far, and made such an effort."

Trosper cocked his head and raised his eyebrows, miming, he hoped, a slight surprise and noncommittal interest.

Zitkin tugged a worn black wallet from his pocket and extracted a tightly folded wad of paper the size of a matchbook. "I think this was intended for you. Please to read it."

Trosper unfolded the flimsy paper. He grimaced and shook his head in disgust as he read the blunt salutation, "Anderson." He glanced up at Zitkin, who smiled slightly as he took another sip of coffee.

The typed single-spaced message was without margins. "I know you will not pay money without some proof of my data. Here is sample, for which you will pay me $Ten Thousand, or Swiss francs to same value. *Lt. Col. George Pickett working Heidelberg Germany was KGB nash* from long time. Completely trusted. I will leave data at hotel for vis-à-vis tomorrow when you will bring valuta. Sinon."

Trosper read the message again. He shook his head wearily and glanced across the table at Zitkin before saying, "And that, as the Bishop said to the actress, just about does it."

"Please . . . ?"

"It's just something we say," Trosper murmured.

Zitkin shrugged. "Yesterday, it would have been difficult for me to explain, Mister Anderson, but there are some things you must know."

"I'm sure of that . . ."

"When we noticed your man—does he call himself Sinon?"

"He is not *my* man," Trosper said, "but that *is* the name on this note."

"When *this* man came to our attention, my young officers assumed—correctly, it seems—that one or maybe more foreign special services are involved in some illegal activity on our territory."

All things equal, Trosper realized glumly, Sinon, the master operative, must have attracted the attention of the hotel staff, among whom, in the best traditions of inn-keeping, was a police informer.

"You must know, Mister, that whatever our sympathies may be, we cannot allow our laws to be violated."

"I understand what you're saying," Trosper said softly.

"But you do not agree with me?"

"My inclination, and I gather from what you said yesterday, yours as well, is to fight. And to fight successfully, allies can be helpful."

"Oh, yes," Zitkin said. "We learned all that in the Nazi time—when France and England sold us to Hitler without so much as a warning or a crocodile tear."

"But some fought—there was some resistance here, and from your people abroad." Trosper decided to drop all pretenses. "You mentioned Moravec—but there was General Ingr, as well as all the Czech military and air force people based on England." The reference to General Ingr, who Trosper remembered vaguely to have been chief of staff of the Czechoslovak forces abroad, would probably confirm Zitkin's suspicions.

Zitkin waved his hand, brushing aside Trosper's comment. "The Germans were clever. They needed our industry, our manufacturing. So, they bought some of us. Heydrich called it '*Peitsche und Zucker*'—whip and sugar—good wages, beer, and good rations meant no strikes, little resistance, and mostly no problems. Only a few, the very best, joined in the fight."

"That was all before my time," Trosper said. "That, and the Soviet occupation, are behind us now."

"Not entirely, Mr. Anderson. The Soviet Bear has been here for forty years. I worked more than twenty years in the criminal police—until judged politically unreliable by the former regime and dismissed. When the government changed, I was called back, not to the criminal police but to the new security organization. But the Bear had long claws and they dug deep into this country. Now that we're again on our own, it will be a generation before we can be sure of one another."

"But surely Moscow has throttled back here . . ."

Zitkin glanced slowly around the cafe. "Of course, of course—some changes, less money, some confusion, for a while a little less attention to business. As far as I could tell there was some cutback in staff, but only of the weaker officers. At first some of the Moscow case men were at a loss to know what to say to their collaborators. After a few months, security intensified, their excellent craft resumed slowly with an apparent weeding out of some activity. Things that may have been peripheral were abandoned, left to wither." He paused as if he were making a continued evaluation of Trosper. "In the days before what you people called 'the liberation,' I had established three double agents . . ."

Zitkin stopped and, scarcely moving his head, checked again for eavesdroppers. "About the time the *rezidency* appeared to be reorganizing, my three cases came to an end. One man—the weakest case—was simply cut off. His attempts to make contact were disregarded, his communications not answered. The two other cases—sound, I had thought—were put on vacation. 'No funds, no need for your cooperation, we will be back, and here is a small farewell present.'" Zitkin paused before adding, "A fistful of kronen, maybe a small tin of fresh caviar . . ."

"That sounds plausible," said Trosper.

Zitkin nodded. "To be sure, plausible. But the timing worried me. It was true the *rezidency* was cutting back, but the double-agent cases were dropped a few months after my office expanded, after we took on new men from the police and university." Zitkin raised his eyebrows and shook his head. "Was it a coincidence of timing, Moscow cutting back just as we were expanding? Or had our security been violated by our own new staff?"

"I take your point . . ."

"So, Mr. Anderson, I have to be careful. When we were alerted to your activity, my young men wanted to wait until we could take both the courier and his agent—shall I say *in flagrante*? Their notion was that two arrests would remind foreigners, all foreigners, that we were again independent. I did not agree, and ordered that Mr. Anderson be taken as he emptied the drop. In their eyes I acted too quickly in taking you into custody." Zitkin smiled. "Of course, I had not thought you would be accompanied, and must apologize for having had to take your lady as well."

"I understand."

For a moment, Zitkin busied himself with the jelly doughnut and coffee. "So, to keep my hotheads at bay, I had Pika—we have worked together for twenty years in the criminal police—remove Sinon's message while he was photographing the canister." He smiled. "Thus no problem with our law—only an empty canister."

"I appreciate that," Trosper said. "I'm not at all sure of this source, or how important this matter might be, but having this message securely in hand is a big step ahead for me."

"Pika and I are the only two who have seen the message—and Pika does not have a word of English."

"If, when things develop a bit more, there appears to be any Czech aspect to the information, I can promise that you will have it."

"Understood," Zitkin said. "We have not identified this man Sinon—which makes me think he knows Prague well and is staying under good cover, certainly not in a hotel or pension."

Trosper nodded. "Perhaps with a woman?"

Zitkin raised his eyebrows. "Possibly so."

"If there is ever anything I can do for you concerning this case, or anything else, you can write me at this address." Trosper tore off a piece of paper napkin and printed the address of his letter drop.

As the young waiter scribbled the bill, Zitkin spoke sharply to him in Czech. The young man looked surprised, but plucked a coat from the rack and scurried out of the cafe.

"My young enthusiasts will have you under surveillance until you depart," Zitkin said. "I told them that I was meeting you here for a final, very fierce warning, so I think we should leave here separately, you had better go first—try to look a little depressed."

As Trosper slipped into his coat and turned to shake hands with Zitkin, the waiter hurried in through the front door. Carefully, he placed a small, dripping bouquet on the table in front of Zitkin. He waited, half at attention, as if expecting another order or at least an extra tip. Zitkin whispered a few crisp words of Czech and waved the waiter aside.

"A small *bon voyage* gift for your lady," Zitkin said. "She behaved very well, and I am truly sorry for her inconvenience." He handed the flowers to Trosper. "Please to keep these under your spy-coat until you get back to the hotel."

21 MUNICH

Trosper spoke slowly, attempting to mask his irritation with Widgery. "And just how did you come by all this information?"

Grogan dropped a sugar cube into his coffee and glanced expectantly at Widgery.

Before Trosper's attempt to empty the Prague drop, he had specified a fallback plan. If anything should happen that made a subsequent meeting with Grogan and Widgery in Prague impossible, Trosper would telephone Grogan's hotel and leave a message that Mr. Johnson had called, and would telephone later. Their next rendezvous—or bugout *Treff*, in Widgery's newly acquired operational vocabulary— would be at the Vier Jarhreszeiten Hotel in Munich for either eleven o'clock coffee or four-thirty tea, daily until contact was reestablished.

Widgery took a sip of Apollinaris water, frowned slightly, and leaned confidently back. "It was easier than I thought. All I did was telephone the consulate . . ." He turned to Grogan. "Actually, it's a consulate general here in Munich."

Grogan nodded, gratefully.

Widgery's nasal timbre had never been more apparent to Trosper.

"I asked to speak to Seth Rigsby—we were at Choate together— and told him I was in town and available for lunch. He said I should drop around . . ." The flow of Widgery's explanation slowed as he attempted to read Trosper's expression. "Riggo—that's what we called Seth at school—went into State six months after getting his M.A. at Harvard. We're not close, but we've always stayed in touch . . ."

"And when you dropped around . . . er, Riggo told you Lieutenant Colonel Pickett worked at Campbell Barracks, lived in army housing in the Heidelberg compound, and was on leave?" Trosper's irony was not lost on Widgery.

"Not exactly . . ." Widgery tilted forward, lowering the nasal element of his accent. "I mean, Rigsby is straight State, plans to be an ambassador before he's forty." Widgery managed an uneasy smile. "I mean, while I was waiting for Riggo to leave for lunch, I just used the military phone book in the outer office to find Pickett's address and home telephone. Only there isn't any *Lieutenant Colonel* Pickett in the phone book. There was only a *Captain* George Pickett. I mean, I called and spoke to the maid—she comes every Tuesday." Widgery's smile became more tentative. "If anyone in the family had been there I'd have said I was dealing encyclopedias, and would have asked permission to come around for a demonstration." Widgery's expression brightened. "Of course, I wouldn't ever have shown up."

Trosper glanced uneasily at Grogan, who shook his head slowly and less in anger than disbelief.

"Are you sure there's no Colonel Pickett in the book?"

"Of course I'm sure," Widgery said. "What's more I checked with the military directory assistance—there's only one Pickett in the Seventh Army area, and he's a captain, on duty in Heidelberg."

"Did you mention our interest in Pickett to anyone else, by chance?"

"Of course not," Widgery said. "If that's what worries you, there's no way anyone in the consulate could have heard me, or have any idea who I called."

"Did the maid have anything else to offer?" Grogan asked. He spoke rapidly in an attempt to sidetrack Trosper's mounting anger.

"She said the key was in the usual place, under a white rock alongside the bushes to the right of the front door, and that I should leave the package in the hallway, just inside the door."

Trosper took another deep breath, and poured himself more coffee. He added milk, and half a teaspoon of sugar. "And just what reason did that good woman have for telling you where the key is hidden?"

Widgery glanced at Grogan as if to solicit his support.

Grogan muttered "Package?" and busied himself with his coffee.

"Since the family wasn't home, I just explained that I'm an old friend in Munich on holiday, and that I wanted to leave a gift for the Picketts before I went back to the States." Widgery's glance flickered between Trosper and Grogan. "Actually, servants must be a bit of a problem here. My German's quite fluent, but Trude spoke with an excruciating Bavarian accent and sounded sort of stupid."

Trosper took a deep breath and exhaled slowly. He got up from the table, walked across the foyer, and passed the reception desk. As he stood staring at lustrous handbags and briefcases in the polished vitrines near the entrance, he remembered his Boston uncle telling him that briefcases were like ladies' hats—one *had* a briefcase. New briefcases were vulgar and one was never to be seen carrying one. Trosper pushed through the heavy doors to the sidewalk. A light rain was falling. He took several deep breaths, stepped back into the hotel, and threaded his way back to the lounge where Grogan and Widgery sat. He took a sip of his cold coffee and turned to Widgery. "Do you have the slightest goddamned idea what you've done?"

Widgery frowned and said, "I was just trying to cash in on an opportunity to get things rolling for you."

"And that you've surely done," Grogan muttered. He closed his eyes and slumped back in his chair.

"What you've accomplished with that goddamned cock-and-bull cover is to risk blowing us right the hell out of the water," Trosper said. "For all I know, Pickett really is an agent. If he is, and when the maid lets him know that he's had a weird call, he could goddamned well take off without even returning to Heidelberg."

"Where's he going to go?" Widgery asked brightly. "Nowadays there's no place for burned-out spies to hide except Cuba and North Korea."

"If you really think Moscow will just let a bought and paid-for agent drift off, you'd better think again," Grogan said. "Or go back to whatever finishing school your Firm may have for failed field men."

"You've goddamned triggered a bomb with a fuse so short we haven't even got the slightest notion how much time we've got before it goes off," Trosper said.

"But . . ."

"No 'but,' you get your ass back to your hotel and get ready to leave. I'll call you there."

"But . . ."

Grogan began to smile. "You'd better just run along, Widge, I think our friend is about to blow a gasket." He waited before saying, "And if he doesn't, I will."

22

MUNICH

"I'll give Widge one thing," Grogan said.

Trosper was too preoccupied to answer but raised his eyebrows in a silent show of interest.

"He's a handsome S.O.B."

"And self-confident to a degree . . ."

They were sitting in the Cafe Odéon. "Do you know who used to have lunch here?" Trosper asked. Sometimes making small talk actually helped him to concentrate.

Grogan glanced around the crowded room. "Hitler," he said with a smile.

"Not bad . . ."

"Shooting fish in a barrel," Grogan admitted. "In Munich, a random question I might possibly be able to answer, who else could it be?"

"All right, smart-ass, who else might I have meant?"

Grogan thought for a moment before surrendering. "You win . . ."

"Do you remember Alexander Foote? A limey Communist that Moscow picked out of the International Brigade in Spain in 1936 or thereabouts?"

Grogan nodded. "The radio operator who was in Switzerland during the second war?"

"That was later. First, they sent him to Germany for a little orientation. Then, more or less as an afterthought, they decided he might help out in an attempt on Hitler's life. It never took shape, but he did see Hitler, a few times, right here."

"What do you make of the discrepancy between 'Lieutenant Colonel' Pickett and plain vanilla 'Captain' Pickett?"

"Nothing right now," Trosper said. "Perhaps Sinon inflated Pickett's rank just making sure we'd meet his price for the information before we could check it out. Perhaps he just got confused, and didn't get it straight." Trosper chuckled. "With my luck, maybe he just sucked it out of his thumb and there's not a thing to it."

Grogan glanced at his watch. "Thanks to Widge's enthusiasm and help, if there's anything in it, we've got maybe three days to sort things out. Even less if the Pickett family comes home earlier than planned."

"I've already called Paul Webster, the Firm's local guy," Trosper said.

"Don't tell me Widge has put him in the picture too? As of right now, Trude Dankeschoen, the obliging Bavarian maid, knows more about what we're doing than my boss—sooner or later I'm going to have to let my headquarters know what the hell is going on over here."

"Paul's the bald guy, just coming in," Trosper said, and got up to make the introductions. Webster shook hands with Grogan and sat down.

"You should have let me know you were coming," Webster said. "I had no idea you were in town."

"We got here last night."

Webster glanced at Grogan. "You both family?"

"In a sense," Trosper said. "Mike's with the Bureau . . ."

"You mean this is business? Another one of your off-the-books stunts?"

"Not exactly."

"Not *exactly* what?" Webster demanded, his face flushed. "Don't bother to answer, I'll tell you *exactly* what's *not* going to happen in my front yard . . ."

"We need a little help, that's all," Trosper said softly. "Nothing difficult."

"Not without specific authorization from the Controller personally."

"First, I need to send an urgent cable, and want an answer in my hands before breakfast . . ."

"*First*, as far as I'm concerned, I need to get permission even to talk to you," Webster said. "The last I heard, you're retired and living in London."

"I'm not retired, damn it, I left . . ."

"All the more reason I'm not doing a thing without authorization."

"We need a car, nothing fancy, but it must have military plates . . ."

"*When* pray, would this be?"

"At breakfast when you bring the answer to my cable," Trosper said. "We really are under the gun."

"What cable?"

Trosper pulled a folded sheet of hotel stationery from his pocket and began to write. "Top Secret, Eiderdown, Controller Only.

"1. Regret attempt empty Sinon drop failed when Sam Anderson intercepted by local security. Released within two hours, but ordered to leave CR.

"2. Altho drop allegedly empty, Anderson subsequently informed by friendly local authority that Sinon message stated subject reference cable is longtime, trusted Moscow Center agent, now stationed US Forces Heidelberg area. Request immediate name search with any indication his access to classified data last several years.

"3. Details aborted Sinon Prague meeting will follow.

"4. Essential have any background subject before 2200 hours local."

Trosper handed the message to Grogan. "This will go straight to Duff Whyte, with a copy to Castle." He waited before asking, "Is there anything you want to say to your people?"

"At this point, I think benign silence is my only hope," Grogan said.

Trosper wrote another few words and turned to Webster. "Send this with the same heading." Webster looked at the cable: "Subject of ref cable is probably identical with Captain (not repeat not Lt. Colonel as reported by source ref cable) George Pickett, listed in Heidelberg area military phone book and presumably assigned Seventh Army Hdqs."

Webster read the cables slowly, shaking his head.

"We really do need the answer and the car before breakfast," Trosper said. "And, I'll have a background cable with some details later this afternoon."

"Is this all Top Secret Eyes Only Oval Office, or can you give a simple country boy some idea what the hell you're up to?"

"We're just going to drive to the army housing complex in Heidelberg and have a look around," said Trosper. "I don't want to do it in a rented car, or a taxi. It shouldn't be any problem . . ."

"When you say there shouldn't be any problem," Webster said, "it reminds me of one of the famous last words in 'Nam—'Don't duck, men, they're our guys.' "

"Before breakfast?" Trosper said.

"Whatever happened to orderly procedure, looking before you leap?"

Trosper smiled politely.

Webster got up and pulled on his coat. "Do you guys know this is a sort of famous place?"

Grogan groaned.

"We pretty well covered that before you got here," Trosper said. "But now that I think of it, it was the Osteria Bavaria where Hitler used to go for lunch. He came here for hot chocolate and those gooey little cakes."

23 WASHINGTON, D.C.

"Mr. Castle is here." Duff Whyte's secretary spoke softly into the intercom.

"Send him in." The Controller looked up from his desk and waited. Despite the intimacy of their working relationship, the chief of Special Operations always paused for a few moments before knocking and entering. Months earlier, on a particularly busy day, Whyte's patience wore thin. "You've got as many special clearances as I have, why in hell don't you just step into the office when Mrs. Sloane tells you I'm waiting?"

Castle was unmoved. "It's only correct to give you time to secure any sensitive paper before I barge in here."

As usual the chief of Special Operations wore an all too snug dark suit, and candy-striped shirt with white collar. He eased himself into the chair to the right of Whyte's desk.

"You've read Alan's message?"

Whyte nodded. "It was decent of that Czech cop . . ."

"Zitkin," Castle murmured.

". . . to give him the message on the quiet."

"If he really was one of Moravec's youngsters, I'm not surprised. The old general knew a thing or two about people and the racket."

"What about this colonel . . . ?"

"First, there doesn't appear to be any Lieutenant Colonel George Pickett," Castle said. "But there is a Captain C. George Pickett. He's on duty with the Seventh Army in Heidelberg. Before that, he was at the Pentagon, and briefly low man in the military attaché office in Prague. I haven't got very much, and didn't want to pursue it until talking to you. It's rather tricky asking the Pentagon for an officer's 201 file and service record without giving any indication of why we're interested."

"Tell me about it." Whyte was rarely ironic, but he had spent an hour reviewing the clerical and administrative manning table and was impatient.

Castle opened his red leather folder and appeared to be studying a single sheet of paper.

"Insofar as I can be trusted, will you please let me in on what you've uncovered." When irony failed, Whyte occasionally resorted to sarcasm.

"Sorry, Duff." Castle looked up, apologetically. "Miss Pinchot has a friend—a close friend I suspect—at the Pentagon."

"I might have known."

"He doesn't know Pickett personally, but he remembers him from the Joint Chiefs—he was either assigned to the SSD or worked closely with them before he was transferred to the attaché office in Prague . . ."

Whyte raised his eyebrows. "Oh, oh . . ."

"He was there for about eighteen months before being transferred to Seventh Army Headquarters at Heidelberg."

"Was this before the end of his regular tour?"

"Yes, but it seems the Pentagon was actually cutting back their staffing of the Prague office," Castle said.

"Is the SSD still the Special Security Detachment?"

"That's it, the ultra-high-security outfit that handles all of the Top Secret special briefing and cryptographic product."

"Just our luck, a wafflebottom."

Castle nodded. It was an inheritance from wartime OSS slang and had originally referred to communications engineers. In recent years the usage evolved and the term had broadened to include the specially cleared personnel who dealt with codes and ciphers.

"Will we never learn?"

"It may not be as bad as it looks," Castle said. "Miss Pinchot's friend described Pickett as a sideboy, one of the career assistants who have propped up the senior staff of every army in history. They remember everything, have a perfect understanding of the pecking order, and know where the bodies are buried. They handle most of the paperwork, meet all the deadlines, and make sure that the right officers get the right papers at the right time. Without these clerks, the generals couldn't even have a war."

Whyte nodded impatiently. "You say clerks, but the SSD is still one of the more sensitive elements in the Pentagon, and Pickett is a captain . . ."

"Clerk is a misnomer," Castle said. "Call them sophisticated executive assistants. Pickett is a reserve officer. As far as Miss Pinchot's source could say, his only qualification for the job was a good memory and a squeaky clean security background. He comes from some small midwestern town."

Whyte wondered what Castle's notion of such a town might be, but he pushed the thought aside and nodded wisely.

"There's a breed of man," Castle continued, "born to push papers. It's a comfortable life, but it's not a fast track, particularly for a reserve officer competing with all the Academy ring-knockers now that the military is, as the Pentagon puts it, 'down-sizing.'"

"There are people like that in every organization," Whyte said, "and they always outlive their value."

"Exactly," said Castle. "If there is anything to Sinon's allegation, somewhere along the line Pickett might have realized that he'd blown his career, and would be headed for selection out at the exact time he needed the most income, educating children and such. Maybe some Moscow Center sharpie on the military attaché circuit in Prague noticed Pickett, and made the right assessment. Maybe they hit him in Prague, perhaps even here in Washington after he got back ahead of his normal tour and was worried about the Pentagon cutback. If Moscow didn't offer him a chance to pile up a tax-free nest egg, maybe he fell for some blackmail caper."

"Perhaps," Whyte said, "He just remembered Johnnie Walker, the navy commo man, and approached the Russians with a cash-and-carry proposition."

Castle shrugged. "There's been a double dozen of these episodes in the last six years, and there's not a dime's difference between them."

"It's plain bad management," said Whyte, "to let any lesser mortal hang around the mighty too long. After a couple of years, they begin to think—rightly or otherwise—that they're just as smart as the boss. That can make for a sour outlook, particularly if there are any money problems."

"That's one aspect that may amuse you—our source says that Pickett's wife is well heeled."

"I'm told this works better in some agencies than in others," Whyte said, with a grin. "But let's not remind the Director of that. Hereabouts that cover went out of fashion about the time Benedict Arnold considered it." He leaned back, his hands behind his head. "You've already sent this, the facts at least, to Alan?"

"He's got it by now."

"Then there's nothing for it—you've got to go to the Pentagon and the Bureau and put it all on the record," Whyte said.

Castle looked decidedly unhappy. "I think we should wait," he said. "All we're working on is an allegation from an unknown source that the Firm is penetrated. And all we have on Pickett is an unsubstantiated allegation by the same unknown source. At this point, it doesn't seem fair to risk compromising what may be left of Pickett's career on what may be just a by-blow."

"What about the Bureau? They've got a stake in this."

"They've got Grogan on the scene," Castle said. "There's no reason we shouldn't do a little checking on our own before we start shouting to the entire community."

Whyte had long realized that Castle's basic philosophy—never tell anyone anything, *ever*—was essentially sound, but like most dogma it needed constant interpretation. "Three days," Whyte said. "After that, we tell the Pentagon and the Bureau exactly what's up. We simply cannot play operations games with anything as sensitive as the SSD."

"Five days," Castle bargained. "There'll be some delay, Alan didn't say exactly why he and Mike Grogan are driving to Heidelberg, but I suspect Alan wants to get some sense of Pickett in his own environment."

"Four days, starting right now." Whyte picked a sheaf of cables from his in-tray. Without looking up he said, "And see that you get a line on the wife—with two out of three spies using rich relatives to explain their cash flow, the security office should be thoroughly experienced by now."

24

HEIDELBERG

"It's hard to tell which is number twenty-four, but I think it's the second house from the corner," Grogan said.

He leaned back in the seat. "Just what is it you really want here? You can't very well drop in on Pickett's boss or even have a chat with the local security officer."

"Just as I told you in Munich, I'm not going to talk to anyone," Trosper said.

"You mean we drove all the way here on that racetrack—the Autobahn—just to case this place? It's exactly like every other house that size in the compound—immaculate duplex, lawn, hedge, flowers, and apple pie in the oven."

"Believe me, if I knew what I was looking for, I'd tell you," Trosper said. "If there were files, I'd study the files, just the way you would. But there aren't any files. When there's no paper, I like to get out and take a look at things. It can't do any harm . . ."

"Instinct," Grogan said. "In ten minutes, you'll be admitting that you guys work by instinct."

Trosper slowed the car to a stop directly in front of the two-story building. "Now that we're here, I'll just deliver this little box." He twisted around and pulled a gift-wrapped box from the back seat.

"You're not going in there . . ."

"I can't leave the candy on the front steps," Trosper said. "If a general saw it, there'd be hell to pay, maybe a court-martial."

"You're fishing without a hook," Grogan said. "I knew damned well we shouldn't have driven up here."

"I won't go in if there's anyone at home—I'll just give them the candy and the card from one of their old friends." Trosper slipped out of the seat belt. "Two o'clock in the afternoon, parking an army-plated sedan right in front of the house, and carrying a gift, is enough to convince any of the nosy neighbors that we're not ripping off the joint."

"*We're* not going to do a damn thing," Grogan said. "I'm sitting right here."

"Okay, if you insist, but one guy sitting in a car will surely look like a getaway driver—don't they teach you things like that in the Bureau?"

"Goddamn it, this is breaking and entering, I don't care what country we're in . . ."

"It's not *breaking* and entering if the key's where the maid said it would be."

"Four minutes," Grogan said. "You've got four minutes in the house and not a second more."

Trosper glanced at the door. Two brightly polished brass locks. Damn and blast. He should have known better than to assume there would be only one lock. If Widgery had understood the maid properly, she said "the key" was beside the door, not "keys." He handed the brightly wrapped candy to Grogan and pushed the bell again as he stooped to turn over the small white stone beside the bottom step. Two keys. Twice lucky. So far, so good. The first key opened the heavy dead bolt, and the second fitted the polished doorknob. He swung the door open and stepped quickly inside.

"Mrs. Pickett, Mrs. Pickett . . . anybody home?" Trosper called heartily.

"Four minutes," Grogan whispered. "Four minutes, we're out of here."

"Stop whispering and talk normally," Trosper said cheerfully. "Scoot upstairs and sort out the bedrooms. Check for anything that looks like the hobbies your everyday spy might have—fancy shortwave radio equipment, odd cameras, darkroom facilities—anything that doesn't quite fit an over-age captain and his family."

Grogan glared at Trosper and went up the carpeted stairs two at a time.

The oblong living room was framed by a fireplace at one end, a picture window facing the street, and a dining area beside French doors leading to a small patio with an elaborate gas grill and green plastic garden furniture. A twenty-inch TV set dominated the living room. Heavy gold velour upholstery brightened the room but emphasized the bulky army-issue furniture. On a coffee table, a heavy crystal ashtray lay between a silver cigarette box and a five-inch, silver cigarette lighter, an exact enlargement of the pocket lighter Dunhill had introduced in the thirties.

Trosper glanced quickly around the room. Enough expensive knickknacks were strewn among the Quartermaster furniture to stock a swank gift shop. Over the mantelpiece, a large oil, à la Cézanne, hung in a heavy, antiqued frame. A side table supported a collection of color photographs of the family. Captain and Mrs. Pickett alone, Captain and Mrs. Pickett with son and daughter, and a separate portrait of the children.

Although he preferred mug shots and candid snaps to studio portraits, Trosper paused to study the photographs, each matted and ringed by broad silver frames. With two exceptions the portraits were conventional, mass-market products, drained of content by the set-piece lighting arranged to erase any hint of character. One photograph of Pickett, which seemed intended to cast him as an aggressive young executive, stood out from the others. The careful lighting and camera angle chosen by a local German photographer showed Pickett's high forehead and large dark eyes to advantage. But by accident or sly design the photographer failed to mask a skewed, tentative aspect in Pickett's expression. The same photographer portrayed Mrs. Pickett, hair freshly sprayed, thin lips pursed, as conventionally plump and utterly vacuous.

Trosper stepped quickly into the hall leading to a study and bedroom. In the bedroom, more photographs of the children, ages eight and ten, Trosper guessed, and a double portrait of an older man and woman. The man, unmistakably Pickett's forebear, posed stiff, in a white shirt, flowered tie, and light suit. His hair, shaved short at the sides, had been slicked down for this uncomfortable session. The starched shirt collar gaped from the man's neck, and revealed a line precise as an equator, separating the tanned upper neck from the bleached area habitually concealed beneath a work shirt. A farmer, Trosper realized, perhaps a cattleman. The woman, less clearly but surely also Pickett's parent, stared gamely straight into the lens. Her graying hair, done within the hour, he guessed, completed an image that said, "I'm as good as any, and better than some." In the lower right corner of the photograph, inscribed in a precise hand, "For Clyde and Tiffany, and little Josh and Kimberly, from Mother and Dad, Christmas 1991." A twelve-inch TV crowded a corner of the room.

Trosper stepped out and into the study. A few signed photographs of Pickett's various chiefs, none of whom Trosper recognized, hung from the side wall. An expensive, high-tech, miniature German TV sat on a bookcase built to fit the leather-bound set of the *Encyclopedia Britannica*. A locked gun cabinet was wedged into the corner. In it, a chrome chain linked two expensive hunting rifles and an over-and-under shotgun to an iron grating. Mounted beside the rifles were two pistols, a Browning 9-mm semiautomatic and a 22-caliber Haemmerli target pistol with custom handgrip. A slightly faded space suggested that a smaller pistol had hung beside the Haemmerli.

In a bookcase protected by a heavy, stoutly padlocked, iron grill and surrounded by a miscellany of large photo books was a row of five leather-bound stamp albums. In the half-light, Trosper could read the gold embossing on two volumes: "Germany, 1933–1945" and "Germany, 1945–1955."

Trosper turned to the desk, but after a moment dismissed the idea of switching on the portable computer. He pulled open the desk drawer, pushed odd bits of stationery aside, and picked up an envelope with a sheaf of color snapshots. A few alpine shots from the balcony of a hotel or apartment and several more of an eighteen-foot daysailer. Two children, a boy and a girl, with Pickett at the helm, on a lake framed by the Alps—summer vacation, perhaps at the Thunersee in Switzerland. At the bottom of the pack, three late-afternoon shots of Pickett leaning against the balcony, eyes fixed on the distant mountains. Trosper slipped two prints into his pocket and closed the drawer.

Grogan stepped into the room. "Nothing special upstairs," he said. "TV sets in each bedroom, lots of gents' apparel, enough underwear to go a month without any laundering, fancy shoes." He glanced around the study. "I don't know, but I'd guess the women's stuff was about as plentiful." He turned to the gun cabinet and nodded appreciatively. "Expensive toys, pricey gadgets. The army must pay better than the Corps did in my day."

Trosper bent over the desk and picked up a travel brochure.

Stapled to it was a carbon copy of an itinerary, "Captain and Mrs. C. George Pickett, One night, Hotel La Clairière, Illhausern, with reservation at the Auberge de l'Ill for dinner eight pm. Six nights, Hotel George V, 31 ave George V, Paris. All travel by personal vehicle, map with preferred route enclosed." Trosper remembered the Christmas photograph—"For Clyde and Tiffany . . ." What hankering for acceptance or status had persuaded Clyde G. Pickett to become C. George Pickett? Clyde Pickett was a solid, straightforward American name.

He turned to Grogan. "I guess the hell he does have a rich wife—the Auberge de l'Ill has got to be one of the most expensive restaurants in France, and that hotel in Paris could cost him more than three hundred bucks a night. They're in Paris right now, and for another three days."

"As long as they're happy," Grogan said. "But we're out of here now."

Trosper picked another folder from the desktop. "He's obviously taking in this stamp show . . . International Philatelic Exhibition, Salle Vincent . . ."

"We're out of here *right now*." Grogan moved toward the door.

"I wish you'd stop saying that, Mike, you're making me nervous."

"I'm making *you* nervous?" Grogan's tone hardened with each syllable. "The minute after Mrs. Jones from next door begins to wonder who is prowling around the Pickett place, we're both looking for a job—as soon as we get out of Leavenworth."

"There really is a problem, Mike . . ."

"If we don't get out of here now . . ."

"If this guy *is* SSD," Trosper said, "Pentagon security is not even going to consider leaving him in place until we sort out Sinon . . ."

"We can talk in the car, get your ass in your hand and let's go . . ."

"If they transfer him abruptly, and after that stupid phone call, and my little gift of bonbons, Pickett and Moscow might have reason to think something's up." Trosper folded the exhibition brochure and stuffed it in his pocket. "I mean, I think we better take a look at him in Paris. We've got plenty of time—at least three days."

"We're bugging out *right* now . . ."

Trosper reached for the door and took a last look around the living room and hall. The candy sat primly on a narrow table beside the hall coatrack. He pulled a felt-tipped pen from his breast pocket and scrawled a note on the card tied to the package. "Thanks again for all of your help." He hesitated for a moment, pleased with the irony. Then he signed the note "Harry". Everyone must know someone named Harry.

Trosper started the car, and turned to glance at Grogan. "What will happen to these people?" He drove slowly, keeping scrupulously to the fifteen-mile-per-hour speed limit posted at every intersection within the Patrick Henry housing compound.

Grogan shook his head, and continued to stare straight ahead. It was not until a crisp gesture form from the immaculate MP had signaled them through the gate and out of the housing compound that Grogan said, "Three families—Captain Pickett, wife, and two kids, his parents, and her parents. I really don't know what happens to people like that when it hits the fan . . ."

25 PARIS

"Why the hell doesn't Widgery call?"

Trosper was impatient. He had been away from operations long enough to have lost his hard-won tolerance for waiting, the part of the racket that he was convinced accounted for the best years of a case man's life. He could not erase memories of the airports, steam baths, phone booths, train stations, street corners, and barrooms in which he was convinced he had squandered half his career. Or even forget the restaurants ranging from a wooden table, a bench, and dirt floor in Nicaragua to a vulgar temple of gourmandise in Dusseldorf that served dainty portions of a mousse allegedly compounded chiefly of the cheek meat of blue trout. Once, he lingered so long at a public swimming pool in Bucharest that he came away with incipient pneumonia and a case of athlete's foot so fierce that Otto Max, the Firm's resident physician, had dubbed it Ceausescu's revenge. He dropped the paperback book beside his chair and stepped to the window.

"He was supposed to telephone as soon as Pickett tucked into lunch."

Grogan looked up from his newspaper. "You're too hard on young Widge. He made Pickett in less than three hours, and was on him all day yesterday without the least trace of—what do you guys call it in your colorful argot?"

"A squeal," Trosper said. "Short for a security problem."

Grogan glanced around the living room of the suite. "Relax," he said. "Take it easy. As safe houses go, this will pass for comfortable."

"It's not a safe house, it's a clac."

Grogan looked puzzled.

"Spelled c-l-a-c, pronounced like clickety-clack, short for a 'clandestine accommodation.' In our salad days, safe houses—an oxymoron if ever there was—were a big budget item. Now that we're on short rations, hotel rooms are all the fashion."

"So how do you guys justify a joint like this?" Grogan glanced skeptically around the suite. The high ceilings, serious furniture, pastel gray walls, and heavy draperies were several steps above the motel rooms most commonly used by the Bureau when operating on its own turf.

"It's just a backup for real emergencies—a hot agent meeting, or perhaps to house an agent for a few days. In the long run, short leases on upscale places attract less attention than something on the cheap."

"And are more comfortable?"

"That too . . ." Trosper glanced at his watch again. Widgery's call was now an hour overdue.

• • •

"If you want to see my pigeon," Widgery said, "I've got him right out in the open."

"Speak up, we've got a lousy connection," Trosper said loudly.

"I can't yell into the phone, there's a dozen people milling around. But he's sitting, plain as day, at a sidewalk table. You know the kind of place—like some movie set, tables on the sidewalk, but permanent, with glass windows, an awning sort of roof for this time of year and everyone talking. It's the Brasserie d'Athos, around the corner from the Scribe, a hop and a scoot from the opera."

Trosper glanced at his watch; it was a few minutes after two. "Is he alone?"

"Just a minute . . ." Widgery's voice faded.

"Is anyone with him?"

"He's alone . . . but wait a minute . . . there wasn't anyone . . . hold everything . . ."

Trosper cupped his hand over the telephone and turned to Grogan. "He's still on our chum, but either Widge is being arrested, or World War Three's just broken out."

"Good," Grogan said, putting down his newspaper. "We could do with a little excitement."

"God *damn*!" Widgery spoke softly. "My friend's just met a woman."

"His wife?"

"He's making a meet. It's a woman. She came into the cafe, looked around, walked right over to him and sat down. There's no doubt about it, she came here to meet him."

"Is it his wife?"

"Can't you understand? It's a real goddamned contact, a *Treff*, right here, right in front of me . . ."

"Once more, can it be his wife?"

"Not unless she's lost forty pounds and had her face redone . . ."

"Stop the crap, I can barely hear you. Where are you calling from?"

"From the cafe," Widgery said softly. "I'm inside, at the phone by the *cabinet*. There's no coin telephone here, you have to use a Télécarte, like a credit card you slip into the phone. So, first I had to buy a Télécarte from the cashier, it's good for several local calls, but it cost a mint—"

"Damn it, just tell me *who's* with him . . ."

"She's absolutely gorgeous, could be five-nine, blond, a hundred and fifteen pounds if that. She's wearing one of those little-nothing dresses that cost eight hundred bucks, shoes you would faint for . . ."

"How long has he been there, where'd the woman come from?"

"Just like yesterday, he spent all morning ogling and negotiating for stamps at that stupid exhibition. He must have dropped a bundle. Then he made two phone calls, and walked over here. He had lunch across the street, and came here, could be for coffee. Ten minutes later, just now while I'm calling you, this girl shows up. Talk about new-look operations! If you ask, I'd say he knows her all right, she's probably handling him. Maybe she even recruited him. God knows she looks like the real thing. She's *authentically* stunning . . ."

"For Christ's sweet sake, stop babbling." Trosper could not hide his exasperation. He turned to Grogan. "Widge is convinced he's caught our friend in a meet."

Grogan got to his feet and stepped closer to Trosper.

"Listen to me now," Trosper said softly into the phone. "*Why* do you think this is a meeting?"

"Because there's no doubt that it was prearranged, that's why. I was looking right at the woman when she came in here. She took one glance around and went straight to our friend. He jumped up like some schoolboy who's been waiting for his first date."

"Okay. Does it look as if they would be there for a while, are they having coffee or something to eat?"

There was a long pause before Widgery said, "The waiter's just brought him a menu, could be they're going to eat something or have a drink . . . Look, I've got to get off this phone, half the *quartier* is waiting to use it . . ."

"We're coming down for a look," Trosper said quickly. "Give us fifteen, maybe twenty minutes. But no matter what happens, don't associate yourself with us in any way. If she leaves before we get there, see if you can stay with her."

"A distinct pleasure . . ."

Trosper put down the phone and turned to Grogan. "Quick like a bunny, we've got to get to Widgery before his chum takes off."

Grogan shook his head. "Why?"

"I've got an idea," Trosper said. "This might be the time for us to have a little chat, maybe get to know Captain Clyde George Pickett."

"No way," said Grogan.

"This could be just the time . . ."

"Just the time?"

"Look, if he was *recruited*, it almost certainly happened in Prague," Trosper said. "There's not much chance of Moscow getting at anyone in his line of work in Washington these days."

"Unless, of course, he volunteered," Grogan said.

"Either way, it doesn't matter, because he's probably been on their payroll for four years. For a year or so,he really sweats security—every strange face on the street, anyone behind him in the supermarket, puts him in a panic. A security briefing in the office is a nightmare. But this wears off. He gets more and more confident, more relaxed, less guarded. It's happened in every case I know—particularly with mercenaries. They always think they've got ten steps on the rest of humanity."

"So?"

"So by now he's cocky. He's a small-town chump who's stumbled into the inner circle at the Pentagon, and then cottoned on to a really plush, tax-free sideline provided by Moscow. In fact he's just a jumped-up small-timer, who thinks he's outsmarted everyone."

"And?"

"Here he is, a big shot, swanking around three-star beaneries, playing with his expensive toys, looking forward to an early retirement and a fat job with some high-tech Pentagon supplier, and all the time keeping his hand in the Moscow honey pot."

"That might be," Grogan said.

"He's a flat-out mercenary, with no political motives at all . . ."

"*If* you've got it right," Grogan said, "he's the kind of a guy who'll keel over in a dead faint or he'll take a swing at the arresting officer and try to brazen the whole thing out. If he folds, he'll whine, talk about suicide, and blame someone else for all his troubles."

"Can you think of a better time to have a little chat? Now, when he's completely off the reservation, isolated, unsuspecting, and living high in Paris?"

"A *little chat*?" Grogan said. "You keep talking about a little chat. There's no such thing as a goddamned little chat with a suspected felon . . ."

"Trust me . . ."

26

PARIS

"Maybe not quite the dish Widge described, but she's not exactly easy to ignore." Grogan leaned forward across the small, marble-topped table. "If she's Clyde's contact, Moscow has surer than hell upgraded its staff in the two weeks I've been out of town."

Trosper looked toward the table across the cafe terrace, took a sip of coffee and shrugged. "It's *l'heure bleue*." Then, with a half-smile he added, "It's *l'heure bleue* all over again."

"It's what?"

"It's like a noonie, only later in the day," Trosper said with a smile. "Some people call it a '*cinq à sept*' though that actually comes a bit later."

Pickett and the woman were seated at the opposite corner of the cafe. She faced the sidewalk, with Pickett at the side of the table to her right. Without moving, Trosper had a direct line of sight to Pickett, and could glimpse the woman in profile. She sat erect, her shoulders squared, her back arched like a dancer's and scarcely touching the chair. No one, Trosper decided, sat like that unless acting a role, in this case a chic *jeune fille bien elevée*, and the very model of decorum. Her ash-blond hair was cut short, presumably to set off her modish high cheekbones and generous lips. Her deceptively plain dress was accented by expensive costume jewelry.

But it was Captain Pickett who interested Trosper. His clothes—a dark red blazer, tan trousers, striped rep tie, and a starched, button-down shirt—looked as if the price tags had been snipped off a moment before he stepped out of the hotel. The best photograph in Pickett's Heidelberg quarters had attempted to cast him as an aggressive executive with a high forehand and an intense, challenging expression. In life, Pickett's lofty brow was more clearly the product of a receding hairline than evidence of a roomy brain box, and rather than projecting a challenge, his expression was blurred by frequent motion, like an actor struggling to compose a face appropriate to his role. His hands kept busy, patting his hair, touching his tie, groping into the sleeves of his blazer to tug at his shirt cuffs and failing each time to keep a bit exposed below the blazer sleeve. Pickett's attitude flickered between a proprietary satisfaction at being seen with an attractive woman and a nervous anxiety that the nature of their relationship might be obvious.

The woman's attention shifted from the pedestrians hurrying along the sidewalk to her attentive host, and then back again to the sidewalk. Although she did not ignore Pickett, her divided interest was so obvious that it could only be part of her role, and calculated to underline her independence. When she did turn to Pickett, Trosper could not be sure whether she was offering a comment or merely answering a question. When for a few moments the early afternoon sun broke through the low-hanging clouds, she reached into a leather handbag to retrieve a pair of sunglasses, distinctive enough to certify an expensive taste in accessories, and dark enough to put even more distance between herself and her host.

Pickett smiled diffidently and for a moment rested his fingers lightly on the woman's hand. She turned slowly, and seemed to speak pleasantly as she freed her hand to reach for the flute of champagne.

"Perhaps not for every day," Grogan muttered thoughtfully, "but she'll do nicely for an occasion."

Trosper shook his head. "She's just an expensive tart, maybe a model who's out-aged the camera and found a less demanding way of picking up a few hundred bucks." He turned to Grogan. "She may even be accustomed to clients who seem less of a hick than our chum."

Trosper had long ago discovered in himself an almost total indifference to the fabled attraction of top-of-the-line prostitutes and even to their supposedly intricate sociology. As many times as he had worked along the fringe of the criminal world, he had never successfully involved a prostitute in an operation which required a trace of discipline or even a briefly sustained sense of purpose. He found call girls, the expensive courtesans who claimed the right to refuse a prospective client, to be relentlessly rapacious and as a rule more wily than the case men who tried to exploit them. At the other end of the income bracket, his experience with street-level prostitutes had been even worse. Their short attention span and inability to identify with anyone who was not in the milieu had in his view ruled them off the field. This experience was further complicated by what he suspected to be a priggish suspicion of the motives of the case men who attempted to involve these women in operations.

"You could be right," Grogan muttered, "but whatever the case, the little creep is batting out of his league."

The waiter interrupted his orbit around the crowded tables to pause beside Pickett. With a flourish he plucked the wine bottle from the cooler and held it quizzically to the light before moving to add a few drops to the woman's full glass. She waved the offer away with a barely perceptible gesture. Pickett, in a man-of-the-world mode, allowed his glass to be filled.

"It's showtime," Trosper murmured, as if talking to himself.

It was one of the moments in an operation that Trosper had always most valued—on his own, free from the layers of supervision, and solely responsible for all the decisions. But now, his sense of excitement lagged. It had been at least twenty years since he had thought that anything but the most improbable series of blunders could cause Moscow to lurch into a global shooting war. Now, the only enemy that might in a suicidal error have cleared the world of much of its treasure and humanity lay defeated, its residual capacity for sustained warfare diminishing by the hour. Did it really matter if an agent of that wasted giant remained in a position to steal secrets for a few more days? Did it matter enough for Trosper to make the decision on his own, or could it wait until a committee authorized the bureaucratic machine to clank into action?

In the past he would not have hesitated. If he moved now, it would be with the advantage of surprise. Captain Clyde George Pickett, caught up in this absurd seduction ritual, fluttering around a woman who for all her apparent style was for sale, and who almost certainly held her customer in contempt, was as isolated, unsuspecting, and vulnerable as he was ever likely to be. At the least, Pickett seemed vulnerable—a man with no obvious ideological convictions, a self-serving careerist, selling out his family, friends, society, to prop up a modest career with a secret income to be spent on expensive toys and ostensibly exclusive whores.

Trosper knew he could wait, avoid the responsibility and the possible conflict, compose a thoughtful cable to Whyte and Castle, and limp back to Washington without having moved the Sinon operation ahead, and with nothing to show except the unsubstantiated allegation that Pickett was a traitor.

It would be easier to go by the book, to walk away, and to let the Bureau and the military investigate, interrogate, and in the end probably convict and destroy Pickett. But the investigation alone would take weeks. Even if everything worked according to the rules, the lead to the penetration of the Firm, if such there were, would be cold, possibly even erased by the countermeasures Moscow would surely initiate the moment a threat to Pickett was perceived.

Trosper turned to Grogan. "Hamlet my ass, I'm going to have a chat with our friend."

"Hamlet? What the hell's that got to do with . . ." Grogan's surprised expression brightened into a smile. Then, without taking his eyes off Pickett, he said, "You better lay off this coffee, Alan. It's too strong, even for a young prince. Besides, you've got no legal authority whatsoever . . ."

"I don't need any . . ."

"Listen to me for a minute," Grogan said sharply. "Even in a friendly court, espionage cases are nearly impossible to prosecute. If you question a suspect without reading him his rights, chances are you'll make it impossible even to bring him to trial and—"

"He's not going to have the slightest idea who I am," said Trosper. "If he comes to trial, I don't exist."

Grogan looked anxiously around the cafe. "For Christ's sake, keep your voice down. Half the people in this joint speak English . . ."

Over his shoulder, Trosper could hear Widgery explaining that he wanted to change his table for a larger one in the sun, and that his friend would be along shortly.

"All I'm going to do," Trosper continued quietly, "is tell the cheap bastard that I know he's a spy and that he'd better tell me all about it before some hard-ass from the Bureau comes along and throws him in the slammer."

"Mother of God . . ."

In the background the waiter continued to argue with Widgery.

"When I get up," Trosper said, "pay the bill at once, and get word to Widge that if our friend leaves without me, he's to stay with him just as long as possible. If the woman leaves first, he's to stay with her until she comes to roost. Otherwise he's to call at the apartment in an hour."

Grogan picked up his empty coffee cup. Without looking at Trosper he said, "When do I get to say something?"

"Right now, but not too much."

"You mean, all I'm supposed to say is, 'Let's go ahead, hit the son of a bitch'?"

"That's right . . ."

"I knew goddamned well that something like this would happen if I hung around you people too long," Grogan said. "So go ahead, hit the bastard. I can always get work as an insurance claims adjuster."

Trosper eased himself out of the chair and away from the small marble-topped table.

27

PARIS

Trosper squared his shoulders, expanded his chest, and stretched to gain his full height before bending slightly, to loom, he hoped, over his quarry. "Captain Pickett?" he asked.

Startled, Pickett ducked instinctively, and then eased himself back in the chair. Staring up at Trosper, he managed a tentative, polite smile, but seemed undecided whether to get to his feet and shake hands or remain seated.

"Clyde Pickett?"

Total surprise. The expression faded from Pickett's face. It was far too soon to congratulate himself, but for a moment Trosper allowed himself to begin phrasing his final report. "Wide-eyed and open-mouthed" were the only words he would remember.

The woman pushed her sunglasses up onto her forehead and favored Trosper with a serene, appraising glance. At close quarters, and in the unforgiving light of early afternoon, her makeup was less convincing. However effective her costume and performance, it had been some time since she was a *jeune fille*.

Pickett's smile faded as he attempted to push his chair away from the table. The back legs of the chair caught against the base of a serving table, leaving him wedged between the chair and table, half standing, and clearly undecided whether to struggle to his feet and shake hands or to ignore social protocol and drop back onto his chair. "Have we met?" he asked stiffly.

"No, we haven't . . ."

Pickett cocked his head, raised his eyebrows, and essayed a superior smile. The effect was lost when with his left hand he checked to reassure himself that his necktie was still perfectly centered.

". . . but I'd like a word with you all the same."

"I'm afraid you've got me at a total disadvantage—I haven't any idea who you are." Pickett abandoned the notion of shaking hands and dropped back onto the chair. He eyed Trosper's tweed jacket and, in what seemed to be a reflex reaction, reached into the sleeves of his red blazer to tug his shirt cuffs into position.

"I've something rather urgent to discuss with you."

"If it's insurance, I'm quite well taken care of." Pickett glanced at the woman, encouraging her approval of his jest.

"It's rather more important than that," Trosper said.

"C'est pas fort rigolo, tout ça, chéri," the woman murmured languidly.

Pickett's expression soured as he turned to Trosper. "This is really not the time or place to discuss *anything*, not to mention being huckstered by a complete stranger."

"I'm afraid there's no reasonable alternative," Trosper said flatly.

"Qui est-ce, ce type?" the woman demanded of Pickett.

"A salesman," Pickett said, putting a gently restraining hand on her forearm. "It seems he's forgotten his box of samples." He looked up at Trosper. "Just who was it you were expecting to speak to?"

"I have something to discuss with Captain Clyde George Pickett," Trosper said, assuming his repetition of the unused first name would at the least suggest his access to records, official or otherwise.

Pickett's face flushed. "God damn it, I might have known who hired you. Did Tiffany—Mrs. Pickett put you up to this?" He tried to peer around Trosper, as if he expected his wife to materialize within the cafe.

"J'en ai eu assez," the woman said quickly. She dropped her sunglasses into her handbag.

"It has nothing to do with your wife," Trosper said. "And I can assure you I haven't come all the way from Washington to participate in a divorce action." The beads of sweat forming on Pickett's forehead heartened Trosper.

"Then what the devil *do* you want, barging in like this? Have you got a card, or some form of identification? Or is it in your sample case?"

Trosper was reminded of one of the axioms in the Firm's briefings on resisting interrogation. Never deliberately irritate or attempt to belittle the interrogator—he will always have the last word.

Pickett strained to scan the cafe.

Trosper followed Pickett's glance. Aside from Grogan at the far corner and the two women at the nearest table, no one seemed to be paying any attention to the confrontation. He bent closer to Pickett. "There is a serious security matter that I want to discuss with you in private and right now." Trosper realized that with the use of "Clyde," the mention of Washington, and now the reference to security, he was rapidly using up his ammunition.

"This is ludicrous, you just breaking in on us like this, and with some cock-and-bull story . . ." Pickett's glance darted around the cafe, apparently still seeking to reassure himself that Trosper had no confederates. "I shouldn't even be talking to you without seeing your ID."

"Isn't this embarrassing enough without my flashing ID and a warrant?"

"A *warrant*?" Pickett exhaled sharply. His right hand groped behind him to grasp the chair. "What the devil do you mean, *warrant*?"

Trosper glanced at the woman. "The first step will be to ask your . . . er . . . *date* to leave us now."

Pickett pulled the carefully folded, white cotton handkerchief from his breast pocket and touched it gently to his forehead. "Don't be so foolish. I'll do no such thing."

"Just tell her to go now."

Pickett's head bobbed from one side to the other as he again attempted to see who might be behind Trosper.

Trosper moved closer, until he was touching the small table.

"This is crazy, you bothering us like this." Pickett brushed the handkerchief across his forehead. "I'm not authorized to talk to you without seeing your ID."

"Do you really want my friend to serve your warrant, right here in the cafe?" Trosper turned, as if to summon the backup Pickett had been attempting to identify. "I've been trying to avoid that . . ." Good cop.

Pickett's mouth moved but Trosper could not hear any sound.

"So stop trying to jerk me around, and tell her to piss off, right *now* . . ." Bad cop.

Sweat showed on Pickett's collar. Like an embarrassed child, his eyes watered and both hands rose slightly from the table in an involuntary gesture of submission. He gulped, sucking air into his lungs, and turned to the woman. "I'm sorry, Claudine, but this gentleman has a problem, something I have to deal with . . ." Pickett moved, as if to begin to get up from the table.

"Je perds mon temps ici avec vous deux." She picked up her handbag and, looking from one to the other, added loudly, *"Sales tapettes."*

Trosper glanced at the nearby tables. The younger patrons had begun to watch with obvious amusement. Those who were older appeared torn between curiosity and the need to express their bourgeois displeasure. For a moment the persistent buzz of French conversation stilled. In the distance, Widgery stood, still locked in argument with the waiter.

Pickett moved to restrain the woman, but changed his mind. He ran his hand down the back of his head and wiped at the sweat with his crumpled handkerchief.

With all his resolve, Trosper silently willed the woman to leave, just to go, right now, this moment, now, before this dumb bastard gets a second wind.

"Enfin, if faut de même régler mon compte, mon cher monsieur." She waited a moment before graciously, adding, "You may think of it as a *cadeau*, a little gift." Her English was almost without accent.

"A *present*?" Pickett rallied. "What for?"

"Just get rid of her," Trosper said. "Give her something, a couple of hundred francs . . ."

"I will not," Pickett said, dignity flaring. "We haven't done anything yet, and that champagne cost plenty . . ."

The woman picked up her glass, and after a glance around the cafe to make sure of her audience, she poured the champagne slowly over Pickett's head, down his tie, and into his lap. She checked the empty glass carefully before placing it upside down on the table.

Trosper closed his eyes as if forever to erase the scene from memory, and reached for his wallet. He extracted three hundred-franc notes and dropped them on the table in front of the woman.

She glanced at the money, stuffed it into her handbag, and raised her eyebrows as she once more assessed her audience. *"C'est fini, cette comédie,"* she said loudly. *"Rentrons au travail tout le monde . . ."* She brushed past Trosper and headed toward the door. *"Fiche toi, Monsieur Pédé, Monsieur La Chouquette."*

"Casse toi, connasse," Trosper called softly after her.

Pickett wiped his face with a napkin and began to dab at the champagne spots on his red blazer.

"It won't fade," Trosper said, easing himself onto the vacant chair.

The waiter spun back toward the table. He glanced at Trosper. *"Encore un verre pour Monsieur?"* He handed a napkin to Pickett and said, *"Monsieur préférerait peut être quelque chose de plus fort?"*

For a moment the hum of French conversation boomed and then receded.

Trosper beckoned to Grogan.

28 PARIS

"What the hell do you people think you're doing here?" Pickett's face was flushed, his eyes moist.

Trosper signaled the waiter, and turned to Grogan. "Something to drink?" he asked, momentarily forgetting that Grogan would consider himself to be on duty.

Grogan shook his head.

The waiter glanced at Trosper.

"Une fine a l'eau, s'il vous plait.."

"I've had enough of this place, I don't want anything to drink," Pickett volunteered.

"You weren't asked," Trosper said.

Pickett dipped his handkerchief into the champagne bucket and began to dab at his blazer again. "Are you going to identify yourselves?" He spoke without looking up.

"I'm here to talk to you," Trosper said. "Isn't that enough?"

"You said you had a *warrant*?" Pickett sounded querulous, as if he couldn't believe what he said.

"In the circumstances, does it really matter what I have in my pocket?"

Pickett looked up, first at Grogan, then at Trosper. "In about ten seconds I'm going to walk straight out of here."

"Unless you want me to knock you right on your ass, you're going to sit there until we're all three ready to leave . . ." Drowning victims were supposed to surface three times; Pickett had fought back twice.

"If this is something official about me, I think I should have a lawyer before I talk to anyone."

"All I want is for you to tell me how you got into this mess," Trosper said. "Nothing you say to me can even be introduced into court. It's a matter of simplifying things, and sorting out a few facts. But if you want a lawyer, you should certainly hire one."

"Who is *he*?" Pickett nodded in Grogan's direction.

"He's with me."

"He's with me, he's with me," Pickett said in a singsong voice. "What's that supposed to mean?"

"I've come a long way to talk to you," Trosper said. "I strongly recommend that you settle down and begin to cooperate."

"I demand to see some identification. I'm not authorized to talk to anyone who's not cleared."

"That hasn't kept you from talking to your Russian friends," Trosper said as harshly as he could. Captain Pickett had surfaced for the third and last time.

"What the devil are you talking about?"

Grogan pulled his folded ID card and gold badge from his breast pocket and held it at arm's length in front of Pickett. "Special Agent Grogan, Federal Bureau of Investigation." He pocketed the badge and put his hand firmly on Pickett's shoulder.

"Oh,God . . ."

"You have the right to remain silent," Grogan began softly.

"For Christ's sake, Mike," Trosper said. "We're not auditioning for some TV series . . ."

The color leached from Pickett's face as he reached for his glass. "You don't understand . . ."

"You have the right to a lawyer . . ."

"Let *him* talk," Trosper said.

"If you cannot afford a lawyer, the court will appoint one for you . . ."

"This isn't happening to me, not here . . ."

"Anything you say can and will be used against you in a court of law . . ."

Pickett's lips continued to move, but Grogan's spirited recital of the Miranda caution drowned him out.

"Just to keep my oars in the water," Trosper said quietly, "how about telling me how it all got started?"

Pickett began to blubber.

Trosper glanced around the restaurant. Pickett was again the focus of attention. "Why don't we get this show off the road and up to my place?" Trosper said quietly. "We can talk things over, get to know one another . . ." But a glance at Pickett made it clear that the sarcasm had passed unnoticed. He caught the waiter's eye and mouthed, "*L'addition*."

Pickett slumped forward, his crumpled red blazer at odds with the subtle gray upholstery of the chair. His disjointed responses to Trosper's questions were punctuated with bursts of teary self-pity.

"Was it in Prague they set you up?" Trosper asked.

Pickett shook his head. "I met this girl in Prague, but I don't think I was set up. She wasn't like that at all . . ."

"A Czech girl?" Grogan asked.

"Of course she was Czech, and couldn't even speak much English," Pickett said primly. "I had intensive Czech at the language school in Monterey, so I was really anxious to try it out with Milada."

"Milada who?" Trosper asked.

Pickett was silent for a moment. "I won't tell you, she's had trouble enough." He looked defiantly at Trosper and then turned to Grogan. "What's going to happen to me now?"

"Where'd you meet the girl?" Grogan asked softly.

"I don't really have to talk to you people . . ."

"Yes, you do," Trosper said flatly.

Pickett's attempt to glare at Trosper failed when he blinked and tugged his tie into position. "She was standing around at a stamp show and auction, just a few weeks after I arrived. She seemed to be looking for someone. There was an empty chair beside me, and I beckoned to her. We didn't even talk, not a word. But later I discovered she had got a part-time job at a stamp dealer I was using. At first we just said hello, she was so shy she scarcely seemed to notice me. Then one time she accidentally brushed against me, and began to blush and everything. It was like the devil in the flesh, you know? I never felt like that before, not even with Mrs. Pickett."

"And then?"

Pickett shrugged. "I just lost my head. It was a few weeks later when she said she was pregnant. She never asked me for anything, except that I go with her to help her to arrange and to pay for . . . you know, a treatment. It was the only time she ever asked me for anything. But after we got there, just like all the security briefings, three thugs burst into the midwife's apartment." Pickett shook his head, and explained, "It's midwives who do that in Czecho—the abortion stuff, I mean."

"We understand," Trosper said. "What about the three men?"

"You know what pee'd me off?"

"I can imagine a couple of things, but why not fill us in anyway," Trosper said. He had had enough of Pickett's piety.

"It all happened just the way we were warned about in the briefings—like a movie I'd seen before, a really rotten movie. I was sore about it, but I still felt bad for Milada. She didn't have anything but the apartment, and she said she'd borrowed that."

"Tell us about the Russians," Trosper interceded. It was not the time to remind Pickett that Milada had been chosen for him, that her job at the stamp dealer's and the borrowed flat had been arranged, and that all of it was just another bit of old-fashioned Moscow Center business as usual.

"If it wasn't for the kids, I'd kill myself." Pickett studied Grogan, looking for some sign of sympathy. "I don't see how I can keep this from them. Whatever happens, the kids will never understand what I've gone through for them."

"The Russians?" Grogan spoke softly.

"They weren't too clever," Pickett said.

"Just barely smart enough to truss you up like a Thanksgiving turkey . . ."

Grogan's frown silenced Trosper.

"I'd had enough Czech to know that only one of them spoke really native. The others were Russians just pretending. Mostly they spoke English. They said the three of us had broken very serious Czech laws . . ." Pickett managed a twisted smile. "That was a laugh—three Russians pretending to be Czechs and worried about enforcing Czech laws."

"Didn't you tell them you had diplomatic immunity?" Grogan asked.

"Of course I did. When I showed them my diplomatic ID, they talked it over for a while and then said I could leave whenever I wanted to. They said they didn't need me because they were going to make a big public case, photographs and everything, against diplomats like me turning Czech women into whores, and that the midwife who was just trying to help us would go to prison. Then, quarter of an hour later, the good guy sidles up to me and says that all this could be avoided if I'd just cooperate a little. Unless I played ball with some harmless information—like who does what inside the embassy—the pictures would go to the ambassador, the Pentagon, and all those magazines that print that stuff. That would have been the end of everything for me. My job, my folks, everything I worked so hard for. And it would be terrible for Milada and the midwife." Pickett kept his eyes on Grogan, obviously hoping for some signal of understanding.

"What was the hook?" Trosper asked. There had to be more to it than Pickett had offered.

Pickett ignored the question, and stared desperately at Grogan. "Does this mean I could be court-martialed?"

"Court-martialed, just for being a venal little spy?" Trosper had had enough. "You're damn lucky there isn't a war on."

Pickett dabbed at his cheeks and slumped forward, his head resting on his hands, the soggy handkerchief pressed against his eyes. "I don't think I can take a trial, or even ask my family to go through what it would mean, the publicity and all . . ."

"I don't know . . . perhaps you can work something out," Grogan said softly.

"If I come to any kind of trial, I might just as well be dead—it means the end of everything, no matter what the verdict is." Pickett spoke without looking up, his voice muffled. "I don't know how I can even tell my folks about it."

"The Russians?" Trosper found it difficult to pity Pickett.

"If I could die now it would only be a little scandal, less publicity," Pickett said as he straightened up and stuffed his handkerchief into his pocket. "There was one guy, who was nicer than the others. His English was pretty good, almost as if he'd been in the States. He was extra kind to Milada, and seemed to understand her. With me he kept harping on my folks. It sounds dumb, saying this to you people, but it got to me. Sometimes when he was talking Czech to Milada, I thought he had taken pity on her, maybe even liked her a little. The other guys were just jerks."

Pickett stopped short, and stared wildly around the room. "I don't understand what's happening to me, what you're trying to do to me. It's as if my life is over and I'm already in hell . . ."

"I want to know about the *hook*," Trosper said. "What was it they *really* stuck into you?"

"What will happen to the children?"

"There's nothing we can say about that now," Grogan said casually. "We're going to need to know about your communications, and when your next drop or meeting is scheduled. After that, I want to have a good idea of what you've been passing to the Russians. The sooner we get through this technical stuff, we can get on with the rest of it."

Pickett nodded. "This one guy, the nice guy, was very good with Milada. He didn't browbeat her, and treated her like a lady, all the while. Once or twice I thought he was even falling for her a little." Pickett glanced at Trosper and then back at Grogan. "If I have to go to court I might as well be dead, no one will believe how this all happened. I never had any friends anyway, and now it's all over."

He reached out as if to shake hands or just to touch Grogan. "I've got to talk to a chaplain—a minister, a priest, I don't care who."

"There'll be time enough for that . . ."

Pickett's shoulders heaved and he shook his head. "They had photographs, everything we did together. I thought I was going to throw up. I come from a small town, it was the first time I'd ever been around a girl like that, ever." He managed a smile. "I know women like Claudine only act as if they feel something, but Milada really liked me."

Trosper got to his feet and moved closer to Pickett. "Listen to me," he said, "I'm not interested in your running off at the mouth about your girlfriend. I've already asked you about the hook, and I want an answer." He touched Pickett's shoulder and then shook him gently, before saying, "There's more to it than your little fairy tale about abortions. It's time you leveled with us."

Pickett's eyes watered as he turned to appeal to Grogan. But Grogan remained stone-faced.

"I want to know exactly what they used to turn you upside down," Trosper said.

"I guess it doesn't matter now," Pickett said slowly. He blotted his face with the sodden handkerchief. "I'd got in the habit of taking papers home to work on. When I knew Milada better, I used to stop at her place—a little apartment, two rooms. Even if it was provided for her, she'd worked hard to fix it up with nice ladylike touches." Pickett stopped, and looked expectantly at Grogan.

"I'm sure she worked hard," Trosper said. "But can't you get it through your thick head that I'm not here to applaud one of your little tarts." Even though it seemed to be working, he was sick of his bad cop routine.

"Easy does it," Grogan said pleasantly. "This fella's been through a lot."

Pickett turned gratefully to Grogan. "So on the way home from the embassy, maybe two or three nights a week, when Tiff thought I was working late, I used to stop off to see Milada. There must have been someone hidden there, and when we were together in the bedroom, they probably took my papers next door and photographed them all . . ."

"What kind of papers?"

"Routine stuff, like administrative things I was working on at the office . . ."

"Was any of it classified?" Grogan spoke casually, like Pickett's big brother.

"Of course, everything in the embassy was classified, but that's one thing I know about. The classifications meant nothing, just routine paperwork, labeled secret but really not important at all in comparison with our briefing material for the ambassador, and cable traffic. Anyway, they must have photographed them over a month or so. It wasn't a big security leak, but my letting the stuff get photographed looked bad, and with the other photographs of us and all, it would have been the end of everything if my boss or the ambassador found out."

"And so you signed an agreement?" Grogan smiled.

"But it didn't *mean* anything," Pickett said. "I was just buying time until I could get transferred out of Prague and away from them."

"But then they put the heat on? And demanded better material?"

"They kept on about it all the time . . ."

"Until you began giving the better material—Top Secret codeword briefing data?"

Pickett shrugged helplessly.

"And this has been going on, what is it now, about two years?" Grogan paused, "Or a little longer?"

Pickett nodded.

Trosper remained silent, admiring Grogan's avuncular manner.

"And after you were transferred back to the Pentagon?"

Another nod.

"What about money, when did they begin helping you out financially?"

"Before we left Prague, they began to help a little with our expenses . . ."

"About how much *these* days?"

Pickett glanced sheepishly at Trosper, and began to twist his handkerchief into a cord.

"It was like a trust for the children . . . good colleges cost an arm and a leg nowadays."

"About how much a month?"

"It depended on what I brought out, but was never less than three thousand a month, usually more, say at least forty-five thousand a year, but depending on what I gave over. I always wondered if my contact kept some of the money that was mine, but I never challenged him on it."

"Who was your contact?"

"In Prague it was Sam, but I was only there another few months or so."

"What about Sam, can you describe him?"

"Of course I can," Pickett said. "He's the one who spoke good English, with some plastered-on American phrases—'loved ones,' 'don't kid around'—a lot of stuff like that."

"How old?"

"Forty-five, maybe older."

If only he could have planned it a bit better, Trosper thought. It would have been done in a proper old-fashioned safe house, not a modern, comfortable clac. All of their chatter would have been recorded. There would be files in the back room and a bright young caddy who could be sent to get a registry photograph of Volin. But this was a new-look operation, with none of the familiar cold-war conveniences. There was one bright spot. From now on, Captain Clyde George Pickett was Grogan's baby.

Trosper got up. The least he could do was make some coffee.

29

PARIS

"That just about does it." Grogan looked up from his sheaf of notes. "One more time, now, just to be sure I've got this straight. You are absolutely certain your wife knows nothing about your relations with the Russians?"

"I'd be crazy to trust her with a secret like that," Pickett said with a smug smile.

"What about the money," Trosper said. "Where does she think it comes from?"

"I've told her that I've already begun to work on the consulting office I plan to set up when we retire. That accounts for the time I have to spend away from home, and I've sworn her to secrecy about the money I'm already making on the side. She knows the army wouldn't approve of my moonlighting, not to mention my not paying tax on it."

"The money?" Grogan said. "Where is it?"

"Mostly in Switzerland, a bank in Bern. I've got a little reserve in my checking account in Washington, and a safe-deposit box."

It had taken less than three hours to determine the essential details of Pickett's recruitment, his communications, the data he was asked to deliver, and the information he had actually provided. Grogan pocketed his sheaf of notes and turned to Trosper. "Have you got anything else?"

"Not now, but we'll need detailed physical descriptions of the Russians he dealt with, and particularly the fellow he called 'Sam.' But there'll be time enough for the follow-up once we're back in Washington."

Grogan nodded. "Right now the thing is to get him the hell out of here and into the hands of the military in Germany . . ." He glanced at Pickett, curled on a delicate chaise longue at the far side of the room, his face buried in a towel.

"We'd best rent a car, and drive straight through," Trosper said. "I'll have my people here cable Washington to alert the Pentagon and your office."

Pickett sat up and tossed the towel aside. "In about an hour, Mrs. Pickett will be expecting me," he said hoarsely. "I'll have to pick her up, pack our things, and check out of the hotel if I'm going to drive all the way back tomorrow." He paused before saying, "We've got to pick up the kids who are staying with friends down the street . . ."

"You'll stay right here tonight, and leave the driving to us tomorrow," Grogan said sharply. "We'll take care of your wife, your luggage, and the hotel." He turned his back to Pickett and spoke softly to Trosper. "That silly bastard still hasn't got it—he's not leaving my sight until I hand him to the military cops."

Over Grogan's shoulder Trosper saw Pickett flinch. With an obvious effort, he straightened up, and began to take deep, measured breaths, as if this were a silent mantra, guaranteed to mend his broken nerve. He wedged himself firmly against the back of the chaise and said, "I've had as much of this as I can take. I want a lawyer, and I want to see a chaplain . . ."

Trosper glanced at Grogan and shrugged. "I've no idea how to arrange any of that tonight . . ."

"I don't think it will be possible until we get back to Heidelberg," Grogan said. "It's almost nine, and there's no chance we could find anyone here."

"I need to talk to someone . . . I want to have someone on my side . . . I want help."

"Tomorrow," Grogan said. "We'll be able to work something out tomorrow."

"This is the pits, the end of everything." Pickett's voice broke. "I'm better off dead . . ."

"Easy does it, fella," Grogan said. "It's been a rotten day, but the pressure's off now, things are bound to look better in the morning." He gestured toward the bathroom. "Go in and wash up, take a shower or something."

The phone rang. Trosper picked it up.

"Alan? This is Widgery."

"Yes, indeed. How's everything going?" And, he thought, why use our names on the phone? Why not John, or Jack, or Fred? Unless you think I'm too dumb to figure out who you are unless you advertise us both to anyone who might be on the wire?

"First, our friend did a little shopping at Fauchon's. It's absolutely fantastic, what a place. They've got fresh asparagus as big as bananas—where do you think they come from this time of year? You really have to go there sometime. You don't have to buy anything, just check the place out."

"I'll keep it in mind. Meanwhile, what happened after Fauchon?"

"She took the metro to Passy, walked straight to the Rue Pergolèse, and ducked into a really neat apartment building. I'd say she lived there. I hung out almost two hours in the cafe across the street, but there was no sign of her. Before I left the cafe, I made a collect call to Dad's secretary in New York. Remember, I told you my parents were planning their annual trip? Well, they're already here, at the Crillon. They had no idea where I was, but I called them. They're leaving for Rome tomorrow, but I'm going to stay with them tonight. Incidentally, Dad invited you for breakfast if you can make it . . ."

"We're a bit busy right now. How long will it take you to get here?"

"Give me ten minutes . . ."

"Stop at a cafe. Pick up some sandwiches, some cheese, and step on it . . ." Trosper put down the phone and glanced at Pickett, still rigid on the chaise longue, staring vacantly at the wall. He turned to Grogan. "Our friend's nearly under the weather—do you think a drink's in order?"

"Only if it's a stiff one."

Trosper walked over to Pickett. "The bar's open—as far as I can tell, there's just about anything you might want from bourbon to vodka, white or red wine, sherry or port. Whiskey or vodka?"

"I'll never touch vodka again . . ." Pickett stared across the room at Grogan. "Not as long as I live . . ." His shoulders began to shake. It was as if he were sobbing, but there were no tears.

"Scotch it is . . ." Trosper took a tray of miniature ice cubes and a bottle of Perrier from the refrigerator in the Pullman kitchen and mixed three drinks.

Grogan picked up a drink and walked back to Pickett. "When you've finished this, take a good relaxing bath, you could swim in that tub. Or, maybe take a hot shower. Then we'll have something to eat and decide about your wife and what we do tomorrow."

Pickett gulped some of the drink, and walked unsteadily toward the bathroom. Grogan reached around the doorjamb, turned the lights on, and told Pickett to leave the door ajar.

Trosper took a deep drink and shook his head. "He's not in such hot shape . . ."

From the bathroom came the sound of the shower at full volume.

"I know," Grogan said. "What the hell are we going to do about his wife?"

"These days there's probably at least one woman officer assigned to the military attaché's office here. If so, maybe she could come along when we drive her back . . ."

From the bathroom, the muffled *whap* of a pistol shot. Then a plop, like a full teapot dropped onto a tile floor.

Grogan leaped toward the bathroom.

A choked, unarticulated shriek came from the bathroom.

A second muffled, but louder, pistol report.

Trosper jumped to his feet, two steps behind Grogan.

There was a second of silence before Grogan, reeling back from the open bathroom door, cried, "Oh Christ, Christ Almighty."

Trosper pushed Grogan aside and stepped through the door. He retched and vomited into the bidet, and stumbled back into the living room.

Grogan stood leaning against the wall beside the bathroom door. He took several deep breaths, turned, and stepped back into the tile-walled room.

Trosper picked up his drink and walked slowly to the small sink beside the minibar. He splashed cold water on his face and took a mouthful of the scotch. He rinsed his mouth, and spewed into the sink. He repeated the process, and spilled the remains of the drink into the sink. He tossed the glass into a wastebasket, and slumped into a chair beside the coffee table. In the soft light, he could just make out the spots left by the champagne on Pickett's red blazer, carefully hung on a chair beside the chaise longue.

Grogan stepped back into the living room, wiping his hands on a heavy, blue bath towel. "I'll take that drink now."

Trosper added another tot of scotch to the untouched drink and handed it to Grogan. "Is it my imagination, or were there two shots?"

Grogan took a long swallow of the drink. "For some reason, that poor, suffering bastard wrapped the gun in a towel. Maybe so the neighbors wouldn't hear and cause us any trouble."

"But two shots . . ."

"Thanks to the damned towel," Grogan blurted, "he nearly missed with the first shot. What he did was blow some of his face off, half his jaw, teeth and everything right across the floor and against the toilet." Grogan's eyes watered. "He must have fallen to his knees. He was blind, and couldn't even scream. All he could do was make that Christ-awful sound. But then he got the gun up to his ear and fucking blew the back of his head off with the second shot."

"Where the hell did the gun come from? I'd swear he wasn't carrying . . ."

Grogan stared at the floor. "It's a 9-millimeter P-12 Grendel. Probably the smallest 9-millimeter made. Who'd have thought the poor bastard would carry a piece like that in an ankle holster?" Grogan pulled a handkerchief from his pocket and wiped his mouth and eyes. "Damn all blackmailers to hell . . ."

"I'd better get hold of someone . . ."

"Call the Pope, he's the only one can straighten out this mess . . ."

As Trosper began to dial, he willed David Hutton to be at home.

"I'm glad I could reach you this time of night . . ."

"Always here, ready to help any passing friend," Hutton said, his voice tight with irritation.

"I wouldn't have called you this late, but something has come up . . ."

"Damn it, Alan, you promised. What the hell is it with you these days?"

"Believe me, I'd have preferred not to have to call this late."

"All right, already," Hutton said. "I'll make my case directly with the boss in my monthly letter. What is it this time?"

"I'm afraid I'll have to ask you to drop by . . ."

"At half-past nine? Won't it keep?"

The doorbell rang. Three short rings.

"Hold for a minute, Dave, there's someone at the door . . . with my luck, it's Mitterrand."

Trosper kept the phone to his ear as he stretched to open the door.

Widgery dropped his raincoat and a plastic shopping bag on a chair and mouthed, "Where's Grogan?"

Trosper gestured toward the open bathroom door, and continued to speak into the phone. "I'm afraid there's no choice, Dave. You really will have to come over."

As Widgery strode across the room, Trosper shouted, "Don't go in there, it's a mess . . ."

Trosper heard a sharp curse, the thud of a falling body, and a long, keening groan. Then Grogan's harsh voice, "You goddamned idiot, that's evidence you're rolling around in . . ."

"What the *hell* are you people up to down there?" Hutton wailed.

"Three short rings when you get here," Trosper muttered.

30

PARIS

Widgery looked up from his fourth, generous Johnnie Walker and water. "What kind of a place is this, 'Le Paddock,' right in the middle of Paris? If it was any more authentic you could smell the horses . . ."

"It's called '*The* Paddock,'" Trosper said. "I don't know why it's made up to look like a tack room, but it's a photographers' hangout. You can always tell, none of the girls who've been eyeing you weighs more than a hundred and five pounds, or drinks anything but designer water that probably tastes as if it had been bottled by Kodak." Trosper was not sure whether he resented the instant impression Widgery made on women more than he did the fact that Widgery seemed oblivious to it.

"This has been the worst twelve hours of my life," Widgery said. "I was all steamed about spotting poor old Pickett's date. If I hadn't been in such a rush to tell you he was making a meet, he'd still be alive . . ."

"It's a mistake to confuse the racket with the Boy Scouts, Widge," Trosper said softly.

"I feel like punching somebody . . . anybody."

Trosper looked at his watch. "It's after midnight, time for the good guys to go home . . ."

"You should have taken a swing at Hutton when he made that crack about the only contribution Mr. Bates ever made to the Firm was bouncing you out . . ."

"Hutton's all right, liaison people tend to go prissy when there's work to be done . . ."

"Even so, how could you justify leaving Grogan and Hutton with the crazy-eyed Frenchman who came boiling in just as we were leaving?"

Trosper signaled for the bill. "Look at it this way—no laws were broken, Grogan is legally in France, he was operating entirely within his rights, and by now he's squared everything with the legal attaché at the embassy. All he did was question an American citizen who freely admitted to a serious crime."

"Yes, but . . ."

"Don't forget," Trosper said with a slight smile, "whatever their peculiarities, the French have always been keen on military security. You remember the fuss they made about Captain Dreyfus, not to mention Mata Hari?"

"But neither of them was really a spy . . ."

"Exactly."

"Can't you be serious?" Widgery's face was drawn and there were dark circles under his eyes.

"In truth, Widge, I find it difficult to be serious after a day like this," Trosper said slowly. "The fact is that the French have good reason to help squelch any scandal. NATO doesn't mean anything to them, but that's an expensive apartment-hotel our friend messed up. Neither the management nor the tourist office want that kind of news on the front page."

"But . . ."

"If we'd hung around until the Frenchman and Hutton cooked a story and the cops had dealt with the hotel, it could only have complicated things."

"I think it's rotten, what happened to Pickett, and the mess he left for his family . . ."

"He did it to himself. He violated orders and common sense when he got mixed up with the Czech girl. When the Moscow thugs began the blackmail, he should have gone to his boss, or the ambassador. He'd probably have been cashiered, but he'd be alive and in a position to take care of his family. As it was, Moscow read him perfectly—he was weak, greedy, and, up to the last moment, feckless." Trosper took a sip of whiskey. "Pickett was a self-serving villain. He sold his family, his society, and his country for cash on the table."

"Yes, but . . ."

"If you can put the Grand Guignol out of your mind for a moment," Trosper interrupted, "you might question Pickett's story about the boudoir photos. It's possible they merely threatened him and then offered some heavy money, perhaps even more than he admitted. Creeps have been known to use dirty pictures and blackmail as an excuse for their treason."

"I still feel like whacking somebody . . ."

Trosper glanced at the bill, decided he would need an adding machine to check it, and dropped a credit card on the serving platter. "There's more to this than congratulating ourselves on having closed a serious leak, and brooding about the blood we didn't spill."

Widgery's expression teetered between hostility and interest.

"When you get around to thinking about it, remember that Sinon said he told us about Pickett to prove his access to important information. Has he got any more data, or has he used it all just to set us up for some serious money?" He finished his drink. "We've got to find it out before Moscow takes steps to protect its own interests—which will be damned soon now." That, he decided, should give Widgery something more than the bloody bathroom to think about.

Widgery drained his glass. "It's too late for me to analyze it tonight, if that's what you have in mind."

"It will keep," said Trosper.

"This has been a dreadful day," Widgery said grimly. "My parents expected me two hours ago. I'm a mess, and there's no way I can change before I get to the Crillon. I haven't had so much to drink since I graduated, and I intend to have more if my old man has his usual bottle at the hotel." He shook his head and managed a wry smile. "The only hope I have in keeping a penny of my trust is that it's a suite, and the parents are in a deep and dreamless sleep."

He got to his feet. "Dad expects you for breakfast at nine, but it's not a command performance."

Breakfast in a good hotel always gave Trosper a sense of well-being. Yet the food—in France his choice ran to soft scrambled eggs, café au lait, and a croissant or brioche—and even the tableware and napery could more easily be reproduced at home than any other restaurant meal. He had never uncovered the root of his enthusiasm for breakfast out, but was satisfied to accept it as a fact. The sparkling breakfast room of the Crillon met his standard in every respect.

"I'm sorry that Nellie—Mrs. Widgery—couldn't join us this morning, Mr. Trosper."

His reverie broken, Trosper looked up and said, "Alan, please, Mr. Widgery."

"I'm called Tom. It was my father—who lived to be ninety-two—who had exclusive use of 'John' most of my life." John Thomas Widgery smiled across the table. "Except for young James Russell here, Widgery men are always called some variation of John Thomas. If there are two boys, the first is John Thomas, and the second Thomas John. James, here, broke the spell. He's the only third son the family ever spawned. The custom gets even more complicated if the generations begin crowding in on one another, but that's too confusing a story to go into over breakfast."

Trosper nodded thoughtfully. John Thomas Widgery's lean six feet and an inch of height, straight, carefully trimmed hair, light blue eyes, and winter tan combined to present an all but ageless member of the New England patriciate.

"Young James, here, *rolled* in rather late last night, and Nellie wouldn't let him go to bed until she had a full report."

Trosper glanced from Widgery to his father. No wonder the young man had problems. Just sipping his coffee and adding a dab of apricot jam to a croissant, Tom Widgery's understated presence was spectacular.

"Come on, Dad," Widgery said, "Mother just hadn't seen me for a bit, she wasn't all that exigent."

"I'm afraid I was the *exigent* one," Trosper admitted with a smile. "We had rather a night of it, one way and another."

"James is our youngest—and quite a surprise he was. What with both his brothers having already tottered into premature middle age, it's no wonder that Nellie can't understand why her youngest has got so far off the straight and narrow in just two years." Tom Widgery smiled as he raised both eyebrows for an instant. It was, Trosper realized, an Olympian version of a wink.

"For God's sake, Dad, let Alan have something to eat."

"You look as if you could use some more coffee yourself," Tom Widgery said. "Why don't you go up and have another cup with your mother?"

Widgery turned to Trosper and shook his head in mock despair. "You can see why the youngest are the first to leave home." He dropped his napkin beside his plate. "I'll be back in fifteen minutes."

Trosper watched the young man hurry out of the dining room. "You'll understand that it's a little difficult for me to say very much about what James is up to . . ."

"I realize that," Tom Widgery said. "I've known Darcy Odlum ever since he wasted a winter chasing my older sister around Wellesley. That was before he signed on with General Donovan and that gang of his. Years later, Darcy was just as close-mouthed when he set up what he persisted in calling 'the Firm.' I suppose it still goes with the territory—insofar as you have much territory left?"

"I've been more or less out of it the last three years, but I'd say that's about right," Trosper said. "Things have changed tremendously since the breakup of the Soviet Union, but it's my guess that the Firm, or something much like it, will be in business for a long time. The Ames fracas even reminded some of the op-ed moralists that people have been spying on one another since the creation. Now, with nuclear weapons and biological warfare devices proliferating, and every country on earth trying to keep significant parts of its activity secret, I can't imagine any of the world powers gratuitously striking themselves blind."

Tom Widgery raised his eyebrows again. "Money, perhaps?"

Trosper shook his head. "Actual spying comes cheap—the cost of a military aircraft and a tank or two would more than cover most espionage budgets. It's the technical operations that chew up the budget."

Widgery's expression did not change. "Is the boy qualified, is he doing all right?"

"He's well qualified, and he's certainly up to speed with his contemporaries," Trosper said. "Like most of us, he'll profit from more experience." He took a final morsel of croissant. "There's just one bit of advice I plan to give him. In the next twelve months, he should be sure that he's prepared to make a full commitment to the life he'll have to lead if he stays on."

Widgery gazed speculatively at Trosper. "That's fair, and I appreciate your saying it."

Trosper managed another bite of his cold eggs.

"When James came in last night, I was reminded that just about dawn on June 11th, 1944, I got a little too close to some incoming fire in Normandy," Widgery said. "I had a platoon in the old 29th Division. My radio man lost his arm, but I just got nicked. Not much of a wound, barely enough for a Purple Heart."

Trosper nodded.

"So you can believe me that when James came in last night, I was surprised, to put it mildly, to see the condition of his trousers. Once you've seen bloodstains, you're not likely to forget what they look like." This time, Tom Widgery's eyebrows remained raised a full two seconds. "I was *also* surprised to see him dip into the scotch that late at night, and in front of Nellie."

"We tried to clean him up, but it was impossible, and he had no chance to change. I hope Mrs. Widgery wasn't upset?"

"She hadn't the foggiest notion of what she was trying to sponge out of his flannels," Widgery said with a slight smile. "But it was the first time she'd seen James quite so crocked."

"All in all," Trosper said thoughtfully, "we had a really rotten eighteen hours."

"Frankly, from what I've heard from a couple of Washington people, I thought the cowboy stuff was a thing of the past."

"So did I," Trosper said softly. "But at least this one was pretty much in-house."

"I felt I had to ask," Tom Widgery said.

"The fact is, James was never in any physical danger. None of us were." There was no point in mentioning the emotional wear and tear.

31

WASHINGTON, D.C.

Duff Whyte picked up the phone. "Yes, indeed, he's here with me now . . ."

Trosper glanced at Castle, well settled into his preferred chair. To avoid appearing to eavesdrop on the Controller's conversation, Trosper turned to the pictures along the wall at the side of Whyte's desk. As he studied the print of Cornwallis's surrender at Yorktown which attested to Whyte's membership in the Yorktown Phyle, he recalled that the noble lord had pleaded indisposition, and remained in his tent, leaving his troops and second in command to accept defeat on their own.

"As far as I can see," Whyte said into the phone, "and with the help of everyone concerned—our French friends, the Pentagon, and the Bureau—things are pretty well in hand." After mumbling "Yes . . . of course . . . that's right . . . yes . . . yes," Whyte said, "I'll do my best . . . thank you . . . yes . . ." and hung up. He turned to Castle and said, "Today's call from the White House." He glanced at Trosper. "Where were we, Alan?"

"There's really not much more I can tell you," Trosper said. "Of course we should have searched Pickett the moment we got into the apartment. In truth, it simply didn't occur to me. Even if it had, I might not have patted him down. Once we'd lifted him, the objective was to get him talking, not to convince him that he was on the way to the gallows."

"I suppose I've known my share of suicides," Whyte said. "Except for a couple of cases, I've never been sure that I knew the real reason for any of them. Am I right in assuming that this one is as obvious as it seems?"

Trosper nodded. "I think it is . . ."

"Pickett never should have had any of the assignments he was given," Castle said. "He was in over his head from the day he was cleared for codeword material."

"He was right about one thing," Trosper added. "By killing himself, he closed the door on any possible media frenzy."

"Right now, I'm more interested in where we go from here," said Whyte.

Castle, rarely one to lead the charge, looked up from his notepad and nodded in Trosper's direction.

"First, although there's obvious reason to assume that Sinon, as he calls himself, is none other than our old acquaintance Volin, there's also reason to think that if he is involved, he's not alone . . ."

Castle glanced up. "Agreed."

"The basic scam—an illegal being recalled and anxious to establish himself in the West—could come straight from Volin," Trosper said. "After that, everything we know about Volin and what Sinon has told us about himself are almost an exact match—illegals training, service in Prague, involvement in Pickett's recruitment, a deft hand with women. Sinon's glib reference to Troika would seem to confirm that he is Volin, or that he's been told about Troika by Volin. The fact that Zitkin couldn't locate Sinon might mean he went to ground with a woman in Prague."

Castle nodded agreement.

"But what doesn't fit *either* Volin as we know him, or Sinon as he has presented himself to us, is Sinon's precise knowledge of the Tomahawk letter drop and pseudonym, his identification of Winesap as our agent, and the allegation that Winesap has been doubled against us."

Whyte glanced at Castle. "Agreed?"

Castle nodded. "On form, there's no plausible reason for either Volin and/or Sinon to have known those facts."

"In Prague, no one was close enough to identify the shabby watcher apparently keeping an eye on us when I emptied the drop," Trosper said. "There's no proof, but logic suggests it was Volin."

"Does logic also suggest that Sinon is identical with 'Sam,' the most fluent English speaker among the Russians who jumped Pickett?" Castle asked.

"It does, indeed," Trosper said. "The impression he made on

Pickett, his command of American, his attention to the girl, Milada.

It all adds up."

"But it doesn't account for Sinon's referring to Pickett as a colonel," said Whyte.

"He probably gave Pickett the promotion just to hype our interest," Trosper said. "Sinon isn't half as bright an operator as he seems to think he is. First, he lands us in the soup with the stupid letter he left at the hotel." Trosper laughed. "The message in the drop was worse—addressed to me, with Pickett's name, and Moscow affiliation for good measure."

"So, where does this leave us?" Whyte's glance drifted uneasily toward the cables piled in his in-tray.

"It's up to Sinon to get back in contact with us," Trosper said. "At this point, he won't take any such roundabout as the *Blood 'N Guts* route, but will go back to the Womack drop in Baltimore." Trosper turned to Castle.

"I've arranged to keep it open," Castle said. "Anything that comes in will be in our hands in two or three hours."

"Good." Whyte reached for his in-tray.

"Sinon will expect to meet us in Europe," Trosper said. "There's no reason to think he'll risk a contact in this country where we might persuade him to continue our chat in a safe house."

Castle began to smile. "It may come as a surprise, Alan, but you'll need an honest-to-God warrant and a policeman to lift him in this country."

"I doubt Volin thinks we need any authority but a gun," Trosper said.

"Once more, where do we go from here?" Whyte asked.

"I've got to get back to London before Emily files for divorce," Trosper said. "But I'll be able to respond much more quickly to any meeting Sinon may propose." Trosper got up to leave. "While we're waiting," he said, "I'll have time to stop by Salzburg. There are still a couple of odds and ends that Lotte Friesler should be able to help me with."

"What?" Whyte lost interest in the cables. "Until Freddie Tuttle has sorted out her pension problems, I don't want either of you riling her up." He scribbled a note on a pad and stuck it on his intercom.

As he moved toward the door, Trosper hesitated before saying, "Actually, Duff, I think things may be a bit more complicated than I first thought."

Five minutes later, Duff Whyte said, "All right, Alan. Have your chat with Lotte, and try to arrange your next session with Sinon on more familiar ground." He reached for the note he had stuck on the intercom. "I want this wrapped up, but I expect you to keep your activity a country mile away from our advisors at the White House and helpers at the Pentagon."

"You know you can count on me," Trosper said solemnly.

Castle snapped his leather folder shut.

Trosper hurried along the corridor from the Controller's office. For security reasons only Jake Green was authorized to handle the expense accounting for the few operations run directly out of the Controller's suite. Green's office, officially cloaked as Project Management, was more informally known as the *Mont de Piété*. The two small booths in which operations officers struggled to document their accounts had reminded some early operative of a cross between a confessional and an upscale pawn shop.

It took Trosper more than an hour to work his way through his accounting, and, as usual, he left convinced that he had failed to record at least twenty percent of his out-of-pocket expenses. As he stepped out of Green's shop, he was hailed.

"Hello, Alan, old hoss, I heard you were back here for a while."

As always, Squint Foley looked as if he had just dismounted from a cow pony and was on his way to the bunkhouse behind the corral. The leather patches on the elbows of his faded corduroy jacket were almost as worn as the cloth they covered. His tightly fitted blue jeans were stuffed into the tops of dusty, but extravagantly detailed cowboy boots, with pointed toes and high heels. The scalloped breast pockets of his shirt were trimmed with bright red cord which matched his knit necktie.

"Howdy, stranger." Trosper wondered if all of Foley's interlocutors lapsed into their own versions of cowpoke.

Foley glanced along the corridor, stepped closer to Trosper, and whispered, "Did you hear what happened in Paris?"

"Nope," said Trosper, shaking his head. Foley was recognized as one of the most inventive audio technicians in Washington. Security notwithstanding, he was also known for his genius at ferreting out the classiest gossip in the rumor-ridden city. He never discussed his own activity, or anything he might have learned through it, but despite repeated warnings from the Controller, he continued to regard the activity of others as fair game.

Foley moved closer. "Our old friend Dave Hutton and some Bureau big shot were working over an army officer in one of Hutton's million-dollar apartments when the guy up and blew out his brains."

"Good grief," said Trosper.

"There's one hell of a flap, everybody from the Joint Chiefs to the White House busybodies have got their tonsils in a wringer."

"Golly, Squint, that doesn't sound much like the Dave Hutton I used to know . . ."

32

SALZBURG

"Really, Alan, I thought I'd seen the last of you for a while." Lotte Friesler hung the dripping trench coat and hat on a wooden peg in the hall beside the door.

"It's the weather, Lotte, I simply can't get enough of it. What is it they call it—*Schnurlregen*?" He handed her a tightly wrapped package. "A wee gift."

Lotte executed an abbreviated curtsey, and affected to simper, "Thank you, kind visitor." As they stepped toward the chairs by the fireplace, she began to unwrap the package. "*Yikes*! Johnnie Walker

Black, no less." She examined the label for a moment and glanced quizzically at Trosper. "You really are here on business . . . " It was almost, but not quite, a question.

Trosper dropped into the chintz chair near the fireplace. She called from the kitchen, "With soda, as I remember it?"

"A splash, if it's there."

Lotte put her drink on a table beside the sling chair and sank to her knees in front of the fire. She rummaged in the bin beside the fireplace, selected a slim log, and placed it gently on the fire. With a long poker, she adjusted the log's position as carefully as if she were adding to a house of cards. Still crouched beside the fireplace, Lotte turned to face Trosper. "*Is* this business?" There were dark circles beneath her eyes, and her face seemed drawn, as if she had been drinking.

"Yes, this is business." He lifted his glass in a faint suggestion of a salute to the business at hand, or an ambiguous toast to Lotte.

She rose as effortlessly as a dancer, and stepped back to the sling chair. Her black turtleneck sweater and sleek black trousers, drawn tight by their stirrups, emphasized her thin, wiry body. As she sat down, she tucked her legs beneath her and picked up her glass. After a long, speculative glance at Trosper, she took a deep swallow of the straight whiskey and said, "All right, enough of all this rapport building, what is it you want?"

"I think it's up to you, Lotte, to tell me what is going on."

She held her glass at arm's length and peered through it at the flames in the fireplace. "Why me? Letting bygones be bygones, I'd help you any way I could, but you baffle me. I haven't the faintest idea what you're talking about."

He took a sip of his drink and said, "I think you do."

She turned away from the fire. "No, Alan, I don't. And what's more, I've no intention of playing charades with you."

"It's not a game . . . "

"Call it what you want . . . "

"It's dead serious," Trosper said. "And that's the simple truth. There's already been a suicide."

"It's me you're talking to, not some suspect source you're sweating."

"We've rounded up one agent," Trosper said. "An army officer, very well placed, a source that Moscow will be sorry to lose."

"It's got nothing to do with me, no matter what the game is." She kept her eyes on the fire, mesmerized.

"Maybe two dead, it depends how you're counting," he said. "As of now, I'm not even sure what the stakes are."

"I'm impressed, but I'm afraid that I can't be helpful," she said. "You seem to forget that I'm a security risk and that I've been fired."

"I want you to tell me what you know."

Lotte took another deep swallow and, as if for reassurance, reached to touch the bottle at her side. "You're really more of a bastard than I thought you were. I knew that was a gimcrack cover story you had the first time you were here, and I knew you'd be back. I remember your reputation from the old days: never satisfied, always mousing around, looking for another bit of data, one more fact. Now you come all the way here, fronting for Duff and his pal—the majestic, the mysterious Thomas Augustus Castle." She finished the drink and poured herself another. "You know what my niece said last summer?"

Trosper shook his head.

" 'Get real, Auntie Lot, get a life.' She's thirteen years old, Alan, but her advice applies to you just as much as to me."

"This is business, Lotte . . . "

"And you're here representing Duff Whyte and 'Tommy' Castle, as Duff delights to call him," she said, her eyes locked on Trosper. "If it has never occurred to you, they're just Rover Boys, bonded like preppies in some silly secret society. Except now they're all grown up, and call it 'The Firm—diplomatic and military secrets stolen to order.' Like the Knights Templars, women need not apply."

Trosper took a sip of his drink. Lotte had been around long enough to understand the uses of silence, but he would remain quiet as long as possible.

Lotte offered the bottle to Trosper. "I mustn't forget my duty as a hostess, no matter that the guest invited himself, or that he hasn't even got the face to tell me a cover story like, 'I was just passing through Salzburg and wanted to see my pal from our working days, good old laid-off Lotte . . . ' " She stopped as though amused, then smiled faintly and added water to her drink. "Erase *'pal,'* " she said, "and make it, 'my old *acquaintance*, Lotte.' Trosper the magnificent, handmade shoes, fancy threads, and real tight-ass self-discipline, doesn't fraternize with everybody—just the real brass, from the old days, Duff Whyte, Odlum, the good old boys, but no women allowed."

Trosper poured himself a tot more whiskey and reached for the soda bottle.

"Can't the army officer you mentioned tell you what you want to know?" Lotte asked impatiently.

"Unfortunately, he's joined the great majority."

"He's what?"

"He's dead, the suicide I mentioned."

"I'm sorry . . . "

"Tell that to his wife and children . . . "

"I know nothing about it."

Trosper put his glass down and began to fumble with the hinged top of the soda bottle. It opened, spraying his tie and shirt front. He brushed the soda from his jacket and pulled a foulard handkerchief from his breast pocket and began to blot the remaining water from his tie.

"Are you going to say something, or just sit there, fussing with that stupid bottle, waiting me out?" Lotte demanded.

"What more is there to say, Lotte? What would you like me to say?"

"I'd like you to tell me exactly why you're back here, with expensive whiskey, and even stuffier than usual . . . " Tears welled in Lotte's eyes, and rolled down her cheeks. She twisted in the chair, and tugged a handkerchief from her trouser pocket. "Damn you to hell anyway, you and Castle . . . " She put the handkerchief over her face and turned away, her thin body twisting as she tried to control her weeping.

"Easy does it, Lotte," he said. "It's going to be all right."

"I'm sorry, Alan, sorry, sorry, sorry . . . " She looked up, her drawn face blotched with tears.

"It will be all right . . . "

"It's not fair," she said, "your just sitting there, all the time beating on me but not saying anything . . . " Her voice, muffled in the handkerchief, rose and choked and fell with each spasm of sobbing.

He got up, stepped to her chair, and pulled her gently to her feet. He wrapped his arms around her and said, "Here, here's a shoulder, I think you can use one." In his arms Lotte seemed smaller, fragile and throbbing like the injured bird he had once picked up, its eyes darting in terror, too frightened to struggle. He had had enough bad cop for a long while.

Still sobbing, she pushed herself away. "I feel like a perfect fool—mixing good scotch with the vodka I'd braced myself with." She dabbed at her eyes. "Mustn't drink alone. A writer said it's opening bottles when you're alone that makes drunkards."

"It was Hemingway," Trosper said. "And now it's coffee time. If you've got a machine, tell me where it is, and I'll show you some fancy coping."

"I'll do it," Lotte said. She wiped her eyes. "Just let me make some repairs." As she turned and headed for the hallway to the bathroom, Trosper leaped after her. "Just a minute!" he shouted.

Lotte whirled around, staring at Trosper in surprise. "All I want is a cold towel for my eyes, and a little lipstick . . . " Still bewildered by his cry, she asked, "*Who* have you been hanging out with? I'm not about to crawl out the bathroom window and make my escape." Her surprise faded, and she began to smile. "Or even take the easy way out, if that's what bothered you."

Lotte looked up from her plate of scrambled eggs. "I'm not supposed to eat this stuff, but these aren't bad."

"God created eggs, a perfect food—the Devil filled them with cholesterol." They sat at the heavy peasant table at the side of Lotte's living room.

She pushed the empty plate aside. "Will you tell me one thing?"

"I can't promise," Trosper said with a slight smile.

"I like that," she said. "It's the kind of answer that sorts the professionals from the plebes." She took a final sip of coffee. "What made you come back here?"

"I want you to explain a few things." It was showtime, but Trosper had no enthusiasm for the struggle.

"Like what?"

He took a deep breath. "A few weeks ago an anonymous letter

came through the Tomahawk letter drop, addressed to the Controller by name. The author allegedly got his information while he was on the old Moscow Center payroll." He waited to see if there was any reaction from Lotte. None.

"You know as well as anyone," he continued, "that most of the unsolicited, over-the-transom stuff we get is junk, lunatic frothing, much of it unintelligible. If we're lucky, maybe one letter in a thousand has a nugget, just enough gold to keep us sifting through all the junk."

Lotte raised her eyebrows and shrugged. "What else is new?"

"This letter is different. It has the right flavor."

"I'll take your word for it if you'll tell me what you're driving at."

"The letter strongly suggests that the writer had access to data that almost certainly came from Moscow. It is also laced with some stuff that could only have come from within the Firm."

"Fascinating, but what on earth has that got to do with me?" Lotte rolled her eyes in an exaggerated and mocking manner. "You can't be suggesting I wrote it?"

With an impatient gesture, Trosper waved the question aside. "In passing, the writer mentioned the Troika investigation in a rather knowing way."

Lotte smiled and shook her head in disbelief. "Come on, Alan. Dwyer may have thought he kept his great investigation a big secret, but I can tell you that almost everyone in the Firm knew about it by the time the three of us were fired. That's a pretty thin reason to connect me with your investigation."

"You're right, Lotte, and until you told me that you did your army reserve duty at Heidelberg, I certainly couldn't see any connection. At least not until I remembered that our anonymous pen pal wanted us to give him a signal in a damned odd publication—*Blood 'N Guts*. I couldn't see why he had chosen such an obscure magazine, or even where he'd got his hands on a copy. But it is sold in PXs everywhere, including Heidelberg."

"For God's sake, Alan, that's a thin thread, even for you. There are probably three or four hundred reservists living in Europe who do their annual training stint with the Seventh Army in Heidelberg."

"But you *are* in a position to have picked up a copy of *Blood 'N Guts*."

"I'm also in a position to have a lifetime subscription to *Cosmopolitan*, but I'm not 'that Cosmo girl' either."

"You're also one of the handful in the Firm who were involved in the Tomahawk case. In fact, you were the primary backup. You knew the case inside and out, and handled the mail coming through the Baltimore drop . . . "

"That case was splashed all over the Russian press when Tomahawk was arrested," she said derisively. "You know that."

"The letter drop was never mentioned . . . "

Lotte shook her head. "Have it your way. But aside from the fact that Tomahawk is long gone—dead and gone, if I may say so—there are at least six others in the Firm who know the case as well as I do." Lotte blinked rapidly. "And I'm not even counting how many might know the details in Moscow."

"You've also let it be known that you're feeling the pinch . . . "

"From what you implied last time, that's just sad apples for me as far as the Firm is concerned."

"You're the only one of our people even remotely involved who knows all the particulars as mentioned in the letter." Trosper waited before saying, "Except, that is, what our pen pal told us he knows about a penetration of the Firm, and a low-level agent doubled against us in Vienna. He also mentioned a mysterious case that the new Russian service will hang on to at all costs."

Trosper shoved himself back in his chair, putting a little more distance between himself and Lotte. He waited before saying, "You also met Viktor Volin, and you sat in on two sessions of his debriefing. Not for long, but long enough for you both to get an impression of each other."

"Now you really *are* fantasizing . . . "

He watched carefully, hoping for some signal, a flicker of expression, an unguarded body movement. Even an impulsive, irrelevant observation. Nothing.

"From what I've learned, Volin wouldn't seem to be your type, Lotte. But if he has nothing else to offer, he has a sure hand with women. In and around the racket I've run into men like that, guys who seem to have a God-given ability to make women fall for them. Most of them aren't particularly bright or subtle, a couple I've encountered didn't even like women. But the rare ones more than make up for the rest—they're genuinely fond of women, all shapes, sizes, and ages. These paragons understand and appreciate women as a distinct class of human being."

"Along with no-cholesterol eggs, perhaps God should have made a few more of them," Lotte said as she took a final bite of toast. "There are times when most women would settle for a little attention from any of them."

"That may be true, but it's not such a hot idea," Trosper said. "You know that if Charlotte Mills hadn't been killed, Volin would have denounced her. Now, I think he's set off a chain of events that resulted in the suicide of an officer who, for all his faults, might have lived to take care of his family."

Lotte shrugged indifferently. "Is this the moment when I'm supposed to say, 'Is that the whole story'?"

Trosper smiled. "Say what you want to, but I've come back because you're the only link to all the facts I've been able to turn up."

"Nonsense."

He watched carefully—not the slightest bit of body language, or even a thoughtless attempt to explain away a bit of evidence. Nothing.

Now or never. One last shot.

"Lotte, Lotte," he said, leaning forward. "You haven't been away from the racket so long that you can't see that it's not entirely preposterous to wonder if someone might have spilled enough inside poop for Volin to set up this scam?"

She sat silently, toying with her coffee spoon.

"Even if I'm right, it's much less important now than the allegation that Moscow has an important source somewhere in Washington." He waited. Nothing. "One thing is certain. The man who wrote the letter sold us a damned important Moscow Center source—an agent possibly even more valuable to them now than before the breakup and all the changes. Whoever wrote the letter also said that he'll sell us another, even more important Moscow source. That's what I'm after." He shrugged. "Right now, I think Volin wrote the letter. But come what may, I'm going to run it to ground."

He took a sip of cold coffee, grimaced as he always did, and pushed the cup aside. "If Volin talked you into helping him with some unimportant inside data that would support the role he has created for himself, I'll do my best to see that Duff Whyte will be the only other person who will ever share our secret."

This was another of the moments when Trosper wished that medical science still permitted him to smoke a pipe. With care, the business of fumbling for a tobacco pouch, filling the bowl, patting various pockets until a box of matches is found, and the climactic, successful lighting of the pipe could be played to almost any length, with the onus of silence always left on the interlocutor.

When at last she spoke it was with an air of curiosity. "Are you offering some kind of a deal?"

As the last word fell from her lips, Lotte turned abruptly away from Trosper. It was as if she realized only as she heard the words she was saying that beneath the surface bravado, she had uttered a confession of broken trust.

"There can't be any deal, Lotte. You know better than that. Tell me what you know, and when we get this sorted out I'll see what can be done." But what could be done? Of the few precepts that had evolved in the long history of the racket, none was more basic than that trust could only be broken once. To be known to have violated trust was never to be trusted again.

Lotte glanced up at Trosper. Her eyes filled with tears. She knew it was over as surely as if she had heard him speak his thoughts.

"I'll say this for you, Alan," Lotte murmured as she turned away to stare at the rain slashing against the window. "Your timing is damned near perfect." She got up from the table and stretched. "I was close to rock bottom when you came last time, and in even worse shape when you telephoned this afternoon." She glanced toward the fireplace. "Let's go back and sit by the fire, they say there's something healing about an open fire."

It began, she guessed, a few weeks after Volin walked out of the safe house. "I had already settled here—I know it's an odd place, but I've liked it ever since I first came here with my parents. I was in shock after being fired, and couldn't face living in Washington and becoming a permanent extra woman. Even worse, because I'd been fired, I would have been a kind of security pariah.

"I got a good deal on this apartment, and had some nutty idea that after I got my feet on the ground, I could tide myself over by latching on to some part-time teaching at one of the schools for army brats in Germany. But those days are over, and there are more teachers than brats now that the army is cutting back.

"I probably could have squeaked by for a while but by the time I got here, the dollar had gone to hell and the bottom had dropped out of the money I'd counted on keeping me afloat. I was fighting off the decision to admit defeat and go back to beg for some kind of a job in Washington when I got a call. Do I have to tell you who it was?"

"Tell me anyway."

"You were right the first time—it was Volin, all decked out with a new identity, and an Austrian passport to match."

"Did he tell you he'd done a bunk?"

"No, but he was so cagey I knew something was wrong," Lotte said. "For a while I thought I'd give the Vienna office a ring, and say that I'd seen Volin, and mention that he had new documents. Then, I thought the devil with it, I just didn't want to get involved."

"How did he learn your name?"

"He never would say, but I suppose one of the morons Dwyer used for the interrogation let it drop—if it were in his interest, Volin could hear an astronaut stub his toe on the moon. As it is, I can picture him chatting with one of the secretaries involved in the debriefing, and asking—'By the way, whatever happened to old Miss Friesler?' And I can see her shaking out her blunt cut, and lisping, 'Oh, she's gone off to Austria—maybe Germany? Wherever Salzburg is.' "

"And so you began seeing him?"

Lotte blinked rapidly. "There's no fool like a lonely woman. I hated myself for making the stupid decision to come here and for not having found a career in real life where I could have lived a normal existence. Much as the work means to me, I hated the Firm for what was done to me. And I loathed Dwyer."

"That's quite a load to carry all alone," Trosper said. "No family?"

"I have a sister in Chicago, who's married into academia, and a niece I love more than anyone."

"So, what happened?"

"Volin said he was establishing a business, cashing in on the new look in Eastern Europe. He seemed to think it's like the Yukon in the old days, gold piled up on every corner. It made some sense, I suppose, but in truth I never paid too much attention. He would come through Salzburg every ten days or so and we'd have dinner. Before long, he was staying here, and I was besotted."

Lotte got up and went to the kitchen. "I'd better make some more coffee."

Trosper stretched and walked to the bookshelves beside the kitchen. "Why Volin, Lotte?" he asked softly.

Lotte laughed. "You really surprise me, Alan. From what I've heard you've been on the fast track with some pretty high flyers in your time . . . "

He shook his head. "Even if that were true, what does it have to do with Volin?"

"Just because you're all settled down with your feet up doesn't mean everyone else is. Put yourself in my place. Because my parents were too busy with their careers to have had children, they raised me as if I were already an adult. It was years before I realized that I'd spent *my* childhood raising my younger sister. Despite that, perhaps because of that, from the time I was twelve I've been cast as an iron maiden. Something about me has always turned people away—in school, in college. By the time I started work, I suppose I'd begun to expect rejection, and in some unconscious way had decided to hit first, to fend people off before they could do as much to me." She raised her voice to be heard above the clatter of cups and cupboard doors. "And that, dear Abby, is the sad story of Lotte Friesler's life."

"I think you're pretty hard on yourself . . . "

Lotte shrugged. "When I walked into the debriefing, Volin was the first Moscow Center man I'd ever dealt with. After the years in the back room, and handling a few tame agents, there I was face-to-face with the real thing. What's more, he was the man Moscow had sent to the States with only one job, to handle Charlotte Mills. Why shouldn't I have been impressed?"

"You had all the judgment and experience to have handled that job."

"Dwyer didn't think so," Lotte said quickly. "But whatever the truth, when Volin called me here, I was at ground zero, the low point in my life. Of course I was suspicious of his motives, but I had a professional curiosity in what he had to say and, when you get right down to it, I suppose I was a little flattered that he'd taken the trouble to find me in Salzburg."

She put the coffeepot and cups on the table by the fireplace. "By the time he began staying here, I'd actually convinced myself that maybe, in his cynical way, he'd discovered—perhaps even by accident—that he'd begun to care just a little for the real me." Her face twisted, and for a moment Trosper thought she might begin to cry again.

Hardheaded Lotte, so tough she couldn't bring herself to admit that even she might be loved. "And why shouldn't he care, Lotte?"

"Why shouldn't he care?" she said, her voice low in despair. "Because I'm old and plain and poor—that's why." Her voice caught, and she turned away to dab at her eyes with a crumpled handkerchief.

"For Christ's sake, Lotte, you're not at death's door—you're fifty-two."

She straightened and managed a smile. "Of course, on a good day I'd say it was because Volin's a no-good, self-serving bastard."

"That's more like it," Trosper said. "How long was it before he got down to business?"

Lotte tossed her head. "He took his time, but it began when he explained his allegation that the Firm was penetrated . . . " She hesitated before saying, "I'm afraid this is going to disappoint you."

"Try me."

"It was phony, just as I thought at the time," she said. "Volin really had heard some chatter by two of the Russians he was working with in Prague. The gist was that one of them had been sent to Vienna on TDY to help support and supply security for some very important meetings with a very sensitive American source. A high-ranking hotshot came out from Moscow every time the American called for a meeting. Volin said that when he mentioned it in Washington, one of the interrogators misunderstood and jumped to the notion that the American was in the Firm. Volin was smart enough to let it stand. The meetings were always in different areas—probably wherever it was convenient for the American. Aside from the fact that the agent preferred meeting on Sundays, or holiday weekends, Volin just faked the data on the meeting places he reported, and the notion that the agent's name began with an 'F.' He sucked it all right out of his thumb—and in the process ruined the three of us, the three F's, Folsom, Findley, and little Lotte Friesler."

She looked sharply at Trosper. "You may not remember, but I did my best to get this across to you the first time you came here, asking about the Troika and Volin. As best I could make out, you just didn't get it."

Trosper shook his head in disgust. "You're right. It didn't really come through to me until a week ago, sitting right in Duff Whyte's office . . . "

"And I always thought you were so fast on your feet . . . "

Trosper winced. "What about the story he's trying to sell us now?"

"One night, after we'd had a bottle of wine and some brandy, he got around to it. He couldn't have been more casual. All he said was, 'Your precious Firm owes you, Lotte. They owe you plenty. They owe us both.' Then, maybe five minutes later, he explained. 'I've been thinking,' he said, 'I knew they'd try to cheat me, and kick me out as soon as they thought they'd bled me dry. But I'm not that stupid. I kept back some of my best stuff, an insurance against the day they would make their move.'" She turned from Trosper and again began to readjust the fire. "It sounds so dumb when I tell it like that, but that's exactly what he said."

"It's not the first time something like that has happened . . . "

"He laid the whole thing out in about ten minutes. Later, when I thought about it, I realized he must have rehearsed himself. No one could have got it so perfect. It was like one of those Japanese poems, a haiku, every syllable measured and in place. He delivered it like a sleazy baritone, but by heaven, he sang in perfect pitch."

She waited for Trosper to speak, but then rushed on. "'Between us,' Volin said, 'we can get some of our own back.' I remember his exact phrase, 'Share it equal, fifty-fifty. We'll have enough to get us started again, with no harm to your damned Firm, and we'll give Moscow a kick where it hurts the most.' Even if there hadn't been any wine and brandy, I probably would have gone along with him anyway."

She remained quiet while she stirred the embers and arranged two pieces of wood on the grate. Without looking up, she said, "So, in the morning we worked it out. I gave him enough peripheral—and I swear to God, non-sensitive—data on Tomahawk to be convincing. I probably shouldn't have given him the Baltimore letter drop, but I figured it was thoroughly compromised and would never be used again. I told him what I thought about the way Dwyer had handled the Troika investigation, and helped him cobble up the first letter. It was his idea to pose as an illegal who'd been put on the shelf, but you were right about that stupid magazine, I did see it in the PX, and thought it might put a little sand in Castle's gearbox."

"What about Gholam, the agent in Vienna?"

"That was something Volin elicited from one of his Russian friends in Prague who had been involved with Gholam when he was stationed in Vienna. From what Volin said, Gholam wasn't very important, but even so I suggested that he mention it just to let the Firm know he was a double."

"Why Prague as a meeting place?"

"That was Volin's idea because he knew the area so well, but it was reinforced when I remembered that in my day the Firm had no muscle there at all."

"What did he tell you about the data he was going to sell us?"

Lotte pursed her lips and shook her head. "Foxy Viktor Feodorovich was too smart to risk my making a unilateral pitch to the Firm. All he told me was that there was one military operation he would sell as a bona fide for two thousand dollars. It was worth a lot more, he said, but he planned to let the Firm have it as a kind of loss leader, something to convince you people that he really knew what he was talking about." She got up from the fire and sat back in the chair. "From what you said about the suicide, I guess you got full value."

"For what it's worth, his asking price was ten thousand dollars,"

Trosper said. It would do no harm to remind Lotte that Volin had his own priorities.

"I might have known," said Lotte, "that Volin's idea of splitting fifty-fifty would be to keep nine thousand, and give me a thousand, minus my share of his operating expenses."

"What about the rest of what he claimed to have?"

She shook her head. "All he ever said about it was that if the Firm paid what he wanted, he would provide a lead to an important in-place source."

"Where can I find Volin, Lotte? Where is he living?"

She laughed. "I don't know, but I doubt if he even has a permanent place. My guess is he moves from woman to woman, a pad wherever he wants to hang out for a few days. Aside from that, I suppose he just flops in cheap hotels."

"What name is on the papers he's using now?"

"It's been some time since I've heard anything from him . . . "

"His name, Lotte . . . "

". . . and that probably means he doesn't need anything more from me."

"Lotte . . . "

Her eyes watered, and she turned away from Trosper. "Despite all the things he said and the promises, I doubt if I'll *ever* hear from him again . . . "

"Why is that?"

"He's got everything he wanted from me. Besides . . . "

"Besides what, Lotte?"

She turned to Trosper, her eyes red-rimmed, her face crumpled. "Because after your first visit, I realized what I had done, and I tried to correct things."

"*Correct* things?"

"I wrote a letter—an anonymous letter—to the Russian ambassador in Vienna, to be passed to his intelligence man. I said that an important Soviet spy had defected and, after peddling secrets to the Americans, was now beginning to blackmail a few select agents he had not already sold out."

If he had been dealing with an agent, Trosper would have leaped to his feet and shouted his next question. As it was, he spoke softly. "*Why*, Lotte? Why on earth?"

"I knew they would run him down as soon as they found out that Otto Karlheinz Gruber, born in Linz, residing in Chicago on an immigration visa, was identical with their man, Viktor Feodorovich Volin." Her shoulders sagged as she added, "The Gruber passport was part of the escape kit Moscow Center had cached in the States against the day something might go wrong with the Charlotte Mills case and Volin would have to bug out. The Center also had given him a cooked American passport, but I don't know what name it's in."

Trosper exhaled sharply. "That tears it wide open . . . "

"I'm sorry, Alan. Really sorry. I was trying to help out, to put an end to that bastard, to undo some of the damage . . . "

"He's the only lead we've got, if Moscow Center gets to him first, that's all she wrote . . . "

Lotte looked puzzled.

"It's a bit of Charlie Parker's jazz talk," he said, welcoming the aside. "In this case it means Moscow *will* kill Volin, no matter where they find him."

It was dawn when Trosper scraped the sleet from the windshield of the rented car and headed back across the border toward the Munich airport.

33

LONDON

Alan Trosper had no difficulty spotting his luggage on the carousel at Heathrow. The stout leather kitbag was a gift from Emily's mother, and had probably been acquired by her late husband sometime before the outbreak of World War II. In all but one respect it was the most practical piece of luggage he had ever owned. Packed carefully, the contents would weather the most savage handling, exposure to blizzards or hurricanes, and survive dry, intact, and unmussed. The bag wore its years comfortably, and still displayed the unmistakable grace of skilled handwork. The hitch, Trosper was reminded as he tugged the bag from the hotch-potch of plastic luggage tumbling out of the chute, came in carrying the damned thing. Even empty, it weighed nearly as much as a piece of fully packed, contemporary luggage. Given the mood he was in, Trosper could but admit that along with being a handsome, antique artifact, the bag was in fact a pretentious affectation, and that he would be better off with a plastic two-suiter.

Shifting his burden from one hand to the other, he struggled toward the stairway leading to the Underground, the fastest transport from Heathrow to Knightsbridge.

"Alan Trosper! Is that you, Alan?" a voice called from behind. Trosper disliked being hailed in public and, ever since he had first begun to travel under a pseudonym, had disciplined himself not to react spontaneously. He took another few steps before turning casually to see who might be calling.

"I thought that could be you," Harrison Slocombe said as he stepped across the walkway to eye Trosper more closely. "I must say, you've developed a bit more panache than some of your colleagues, those gray little fellows you usually chum around with." He stepped back in mock admiration. "That may be the only leather kitbag that has cleared customs since the BEF came back from France in 1918."

"Hello, Harry." Trosper studied Slocombe's ostentatiously formal garb—black chesterfield, black homburg, and glistening black shoes—for a moment before muttering, "Not a death in the family, I trust?"

"Just my work clothes, Alan. Not everyone is required to traipse around in a spy cloak the way you do." Slocombe glanced at Trosper's trench coat and wrinkled his nose in disapproval.

"It's because I can still get a trade discount," Trosper admitted.

"I've just got in from a weekend in Bonn, en route from Moscow," Slocombe said cheerfully. "I'll be here for a week before going on to Washington. Things are definitely looking up these days."

Trosper nodded politely, and asked, "In Moscow or in Washington?"

"In Washington, old fellow. If things work out, I'll be stepping up soon."

"That is good news . . . "

"Actually, our meeting like this is most fortunate. I'd planned to give you a call."

"Had you now?" Trosper was surprised.

Slocombe glanced over his shoulder and stepped closer. "There was something I wanted to mention about that secretary, the spy woman . . . "

"Charlotte Mills?"

Slocombe checked again for any possible auditors, and said, "Yes, of course, it's just that I'm rather bad at names."

"I'll come around to the embassy tomorrow, any time you like . . . "

Slocombe glanced over his shoulder again. "Actually, one of the embassy drivers, the man who picked up my luggage, has a car outside. If none of your co-conspirators are waiting in the bushes, perhaps I can give you a lift into town, two birds with one stone, so to speak?"

"No one's waiting for me—at least no one on our side," Trosper admitted. "I'd like a ride."

Slocombe took off his homburg, laid it gently on the seat between them, and ran both hands through his hair, flouncing it. It was an oddly vain movement, something Trosper had never seen a man make.

"After our little chat in New York, I began to wonder what made you ask about that woman at this late date."

"It's not very complicated," Trosper lied. "When you get down to it, counterintelligence has something in common with murder—once you begin to shake it out, to look at an event backwards and forwards, upside down and every which way, there's no telling what will turn up." He smiled brightly. "And like murder, there's no statute of limitations in counterintelligence."

"I wouldn't know about that," Slocombe said with a frown.

"As it has turned out, some of the people Mills knew seem to have been involved in another matter, a different problem," Trosper said, his voice flat.

"Aside from whatever your mysterious 'different problem' may be, there was something you said about the woman that bothered me."

"Tell me . . . "

"You mentioned an actor . . . someone you said the woman picked up at a party somewhere in Moscow."

"It was the other way around, *she* said *he* picked *her* up . . . "

"That's hard to believe . . . "

". . . and seduced her."

"Even harder to believe," Slocombe said with a tight smile.

"It's also quite possible that somewhere along the way, he drugged her."

Slocombe shrugged. "That's more in your field than mine . . . "

"It is now," Trosper said thoughtfully. He leaned back in the seat and watched the surging stream of the rush-hour traffic for a while before saying, "What was it you were saying about stepping up?" He would let Slocombe indicate his degree of interest in Charlotte Mills.

"I probably shouldn't mention it to you," said Slocombe, "but I'm up for a new assignment."

"I hadn't heard," said Trosper. "Something good, I trust?"

"Damned good, and about time," Slocombe said. "I've been carrying other people's responsibilities long enough."

"A command of your own, an embassy?"

"Not exactly," said Slocombe. "But in a few days, I'll be given ambassadorial rank, and made responsible for the political side of all our new aid programs for Russia, and the other components of the confederation."

"Wow," said Trosper. "Congratulations *are* in order."

"You're damned well right," Slocombe said confidently. "All the time I've put in as deputy and carrying the can for the political hacks and thimble merchants the White House rewards with embassies these days, this is the least I deserve."

"It's a rotten system . . . "

"I'm really quite pleased," Slocombe said with a slight, satisfied smile. "But along with everything else, and being in Moscow again, I got to thinking about that woman . . . "

"Mills . . . "

". . . and what you said about her claim that some actor had done her wrong."

"Yes?"

"Well, I asked about it in Moscow," Slocombe said.

"For God's sake, Harry, why didn't you ask one of us before taking an initiative like that?" Trosper groaned in dismay. Now, Moscow knew that the Mills case had been reopened, and for no apparent reason. Thanks to Lotte's letter, the Center also knew that Volin was on the loose and preparing a blackmail program. Although Pickett's suicide had not been mentioned in the French press, it could not be long before Moscow Center learned it had lost an important agent. There was at least one plus, Trosper told himself. Because Moscow Center looked at the world through its own eyes, chances were that in their assessment of Pickett's death, Moscow would factor in the possibility that he had been murdered by American security forces to avoid the bother and publicity of a court trial for espionage. That, at the least, might add a complication to their evaluation of the suicide.

Slocombe was unabashed. "Aside from the fact that you didn't indicate that the Mills story was sensitive, I'm not under any obligation to clear any initiative I may choose to make with anyone—let alone an unofficial organization," he said stiffly. "Besides, it turned out to be of no importance anyway."

"Whom did you ask, Harry?"

Slocombe turned full face to Trosper. "One of my sources, a fellow I've used in the past."

"Who, Harry? Who was it? This is rather important."

"If I may say so, Alan," said ambassador apparent Slocombe, "I'm a better judge of that than you are. You seem to forget that I spent three years in Moscow in the old days, not to mention all the temporary assignments I've had there since then. Experience like that gives one a real feel for things. And that's something quite different from what you fellows who never set foot there, and who are still wallowing in all that cold-war claptrap, are ever likely to have."

"Just what was it you asked?"

Slocombe sniffed angrily. "All I asked was if my source knew anything about the fellow you questioned me about—Yuri Krotov."

Trosper blinked. "And what did your good fellow have to offer?"

"Needless to say, he had never heard of any Krotov, and when he checked with the people who used to be at SovFilm—even the name's changed now—they had no record of him either." Slocombe smiled again. "And that, I believe, puts paid to the silly story that foolish woman fobbed off on all you security people."

"In a way, I suppose it does," Trosper admitted. He leaned back in his seat, his black mood unexpectedly cheered by having accepted Slocombe's offer of a ride.

34

FRANKFURT

"What we're getting into is going to be ad hoc, and maybe a little sticky," Trosper admitted.

Widgery's expression edged from its customary sardonic tolerance to uneasy anticipation.

"Not quite downtown Prague," Trosper mused as he bent over the street plan. "But close enough by tram or subway."

By the time Sinon's urgent call to the Peach telephone was relayed to London, Trosper had less than thirty-six hours to pick up Widgery in Frankfurt and make the scheduled mid-afternoon rendezvous in Prague.

"Couldn't we just fly in?" Widgery asked. "I checked, and there are two flights this afternoon that will land us there with plenty of time to get our bearings."

Trosper shook his head. "If the Czech security people monitor *any* travel these days, they concentrate on airlines. My passport says I'm Sam Anderson—you're still traveling as Peter Lynch—and these are the names Zitkin has in the files. He may not have bothered to lift all three of us last time, but he's too much of a pro not to have made you and Grogan, and not to have registered us all on the watch list—maybe even on an automatic arrest roster."

"But we'll only be there a few hours . . . "

Trosper shook his head. "Under the Russians, Czechoslovakia was sealed vacuum-tight and the police were hated. When the Czechs shook off the occupation everything touching on the police and security services was throttled back. The cops are still in bad odor, but the uniformed staffs are being rebuilt and normal police controls are in effect. As we . . . er . . . learned, a 'politically correct' security service is functioning, and on the basis of what we saw of Zitkin, it is working quite well."

"Judging by that airport," Widgery said, "I'd be surprised if they even have a telephone."

Trosper shook his head. "Even if Slovakia hadn't broken off, I'd be dead certain that the old passport controls are functioning as efficiently as ever. Zitkin knows there's enough nasty international political activity, terrorism, and drug traffic to warrant keeping up their guard. That means *airport* controls come first if for no other reason than that cops assume that almost everyone of police interest—including the odd spy—travels by plane. The passenger manifests are telexed from the airport to a central computer for tracing within minutes. The few incoming flights this time of year make control all the easier. There's no way we can count on beating the system."

Widgery shrugged. "What's so different about the train?"

"No passenger manifests on the train, and on night trains only a perfunctory passport inspection at the border, around three A.M. Even if they make a note of our names, we should be on our way out by the time Zitkin learns we were there."

Trosper turned back to the street map. The small Krizikova Park was four subway stops from Republiky Square. The afternoon *Treff* would be better than the mid-morning fiasco at Karlovo Square, but less than desirable. Even if the weather were good, two men strolling through a park at three-thirty in the afternoon might plausibly spark the attention of even a street cop otherwise occupied with parking violations.

"So, we go in by night train from Frankfurt, have breakfast, drop our luggage at the station, take a taxi to Republiky Square, and the subway to the vicinity of the park. We'll have a quick look around, and make it back for the *Treff*. Then, all things equal, we'll take the midnight train back to Germany." Trosper attempted a reassuring smile. "This is what we used to call a quick in and out." He thought for a moment before saying,"With any luck, we should have time enough."

"When you say we *should* have plenty of time, it reminds me of something Fred Burke used to say at his ops seminar at the Fort."

Trosper nodded.

"Actually, it's a couplet . . . "

"A couplet?"

"'*Would have* and *should have*, are words we don't use, 'cause if we do, they give us the blues.'"

Inspector Zitkin stood at the head of the platform, his hands thrust deep into the pockets of his leather coat.

"So much for avoiding airport controls by sitting up all night on that unwatched train," Widgery muttered.

35

PRAGUE

Inspector Zitkin leaned forward, elbows on the small table, fingers laced together, his thumbs forming a shelf for his chin. He looked down at Trosper. "Tell me, Mr. Anderson, do you believe in miracles?"

"In the circumstances, I suppose I've little alternative," Trosper said as he shifted uneasily on the low-slung sofa in front of Zitkin.

Zitkin's expression had not changed from the moment he beckoned Trosper and Widgery to follow him from the *Praha hlavni nadrazi* to the unmarked car, standing alone in a No Parking zone directly in front of the busy entrance to the central rail terminal. After cautioning them not "to essay anything foolish," Zitkin remained silent. With Trosper in the front seat, and Widgery in the rear, he drove a twisting route across Vinohrady to a shabby apartment building. Once inside, they walked up two flights to a sparsely furnished studio apartment. Zitkin relegated Widgery to a stool in the minuscule kitchen, and motioned Trosper to the sprung sofa in the bed-sitting room.

"When we talked last time, I thought you were too experienced to trust your work to a miracle," Zitkin said heavily.

Trosper took a deep breath. "I can explain . . ."

Zitkin dismissed the offer with an impatient brushing movement of his hand. "You realize, I trust, that you have disappointed me."

Trosper nodded. "I'm truly sorry that in the circumstances I had no alternative but to act as I have."

Zitkin leaned back in his chair and folded his arms across his chest. "When I released you the first time, I thought I made it clear that neither you nor your confederates were to return to the Czech Republic for at least twelve months."

"You did indeed make it clear, and I had every intention of respecting your wishes. Unfortunately, it was urgent business, not merely, as your writer put it, that 'Prague doesn't release you. This *Muetterchen* has claws' . . ."

"Don't quote Kafka to me," Zitkin said sharply.

"What I'm trying to say is that the urgency and the importance of the trip made it essential for me to return on almost no notice. There simply wasn't time to inform you of the problem and to ask your indulgence for a few hours."

"That's not good enough . . ."

"I understand," Trosper said.

"I'm not sure you do," Zitkin said.

"Let me tell you why we're here . . ."

Zitkin's nod was barely perceptible.

"My service is in touch with a Russian, a former Moscow Center man who had been trained for a mission in New York, but who defected to us even before he started work in the States."

Zitkin remained impassive.

"He left our custody a few months ago, and since then has become a renegade, working on his own. Using a false identity, and pretending to be someone else, he wrote to us demanding a large amount of money for information on an important Moscow Center operation in Washington, an activity he claimed the SVR will not possibly give up, even in these days of improved relations. Because he knew Prague well, and assumed we had no facilities here, he demanded that we meet him here. As you know, that meeting was aborted."

"Yes, yes," Zitkin said impatiently.

"You will also understand that the one bit of information the Russian gave us in the canister you so kindly protected turned out to be much more important than the man thought. It led us to a serious communications leak."

Zitkin raised his eyebrows, but remained silent.

"Forty-eight hours ago the Russian reached us through a roundabout channel he set up, and again demanded a meeting in Prague. This time, he said he would pass us the information on the other, allegedly more important, Washington operation."

For the first time, Zitkin showed interest.

"As a matter of background I can tell you that the man spent a year, possibly longer, in Prague during the Soviet occupation, working with the *rezidency*. He left our custody before we could finish the interrogation, so I've no idea how much he knows about their activity here. I can say he's aggressive and wily enough to have picked up quite a bit."

Zitkin nodded. "As you may know, we saw this man when we picked you up last time. We've continued to look, but we haven't been able to uncover him in Prague. There's no record of him in any hotel or pension or in criminal circles."

"I can tell you where to find him today . . ."

"Well now," Zitkin said, "are you offering me a compromise—I let you go, you tell me where I can find this renegade Russian?" He shook his head in mock surprise. "Have you already forgot that we're an independent country, forced to be even-handed with our friends, and our not-so-friends? Do you understand?"

"No, I do not understand," Trosper said. "We face the same antagonist."

"Your enemy is my enemy? Those days are over . . ."

Trosper shook his head. "I said *antagonist*, it's you who said enemy. There's a difference. I don't have to remind you that the cold war is gone, and the world is almost back to what it was sixty years ago. Traditional friendships, generations-old political hostilities, half-forgotten antagonisms, centuries-old ethnic—even tribal—hatreds, have all rekindled. I know of no country that's not actively keeping an eye on its antagonists and, as you surely must know, its neighbors as well."

"I must enforce our laws even-handed, treat everyone the same," Zitkin said. "I let you all go once, I can't do it again without my people finding out. If I arrest anyone, I must arrest all."

"Good enough," Trosper said. "Since my friend and I haven't committed any crime, and you've no reason to suspect that we have, perhaps you could settle on merely *detaining* us until we leave." Trosper leaned closer to the table. "Let me explain . . ."

36

PRAGUE

"So, Mr. Anderson, we meet at last." Viktor Feodorovich Volin, a.k.a. Sinon, a.k.a. Sam, a.k.a. Otto Karlheinz Gruber, thrust out his hand. "Not the best weather for our little get-together . . ."

"Not the best place, either," Trosper said, peering through the rain-spotted, clear-glass cheaters he had decided to wear. Volin was about five-ten. The excellent camouflage of his worn lodencloth top-coat, heavy shoes, and sodden black *Steierhut* pulled well down over his forehead reinforced the bleak aspect of the park.

Volin nodded approvingly. "Security comes first, I've always said that."

"If so, isn't there some place we can get out of the weather long enough to conduct our business?" Trosper glanced uneasily along the length of the park.

"There's a little *kavarna*, on the other side of the park, not too far. It's all right for a *Pils*, or coffee and a sandwich."

"Good enough." As Trosper turned to step beside Volin, he

glanced quickly around the barren park. In summer, he supposed, there would have been annuals sparingly planted in the desolate beds beside the sidewalks that twisted through the patchy, yellowed grass in a series of loosely linked oval patterns. The leafless trees gave a clear line of sight from one end of the park to the other, perhaps a hundred and fifty yards. At the top of the park, one man huddled so implausibly on a bench that Trosper dismissed the possibility that he might be a watcher.

"Just one thing," Volin said as they moved slowly along the graveled walkway.

Trosper expected Volin to assert himself early in the meeting, and would wait for the right moment to restore the balance in their relationship.

"The money?" Volin offered an ingratiating smile.

"What money?"

"What you owe me for the information I gave you on Colonel Pickett . . ."

Trosper shook his head. "There isn't any colonel . . ."

In his surprise Volin stopped short, and tugged at Trosper's arm in an effort to turn him around. "Of course there is, you're lying."

Trosper pulled his arm free. "You're making yourself conspicuous . . ."

"Colonel? Major? What difference does his rank make? I gave you all the information you need to find that guy."

"What makes you so sure the information you gave us on the man you call 'Colonel' Pickett is *news*?"

"What the hell are you talking?" Volin demanded. "My sources are perfect, that's an important guy, I should have charged you more."

Trosper stopped walking and faced Volin. "Look, if you want to call yourself Otto Gruber, that's your business—something between you, the Austrian passport people, and any country that doesn't like visitors traveling on false papers." He took a few steps more. "But don't try to pull that Sinon, high-level Moscow Center crap on me."

Volin's face flushed, his eyes narrowed. "That woman, that damned Lotte, I'll teach her some lessons . . ." Cursing, he turned away.

Trosper grabbed Volin's arm and spun him around. "One step in her direction, comrade, and you'll think you've been run over by a goddamned train." Volin wrenched his arm free and drew back a clenched fist. Trosper braced himself and with both hands shoved Volin hard in the chest. Caught off balance, Volin lurched backward, sprawling onto one of the wooden benches ranged alongside the gravel walkway. As he hit the bench, his hat jarred loose and fell brim down onto the wet gravel. He pulled himself into a sitting position.

Trosper picked up the hat, slapped the brim against the sleeve of his trench coat, and dropped the hat in Volin's lap.

"Don't try that again," Volin said. His voice, as he gulped for air, was too high-pitched to convey a threat.

"Don't *you* ever, and I mean *ever*, make threats to touch any of our people." Like a dancer after a strenuous solo passage, Trosper struggled to mask his own deep breathing. He was, he realized glumly, gasping almost as heavily as Volin.

"Big damn deal," Volin said. "You people squeeze me like a lemon dry, then throw me in the garbage . . ."

"I haven't got time to listen to that self-pitying crap," Trosper said. "The minute you thought you were out of Moscow's reach and had something to sell, you came to us begging for asylum. You got it and we were paying you a better salary than anything you had ever wheedled out of Moscow when you decided to sneak off and start this stupid swindle. If you think I'm going to pay for information you held out after you signed our agreement, you're just plain dumb."

Volin remained seated as he flicked the remaining specks of gravel from his hat. He glanced up as if to speak, but stayed silent, and for a moment Trosper glimpsed him full-face in the cold gray light. Thick black hair, touched with gray, combed straight back, with a receding hairline forming a crescent that gave the impression of a high forehead and broad brow. Prominent, Slavic cheekbones crowded the dark eyes set deep beneath heavy black eyebrows. Volin's jaw was broad, but tapered sharply as it formed his chin. For a man to have been so prized by women, he was neither handsome, prepossessing, nor even interesting. The most that could be granted Volin was a bland, shifty expression, and a slight feral overbite.

"Let's stop this nonsense, and get to business before something else comes unstuck," Trosper said. "The last time I was here, your stupid letter attracted so much attention at the hotel I nearly went to jail . . ."

"How could I know the clerk was on the security payroll?"

"Now, you've got me standing around in a park, conspicuous as a bowling ball on a billiard table . . ." Trosper scanned the park. Still no sign of surveillance. "Let's stop the nonsense and get down to business."

"All right, you can give me the money at the *kavarna*."

"Just to speed things up," Trosper said, "did it ever occur to you that we might *know* the fellow you mentioned, the man you said was a colonel?" It would do no harm to keep Volin on the defensive.

Volin's eyes widened. "I don't believe you . . ."

"Or that all you did by butting in was to jeopardize another activity?" If Volin were ever in a position to peddle this story in Russia this might add a confusing dimension to Moscow's analysis of the Pickett case. "I don't know who the hell you think you're dealing with, but if—"

"*If*?" Volin interrupted loudly. "What '*if*' can there be? I told you about the guy, and where to find him. Now you tell me you knew all about it anyway. Do you expect me to believe that?"

"I don't give a damn whether you believe it or not," Trosper said.

"So, pay me . . ."

"It's the other matter that interests me, what you described in your letter as the important case."

"Look, you've checked on Pickett, you know that I know what I'm talking. You know I have sources."

"Up to a point," Trosper said.

"I'm not trying tricks. There's money to be made in Eastern Europe, particularly in Russia. To get in on the floor, I need some capital. I have things to sell, but I have to pay my sources. These are tough guys, used to having things just so. I can't play fools with them." Volin shook his head in wonder, a fair imitation of an honest man perplexed when his true character is not immediately perceived. "Where do you think I learned about Pickett if I don't have sources?"

"For Christ's sake, you learned about Pickett when you were in on his recruitment, right here in Prague . . ." Trosper took a few more steps before saying, "Why didn't you explain this in the first place? Why all this crap about Sinon, the illegal who had been offered the chance to return to Moscow or stay in the States at his own expense?"

"I handed you Mills, the embassy woman, and that's worth ten times what you paid me," Volin said. "Why should I make a gift of Pickett? You people wouldn't pay any more for him than I was getting. You already had me, just a dumb defector you thought didn't know enough to get decent treatment . . ."

Before Trosper could respond, Volin pulled himself off the bench and stared nervously across the park. "You smart people would have laughed at me, and stolen what I know, and that's all what would have happened."

"Why all the nonsense of coming here to meet you?"

"It's the best place I know where you couldn't just grab me up . . ."

Trosper glanced over Volin's shoulder. The park was empty but for a thickset woman at the far corner, slowly wheeling a pram. He wondered if there was a baby in the carriage or a walkie-talkie. Maybe both.

"I have five thousand dollars with me, a retainer. But first I want to know about the other activity . . ." Trosper's voice trailed away. From the corner of his vision, he saw the woman bend over the pram and then straighten and begin to move briskly toward the street. At the bottom of the park, a Skoda pulled to the curb. Two men, both wearing hip-length leather coats, stepped out and stood leaning against the car, staring directly into the park. At the top of the park, across from the Krizikova church, a four-door Fiat pulled to the curb. Three men spilled out, stepped across the sidewalk, and strode rapidly into the park.

"Damn," Trosper said loudly. "Damn and blast."

Volin muttered a curse in Russian. He eased himself sideways as if getting ready to run.

Trosper touched his arm. "It's not worth it, they've got us staked." He nodded in the direction of the two men leaning motionless against the car, and turned to direct Volin's attention to the three men who were advancing like beaters herding game toward marksmen at the far end of the park. "Keep to your cover," Trosper murmured. "They haven't got anything on us . . ."

A second small Fiat drew up at the side of the park. Zitkin thrust himself out of the front seat and strode deliberately toward the bench where Trosper and Volin were being patted down. Still at a distance, Zitkin shouted "*Haendkaf*" and something less intelligible in Czech.

"Restraints," Zitkin said as he reached the group. "For two such dangerous spies, the new regulations say we need handcuffs." He turned belligerently to Trosper. "Some damned security you've got, two meetings and you get arrested each time. Now you're really in trouble."

Lieutenant Syrovy, still in his tweed cap, grasped the chain linking the cuffs and prepared to lead Trosper away. "You are under arrest and will be at the disposal of the Inspector." He turned to Volin and said something in Czech. "*Ich verstehe Sie nicht*," Volin said angrily.

"There's not to be talk between you two." Zitkin spoke directly to Trosper, and then repeated the instruction in German to Volin.

Hampered by the handcuffs, Trosper wedged himself into the rear seat of the Fiat. From the side window, he could see Volin being pushed into the Skoda.

Zitkin leaned forward, his hands palm down on the desk. "It will be easier for us both," he said in German, "if you realize from the beginning that I know who you are, and have a good notion of what you are doing in Prague."

The wainscoted walls, leaded windows, and what Trosper assumed had been a decorative plate rack encircling the room suggested that Zitkin's interrogation area had once been the dining room of the small villa on the eastern outskirts of Prague.

The binaural audio was high quality, pitched to monitor voices without magnifying the distracting barrage of peripheral sounds—doors slamming, windows rattling, papers being shuffled—that can make monitoring an interrogation a nervous agony. The see-through mirror was sited to give the viewer an unobstructed view of Zitkin and the prisoner. Trosper pulled his chair closer to the glass and adjusted the earphones.

Zitkin plucked a sheaf of papers from a tray at the side of the desk. He scanned a few pages and tossed the papers back into the tray. "We will begin," he said heavily, "with your passport." He leaned forward, both elbows on the desk. "My technician doesn't like it. What's more, I don't like it."

Injured innocence flickered across Volin's face. "There's some mistake . . . I don't understand."

"There'll be time enough for that tomorrow, when we check with the Austrian authorities, our friends in Vienna."

"What problem can there be?" Volin's voice rose. "My passport is just like all the others, all the Austrians who come here for tourism or business . . ."

"Perhaps," Zitkin said. "But all in good time." His German was fluent, almost without accent.

"Why am I here, why all this unpleasantness . . . ?"

"You're a sophisticated man," Zitkin said. "I'll not insult your intelligence with a lecture on the laws of the Czech Republic." He paused before saying, "And so, I urge you not to insult me with any foolish cover legend. What you do not tell me, I can assure you my colleague is getting from your Mr. Anderson."

"I'm a businessman, here to meet a man who promised some export opportunities. It doesn't matter what he may have to say about it . . ."

"I warned you once," Zitkin said. "Do not waste my time."

"What can I say . . . ?"

"You can save me the trouble of explaining all this to my Russian liaison contact at the embassy here. I'm less interested in your documents than I am in just what it is you have to sell the American and your earlier work here in Prague."

"What work? You have my papers, the passport will show only one previous visit . . ."

"You tax my patience . . ."

Volin raised both arms, his hands upturned, fingers spread, his life an open book, nothing concealed. "There's some mistake, you have me confused with someone else. I'm an Austrian trying to establish a business. I know nothing about Russians or embassies. What more can I say?"

"Let's begin with what you've got for Anderson," Zitkin said.

Before Volin could speak, a light flashed on the intercom, the timing so perfect Trosper suspected Zitkin had summoned the interruption by pressing a hidden button beneath his desk. Zitkin picked up the phone and barked, "*Jes* . . ." He listened a moment, spoke a few words in Czech, and switched back into German, "*Ich komme gleich* . . ." He dropped the phone onto the cradle and turned to Volin. "By the time I get back, you will begin speaking freely." Zitkin took the sheaf of papers from the in-tray and walked around the desk. "If your statement doesn't check with what the American is already telling my colleague, you will be in deep trouble indeed." As he stepped toward the door, Zitkin paused. With his closed fist he tapped Volin firmly on the shoulder. "*Verstehen Sie*?"

Zitkin pulled the door open and shouted, "Pika!" The short, thickset technician stepped into the office. Zitkin pointed at Volin, said a few words in Czech, and strode out of the room.

Trosper turned away from the screen as Zitkin stepped into the observation room behind him.

"So," said Zitkin, "please to spare me any critique of my performance."

"Just two words," Trosper said. "*Exactly right* . . ."

Despite himself, Zitkin smiled and stepped to peer through the one-way glass. "What do you think? Will half an hour do it?"

"I should think so," Trosper said. "Just enough for him to figure that I'm talking freely, but not so long that he thinks your staff is having to beat down my resistance."

Zitkin nodded. "Time enough for a sandwich and coffee, or perhaps a *Pils*?"

37

PRAGUE

Zitkin settled himself in the heavy wooden chair behind his desk and pulled on his reading glasses. He scanned a sheaf of handwritten notes before looking up to study Volin. "Now, Herr Gruber, start talking."

Volin pulled a crumpled handkerchief from his pocket and dabbed at his nose before wiping at the sweat forming along his shirt collar. "This is all a great mistake." He glanced hopefully at Zitkin. No reaction.

"Perhaps more a misunderstanding than a mistake," Volin suggested. "I can explain it all if you will listen . . ."

Zitkin remained motionless, hunched forward, elbows on the desk, fingers laced together. He peered, unblinking, over the rims of his half-glasses.

"The Americans bled me white, then tricked me . . ."

Zitkin leaned back from the desk and folded his arms across his chest.

"All I need is a little cash, enough to get me out of this mess, and to give me a chance in business. I swear to God that I . . ."

Zitkin raised his hand, a bored policeman bringing traffic to a halt. "What are you selling?"

Volin took a deep breath. "I told him about a spy, an important agent, a bad leak in their security . . ."

"That was the first trip," Zitkin said.

"He gave me nothing, not a penny . . ."

With an impatient gesture, Zitkin brushed Volin's comment aside. "For the last time . . ."

Volin began to rock from side to side, a frustrated infant about to begin shaking his crib. "You've treated me decently, there's something I can share with you," he said. "Like all those people, Anderson has money, plenty of it. He'll pay whatever I ask for the information I have. We can share, there'll be plenty." For the first time, Volin hazarded eye contact with Zitkin.

The fury in Zitkin's expression skewered Volin as effectively as a bayonet thrust. In the instant the impact of his mistake registered, Volin's expression flashed from a tentative affinity to panic.

Zitkin rose from behind the desk. Volin attempted to push his chair back, beyond reach of the Czech, and blurted, "I mean you can use the money for expenses in your operations, it can go to your service."

Zitkin stepped to the side of the desk and with both hands grabbed the lapels of Volin's jacket. With a single movement, he heaved Volin to his feet. "*Du unverschaemter Scheisskerl*," he shouted. "In my own office, you offer bribes to me!" He shook Volin free of the floor and like a farmhand heaving a bale of hay, flung him across the room. The Russian crashed backwards against a small table. Striving to keep his balance, he stumbled sideways, and fell. A lamp toppled off the table onto the floor. The bulb broke with a pop.

As the Czech moved quickly across the room, Volin pulled himself to his knees and raised both arms, uncertain whether to defend himself against Zitkin's fists or heavy shoes.

The door flew open and Lieutenant Syrovy burst into the interrogation room. He glanced quickly at Volin, then turned to Zitkin and said in German, "Did you ring, *Chef*?"

Zitkin whirled to face Syrovy. Then, his back to Volin, he winked. "The prisoner appears to have taken a fit," Zitkin said in German. "Please get him back to his chair before he has another seizure."

Trosper hitched his chair closer to the one-way glass.

Zitkin continued to leaf through the sheaf of notes until he glanced up at Volin. "All recovered?" he asked. "Ready to talk?"

Volin stuffed the sweaty handkerchief back into his trouser pocket, heaved a deep sigh, and said, "First, I will admit that I was with the Center, forced by a stupid indiscretion when I was at university in Kiev. A colonel's daughter—an important man in the security service—accused me . . ."

"Quickly now," Zitkin said heavily.

"She told her father I had seduced and abandoned her." Volin smiled. "A tramp like that, nobody needed to seduce."

"And then, of course, the colonel forced you to become an informer?"

"He had the girl aborted, and blamed me for everything . . ."

"Am I supposed to believe this impressed the Americans?"

Volin shook his head. "They know me as a senior agent formerly with the First Chief Directorate, Line S, the illegals component."

With an impatient beckoning gesture, Zitkin hurried Volin along.

"I was a good student, but my work for the security organs wrecked my university career. When I failed my examinations, I was ordered to Leningrad—St. Petersburg—for work among the American and foreign students at the university there . . ."

"Could any of this have interested Anderson?"

"You misunderstand," Volin said. "What I'm saying is that because I was successful and good at languages, I was transferred to the 'S' Directorate for higher training. By the time I realized what was happening it was too late, I couldn't get free of them, they wouldn't release me."

"Of course not, there are so few good people for that work," Zitkin said, his sour expression intensifying the irony of his tone.

"I'd learned good English, and went quickly through the other studies to prepare for serious work as an illegal agent in America. I knew that once there I could escape, and find a decent life. As a final step, I was sent to Prague, a safe place for me to accustom myself to Western ways and to get more practical experience. After months, I was called back to Moscow to be fitted with a legend and new papers to support it. It was then I learned I would be sent to New York, and was given the file of the important agent I was to handle. When I read the file, I knew I couldn't do it—the agent was a woman who had been blackmailed, quite innocent until they set someone against her. It was a crime, I would have no part . . ."

"But you did go to the States?"

Volin raised both hands as if in surrender, the exposed palms framing the image of a simple man snared by fate. "What could I do, what could any of us have done against the power of that service?"

Zitkin shrugged. "And so you turned yourself over to the Americans?"

"I went to them in Germany, before I even began my mission. They took me to the States, where I told them everything, explaining that the woman was innocent . . ."

"And they rewarded you handsomely?" Zitkin's smile flickered.

Volin snorted. "They put me in a camp and squeezed almost everything from me. They had the woman killed, pretending it was a robbery in the park in New York, just to avoid the publicity of a trial. There was nothing I could do to save her . . ."

"And then they threw you aside?"

"They said that if I ever spoke about it, they would turn me back to the Russians." As he gained confidence, Volin risked an ingratiating smile.

"But your interrogation continued?"

"It went on until I escaped from their custody. But once I was on my own again, it was clear I didn't have enough money to get started. As much as I distrusted the Americans, I knew it was more important to put an end to the old Soviet apparat, because I knew the new people would cling to the old ways, keep the old agents in place. For once my two objectives matched. I would disclose more of what I knew—priceless for American security—and ask to be paid enough to get myself started again."

"And so you arranged for Anderson to come here," Zitkin said, "and you gave him enough information to close the leak?"

Volin's smile broadened. "Yes, that was my purpose. I left some information—a bona fide—for him hidden on the park bench where you arrested him. You must have found it."

"I see . . ."

"But as usual dealing with these people I got nothing for it."

"Still, you carried on?"

"Only because I had even more important data that I felt I must disclose," said Volin with a shy smile. "And, to be blunt, because I still need money for business purposes."

"I've been patient with you," Zitkin said sharply. "Now I'm going to check what you've said against what Anderson is telling my colleague.

When I come back, you'll have a last chance to tell me what it is you planned to sell to Anderson . . ."

"But, he will lie . . ."

Zitkin got up and moved toward the door. "On the basis of what you tell me when I get back, I'll decide whether to deliver you to the Russian embassy, or hand you and your counterfeit passport over to the Austrian police at the border. I gain credit either way. If you're smart, you'll tell the truth, and not try to hand me another dish of *Schmarrn*." He waited before saying, "It will be up to you, but make no mistake, you'll have five minutes to make your case."

"But . . ."

Zitkin opened the door and bellowed for Pika.

Trosper pulled back from the glass as Zitkin stepped into the monitoring room.

"I'd heard that you people played rough," Zitkin said as he closed the door behind himself. "But shooting some poor woman in the park?" He laughed. "I suppose it was cheaper than staging a trial . . ."

"That's not quite what happened," Trosper said. "She died in a mugging days before Volin made contact with us. He didn't even know she'd been killed when we brought him to the States." Zitkin listened attentively until he glanced at his watch.

Trosper picked up the earphones as Zitkin stepped back into the interrogation room.

38 PRAGUE

"Quickly now," Zitkin said. "Why is Anderson back in Prague?"

Volin looked up but avoided eye contact. He coughed and cleared his throat. "Some coffee—water, anything," he said, pleading.

Zitkin flipped a switch on the intercom and muttered in Czech. Syrovy pushed the door open, spoke a few words to Zitkin, and handed Volin a tumbler half filled with water.

Volin nodded his thanks, and said, "When I came to Prague, I worked with Oleg Kozlov, the culture attaché at the embassy, you can check in your files. In truth, Kozlov was the 'S'—illegals—representative. Before coming here, his first field job was in Tehran. From what he said, he did well, got good promotions. But there wasn't much for him here in Prague, just small matters, getting blank copies of Czech documents, passports, ID cards, things like that . . ." Volin caught Zitkin's expression and said quickly, "It had nothing to do with Czech security, just documentation for illegal work in other countries . . ."

"I'll judge what concerns Czech security," Zitkin said, adding a note to the pad on his desk.

"Of course, of course," said Volin, taking a deep breath. "Aside from that, Kozlov had little to do here unless an agent was staging through Prague en route to assignment in the West." He waited for a reaction from Zitkin. None.

"To understand my relations with Kozlov, you have to know he was here alone, no wife, no girlfriend. It was natural that I introduced him to a woman I knew, not too young, but nice enough." Volin smiled, a man of the world inviting Zitkin to share his sophistication. "Of course Kozlov was grateful, but I would have done as much for anyone. So, we became friends. One night when we were having drinks, Kozlov began talking about Iran, the intrigues and back-biting in the Tehran embassy and how bad the operating conditions were for the *rezidency*."

Volin's speech came faster as he gained confidence. "From what Kozlov said, the best thing that happened to him in Iran was getting to know his chief, Colonel Golobev, in charge of illegals work in Iran. Golobev was developing a woman—half Iranian, maybe with an Armenian mother, I'm not sure. Her family came from the border area in the north. In the old days, that part of Iran was under Russian influence. No one cared too much about nationality, and Armenians moved back and forth across the border like it was one country. But under Lenin, things tightened. The Armenians who settled on the Soviet side of the border were told to become Russians or get out. Some stayed, the smart ones fled into Iran. The strange thing is that even after a few generations in Iran, some families continued to keep their ties to Russia alive. They spoke Russian, celebrated holidays, and mixed in with the White Russians who came over after the defeat of the White Army."

"Your point?" Zitkin demanded.

"Simple enough—Kozlov's boss fell in love with this half-Armenian woman, completely infatuated." Then, as if taking Zitkin more deeply into his confidence, Volin added with a leer, "Believe me, it's been known to happen, even to a widow with a son fourteen, maybe even a year or two older. The point is that under the pretense of bringing her to the U.S.S.R. for training as an illegal, Golobev smuggled the woman and her son out of Iran and into the U.S.S.R. This was in 1982, maybe 1983, but Golobev already had a big reputation, and knew everyone, so no questions were asked. Of course the woman never returned to Iran."

"What about the boy?"

Volin nodded his head shrewdly. "I think he was called 'Gholam,' a very Persian name. A few times Kozlov slipped and called him that. But Anderson will have no trouble identifying him—an Iranian and recruited by the Firm in Vienna. There can't be very many who fit that description." Volin took another sip of water. "The boy was lazy and spoiled, with no interest in anything but a comfortable existence. All he really wanted was to go back to the life he knew best, Iran. But Golobev had another plan—he had had a death certificate fabricated showing that the mother had died in Iran about the time he smuggled the boy and her out. After long training in the special school, he had the service slip the boy back into Iran, to Tehran, where some of the mother's relatives took him in. Blood is thick in that culture, and no one else even knew that Gholam had ever left Iran. Golobev's idea was that as soon as Gholam was old enough, he would apply for the Iranian diplomatic service, or the interior ministry. In either place, even as a clerk, he would be of use to the 'S' Directorate, for documents, things like that."

Volin stopped to take a sip of water. "And that is just what happened. Gholam was a bona-fide native speaker, not a trace of accent—a real clerk type, educated, but not too ambitious, a dreamer interested in music and books, but always on the watch for an extra bit of cash. Perfect for a support agent."

"Do you really think Anderson will pay you for that story?" Zitkin said.

"He'll pay, because what I haven't explained is that Gholam married and got a job in the foreign ministry." Volin waited before adding slyly, "If I were an active intelligence man, I might wonder if Golobev had a man inside the ministry who helped to arrange Gholam's job, and I might even think of having someone with experience in this work find this guy and shake him down for work on my behalf."

Trosper leaned away from the see-through mirror and laughed aloud.

Zitkin waved the proposition aside and beckoned Volin to continue.

Volin shrugged, and began to speak more rapidly. "Whatever the reason, Gholam was assigned to Vienna, a clerk in the embassy there. He'd only been there a few weeks when he met an American, a young guy, who'd been circulating around the coffee houses where some of the Iranians and their friends hung out. The American pretended to have some money to invest in developing a business in Iran, but typical American, he was so conspicuous and naive that he might as well have paraded himself as an agent. After three or four meetings, he propositioned Gholam to feed him information from the Iranian embassy and community—'just a little inside stuff that would help set up a business.' But Gholam had spotted him right off and had already told Golobev's man in the embassy about it. The Russian told him to accept—'Tell the stupid Americans anything they want to know about Iran, just don't make yourself too important, don't risk exposing yourself.' "

Volin's smile was ingratiating. "There you have it," he said, his hands palm up as if offering Zitkin an invisible gift. "The scheme that Golobev had started years earlier was beginning to take shape. What deeper cover for a Russian illegal than to be a trusted clerk in the Iranian foreign office, *and* an American agent as well?" Volin snickered. "Don't you see? No trace of the Russian service anywhere?"

"Yes," Zitkin said. "I see."

"Later, Gholam, who'd been studying English, is transferred from Vienna to New York—the Iranian mission to the U.N." He touched his finger to his nose and cocked his head. "Again, it made me wonder if Golobev had a little help from someone inside the ministry . . ."

Zitkin nodded.

"Whatever the explanation, the move was exactly what Colonel Golobev wanted—a deep-covered illegal agent completely unknown to anybody, with a perfect job, and able to service any agent, no matter how sensitive and in an area tough to work in. So, Golobev goes to New York to brief Gholam on his role. All Gholam knows is that he's to be the contact point for a big shot agent. Even the local *rezidency* is cut out—all they have to do is pick up the agent's encoded messages from Gholam and hand the incoming Moscow messages to Gholam to pass to the agent. Once, maybe three times a year, Moscow sends a colonel to meet the agent. The most that anyone outside Moscow knows is that they're servicing a high source—aside from that, nothing. Perfect security."

Volin paused to consider the impact of his story, and to encourage a favorable comment or at least a smile. But Zitkin remained silent, tilting back in the heavy wooden chair, his arms folded across his chest.

"Perfect security, you think?" Volin said. "Not quite. There's one big problem. Crafty as he is, Golobev had a bit more business that required him to stop in Prague on the way back to Moscow. After business, he has a big vodka dinner with Kozlov. Then, like he's talking at the training center, impressing everyone with how to do long-range business, Golobev tells his old protégé Kozlov the whole story."

"And later," Zitkin said, "Kozlov tells most of the story to you?"

Volin nodded. "It was at our last meeting here in Prague, before I left for Germany and New York. This time, it was Kozlov who was drinking heavily and trying to impress me with how much he knew and how important my work as an illegal agent would be . . ."

"Did he give any particulars on the agent—name, description, even a codename?"

Volin shook his head."Not a word of description, nor any name at all. The only hint, and I can't be absolutely sure, but there was one hint. Once Kozlov seemed to slip and say something that sounded like *Bronze* when he referred to the American agent. But I'm not sure, and he only did it once . . ."

In the monitoring room Trosper shook his head and muttered, "It ain't *necessarily* so, Inspector. Three of my colleagues were sacked because that creep chose to authenticate one of his stories with the lie that a Moscow agent's last name began with an 'F' . . ."

In the interrogation room, Volin grinned broadly, his confidence restored. "And that is some of what Anderson will pay us a lot of money to learn . . ."

Zitkin leaned forward and picked up the papers on his desk. "Have you any other information on the agent?"

Volin shook his head slowly before saying, "Not enough to make much difference. The guy is supposed to be so important, he tells Moscow when he will meet his case man—weekends, or holidays, when the man is free of his government work. Otherwise he's either a high government official, or very close to someone able to report information and to influence policy as well. He's a mix, part a highly paid mercenary, a little bit idealist. But as Kozlov said, a valuable friend of Russia."

For the first time Volin leaned back in his chair, for a moment relaxed. "All I—all we—have to do is tell the Americans to follow Gholam and he will lead them straight to the important source."

"Is that everything you have for sale?"

Volin lowered his eyes and shook his head in apparent disbelief.

"Isn't this enough? Just a whisper to Moscow could mean the end of everything for me . . ."

"Quite possibly," Zitkin said with the semblance of a reassuring smile. "If not one way, another . . ."

Trosper moved closer to the false mirror. He could see Volin's confidence melt.

Zitkin made another note on the pad in front of him, and looked up to stare speculatively at Volin. "On the basis of what you've freely told me, you're in this country illegally, traveling on false papers. So, before you start peddling information, any information, to anyone, there's a legal problem to straighten out. In the circumstances, I have the option of recommending that you be deported to Russia or sent out of the Republic to Austria or Germany. If you work it right, the choice might be yours. These decisions will be strongly influenced by what you have to say about the time you spent here, in Prague, while still affiliated with the Russian intelligence services."

"But . . ."

"You should think of this detention as being as much in your interest as in ours," Zitkin said. "Sometime, and it could be very soon now, your former comrades will learn what you've been up to. At that time you'll need whatever friends you can find." Zitkin smiled. "In the meantime, I urge you to be very careful indeed."

Volin moved, as if to protest again.

"In the interests of keeping you alive, you will remain in custody for the present."

Zitkin flipped a switch on the intercom and bellowed, "Syrovy!"

39

NEW YORK

"I'm going to look damned silly if this doesn't come off," Grogan said. "Thanksgiving morning, and I'm responsible for putting two teams on the street and for God knows how long." He glanced at Trosper. "What's more, I've got a boss sitting on each shoulder."

Widgery leaned back from the video screen in the surveillance van. "If there's any more coffee in that thermos, I could use another splash."

"It's ten-fifteen, and you're the only one who can put a positive make on Winesap. Maybe you ought to slow down on the diuretics until you've got some idea how long we're likely to be in here." Mike Grogan had logged his share of stakeout time.

Widgery rubbed his eyes and turned back to the screen.

There was no rear exit from the apartment building and both the lobby entrance and the narrow passage along the side of the building leading to the back service door opened onto the sidewalk on East 81st Street. Winesap could not step out of his apartment building without passing the surveillance van parked across the street, nor could he avoid the stakeout and backup teams positioned to cover the intersections at Lexington Avenue and at Third Avenue.

The Winesap surveillance began Thanksgiving morning at six, the day following the meeting in Whyte's Washington office. It was not the stormy session Trosper expected when he learned that Grogan would be shepherded by a delegation from FBI headquarters—the deputy chief of operations, the chief of counterintelligence operations, and the deputy chief of the legal staff.

Thomas Augustus Castle's entrance, five minutes after the group had assembled, brought the clatter of coffee cups and perfunctory joking to term. With his red leather folder and thick gold fountain pen in hand, Castle quickly made the rounds of the visitors. He clapped Trosper on the shoulder and said, "Handcuffs, I do declare . . ." From across the room, Grogan raised his voice: "It would have been worth a second trip to Prague to see that."

"We've got the makings of a long weekend," Whyte said as he slipped into the chair behind his desk. He glanced at Castle, who, in apparent deference to the guests, had refrained from doodling. "Why don't you get things started, Tom?"

Castle touched his reading glasses, and cleared his throat. "This holiday weekend could give us a shot at catching our man Winesap at his real work— a *Treff* with an American agent important enough to be handled with unusual security precautions . . ."

"Since we're talking on the record," Charlie Mayo interjected, "can we say an '*allegedly* important American agent'?" The FBI's deputy chief of operations was not one to miss the opportunity to make the Bureau's presence known.

Castle stopped abruptly, adjusted his reading glasses, and took a deep breath. "By all means, let's call him an *allegedly* important American agent."

"That's not what I was driving at," Mayo said quickly. "I meant, could this guy be a sleeper, who's on the shelf now, but to be activated later? That might account for his being dealt with by a low-level type like Winesap?"

"Perhaps," Castle said. "But with things the way they are in Russia, I wonder how long Moscow could afford to let any agent doze?"

Roger Brooks, chief of FBI counterintelligence, scowled, "I've always thought sleepers were invented by the hack who dreamed up the nutty notion that Moscow Center had built a perfect little American town just to condition agents for life in the States . . ."

Grogan laughed and said, "Sure, and about the time they finished the village, some youngster would have recommended the agents do it the easy way—apply for a scholarship and spend an all-expenses-paid year or two at MIT or UCLA."

Castle continued to speak. "If Volin had it right, Bronze may be a prima donna, but he's obviously of real value to Moscow. And that means bales of cash and lots of tender care."

"All the same," said Charlie Mayo, "we've seen some cutbacks in personnel, and a few agents discarded. That suggests money and manpower problems . . ."

Roger Brooks stirred, but before he could risk his future by modifying his chief's assessment, Trosper intervened. "The new management obviously intends to clear out the mare's nest they inherited, but I can't see any of the young Turks dropping a useful contact, let alone a productive spy, no matter how risky and expensive the case might be to handle . . ."

Brooks glanced gratefully at Trosper as Whyte impatiently signaled Trosper to leave well enough alone.

"The new Moscow crowd are anything but 'young Turks,'" Castle said sharply. "They're the cream of the crop of operations men whose entire experience came in the last ten or fifteen years when ideology played no role at all in Moscow operations." He pulled his half-frame glasses farther down his nose and gave each of the Bureau men a momentary glance. "So, let's table the speculation and agree there's reason to hope that this is a plausible weekend for Winesap to service his unknown chum—and while we're at it let's start calling him Bronze. If the codename is good enough for the SVR, we might just as well use it. If we're as lucky as we deserve to be, Winesap might even go face-to-face."

"Come on, Tom," Mayo said. "You're not suggesting that we actually *plan* to be lucky?"

Castle shrugged. "At this point, I'll settle for Winesap leading us to a dead drop."

Mayo and Brooks groaned in chorus. "If all Winesap does is service a dead drop, we've really got our toe in a crack . . ."

Whyte nodded. "If there's no personal contact—and we'd better knock wood—we'll all have something to look forward to over the Christmas and New Year season." The raised eyebrows and grim smiles were gratuitous. The cost and logistics involved in an around-the-clock surveillance in New York City during the Christmas shopping and tourist season lay well within the collective imagination.

"But why *is* Moscow using your man Winesap?" Brooks asked. "At best he doesn't seem any more than just up to the job?"

"Because Winesap's a near-perfect live letter drop—well established in New York, and covered as an Iranian clerk and as an American spy," Trosper said. "Aside from the few seconds a month in brush contacts, there's no way he might be linked to Bronze. When Moscow wants a substantive face-to-face with Bronze, the Center can set it up anywhere—hereabouts, or out of the country, perhaps even in Moscow. Winesap would never even learn about it."

They talked until Mayo said, "Just remember this. Money is tight. I'm understaffed. Time is precious."

"Tell me more," Whyte said pleasantly.

Charlie Mayo nodded and snapped his briefcase shut.

As Ralph Nugent got up to leave, he spoke for the first time. "Before we break, I must remind everyone that the law comes first." The lawyer's glance passed swiftly over Whyte but lingered on Grogan and Trosper. "The rules of evidence are to be scrupulously respected. There will be no intimidation. No provocation. No deals. No kidnapping." He turned slightly, just enough to focus on Trosper. "And certainly, no citizen's arrest."

"Yes, indeed," said Whyte. He got to his feet and glanced at Trosper. "I'm sure we all understand that."

Widgery clapped his hands and thrust himself closer to the screen. "Tally-ho," he whispered, pointing at the screen. "Right there, raincoat, baseball hat, airline bag . . ."

"For Christ's sake, speak into the mike," Grogan said in a low voice. "Put it on the air, and stop the fox-hunting crap."

Widgery fumbled with the microphone. "Tango, Tango . . ."

The Tango team was in place at Third Avenue and 81st Street.

"Damn it all anyway," Widgery spluttered. "He's done a spin, reversed, and headed in the other direction . . ."

"On the air," Grogan demanded. "Into the mike . . ."

"Erase Tango, erase Tango," Widgery cried. "It's Love, repeat, Love . . ."

The Love team was at Lexington and 81st Street.

Grogan and Trosper leaned over Widgery's shoulder to watch as Winesap walked slowly out of the surveillance camera range.

"You know what?" Trosper's voice was low and confiding as he turned to Grogan.

"Nope . . ."

"It wouldn't be much of a problem if we were to tag along—Comrade Winesap's never laid eyes on either of us."

"Don't be so damn silly. I'll have seven or eight people on him, and just as many in a floating reserve by the time he gets to the corner."

"Just stick the radio on your belt, rig the earphone, and no one will be the wiser."

"No."

"Why not?"

"It's not procedure," Grogan said slowly.

"We're both of us better able to tell if Winesap is making a meet than any of your guys . . ."

"Nonsense, my people are as good as they come . . ."

"There's no risk if we just tag along . . ."

"You haven't got the slightest idea where he's heading . . ."

"You want to bet?" Trosper pulled on his raincoat.

There was a static squawk as Widgery turned up the volume on the radio monitor. Then, "Sugar Sugar, Love Love."

"He's going south on Lexington," Widgery explained to Grogan. "From now the teams will use numerical codes," he added helpfully as he picked up a red china pencil and turned to the plastic-covered street map.

Trosper glanced uneasily at Grogan's darkening face. "There's nothing we can do here, why not just tag along for a while?"

"Damn it to hell." The sleeve of Grogan's raincoat snagged as he wedged through the narrow door to follow Trosper out of the van.

40

NEW YORK

Trosper edged toward Grogan until they stood like strangers impatient for the traffic light to change.

"Even money he's headed for the parade?"

"In your hat," Grogan said. "It's been a one-to-ten bet ever since he crossed 71st Street at Lex." He spoke softly, exhaling his words in a monotone, without glancing at Trosper or moving his lips. "I wish to hell we'd figured this out yesterday and planned for the traffic. We're not in the best shape." Without waiting for the light to change, he sprinted across 69th Street, a perfect rendition of the jagged, twisting style of a broken field runner.

Trosper lingered, waiting until the light was green before crossing.

On the opposite side of Lexington Avenue and a hundred yards ahead, Winesap strode purposefully along.

Across town, the annual Thanksgiving Day parade had begun to move from Central Park West down Broadway toward Herald Square.

The heavy, low-hanging clouds and scattered light rain had reduced pedestrian traffic, making it easier for Grogan's squad to keep Winesap in a long box—three watchers ahead and four behind, all moving in tandem with their target.

On the west side of the avenue, a man and woman ranged eighty yards ahead, their measured pace keeping a constant distance ahead of Winesap. Across the avenue, and more nearly abreast of the target, a single man carrying a plastic shopping bag strolled as if unaware of the threatening clouds. Behind Winesap, two men, one with a furled umbrella, the other wearing a raincoat and cap, chatted amiably as they kept Winesap in view. On the opposite side of the avenue, two women kept pace with the men.

A box is not the easiest surveillance to maintain, but Grogan's team executed it as deftly as any Trosper had seen.

Behind the box, the second and third teams of watchers—the

float—were ready on radio signal to take over from the deployed team, to spill into the subway, dash for a bus, or take up a stationary watch if Winesap were to step into a building. To the rear, and out of Trosper's sight, a radio van with masked antennas served as a mobile control base in contact with the watchers on all four corners of the box and with the float. Strung out behind the float, three nondescript vehicles leisurely leap-frogged one another, ready to respond on the signal that Winesap had hailed a taxi or been picked up by a moving car.

Pedestrians were still sparse as Trosper stepped up his pace to close within a few feet of Grogan, now only a block behind Winesap.

"You want a bet on the time for the meet?"

Forcing a smile as if he were giving directions to a stranger, Grogan said, "*If* it is a meet, and *if* our chum isn't so anxious he allows himself an extra hour, it could go down at quarter to eleven. Whatever the plan, they'll have fallbacks every forty minutes or so until the parade's over, or the crowd thins out. They must have read those procedures in one of your manuals."

"We read it in one of theirs . . ."

Grogan eased his pace as Winesap on the west side of the avenue halted for a red light. "These guys like a crowd for a brush contact, so it'll be one of the four-lane crosstown intersections—probably 59th and Broadway."

"Not 42nd?"

Grogan shook his head. "Too much crime, and that means too many uniforms, even PCs."

"PCs?"

"Plain clothes, sometimes 'suits' . . ."

It had long been the practice to avoid meetings in heavily policed airports, and bus and train stations; the notion that one of the busiest crossroads in the world was off-limits was news.

Grogan stretched slightly as he strained to reassure himself on the progress of his team. Apparently satisfied, he said, "I like that stupid airline bag he's carrying. What the hell does he think anyone might imagine he has in it? It's like he's carrying a sign, 'Hotshot agent about to make a meet and do a switch.' He should have a camera bag, maybe a kid, like everyone else."

"Count your blessings," Trosper said softly. "All you've got to do is start looking around Manhattan for anyone else who's toting a United Airlines bag . . ."

"If the *Post* had it right, there'll be more than half a million people lined up along Broadway—and another few million glued to the tube," Grogan said. "With my luck, every one of them will spot my guys."

Seconds before the light changed Winesap crossed 67th Street and continued briskly along Lexington Avenue. Across the avenue, Grogan gave Winesap another few yards.

Trosper loitered at an antique shop window until he was a full block behind Grogan. He could not see Winesap at all.

At 59th Street, Grogan flipped up the collar of his raincoat. Winesap had turned west.

Trosper lengthened his stride as he turned onto 59th Street. Across the four lanes of stalled traffic, he could see Winesap moving more rapidly toward Broadway.

With the shift from the near-empty sidewalks of Lexington Avenue to the crowd of latecomers moving along 59th Street toward the parade, the second team eased into place and the box formed more tightly around Winesap. Trosper would stay on the far side of 59th Street until the team had settled down.

In the distance Trosper caught glimpses of the huge, inflated caricatures of cartoon and folk figures, and heard occasional echoes of the thunder and blast of the drum and bugle corps and marching bands.

The annual Thanksgiving Day parade beckoned thousands of automobiles into midtown Manhattan and erased established traffic patterns. Auto and bus routes were dislocated as crosstown traffic was corralled into a few scattered streets where vehicles were allowed to inch across the parade route in the intervals between the floats and marchers.

Along Broadway, spectators ranged three to five deep at curbside. Children pushed forward, wriggling their way to the front. Behind them, restless adults jockeyed for a better glimpse of the passing show and then, bored, moved on again. A younger child perched high astride his father's shoulders, and more bewildered than entertained by the spectacle, seemed happy just to be with the parent. Trosper wondered if this outing would be logged under bonding or quality time in the notes for the next session with the family guidance counselor.

At the barricaded cross streets, the crowds of viewers clustered six to ten deep provided textbook-perfect cover for a brush contact or even a few moments of casual conversation, as if between strangers strolling along the parade route.

As he threaded his way along the teeming sidewalk, Trosper made no attempt to keep Winesap's visored baseball cap in view, but sighted on Grogan. Buffeted by the crowd moving along with the parade, Grogan kept edging closer to Winesap.

Suddenly, beyond Grogan, the blue cap came clearly into Trosper's view. Winesap had stepped away from the crowd at the curb and stood with his back against the façade of a shuttered drugstore, his attention apparently fixed on a helium-filled, sixty-foot representation of a comic-strip beagle. Like a fractious puppy, Snoopy tugged against the ground lines binding him to the handlers struggling to keep him moving along the route.

Trosper eased his way to the rear of the curbside crowd, a scant hundred feet from Winesap. Too close. This was a Bureau stunt. He was a spectator, and had no business even being in the vicinity.

But where in hell was Grogan's team? As he shifted slightly to scan his nearest neighbors, Trosper remembered a bit of wisdom from the Fort. Great street men have one common trait, fantastic peripheral vision—legend had it that a really gifted watcher could see his own ears.

Trosper had no such advantage. He used the excuse of stepping aside for a child to peer quickly in Grogan's direction. Nothing. Could the float have lost Winesap when he crossed onto 59th Street? Unlikely. Without turning his head, he occupied himself sorting out the spectators carrying photographic equipment. He ignored those encumbered with expensive, wide-angle or bulky zoom lenses, some with the protective lens caps in place. He had never seen a working photographer trouble to cap a lens. Low-cost equipment, the least conspicuous and non-threatening gear, would be the choice of any surveillant prepared to work close to his target.

Grogan moved close enough to nudge Trosper's elbow. "Ten forty-three," he breathed, his lips motionless. "Like he's wondering if the turkey's done, the stupid bastard keeps checking his watch. It's like he wants *everyone* to know the *Treff*'s right now, in front of the drugstore."

Trosper kept his eyes on the parade as Grogan inched away.

Still no indication of the float. Either the second squad had split and been replaced by an invisible third group, or something had gone wrong . . .

Trosper eased his watch to the inside of his wrist and, as if adjusting his glove, checked the time. Ten forty-four. He risked a quick look in Winesap's direction.

At the moment their eyes met, Winesap pulled off his baseball cap and thrust it into the pocket of his raincoat.

Trosper blinked as the adrenalin spurted into his system.

With an effort he caught himself, and managed to keep from averting his eyes and twisting suddenly away as if aware he had glimpsed an embarrassing moment. Keeping his expression blank and uninterested, Trosper continued to turn slowly, a bored spectator, absently looking for some slight distraction. When his back was to Winesap, Trosper leaned forward, feigning an interest in a marching band of pudgy high school cadets.

He had broken an absolute commandment—a surveillant is never, ever, to make eye contact with a target. If it happens, the watcher is blown, and must break away at once.

Trosper cursed his stupidity. His one direct look at Winesap could not have been timed more perfectly to intercept the single bit of standard security procedure the agent had permitted himself that morning. When Winesap pocketed his cap, he had signaled an all-clear, at precisely the moment he caught Trosper's eye.

Damn and blast . . . damn and blast . . . damn . . . damn . . . damn.

He stood motionless, his attention fixed on the Marshfield Senior High School Marching Tigers band. Neither the elaborate black uniforms nor white shako hats could lift his spirits. Not even the pleasant young faces, absorbed in the music and keeping step, were any distraction. He had blown Grogan's stunt well and truly. Worse, it was none of his business. All these years in the racket, and here I stand, a damned freeloading spectator, with no reason to be anywhere near the scene. Just my stupid curiosity, a dumb desire to see how things would work out.

Damn . . . damn . . . damn, he recited in time with the thumping drums and blaring brass—more than a hundred strong, he estimated bleakly.

A jostling from the left. Trosper pulled slightly away, now attempting to distract himself by making a more accurate estimate of the number of Marshfield marchers. More than a hundred, maybe two hundred marchers was his final, sour guess.

Jostled again. J. Edgar Hoover's enraged ghost, he thought as he risked a quick glance. Not J. Edgar, but Grogan, his face drawn.

"He's moved," Grogan whispered, his eyes on the final rank of the Marshfield marchers.

"I'm not surprised, Mike," Trosper murmured. "I think he made me, eye-to-eye . . ."

"Not that horse's ass," Grogan said. "He's stuffed that stupid hat into his pocket. All signals are go. He's hot to trot . . ."

Trosper turned away, glancing over Grogan's shoulder. Winesap was moving slowly along the sidewalk, apparently following the parade, south along Broadway.

Grogan moved along, now fifty feet behind Winesap.

Trosper gave him a few steps and then followed.

In the distance, more than a hundred yards, striding north, and conspicuously tall against the opposing flow of spectators—a tweed cap, and dark green, country gentleman's waxed rain jacket. Black airline bag in left hand. Not even a glance at the Marshfield Marching Tigers, now in full cry.

Bingo.

"It's a make," Trosper said to himself as he turned away.

"I'm out of here," he murmured aloud, but to no one in particular.

I should have known, he told himself as he hurried away.

But I did know, he told himself as he turned east on 56th Street.

I knew, damn it. I knew it.

41

NEW YORK

With the now familiar move, Grogan thrust his ID card and badge at arm's length toward Winesap. "Mike Grogan, Special Agent, FBI."

Startled, Winesap rose from the chair beside the coffee table and then dropped back. He turned to Widgery. "What is happen . . . what the hell this guy doing here?" Grogan's confrontation had rattled Winesap's command of English.

"These gentlemen have a few questions for you," Widgery said, his nasal drawl amplified by his evident pleasure in Winesap's surprise. "Mr. Grogan is with the FBI. You should think of the FBI as our security police."

"I know FBI," Winesap said. He started to get up again, pushing both hands on the arms of his chair.

"Sit down," said Trosper. "And stay right where you are." Winesap's black hair, thick mustache, and heavy eyebrows that stretched in an almost unbroken line above the black frames of his glasses limned his face like the bold strokes of a caricature.

"That's our Mr. Jones," Widgery said, nodding in Trosper's direction. "He's a colleague of mine."

Winesap had come to the East 31st Street safe house for the regularly scheduled meeting with Widgery. Ten minutes after his arrival, Trosper and Grogan let themselves into the apartment.

"I have a few things to discuss with you," Grogan said stiffly. "But first I want to be sure you know your rights . . ."

"I am Iranian diplomat," Winesap said. "I already know I have the right to immunity from arrest and any questioning by police." He brushed both hands through his thick black hair and glanced anxiously at Widgery.

Grogan shook his head. "You're a clerk at the Iranian mission to the U.N. Only diplomatic officers have immunity. As a clerk, your immunity is granted at host country discretion." The definition might not have cut much ice at the U.N. protocol office, or even with the State Department, but Trosper found it fitted the situation at hand.

Winesap pulled a green-bordered ID card from his wallet and handed it to Grogan.

Grogan glanced at it. "This identifies you as Gholam Alizadeh, born Tabriz, Iran, 6 May 1964 . . ."

"What?" Winesap appeared not to understand Grogan's pronunciation.

"Hereabouts most people just call him Ali or Gholam," Widgery interceded.

"If it's all the same," said Trosper, "I'll continue to think of him as Mr. Alizadeh." He waited thoughtfully before saying, "In return, he'd better understand that we know he's a Russian agent inserted into the Iranian foreign office by what used to be the Soviet intelligence service."

Alizadeh's eyes blinked shut and he twisted back into the heavy chair. "You're crazy people," he said. "You don't know what you're talking, I am Iranian official, assigned to Islamic Republic of Iran Mission to United Nations in New York." He turned to Widgery. "Tell him we work together. You know me . . ." Beads of sweat formed on his forehead.

Widgery smiled slightly before saying, "They're both well aware of your record."

"Then that's enough of this crazy talk," Alizadeh said. "I demand to leave."

"Where do you plan to go—to your friends at the Russian mission?" Trosper said. "They won't let you in the door."

Alizadeh turned angrily to Grogan. "I'm going from here . . ."

"If you try to leave this room, I'll arrest you for conspiracy to commit espionage," Grogan said.

Alizadeh jumped to his feet. "Conspiracy! What conspiracy? You're all crazy . . ."

Trosper sighed and stepped behind Alizadeh. He disliked violence but had learned that a bit of it early in a confrontation tended to demonstrate who was in charge and to focus attention on the problem at hand. He grabbed the collar of Alizadeh's blue blazer and yanked him backward. As the Iranian struggled to avoid flopping back into the chair, a brass button popped from the front of his blazer and arched across the coffee table. Widgery fielded it in midair and tossed it back to Alizadeh, now sprawled in his chair.

"I sincerely suggest you listen to my friends," Widgery said, his drawl as astringent as iodine.

"You have a choice," said Grogan. "You can cooperate by giving us the details of your background and clandestine activity here. If that doesn't suit, I'll arrest you right now for illegal entry into this country, and charge you with resisting arrest. After that, we'll have to see about the conspiracy to commit espionage."

Alizadeh pocketed the button. "I am a diplomatic official, legally here at U.N. I protest this treatment and demand to see my ambassador." He twisted angrily to stare over his shoulder at Trosper.

"If it's the new Russian ambassador you're talking about, he'll be some damned surprised to find you on his doorstep," Trosper said, as he stepped from behind Alizadeh's chair. "Since he's trying to get off on the right foot with the U.N. Secretary General, I can't think of anything the ambassador would be less willing to do than try to explain why he's representing an Iranian clerk who claims he's a Russian spy." Trosper had no idea whether there was a new Russian ambassador or not. He wanted to challenge Alizadeh, to maneuver him into talking about anything but his immunity and nationality.

"Iranian ambassador," Alizadeh said without looking up.

"Do you really think the Iranian government will protect you after we show them that you're a Russian agent, foisted on Iran by the KGB?"

"KGB is finished, everyone knows that . . ."

"But there used to be a KGB," Trosper said. "And as you damned well know, now there's something called the SVR—the same people, just a little tarted up."

"Everyone are friends now," Alizadeh said. "All this spy nonsense is over except for you crazy people."

Trosper glanced at Grogan—come on Mike, he implored, he's begun to argue with us, take a shot.

"What do you think VEVAK will say when we show them that you're a Russian national, inserted into their Islamic Republic's diplomatic service?" Without waiting for an answer, Grogan forged ahead.

"It still is VEVAK isn't it?" he asked, and reeled off a string of nearly incomprehensible sounds.

Alizadeh stared blankly at Grogan.

Trosper masked a smile as he realized that he was not the only one who had boned up on Iran. Grogan had rendered what seemed to be an anglicized version of Persian—*Vezarat-e Ettela'at Va Amniyat-e Keshvar*, the Islamic Republic's security and intelligence organization.

"I mean the *new* security muscle, the VEVAK," Grogan said. "Aren't they still trying to prove they're tougher than the Shah's thugs, the SAVAK, used to be? Or don't you agree?"

Alizadeh began to speak, but Trosper interrupted. "I'll tell you one thing for sure," he said. "When the VEVAK people learn what you've been up to, they'll have you back in Tehran on the next plane. And if you don't agree to leave New York, they'll take you back on a stretcher, straight to Evin prison. If they don't hang you in a public square, maybe they'll turn you over to some of the vigilantes, the *Komitehs*, who'll probably arrange to stone you in a pit. Those guys and your Revolutionary Guards like public executions, it builds morale—of a sort."

Alizadeh bent forward, elbows on his knees, clasping his head with both hands. The room was quiet until he looked up, his face drawn, his dark eyes moist. "I'm an innocent fellow . . ."

"Stop that crap," Trosper said loudly. "You know what we're talking about."

Alizadeh's glance darted between Trosper and Grogan. "I knew something like this would happen. My whole life, everything about me, every decision, always in the hands of others." He leaned sideways and began to fumble in his blazer pocket.

Grogan shifted his weight, and eased his jacket to free his shoulder holster.

"I need a cigarette," Alizadeh said.

Trosper relaxed and nodded to Widgery.

Grogan pulled an armchair closer to Alizadeh and sat down. "You were saying?"

Widgery tossed a package of Winstons onto the table beside Alizadeh.

"Now, it's all over, my life half gone and I have nothing. No career, no country, not anything. My wife is miserable, one day crying to go back to Iran where she'll wear that stupid veil and spend the day gossiping with a bunch of other *chadori*." He stopped, his glance still wavering between Grogan and Trosper. "The next day she say there's nothing in Iran for us, so we must stay here. One day one thing, next day another. It makes me crazy."

"I'm more interested in your Russian friends than your marital problems," Trosper said.

"I'm not involved in any conspiracy," Alizadeh said, shaking his head. "And I don't have any special Russian friends."

"No *special* Russian friends?" The Iranian was folding more easily than Trosper expected.

"I do no harm, I swear that. You can ask him . . ." Alizadeh turned to Widgery. "Tell them I never try to get information from you. All I ever do is tell you what I know about things at my office and about Iranians I know . . ."

"No harm?" Trosper interrupted. "Then why haven't you told us your mother is in Russia, that her Moscow Center friend got you both out of Iran, that he had you trained and sent back to Tehran . . ."

"I've done nothing against United States, I swear it . . ." Sweat moved along his hairline to the collar of his light blue shirt.

"If you've done nothing against us, what is it you have been doing for your Russian friends?" Grogan asked.

"I never did anything for Russians but training until I met Peter Lynch in Austria." Alizadeh turned to Widgery again. "Tell them I'm telling the truth . . ."

"They know all about us in Vienna," Widgery said.

"Then you smart people know that all I did was tell my Russian that I met this American guy, almost too friendly to be real." He glanced anxiously at Widgery. "The Russian said go ahead, find out what he wants. When it got certain he was going to make a proposition, my Russian said okay, go along, tell Americans anything they want to know about."

"Didn't *your* Russian ask any questions at all?" Trosper said.

"Just details about Mr. Lynch—where he lived, how much he drank, if he's a gay-boy, if he has money enough, if he cheated on my pay . . . things like that." He turned sheepishly to Widgery. "I couldn't answer most of those questions."

"That's all they ever wanted?" Trosper asked. As Alizadeh recovered from his surprise, his English improved and he appeared to be more like the few other Iranians Trosper had encountered, a good linguist with an actor's facility for adopting the manner of other cultures.

Alizadeh shrugged. "Once the Russians were satisfied I'd told them all I could about my friend, Mr. Lynch . . ." Alizadeh hesitated, and glanced at Widgery. "After that they never bothered much more . . . except every now and again to ask what you people want to know about Iran."

Grogan picked up his notebook, took a pen from his pocket, and slipped into the chair across from Alizadeh. "Okay, now let's get started—at the beginning, please."

But it was too soon to expect cooperation. The Iranian had not begun to unwind and wasn't even aware that he'd already confessed. There was no way Trosper could deflect Grogan's direct question.

Alizadeh stiffened. He fidgeted with the threads where the button had torn from his blazer. Then he said, "No."

Surprised, Grogan glanced quickly at Trosper and turned back to Alizadeh. "No?" he asked. "No what?"

"No talk," Alizadeh said. "Why should I keep answering any questions?" For a moment the Iranian looked older than his twenty-nine years. "What do I get out of it?"

"I can tell you what you'll get if you don't cooperate," Trosper said.

Alizadeh shook his head. "What you want is that I tell you everything so you can say it's of no interest and give me nothing . . ."

"We don't work that way," Grogan said. "But you'd better keep it in mind that you've committed a felony and are subject to arrest."

"I want to stay here, have asylum and enough money to get started again . . ."

"There's no money up front," Trosper said. "First we talk, and then we decide about staying here."

Alizadeh shook his head.

"Unless you speak up, our hands are tied," Grogan said.

Alizadeh looked at Widgery as if to ask for help.

"It's now or never, Gholam," Widgery said.

Alizadeh shook his head in disgust. "You people forget some things—I have friends, what do I need you for?"

"What friends, Gholam?" Widgery asked politely.

"You smart people know so much, you know next to nothing. How do you think I got into the foreign office? Someone told some big shot in Tehran foreign office to make sure I get a job without any troubles. A while after I got the job and was assigned to Austria, the same fellow—maybe even someone else—offered someone a big . . . *roshveh* . . . a gift, like a bribe, to make sure his good friend Alizadeh gets assigned to United States. Can't you people understand that?"

"I understand," Trosper said. "But I'm not sure who in Moscow could have arranged it all." He wanted to make it a matter of fact that Moscow was involved.

Alizadeh shrugged. "A big shot colonel, a family friend . . ."

"Who?" Grogan said sharply.

"Sergei Golobev, he's my mother's friend, an important man. He got us out of Iran, and to Moscow. He fixed it for me in Moscow schools."

"And got you back to Tehran?"

"Of course."

"And got you trained for this job?" Trosper asked.

Alizadeh nodded.

"And made sure that you were assigned here?"

"Of course," Alizadeh said. "He was very particular that everything was perfect."

Grogan flipped over a page in his notebook before looking up. "That's a lot of work just to get you an easy job in New York."

"Not for my mother's friend . . ."

"Perhaps not, but it depends on what he's had you doing in New York," Trosper said.

Alizadeh had begun to relax; he drew deeply on his cigarette. "Nothing," he said.

"*Nothing?*" Trosper said.

"*Almost* nothing." The Persian's glance moved quickly from

Trosper to Grogan and Widgery. "The most I've done is write messages saying that Mr. Peter Lynch hasn't told me anything worth writing about, and twice pick up messages from a man here."

Grogan put down his pen. "What man?"

"All I know is codename—Adam."

"Who?"

"Adam, that's all I know." Alizadeh pronounced the name as two distinctly separated syllables, with the stress on the second—Ad-AMM.

"What messages did you pick up?"

Alizadeh shook his head. "All I do is exchange bags, I never see what's inside. But the bag is light, maybe just some letters, or a few rolls of film, something like that. No atom bomb, nothing too serious."

"Where did you meet Adam?" Grogan asked sharply.

"First time at rock and roll records at Sam Goody's at 43rd and Lexington Avenue. When he used some dumb recognition question about Chummy Checks, I knew this was the right guy."

"A question about who?" Grogan asked.

"Chubby Checker," Widgery explained.

Grogan glared at Widgery and turned to Alizadeh. "*Who* was the man you met?"

"Adam, the guy I was supposed to meet," Alizadeh said. "So I put my airline bag down and picked up his."

"Then what?"

"I went to Pan Am building, to news and magazine store at the head of escalator from Grand Central Station and gave the bag to Mr. Wright."

"Mr. Right?" Grogan asked. "How do you spell 'Right'?"

Alizadeh looked puzzled. "V-R-I-G-H-T," he said.

"Sometimes Iranians have trouble with W's and V's in English," Trosper whispered. "The guy's pseudo is W-R-I-G-H-T."

"Correct, Mr. Wright is the man Golobev told me I was to meet in New York," Alizadeh said. "Golobev was worried there could be some mistake, so to be sure, he had Wright come to Austria, so he could introduce us before I left Vienna for New York."

Grogan turned away from Alizadeh and toward Trosper. He wanted to make sure Trosper understood the significance of having an operative travel from New York to Moscow to Vienna and back merely to meet an agent. Trosper did understand.

"Is Wright a Russian?" Grogan asked.

"Sure, but he speaks good English," Alizadeh said. "He's probably at the U.N. or the consulate here in New York." He turned to Widgery. "I want something to drink. Some juice?"

Trosper motioned to Widgery.

"You said you met Adam more than once," Grogan said.

"Just the other day," Alizadeh said. He ran his finger around the sweat-soaked collar of his shirt. "Thanksgiving Day, at the big parade, right on the sidewalk, by 58th Street. We swapped bags, and then I went to the JR record store at 86th and Lexington and slipped the bag to Wright."

Grogan glanced at Trosper and raised his eyebrows, another silent question. Trosper nodded agreement—the method was plausible, well within the usual practice. Grogan turned back to Alizadeh. "Tell us about your friend Golobev."

By the time Widgery came back with the orange juice, Alizadeh had finished the story of his mother's relationship with Colonel Sergei Golobev, a senior officer in the Illegals Directorate, and had described their journey to Moscow.

" . . . from when I first left Iran with my mother nothing has been right," Alizadeh continued. "I was young, just a kid really, but I looked forward to Russia. Of course, once I got there I hated it and wanted to go back to Iran. Finally, Golobev put me in a special intelligence school to prepare for work abroad.

"All I wanted was to get back to Iran and my old life, so when I was ready they sent me on an Aeroflot flight from Moscow in a navigator's uniform. I changed clothes at the embassy, took my new papers—all perfect, exactly as if I'd been in Iran all my life—and went directly to my cousins, no questions ever asked. My Russian is fluent, and I'd been working on English. I wanted to enter the university, but my Russian said I should apply for a job at the foreign ministry."

Alizadeh shook his head in disgust. "I should have insisted on the university, but everything in Iran had changed. I hated the mullahs, their new government, and stupid religious rules. There was nothing there for me, no opportunity anywhere. So I was glad to get away."

Alizadeh attempted a slight, ironic smile. Grogan nodded a measure of encouragement.

"Everything was such a mess—I was so lonely, I even got married. Her family is old-fashioned, the mother always in a *chador*, probably even in the bathtub. Everyone very religious. Like everything else, marriage was another mistake."

"How come?" Grogan asked.

Alizadeh shrugged. "In Iran a job at the foreign ministry does not sound important, but it is all right. Abroad, I'm just a clerk, a nobody. As soon as we got out, even in Austria, and my wife could see the shopping and conditions, she was at me all the time, complaining about money, about people at the mission, about everything. She was worse when we got here. She even thought I should defect, get a good job, settle in Queens." He raised his eyebrows to emphasize the irony. "But when she couldn't understand there's no money for defectors now, I tried to shut her up by admitting I already work for you people."

Grogan looked up from his notebook. "You know you handed her a loaded gun . . ."

"I know *now*," Alizadeh said. "She's already threatened to tell on me . . ."

"Who would she tell?" Grogan asked.

"Ahmed Kazemzadeh. He's the VEVAK security guy. In the old days he was taken by SAVAK and tortured. Now he's a fanatic, and wants to pay back everyone who supported Pahlavi . . . the Shah and his gang."

"Could she have told anyone yet?" Grogan asked.

"One minute after she says the first word I'm done for. Kazemzadeh's full of hate."

"Does she know about your work for your Russian friends?"

"Of course not, I never make that mistake again."

"Which brings us to the point," Trosper said.

"What's that supposed to mean?" Alizadeh's nervous energy had vanished and he seemed listless.

"I mean what you are going to do from now on . . ."

Alizadeh shrugged. "After this, I'm through with you people for good." He took a deep breath. "Your game's over."

Trosper shook his head. "Nothing's over . . ."

Grogan looked up from his notebook, but before he could speak, Trosper said, "There's more to be done, a score or two to settle . . ."

"Not possible . . ."

"You're going to stay right here in New York, in place at the Iranian mission, until you see your man, Adam, again," Trosper said. "After that, something will be worked out."

Alizadeh shook his head. "Not possible. Golobev gives me my orders—he knows what he's doing."

Trosper laughed. "If Golobev knows so much, how come we've got you under arrest?"

Grogan started, as if to protest, but Alizadeh, his energy rekindled, cut him off. "No matter what you say, you can't arrest me . . ."

"You're in *custody*," Trosper said with a reassuring nod to Grogan. "Believe me, it's much the same . . ."

"I've done nothing against United States, and I've got immunity," Alizadeh said softly.

"Immunity may be a big thing for you," Trosper said, "but if something blows, just how much immunity do you think the VEVAK's going to give you? They'll hang you before you can even *say* you're innocent."

Alizadeh shook his head. "Not possible."

"And what about your wife?" Trosper said. "How long will they have to slap her around before she admits that you told her months ago that you're a spy for the Great Satan? Do you really think they won't hang her?"

Alizadeh dabbed again at the sweat running down his cheek.

"How will they dispose of your kid? Some special orphanage—a place where they can really impress him with the error of your ways?"

Grogan remained motionless, his eyes on Alizadeh.

Widgery shifted uneasily in his chair and avoided looking directly at Alizadeh, slumped forward, staring at the floor. In the half-light, he might have been a rug dealer about to offer a few dollars for the cheap safe-house carpet. He did not look up when he said, "Okay, you win . . ."

Grogan beamed at Trosper.

"There's just one thing," Alizadeh said. "I've been ordered back to Tehran. We're scheduled to leave any time after Tuesday . . ."

"That's four days," Grogan exclaimed.

Alizadeh nodded.

42

WASHINGTON, D.C.

"Exactly what does this leave us?" Duff Whyte tilted back in his chair and crossed his arms.

Castle flipped his red leather folder shut. "In the words of the poet, we're left with 'but a mouthful of air.'" His glance lingered on the three FBI representatives ranged in front of Whyte's desk.

"Zilch," said Charlie Mayo, deputy chief of FBI operations. "Big-time zilch is what we've got."

"It's not all that damned bad," said Roger Brooks. "From a CI point of view, we've identified Slocombe, and we've seen him swap the airline bags with Alizadeh—an admitted Russian agent—who claims to have turned the bag over to a member of the Russian SVR."

"We're talking arrest *and prosecution*," said Ralph Nugent. "On the basis of your evidence, the legal staff sees no grounds on which the FBI can recommend prosecution, or which the attorney general could possibly accept as a basis for going to trial. Even if Alizadeh is able to identify Slocombe in court, all you've got is the word of a defected Iranian clerk against that of a highly regarded State Department officer. Alizadeh may claim that a Russian official instructed him to exchange flight bags with Slocombe but he can't prove it. The

FBI can't prove that Alizadeh turned the bag over to the Russian, and we've no proof whatsoever of what might have been in the bag. Even Alizadeh admits he doesn't know what was in it." He turned to Mayo. "There's not a scrap of legal evidence against Slocombe."

Mayo's face flushed. "Which means our only chance to make a legal case is to tape and photograph a meeting between the two, and arrest Slocombe twenty seconds after he hands over *classified* material?"

"Unless Slocombe's willing to help you out by writing a confession, I'm afraid that's it," said Nugent.

Trosper added to the gloom. "As of now, we've got four days to make the case. Any time after that, Gholam Alizadeh will have to take one of his options—return to Tehran if he's convinced his luck will hold, nip back to Moscow and his sponsor Golobev, or jump ship here and hope that we'll take care of him."

"We're authorized to offer Alizadeh asylum," Mayo said. "But the moment he takes it, he's out of the Iranian mission, and of no use to anybody."

"Why does Alizadeh think he's being called back to Tehran?" Brooks asked.

"It appears to be a routine change of post," Grogan said. "Counting the time he served in Vienna, Alizadeh's been out of Iran for more than two years, and that's about as long as Tehran leaves clerks abroad. Transfer orders are always urgent and come unannounced, presumably to prevent anyone from making a last-moment arrangement to drop out of the revolution. The fact that his transfer follows Volin's blowing the whistle on him appears to be a coincidence."

"VEVAK?" Mayo asked.

Grogan shook his head. "Ten seconds after the VEVAK thugs first suspected Alizadeh, they'd have tossed him onto a nonstop flight to Tehran."

"Moscow?" Whyte asked in an unconscious parody of Mayo. "What's going on there?"

"Right now," Castle said, "a couple of their back-room boys are trying to make sense of some troublesome facts." He opened his folder and glanced at a page of notes. "When Volin defected he had two equities to peddle—Charlotte Mills, whom Volin was going to handle in New York, and Clyde Pickett. Mills was hit a few days before Moscow knew Volin had deserted, and her apartment was burglarized. As Mike Grogan points out, the most plausible reason for two such high-risk stunts in New York would be to protect an even more important source than Mills. Moscow can only have assumed that Mills had become a threat to Slocombe. As far as Moscow is concerned, the Mills case is closed."

Castle stopped to fiddle with his glasses and assess his audience. "Because their files show that Volin was in on Pickett's recruitment in Prague, Moscow must have assumed that Volin would shop Pickett as well. But when Pickett remained in place and as productive as ever, Moscow decided they had nothing to gain by dropping contact or even warning him. They were right, and Pickett soldiered along until last week. By now Moscow probably knows Pickett is dead, and might even have learned he was a suicide. This will suggest either that Volin approached Pickett and attempted to blackmail him, or that Volin belatedly sold him to us. Either way, the Pickett chapter is closed.

"Volin had one bit of merchandise that Moscow does not know he had—Alizadeh. But as of now, I see no reason to think Moscow arranged for his recall to Tehran. As far as Moscow knows, Alizadeh is in good shape."

"All the necessary phone taps are in place," Brooks said. "Given time, we can start surveillance, begin searches of Slocombe's office—government property, after all—and perhaps even sneak a peek into his residence."

"*Forget* having the time," Trosper said. "If we don't move now, Alizadeh will make his own decision. Whatever choice he makes, he's permanently out of touch with Slocombe."

"If Moscow puts Slocombe on ice until they sort it all out," said Grogan, "the most we'll be able to do is question him and he's surely smart enough to tell us to get stuffed. When that happens, all the State Department can do is isolate him in a tame job until he decides to retire and write his memoirs."

"Unless he freaks out and tries to run," Brooks suggested cheerfully.

Mayo scowled and said, "Unless, as has been known to happen in such a case, there's a leak, and the press latches onto it."

"So it's three days?" Whyte peered around the office.

The FBI delegation nodded in unison.

"Perhaps less," said Castle.

Trosper took a deep breath before saying, "Maybe Doc Trestle could buy us enough time to sort this out, maybe come up with something that will force a meet with Slocombe?"

Whyte glanced at Castle.

Castle nodded.

"Agreed," said Whyte.

43

NEW YORK

In the half-light of the safe house, Gholam Alizadeh appeared pale and drawn. "Karem Nabavi, our administrative guy, told me he wanted to postpone my leaving until they knew about my replacement. But it didn't get approved. Now we're supposed to leave on the Saturday flight." He shrugged. "Our stuff gets moved out on Friday."

"But that's just three days," Grogan said.

"Time enough for me to make a decision and get away," Alizadeh said with a glance at Trosper.

"Get away where?" Grogan asked.

"I've done nothing wrong, I still have choices—work something out with you, return to Tehran, or go to Moscow."

"But you agreed to stay here as long as possible, at least until another meeting with Adam," Grogan said.

"Don't you understand I can't stay at the mission now that they've told me we're to leave on Saturday?" Alizadeh turned to Trosper. The other day you offered me asylum. Okay, I accept, we stay here, I do what you want, and you give us some money to start life over again. But I can't stay on at the mission after they've told me I'm leaving this week . . ."

Trosper pulled his chair closer to Alizadeh. "Does the mission have a doctor here?"

"Sure, Doctor Hasan, an old guy. He left Iran for medical school here and never went home. He's been in New York ever since he got citizenship and a license . . ."

"If you get sick, could he tell the mission that you're not well enough to travel for a while?"

"I guess so," Alizadeh said. "But I don't see how I could fool him . . ."

"We have someone who can help," Trosper said. "He can tell you about the symptoms that would make it impossible for you to travel for a few days."

"Old Hasan is no fool," Alizadeh said. "I'm not sure I could convince him that I'm sick enough to postpone my leaving."

"Why don't you talk to our man about it?"

Alizadeh shrugged. "Okay, why not?"

"Just as a precaution," Trosper said, "I brought him along tonight. He's just down the hall . . ."

Grogan got up. "I'll call him."

Although the Firm had its own medical staff, "Doc" Trestle had taken his degrees in biochemistry. As a chemist, he was completely separated from the medical staff, and had no ethical problems with the occasional special demands which might conflict with the Hippocratic oath.

Trestle stepped into the room. Brown suit, light tan shirt, olive-drab knit necktie, chocolate-brown lisle socks, and dark suede shoes. Trosper could not remember ever having seen Trestle in anything but brown.

"Now," Trestle said as he pulled a thick maduro cigar from his breast pocket, "just what's the problem?"

"Our friend," Trosper said with a gesture toward Alizadeh, "is being forced to make a rather long flight. Because we can't be sure about his reception, it's in our mutual interest that he postpone the trip for at least a few days, perhaps two weeks or more."

"I see." Trestle busied himself lighting the cigar.

"Although he's healthy, a sudden and obvious sickness might convince his local doctor that he's too much under the weather to travel right now."

Trestle blew a cloud of smoke across the coffee table and turned to Alizadeh. "Is your physician trustworthy and scrupulous, or will he take your word for being sick?"

"Oh, no," Alizadeh said quickly. "He won't take anyone's word for anything at all . . ."

Trestle shook his head. "What about your health? Any chronic medical problems—asthma, heart irregularity, ulcers, kidneys, liver? Any sort of digestive bothers I might be able to work on?"

"Nothing at all," said Alizadeh, embarrassed by his good health.

"Is your doctor aggressive—one of those dedicated TV-type medics who'll keep probing until he comes up with a textbook diagnosis? Or will he do what most of the medical crowd does—prescribe a couple of pills and wait to see how things work out?"

"I don't know . . ."

Trestle opened a shabby attaché case and began to sort through an array of small bottles. Puffs of cigar smoke floated to the ceiling like tribal signals. He turned to Trosper. "We need a set of symptoms that are difficult to diagnose. Symptoms that cover a dozen sicknesses, some serious, others more like the flu, but all possibly contagious, at the least infectious. That means we have to supply our friend's doctor with a set of clues—fever, stomach cramps, a touch of diarrhea, severe headache, maybe even muscle spasms—that point to a variety of likely medical problems. Depending on how your doctor reacts to his first examination, we might have to provide a few more clues—something suggesting a serious kidney problem might work."

Trestle paused to draw deeply on his cigar. "The Legionnaires' version of pneumonia has a good publicity value these days, but if the local doc thought he recognized it, he might think it was acute." He waved his hands to blow away the bank of smoke and said, "The right virus might give us a useful range of symptoms. If not, we can always fall back, maybe hint at a possible meningitis."

Trosper nodded. "That all sounds fine, but along with keeping our friend from traveling, let's be damn sure he doesn't get slapped right into hospital."

"Of course, of course," said Trestle impatiently. "Because I know exactly what caused the symptoms, I have a tremendous advantage over any local practitioner." He turned to Alizadeh. "If your doctor gets too upset, I can erase most of the symptoms with a few simple antidotes."

Trosper faced Alizadeh. "How does that sound to you?"

"No problem," said Alizadeh, "as long as you have the cure pills right at hand."

"Then we're all agreed?"

"The sooner the better," said Alizadeh.

Grogan's smile was enigmatic.

Trestle selected two small vials from his case and held them to the light. "I want your wife to take this, it's a prophylactic, just so she won't catch any of your symptoms." He stopped to study each vial. "As you can see, there's less than a teaspoon of liquid. Neither the dose itself nor the prophylactic has any color. Both are absolutely tasteless."

"When should we take it?" Alizadeh asked.

"Eight hours before you want the symptoms to appear," said Trestle.

"That means around midnight," Trosper said.

"Perfect," said Alizadeh.

Trestle pulled a fountain pen from his pocket and prepared to label the vials. "There's just one thing I suppose I should mention." He glanced quickly at Trosper.

"Yes?"

"In order to produce the symptoms you want, I'm afraid there's no way around the fact that the patient will *feel* as if he's actually contracted one or two of the sicknesses that cause the symptoms."

Trosper's eyes closed as he took a deep breath and slowly exhaled. He could not tell whether the muffled groan came from Grogan or the prospective patient.

"You mean I'll actually be sick?" said Alizadeh, his voice choked.

"Not *sick*, exactly," Doc Trestle said. "Think of it more as a slight case of poisoning . . ."

Grogan's lips barely moved as he muttered, "That last bit's not very helpful, Doc."

"And remember, I'll have all the antidotes right here in my case," Trestle said.

"You're absolutely crazy people," Alizadeh cried. "I can't knock myself down just at the time everything's at stake . . ."

Trestle took a blue label from his case. "This will go on the vial for your wife—put the potion in her coffee or orange juice, anything at all. It will immunize her so she doesn't contract any of your . . . er . . . symptoms."

"Not possible," said Alizadeh as he dabbed at the sweat on his collar.

Trestle took a red label from his bag. "This will go on the potion that produces the symptoms. Make no mistake about it. Blue for your wife, red for the symptoms."

Alizadeh's eyes widened. "What would happen if my wife takes the dose, would she have symptoms?"

Trestle looked up. "She would have the symptoms just as I've described them."

Alizadeh turned to Trosper. "That's the answer—if she can't travel, neither can I. I'll have my wits with me, and the doctor will say that we must stay here until she can make the trip."

"What about it?" Trosper asked Trestle.

Trestle glanced thoughtfully at Alizadeh. "It's all right with me. If she's in good health, there'll be no problem."

"She's in perfect health, stronger than me, no problems at all," Alizadeh said quickly. "Besides, she doesn't have to know anything about it. She'll think she's really sick and will be completely convincing."

Trosper glanced at Grogan. "Okay?"

Grogan shrugged.

Trestle picked up the vials, checked them against a notebook in his attaché case, and pasted on the labels. "Blue for immunization, red for symptoms—don't forget now."

Doc Trestle was the first to leave. Alizadeh followed ten minutes later.

Trosper handed a drink to Grogan. "Did you get the same impression I did?"

Grogan looked puzzled. "You mean, like the Doc wasn't much impressed when your friend decided his wife should take the fall?"

"That's the bad news, the good news is that I think Doc Trestle switched the labels . . ."

Grogan stared at Trosper. "You know, I'd really hate to get mixed up with you crazy bastards if something important was at stake."

44

NEW YORK

"If Doc Trestle's almanac is right, we ought to know by now just who got the 'symptoms,' " Grogan said.

"Alizadeh said he'd call at noon," Trosper said. "He's only half an hour late."

"Maybe he got confused," Grogan said. "If he drank both the red and the blue potions, he may have croaked—internal combustion."

"I can call him at his apartment," Widgery said. "I've got the number and we have a code—if he can remember it."

"We're not going to do anything until three o'clock," Trosper said.

"Good," said Grogan. "I've always had trouble getting through the first fifty pages of Henry James. It's just my good luck that the only thing to read in this whole damned safe house is Widge's copy of *The Wings of the Dove*."

"Clac," said Trosper. "Not safe house."

• • •

Widgery answered the telephone. "Hello . . ."

Trosper picked up the monitor and glanced at his watch. Two-fifteen.

A woman's whisper: "Mr. Lynch, please."

"I'm Lynch," Widgery said.

"Mr. Alizadeh wants something, please."

"Very good," Widgery said. "Put him on . . ."

"Mr. Alizadeh can't speak, he's too sick. Throwing up, stomach pains, fever, leg aches. Our doctor very worried."

"Who is speaking?"

"I am calling for Mr. Alizadeh, please. I am Mr. Alizadeh's wife and so I am to speak to his friend Mr. Lynch."

"This *is* Lynch, what do you want?"

"Mr. Alizadeh wants to see you and your friend right away. He says come here and bring blue bottles."

"Bring what?"

"Some blue bottles medicine. Mr. Alizadeh's doctor never heard of it."

Widgery turned to Trosper.

"Half an hour," Trosper said.

The varnished furniture supplied by the Iranian mission reminded Trosper of a motel room, and clashed with the samovar, a stack of large cushions, and a small rolled rug. A handsomely framed picture of the prophet Mohammed hung over an empty bookcase, and on the far wall a large portrait of Khomeini testified to Alizadeh's presumed enthusiasm for the revolution. An open box with a baseball glove, scuffed roller blades, and a New York Giants' sweatshirt were the only signs of a child. The packed luggage ranged along the side of the living room was evidence of the Alizadeh family's projected departure.

Mrs. Alizadeh, her hair covered with a tightly tied white scarf, clutched her black smock, and beckoned Trosper and Grogan across the living room and into a bedroom. "He's been very sick," she said. "A high fever, and pains. I hope you brought the medicine."

Trosper nodded as she opened the door to the bedroom. Alizadeh lay propped against two pillows, his dark complexion mottled with patches of gray. He eased himself into a sitting position. "Did you bring the medicine?"

Trosper pulled an unmarked bottle of pills from his pocket. "Take two of these every four hours, drink plenty of liquids—water, tea, juice, ginger ale, no coffee. Stay in bed."

"That's all?" Alizadeh exclaimed. "I'm in hell, and that's all you have for me?"

"It was decent of you to take the wrong stuff just to spare your wife," said Grogan with a comforting smile.

Alizadeh groaned and gobbled two pills.

"Keep taking the pills, and stay in bed until you feel normal . . ."

Doc Trestle's only prescription was unmarked aspirin, plenty of liquids, and bed rest. "A guy like that has never felt normal," he said. "He'll continue to imagine symptoms and stay in bed until he gets too bored to keep feeling sorry for himself. Put the aspirin in an unmarked bottle, but for Christ's sake don't tell him what it is or he'll never get up."

Alizadeh groaned as he pulled himself higher on the pillows.

"Has Dr. Hasan canceled your flight back?"

"Of course he has, I can't travel like this . . ."

"Then we can count on your being here for several more days?" Grogan asked.

The telephone rang and Mrs. Alizadeh hurried into the living room to pick it up. "He's too sick, he can't come to the phone," she whispered. There was a pause before she said, "Yes, I'm sure he cannot get out of bed . . ." Another pause. "Moment please, I will go tell him . . ." From the door of the bedroom Mrs. Alizadeh spoke softly in Persian. Alizadeh shook his head and waved his hand dismissively until his wife made a clear reference to "Mr. Wright." He looked anxiously at Trosper and Grogan, said something in Persian to his wife, and picked up the extension phone beside the bed. "Alizadeh," he said, his voice barely audible.

"Mr. Wright asked me to talk to you," the caller said.

"I don't know any Mr. Wright . . ."

Trosper stepped to the bedroom door and took the other phone from Mrs. Alizadeh.

"Yes you do . . . *Mr. Wright*. He's fallen sick. He asked me to telephone you to say he's sick."

"I'm the one who's sick . . ."

"You're sick too?"

"Yes . . ."

"Can you tell me about it on the telephone?"

"I have fever, headache, stomach cramps, throwing up, and—"

"You mean, you're *really* sick?"

"Yes, I'm *really* sick." Alizadeh shook his head in disbelief. "Who are you anyway?"

"Like I said, I'm a friend of Mr. Wright. He asked me to call you and to say that he's sick. He's too sick to see you. He's so sick that he has to go home to get better . . ."

"I see," said Alizadeh. "What you mean is, he's sick in a different way?"

"Yes, damn it, he's sick in another way. It's important that you don't try to see him or call. You and your family might catch what's wrong with him. Do you understand?"

"I think so," Alizadeh said.

"If you believe you might get sick the way Mr. Wright is, you should think about going home to get better."

"I am home," Alizadeh said weakly. "I'm home in bed, sick . . ."

"I mean you should go all the way *back* home . . ."

"*Which* home?"

"I think you must go home where Mr. Wright is going. It will be more healthy there—good doctors. Do you understand?"

"I think so . . ."

"Do you remember the travel agency plans?"

"*What* plans?"

"I mean the plans for if you had to make a sudden trip home—where Mr. Wright has gone?"

"I think so . . . I have it all written down."

"Then you have everything you need to make a trip right away?"

"I think so . . . Except for money," he added quickly.

"Okay, you'll get a letter tomorrow with some money to help with your travel plans . . ."

Alizadeh groaned loudly, and whispered, "But don't forget there are three of us."

"I know that, but are you sure that you understand everything?"

"I think so . . ."

"Just remember this—Mr. Wright is very sick. He will not see you again. It is important that you not try to reach him until you are both home again."

"I understand everything, but . . ."

"I have to go now."

"But . . ."

"Goodbye, and have a nice trip."

Trosper handed the phone to Mrs. Alizadeh and turned to Grogan. "Did you get any of that?"

"I think so," said Grogan, aping Alizadeh's accent. "The jig's up and everyone is bugging out?"

"That about covers it," said Trosper.

45

WASHINGTON, D.C.

Whyte glanced at his watch as Trosper and Grogan made their way to the empty chairs at the foot of the long conference table. "I know it's almost ten," Whyte said, "and I'm sorry to have dragged you both down here after your long day in New York. It's just that our FBI colleagues and we agree that there isn't much time left."

Charlie Mayo and Roger Brooks nodded agreement.

Castle peered over his half-glasses along the table to Trosper and smiled politely. "At least you got to enjoy a snack on the plane—was it chicken or couldn't you tell?"

"To get things started," Whyte said, with an irritated glance at Castle, "do we agree that the SVR has reason to believe that their creature Slocombe is in trouble?"

Without looking up, Castle said, "Yes."

Charlie Mayo cleared his throat. "That's the FBI's position, and if there's any doubt about it, we have some further information on Boris Danilov, second secretary at the Russian mission to the U.N., the fellow Alizadeh picked out of the mug book as Mr. Wright. Danilov left Kennedy Airport for Moscow last night. We're to understand that he left for a routine consultation in Moscow."

"Danilov has diplomatic immunity, but Moscow whisked him out all the same," Castle said. "They're running scared."

"This confirms what Alizadeh was told on the telephone this afternoon," Grogan added.

"Are we still certain that there isn't enough evidence to bring Slocombe to trial?" Whyte was touching all bases.

Brooks shook his head. "Not unless you can jolt him into a plea bargain . . ."

"Not a chance," said Trosper.

"Two questions," said Castle. "Did the SVR arrange for Alizadeh's recall to Tehran, or has it come as a surprise to them?"

"It was a surprise to the New York *rezidency*," said Grogan. "If Moscow had been behind it, they would have alerted New York."

"Second, has Slocombe been warned that he may be in trouble?"

"Right now Moscow is trying to decide if this is a real emergency," Trosper said. "They'll not tell Slocombe he's looking at life in prison if they can avoid it. The only lead to Slocombe is Alizadeh, and they've ordered him back to Moscow rather than risk VEVAK thumping a confession out of him."

"Moscow may also figure that Alizadeh's only a one-thump prisoner," Grogan said. "One thump and he's changed sides."

"The moment Moscow learns Alizadeh has jumped," Castle said, "they'll have no choice but to offer Slocombe escape and asylum . . ."

Trosper shook his head. "That may frighten Slocombe, but he's got too much of a bump on himself even to consider spending his sunset years in some Kuibychev suburb. He'll have no trouble convincing himself there's no way we can prove a case against him."

Whyte turned to Mayo. "What about his finances?"

"We've found ample money," Mayo said, "but no trace of anything like the cash Comrade Ames was tossing around. Slocombe's just bought an expensive boat, but it's financed through the State Department credit union."

"Slocombe is bright enough not to pay for a boat with cash he carries around in a shopping bag with a GUM Moscow logo on it," Trosper said.

"I've kept State informed of our investigation from the moment we identified Slocombe," Mayo said. "The Secretary has tabled the ambassadorial nomination and will take no action until he hears from us. Then, all things being equal, State Department security officers will confront Slocombe. If he doesn't admit to any malfeasance, they'll lift his diplomatic passport and put him on administrative leave. At that point, we'll begin surveillance." Mayo nodded to Whyte before saying, "An open surveillance tends to convince suspects that we mean business—even more so if the press gets wind of it."

"That gives us two days before Slocombe is warned," Whyte said.

"Thirty-six hours maximum," Castle grumbled.

Trosper turned to Grogan and whispered, "Just about now, I'd like someone to say that the Firm's role is finished."

"You think they dragged us down here to say thanks and goodbye?" Grogan muttered.

Whyte glanced at Mayo, who turned to Castle, who nodded to Whyte, who addressed himself to Grogan and Trosper.

"You may have wondered why we asked you both to fly down tonight when we might have used the red phone," Whyte said.

"Oh, yes," said Trosper.

Grogan smiled uneasily.

"While we still have a few hours to ourselves," Whyte said, "it seems to Charlie Mayo and me that there's something to be said for someone having a little chat, an *unofficial and deniable* chat, with Minister Counselor Slocombe before his Russian friends tip him off and he has a chance to get all iron-assed about everything."

"It can't work," Trosper said.

Grogan's expression froze.

"An unofficial approach, taking him by surprise, is all we have left," Mayo said. "Someone has to do it."

Trosper shook his head. "Not I."

"I'd like you to do it," said Whyte. "There's nobody else."

46

NEW YORK

Slocombe looked up as Trosper came in, and waved casually toward a chair. "Give me a moment with these cables," he said as he continued to read.

No greeting. No notice taken of or apology made for the time spent waiting in the outer office. And no clue as to whether Slocombe had been warned of trouble.

Trosper glanced at the table near his chair and stretched to tug a copy of *Sports Illustrated* from beneath *Foreign Affairs* still snug in its uncut plastic mailing wrapper. He began to flip the pages, ignoring the text and pausing only to study the more spectacular photographs. He knew the first few moments with Slocombe would be critical, and on the Metroliner that morning had tried to fashion a plan for the interview. But nothing worked. It was hopeless to plan without knowing what Slocombe knew. The diplomat held every advantage.

Trosper would not look up from his reading until Slocombe moved to open their interview.

"Your magazine of choice came with this temporary office," said Slocombe as he laid his reading glasses on the desk and squinted in Trosper's direction. He dropped the sheaf of cables into the out-tray and said, "Because I'm treading water with our delegation to this year's General Assembly, I have to take potluck on everything, even office space." He paused to make a minute adjustment in the position of a discreet gold cuff link. "These annual U.N. meetings are tiresome enough, but every new administration pays off their big campaign contributors—undertakers who call themselves obsequy counselors, and used-car merchants who say they're on sabbatical from the motor trade—by making them honorary delegates to the General Assembly. There's no end to the damnable cheapening of our diplomatic service."

Slocombe's sigh was comprehensive, intended to encompass grievances he had not troubled to mention. "Meanwhile, the confirmation of my promotion and assignment rests at the bottom of some clot's 'urgent action' box."

Trosper turned another page before tossing *Sports Illustrated* onto the table and watching as it slipped to the floor.

"And why, pray, are *you* still scuffling around in New York?"

"I've been asked to bring a security situation to your attention," Trosper said.

Slocombe's eyebrows lifted. "A security *situation*?"

"A security *problem*, if you prefer."

"And what might that be?"

"It concerns your relationship with the former U.S.S.R. and the government of Russia." Gently, gently, Trosper counseled himself, just the tip of the knife.

"What on earth are you talking about?" Slocombe spoke without the slightest change of expression or hint of body language.

He had not been warned. No one had that much self-control.

"To be blunt, I've been sent here because there's reason to believe that you're involved in a clandestine and illegal contact with the Russian intelligence services and had the same relationship with the former Soviet intelligence."

Slocombe shoved himself back from his desk. His chest heaved as he took a deep breath. He stared at Trosper, exhaled slowly, and pulled himself forward, his expression stiff with the trace of an incredulous smile. "Is this some lunatic, cold warrior speculation of *yours*? Of yours *personally*?"

"It's well beyond speculation at this point."

"By what authority do you come into this building and to my office with this incredible nonsense?"

"No authority whatsoever," Trosper said, "and that's precisely why I'm here. I've been asked to discuss this with you informally because when the hard-ass authorities take over, and the media arrive, the legal proceedings will come under a public scrutiny so intense that you can't even imagine it."

To slow the pace of the confrontation, Trosper picked *Sports Illustrated* from the floor and tucked it carefully under *Foreign Affairs* on the side table. "The idea is that we might come to an arrangement that will help satisfy the authorities and perhaps lead to minimizing the damage and fallout that are otherwise a dead certainty."

"I should order you the hell out of this office this minute."

Trosper shook his head. "I really don't recommend that."

"You and your confederates are out of your bloody, scheming little minds . . ." Slocombe's face flushed, his fingers drummed along the edge of his desk. "You damned well forget who I am and what I represent."

"I know exactly who you are and what you represent, and I can assure you our data are firm and will be convincing in court . . ."

"In *court*?" Slocombe lowered his voice.

"Where else?"

"What a monstrous world we live in," said Slocombe, "when an acquaintance, even a colleague of sorts, can come into one's office spewing threats without so much as a preamble of any kind, or even an explanation." As Slocombe struggled to control his breathing, the color leached from his face.

"Preambles be damned—you know exactly what kind of a world it is," Trosper said. "And people like you have helped make it what it is." It was like the diplomat, Trosper realized, to appear as concerned about the form of the confrontation as he was to the threat to his career.

"In the time you have left in my office, you'd best come to the point," Slocombe said. "I'll deal with the legal and bureaucratic aspects of your slander in due course."

Trosper shook his head. "I still don't think you understand. You're *known* to have maintained a clandestine relationship with Soviet and

Russian intelligence. I've been sent here to make you an offer *because* I have no official status, and am quite anonymous."

"What offer could you possibly be authorized to make to me?"

"In return for the truth of how you became involved, and exactly what has happened since, you may have a chance to avoid an international scandal, personal disgrace, and almost certainly prison." Trosper waited before saying, "I'm speaking bluntly because everything you have, and everything you pretend to be, is at stake, and there's no room for any misunderstanding."

Blotches of color were coming back to Slocombe's face. "Now that I've heard what you were sent to say, I want you the hell out of my sight. I suggest you tell your various superiors that your allegations are absolute crap and exactly what I might expect from you and those you represent."

Trosper shook his head. "Neither of us has time for that nonsense. You're just as aware as I am of the back-room data and files that have been leaking out of Moscow for the past three years—enough of it has your name on it to make a solid case against you." He waited, hoping to observe Slocombe's reaction. There was none. "And that was before we began making independent observations of our own."

"Just what in the name of Christ do you think would make me even consider any relationship that went beyond the propriety and the documented accounts of my work with the stable of sources and contacts I've spent my career developing?"

Trosper shook his head. "Now, you *really* surprise me. In wartime the motivation for what you so delicately call a 'relationship' is pretty damned simple. People with the guts to fight do so for political and moral reasons."

"By God, Alan, that really is a joke," Slocombe said. "The idea of you and your crowd talking about political and moral values turns my stomach."

"In peacetime, money is the great persuader," Trosper said. "After that there's the need for recognition, even secret recognition, and revenge against a boss or system that doesn't recognize one's worth. For some, there's the adventure of it, for a few, love can be a factor. In your case, I'd say that vanity, a simple, overpowering vanity, played on by someone at least as bright as you, is at the root of it." He moved closer to the desk before saying, "Along with that, your Moscow admirers will have lubricated your conscience with a comfortable secret income."

"Are you actually suggesting that because I've been sidetracked a few times by incompetent political appointees and cretinous civil servants, I leaped into the arms of the first secret policeman who bought me lunch?"

"Not at all," Trosper said. "I'm certain their cultivation of your ego went on for some time."

"Ha . . ."

"And it would have taken even more time before anything tangible could safely have been introduced."

"Tangible?"

"Not necessarily *entirely* tangible," Trosper said. "It probably began with them feeding you background on negotiating or policy positions, perhaps a pending change in the leadership—the sort of data you could use in a brilliant forecast of Moscow policy. And to thicken the broth, I imagine occasional perceptive glimpses into the inner workings of other powers—Germany, Japan, the U.K.—were dropped on your plate. That's the sort of thing your Moscow friends buy from your opposite numbers in those countries."

With his elbows on the desk, his slim fingers forming a temple, Slocombe's eyes never left Trosper. "I find you and your crowd contemptible, as well as quite mad."

"The more 'tangible' aspect comes later in cases like yours," Trosper said. "After the insights and news tips, and a few discreet but pricey gifts, cuff links, a watch, perhaps something in the white gold that most of us confuse with stainless steel, the veil is dropped. A regular stipend, 'A little something to help with expenses,' your worldly friend might have said—'The least we can do for you, what with all the time you're spending putting things in focus for us.'"

"You're talking rot," Slocombe said slowly.

"I'm talking about a really admiring friend," Trosper said. "A senior man, sophisticated, cultivated, gifted in diplomacy, a fellow who understands and appreciates your real stature as no one ever has. That's the kind of friend Moscow has produced for a couple dozen people quite like you."

"Your imagination is sicker than I might have dreamed," Slocombe said.

"Perhaps I haven't gone far enough afield," Trosper said. "On occasion, Moscow has turned up one of those personal eccentricities, something that used to be a bit too indelicate for polite society. Among themselves they call it a hook."

"It's you and your kind who are sick and corrupt . . ."

"I mean an eccentricity that the victim may never even have admitted to himself, something that the right provocation and perhaps a drop or two of a drug might uncork," Trosper said. "The Moscow people have a nose for those things—like what they call 'discipline,' ladies with whips, chains, weird masks, and all the other fittings. Or maybe some youngster, who needs the comfort of an older and experienced man of the world?" Trosper smiled. "Surely some of this must sound familiar?"

"You absolutely disgust me . . ." Slocombe pushed himself back from the desk, farther away from Trosper.

"On a more practical level," Trosper said, "I have to remind you that photographs of you meeting a courier really do exist . . ."

"Photographs?" Slocombe said loudly. "You taunt me with photographs? Come to my study, I'll show *you* photographs. Pictures of me with a score of people, three presidents, prime ministers, foreign ministers, the Pope—and a dozen Russians, *all* of them spies for what I know. Bring along your secret police friends, they should be able to sort them all out."

"Not only photographs," Trosper said softly. "Copies of documents—some with as high classifications as I've ever seen . . ."

Slocombe flinched. Pay dirt.

"Mills!" he cried, his voice choked as if he were struggling to prevent shouting. "It's that little bitch Mills who's behind this." He slammed both hands onto the top of his desk. "That miserable whore actually had the nerve to come to me with stupid lies about having been blackmailed. I ordered her to go to security at once. She promised, but by the time I got back to New York, I heard she'd been killed in Central Park, probably by some of her rough trade. The security people eventually came around to me with the whole story, dirty pictures and all. Now you have the brass to come into my office and try to identify me with the documents that little tramp was peddling like tabloid newspapers."

"You never mentioned that she'd told you about blackmail and passing documents."

"Of course I did, to our security people, either here or in Washington . . . I can't remember precisely, but it's none of your business anyway."

"There's no record of it," Trosper said.

"I'm afraid I can't help that," said Slocombe.

Trosper remained silent. He would not follow up, and was happy to leave the detailed interrogation to others. He kept his unblinking attention focused on Slocombe and waited for the diplomat to break the silence.

"Can you really think," Slocombe said, "that I would behave quite as stupidly as you've suggested?"

Trosper shrugged. Silence was provocation enough.

"Do you have any idea who I am, or the role my family has played in this country? Of the contributions we've made, dating back to the Revolution and before? Do you know that my son graduated cum laude from Georgetown last year, and that my daughter is following right along at Vassar? Do you think I'd risk their well-being for something as sordid as penny-ante spying?"

Trosper remained silent.

"Do you think I'd sell myself and my position in life for a few thousand dollars a month? Can you imagine that even the opportunity to have one's views considered at the highest level by a world power would be important enough for me to risk all of that?"

"I think the answer is yes to every one of your questions," Trosper said. "On a more operational level, there are the photographs of you exchanging airline bags with a courier."

"Just tell your chums to bring charges, and we'll see where the truth lies."

"The truth is that Charlotte Mills was murdered just to save your rotten carcass . . ."

Slocombe got up from behind his desk. "I've had enough of this. You'll leave now, or I'll call security and have you dragged out."

Trosper got up and stepped toward the door.

"You'll understand," Slocombe said, "that you've given me no choice but to report this to the Secretary personally . . ."

"If that's your decision, you're making a serious mistake . . ."

"Now, I'm all but late for a Security Council meeting," Slocombe said, "and that's not my custom."

"You've got twenty-four hours to reconsider the most important decision you're ever going to make," Trosper said. And unless you confess, he thought, no one will lay a glove on you.

47

MOSCOW

"Which brings us to the impending loss of our friend in New York," Koltsov said. The chief of operations hunched forward and peered intently across his broad desk. It irritated him that the section chief had left the most important part of the afternoon briefing to the last.

"True name Harrison Slocombe," Igor Maisky said. "An old family, aristocratic."

"Has the problem been resolved?"

Maisky shook his head. "Slocombe is badly shaken, but he refused our offer of asylum, a comfortable retirement here, and, in time, public honors . . ." His voice faded as he attempted to determine whether the chief of operations was clearing his throat or laughing.

"And all that with a straight face?" Koltsov slouched over his desk, his hand shading his eyes from the desk lamp.

"I don't understand," Maisky said. "Boris Ragulin has been *Rezi-*

dent in New York for three years. He knows the Americans perfectly. I'm sure he stressed the absolute need to avoid arrest and to escape along the route we recommended."

"How are Slocombe's nerves?" Koltsov said. He had worked with Ragulin in Paris and did not need to be reminded that his friend was one of the most able officers in the service.

"Please?"

"Is Slocombe likely to break in fucking pieces?"

"Oh, no," said Maisky. "Solid as a rock, as I said, something of an aristocrat."

"Where's Navrov?" Maisky's assumption that he could discuss Slocombe without the presence of the man who had recruited and nurtured him also annoyed Koltsov.

"He's retired, but—"

"I know he's bloody retired . . ."

" . . . but I have him standing by."

Before Maisky could jump to his feet, Koltsov barked a command into the intercom. The door swung ajar and a slim, gray-haired man stepped into the office.

Koltsov strode across the room to clasp Navrov in a bear hug. "Still the same shit-face spy, who actually liked playing diplomat? Now a businessman?" He released his grip, but held Navrov at arms' length. "Foreign clothes . . . polished shoes . . . there's no end to you." After a second embrace, he shoved Navrov toward a chair beside the desk.

"In case you've forgotten, I'm a *retired* diplomat—now chief executive officer of Moscow Help," Navrov said with a broad smile. "We make introductions, provide researchers, interpreters, secretaries, and an occasional bit of fluff to our visiting benefactors, the representatives of the Western business world." He tossed a business card onto the desk.

Koltsov glanced at the card and turned to Maisky. "Fluff," he said, shaking his head. "In my day we used a different vocabulary." He bent to pull a bottle from the cabinet behind his desk. "A drop of vodka for my prosperous old comrade who probably prefers scotch whiskey?"

Navrov nodded.

"You know that your protégé Slocombe is facedown in the crap?" Koltsov growled.

"I've been told."

"So what happened?"

"Someone must have talked," Navrov said. "Slocombe had four, maybe five years left. A real loss."

"What will they do, the Americans?"

Maisky started to speak but Koltsov waved him to silence.

Navrov emptied his glass. "There'll be no double game, the Americans don't think that way any more. In their hearts they're Puritans, on the job they act like cops. Slocombe sinned, therefore he must be punished. They won't even think about playing him back against us."

"So what will they do?"

"Everything has to be legal," Navrov said. "First they question him. He'll deny everything. The FBI and the State security people will continue to investigate—they're good at that. They'll interrogate again, stiffer questions, more pressure. But they're not so good at that. Slocombe will admit nothing. The investigation won't reveal anything—perhaps a little extra money. Then comes a hearing. If Slocombe offers to retire, the board will accept rather than risk a trial they can't afford to lose. They will deny him a pension—one way the sinner can pay for his broken faith."

"What does that leave *us*?"

Navrov shook his head. "Not much. Slocombe's wife has the social position that Slocombe has always claimed to have. He was a clever boy, but not such a clever man. He spent so much time pretending to be something he was not that he wasted the promise he had. Without our support, he'd never have got as far as he did. Now he'll find that American women of his wife's class don't like to support men. Her friends, who always saw through his pretensions, will begin to piss on him. Soon, everything that means anything to him will have disappeared . . ."

Koltsov moved to refill the glasses. "And then?"

Navrov shrugged. "Slocombe might be tempted to try to make a deal—admit that he may have talked a bit too freely to some of his Russian contacts, and swap this for a resignation without prejudice.

This would let him keep his pension. A good interrogator might be able to work that into a full confession."

Koltsov shook his head. "Aside from the names of two or three of his handlers, and what he can remember having sold to us, the most Slocombe's got to give them is an inkling of just how much else we know, and maybe make them start wondering how we learned it. The Americans won't make a public show of a confession like that."

"There's another possibility," Navrov said with a faint smile. "'*The Slocombe Story*. A respected, senior State Department official—behind the mask, a villainous spy.'" Navrov parodied the pompous voice of a TV newsman. "That's the sort of thing one of your hungry pensioners might sell to the foreign press."

"Possible," Koltsov said heavily. "Always possible . . ."

"A scandal like that will puff up like a case of gangrene, with congressmen threatening to screw our economy just to convince their voters that they're democracy's only defense against the evil empire."

"To be avoided," Koltsov said, glowering at Maisky. "The days when I could stuff blown operations down the boss's throat are over. I used to say, 'If you want top-secret data, you'd better be prepared for an occasional screwup.'" He reached for the vodka bottle. "In the old days an occasional shot of publicity could be a plus. It showed outsiders what we can produce and convinced potential collaborators that our pockets are deep. In those days we could live with a little scandal. Now that we're beggars, we've no choice but to avoid offending our benefactors. So, we keep our ass off the front pages."

"There's no question—Slocombe can't be allowed to go public," Navrov said.

"So what do we do?" said Maisky.

"It's not what *you* do, it's what Slocombe does . . ."

"And what's that?" Maisky said with a smug glance at Koltsov.

"Slocombe dies, maybe suicide," Navrov said. "Once he's dead, even if there's a leak, the scandal will be minimal. The 'useful idiots'—as Vladimir Ilyich used to call them—will rally around and say that the right-wing press is kicking the corpse of a great American who can't fight back . . ."

"Do me a favor, Mr. Businessman, don't quote Lenin in this office . . ."

“Slocombe’s too much of an egotist,” Maisky said. “They don’t commit suicide . . .”

“It’s not his decision to make, you ass,” said Koltsov.

“Talk to Ragulin,” Navrov said. “He’ll be able to recommend something specific . . .”

48

WASHINGTON, D.C.

The State Department security representatives thanked Duff Whyte, shook hands, and filed out. Charlie Mayo, Mike Grogan, and Trosper remained behind. The pocket recorder Trosper had carried was scratchy with static and had little base response, but the fidelity was adequate and they had played the tape twice.

From his chair at the side, Castle looked up from his notepad. “This is depressing enough without you people looking as if you were huddled around a burned-out campfire.”

“The fire may be out,” Grogan said, “but it sure was burning when Alan hit that creep. In ten minutes, the ashes of everything Minister Counselor Slocombe treasured went straight down the toilet.”

Whyte leaned back, his arms folded across his chest, and turned to Trosper. “You were right, of course. It was out of the question for anyone as self-centered as Slocombe to crumble the first time he’s challenged.”

“All the same, Slocombe will have big trouble explaining his admission that Charlotte Mills had come to him with a confession,” Grogan said.

Castle shook his head. “All Slocombe has to admit is that he made Mills promise to tell everything to the security staff, that he didn’t necessarily believe her story but was out of the country and couldn't pursue it. By the time Volin disclosed his version, Slocombe will say that he had nothing to add to it, and admit that he was so embarrassed by having failed to follow up on his instruction to Mills that he mistakenly chose not to bring it up."

"I suppose we ought to be glad you're not his lawyer," Grogan said, his face flushed.

"After that," Castle said, "Slocombe will stonewall every allegation." He snapped his leather folder shut. "I gather that State security will begin with Slocombe tomorrow?"

"Everything has been cleared at the top," Mayo said.

Grogan turned to Trosper. "It's really rotten luck that Mills felt she had to go to a stuffed shirt like Slocombe for help."

"She was desperate," Trosper said. "She'd been living with this every hour of her life."

"Compare her with that money-grubbing little creep, Pickett," Grogan said.

"I have," said Trosper.

49

KEY WEST

Navrov glanced along the narrow sidewalk toward the fence edging the cemetery a hundred yards ahead. Nothing of interest. He had moved idly from the kickshaw commercialism of Duval Street as if uncertain of finding his way along the hushed streets and shuttered houses of the old town. Now he slowed his gait to check the automobiles along each side of Frances Street. Nothing.

"The truth now, did you recognize me at once?" Navrov lowered himself into the sling chair beneath the lazy overhead fan in the living room.

"I was surprised, but of course I knew you," Broom said.

"When you hesitated, it reminded me how much I must have changed since Vienna."

"For God's sake, we were twenty years younger then. You were not nearly so well turned out, but much more intense."

"To lost intensity." Navrov raised his glass. "If that's not too grim a toast . . ."

"It will do," Broom said as she took a sip of wine.

"An old friend insisted I come here," Navrov said. "Until I read the file, I had no idea it was you I would be meeting . . ."

"I'm glad to have been such a secret. There were times when I worried about it . . ."

"I've been out of things for four years—completely divorced from the work," he said. "Now that free enterprise rages, I've got my own business. This is the first time I've so much as been asked anything, let alone to do a favor."

"Rather an odd sort of favor, isn't it?"

"It's the last thing I would have expected—to find you living alone, and as isolated as this."

"I've not always been *all* that alone," she said. "But you must have a wife and family?"

Navrov laughed. "It's a story you've heard a dozen times—Anna enjoyed the privileges, but resented everything else about my work. She left six weeks after I quit the service. The last I knew she was Mrs. General someone or other." He took a sip of wine. "Most of our people tolerate the lonely spells, but it's hard to think of you living in this backwater."

"As you put it, perhaps there's not as much intensity . . ."

Navrov swirled the wine in his glass and glanced speculatively at the paintings stacked against the wall. "The years have been good to you . . ."

"You're being kind . . ."

"Not at all," he said. "It's a simple fact, you're just as I imagined you would be . . ."

"As much as I might like it," she said, "I'm not the person you remember. I'm not even me anymore."

Navrov shook his head. "You make a mistake thinking too much about the work. We've been through a sort of war, but it's not as serious as all that . . ."

"Perhaps not for you."

"Not for any of us," he said. "After a few months on your own you'll begin to see it in perspective."

"I've almost always been on my own."

"Not in Vienna," he said.

She shook her head. "I was terribly frightened in Vienna . . ."

"It didn't show," he said. "I've always thought of you as one of those great cats in Africa, a leopard, quite beautiful, solitary and quick and very strong."

"That wasn't me at all. I accepted Leonid Ilyich's offer because it was like a pardon for what had been done to my family. Even though I thought Brezhnev was an old fool, I have to admit that he made me feel as if I were part of something, like the way people must have felt during the war. I actually looked forward to joining the fight, but like a conscripted soldier I was frightened at leaving home, terrified at the thought of the work, praying that it would all be over before I was called to do anything . . ."

"How long did we have," Navrov said. "Six weeks?"

"Longer," she said, smiling. "Two months, a little more. You were very good for me. So confident, even then so sure that everything at home was on the verge of change, and that our miserable work would help turn things around."

"I never thought I'd see you again," he said abruptly.

Broom stiffened and turned away. "Why are you here now—because *they* think I need special attention if I'm to do something more?"

Navrov pulled himself from the canvas chair. "I wouldn't have come if that was the reason. Surely, you know that."

"Then why? I was promised it would be finished after that thing in the park." Tears spilled down Broom's cheeks. "Why did they have to do that?"

"You mean the woman?" Navrov said, taking her in his arms.

"Of course I mean the woman . . . What could she have done?"

"It was to protect something," he said, touching her hair as if to shape it. "Something they thought they couldn't afford to lose."

He stepped back, and for a moment held her at arms' length. "Surely you know I'm not here to defend the new crowd. Their words would stick to my tongue, but you must have some idea how serious things are at home. The government stumbles from crisis to crisis. The army is almost paralyzed but always a threat to the leadership. It will be five years, maybe ten, before we can live without the life support the West is doling out. Moscow, and particularly the service, can't tolerate any more scandal."

"So why are you—of all people—here?"

"Koltsov sent me, he's at the top now, one of the last of the old crowd still on duty."

Broom freed herself and pulled a handkerchief from her pocket.

"He knows as well as you do that your work—the work of your section—was just a leftover from the old days, when everything was an extension of the war. Even then it was a lunatic defense of the motherland that no one was going to attack. Your work was just an echo of the preposterous battle groups that old Sudoplatov was ordered to get together in the fifties."

"So . . ."

"The whole activity was closed down when the committee was briefed on your last task. Everything like that is officially forbidden."

"Officially forbidden?" Broom said. "But you're here . . ."

"You know how it is, always one more thing to be done."

"If it's over, if it's forbidden, that's good enough for me," Broom said. "There can't be one more thing."

"Koltsov is in trouble," Navrov said. "He has no choice but to cauterize what can become a serious leak and maybe a scandal . . ."

Broom shook her head. "You do yourself no credit, parroting talk like that."

"Koltsov's my friend," Navrov said. "He's a decent man, he does what he thinks best for the work, for the good of the country. I accepted his request in good faith, and before I had any idea you would be involved. He's always been fair with me. The least I can do is present his views."

"You've done that . . ."

"The only way it can be done . . ." Navrov paused, it was important to get this right. "It must be done, as my American business friends say, 'off the books'—behind the back of our administration. It will be done on Koltsov's own authority . . ."

"I won't help, and don't you try to involve me . . ."

"I have the plan and all the materials with me," he said. "Like you, the man's a sailor, every weekend. You can approach his boat pretending distress . . ."

"No . . . never again."

They talked until dark, when Navrov said, "Since learning you were here, I've thought of nothing else. Come to dinner, like old times."

While Broom changed, Navrov studied the paintings. "These are great," he called to her in the bedroom. "I had no idea . . . it's really good work. You have talent and must have worked like hell to produce all this."

In the morning as Broom made breakfast, Navrov said, "I've left the package on the table by the bed. The plan is clear, excellent photographs, good background on the area—everything you'll need, and money as well."

Broom turned away. "What will you do, stay in Moscow and get even richer?"

"I'm not rich," he said, "and I'm not going to stay in Russia. In a few more months I should have money enough to get out and to settle in a decent climate, as far away as I can get."

"So very much money?" she said.

"Enough to resettle, and keep me until I can start something new, something different from anything I've done before."

"In a decent climate?"

"Maybe Mexico," he said softly. "I'm told the light is very good there."

Broom smiled, and turned abruptly away.

"I'll not leave us like this," he said. "Where can I write?"

"You don't understand anything, you can't even know how I've changed . . ."

"Yes, I do . . ."

"I'm not the same . . ."

"Can I telephone?"

"Absolutely not . . ."

"Where can I write?"

Broom scribbled an address on a scrap of paper. "My gallery in New York. They will always know."

"Should I say, 'be careful'?"

Broom shook her head, kissed him quickly, and pushed the door open.

50

MOSCOW

"Well, Mr. Big Business, I see that you've been on an expensive holiday . . ." The chief of operations shoved his friend's expense accounting to the side of his desk. "You enjoyed yourself? Airplanes, hotels, expensive rented motorcar from Miami to Key West?"

"My travel had all the aspect of a business trip," Navrov said with a smile. "I remember the days when you talked about cover, called it mixing with the herd."

"But not for tossing funds like confetti . . ." He scribbled his signature on the accounts. "You've heard what happened with your friend Slocombe?"

"Maisky showed me the press clips."

"Ragulin used our private channel from New York to tell me your report was inconclusive . . ."

"I told him that I found Broom, briefed her, and gave her the materials . . ."

"But Ragulin said you weren't sure?"

"Broom's older now, she's been outside for a long time," Navrov said. "After a while some of the discipline weakens, the intensity fails, you know that."

Koltsov leaned back, his fingers laced behind his head. "I know all about discipline and what you call intensity. Do you know what's happening to some of my people?"

"Do you really want me to guess?"

Koltsov frowned and shook his head. "I'll tell you what's happening," he said softly. "Too many of them are disappearing, dropping contact, refusing to accept meetings. Some move away from the only address we have for them." He leaned forward, elbows on the desk.

"They read the press," Navrov said. "They know what's going on here and how the life is."

"They're Russian—most of them anyway—and they should damned well help."

"Cling to that," Navrov said.

Koltsov peered intently across his desk. "A week ago I saw old Petrov—Pyotr Ivanovich, your boss in Vienna when you were still a puppy."

"I liked him . . ."

"It was a big dinner, vodka like rain, but he asked about you."

"I'm surprised . . ."

"He even asked about an agent you had handled for him in Vienna. He said he always suspected that you'd gone beyond your responsibility for her welfare . . ."

"I was young then . . ."

"You might have told me when I briefed you on the Key West assignment," Koltsov said.

"I should have, but I wasn't sure it was the same person, and I really wanted to make the trip."

"Did she tell you what she was going to do?"

"No, she didn't."

"Ragulin has tried the alternate and emergency contact arrangements, so far nothing," Koltsov said.

"I'm not surprised," Navrov said. "She's been outside so long that she sees us and the homeland through foreign eyes. She's loyal, but perhaps no longer quite as useful."

"I've got an entire apparat to reposition, even rebuild, and I sit here with an old friend who deals with me like a merchant in Ukraine."

"There was no cheating, my cover was perfect, your instructions were followed to the letter."

"I have to report to the committee," Koltsov said. "What am I to say?" Koltsov's voice had lowered to a growl.

"I don't know," Navrov said.

"And that's what you think I should report?"

"If I were you that's exactly what I would say," Navrov said. "And then I'd recommend that since the beast is dead, we should stop kicking it."

"And get on with new business?"

"That's what I plan to do," Navrov said.

51

LONDON

Trosper motioned Widgery to help himself to a drink and stepped across the study to pick up the telephone.

"Did I wake you up?"

"Mike Grogan!" Trosper exclaimed. "What a pleasant surprise."

"Why such a surprise?"

"When people call from the States the first question is always, what time is it."

"What time *is* it?"

"The next question is about the weather . . ."

"I assume it's raining," Grogan said. "Have you heard the news?"

"Nothing interesting enough to make you pop for a phone call . . ."

"It's about your friend, the recently retired minister counselor . . ."

"Widge is here, taking a couple of weeks to catch his breath. He's told me about our friend's stonewalling the panel and retiring."

Grogan laughed. "As usual, you guys are a few days behind the press. My news is fresh, three paragraphs in yesterday's *Washington Post* and one in the *New York Times*," Grogan said. "Your friend Slocombe is dead . . ."

"I'll be damned," Trosper exclaimed.

"He was alone on his boat, and left his mooring Saturday morning," Grogan said. "When he wasn't back by Monday, the marina called the Coast Guard. They found the boat, but it was another thirty-six hours before they spotted the body."

"That really is news," Trosper said. He paused before saying, "Was he in a life jacket?"

"No, just one of those yellow rain things you guys wear . . ."

"What about the weather?"

"A late afternoon squall Saturday, but he might have croaked before that."

"He'd done a lot of sailing," Trosper said, "but in heavy weather one misstep can put you over the side." Trosper passed the news to Widgery before saying, "What was the actual cause of death?"

"According to the local medical examiner, it was natural causes," Grogan said.

"*What* natural causes?"

"Probably a heart attack," Grogan said. "But even with an immediate autopsy it's sometimes difficult to distinguish between a heart attack and stroke. It was three days before the autopsy was done."

"Any medical history?"

"It should sound familiar to you," Grogan said. "He'd been told to cut down cholesterol, get more exercise, and cheer up."

"Thanks . . ."

"It seems he was under some stress, retirement, wife problems, depression."

"Have the . . . er . . . experts been consulted?"

"The medical examiner thought it was open and shut," Grogan said. "But as soon as we heard about it, our guys tested the data against everything in the book. As of now, there's not a scrap of evidence that shows anything but natural causes."

"Is that your opinion?"

"I dunno." Grogan's sigh was clearly audible. "I've been here all night going over the files. We're having a meeting this morning—your people, State, and my crowd. As far as I can see, there's almost a consensus—a heart attack brought on by stress of the past few weeks, the effort of handling the boat alone, maybe intensified by the shock of falling overboard."

"*Almost* a consensus?"

"As of yesterday, your friend Castle had abstained . . ."

Widgery waited until Trosper had put the phone down before taking a sip of his drink. "Well, was it a hit?"

"Mike said there's no evidence of anything but a heart attack, and the boat was found offshore."

"If it was a hit, it would be rigged to look like a heart attack, and there is a motive," Widgery said. "Don't you think Moscow will find the death quite timely?"

Trosper shook his head. "On the face of it, it's hard to see what Slocombe might have known that would justify the very high risk of hitting him."

Widgery waited before saying, "Not so long ago you told me that any time I caught myself saying 'on the face of it' I should check the evidence again and dig deeper."

"Thou art sharper than a serpent's tooth," Trosper murmured.

"Won't Castle say the motive could only be to protect something worth the risk?"

"I suppose he has said that, and for all I know he may be right," Trosper said.

"Mills murdered, Pickett a suicide, and now Slocombe deep-sixed—we can't let them get away with that."

Trosper pushed himself back in the chair. "You know, Widge, we've been in a war. It's taken almost fifty years, but the war is over. If we had anything to work on, I'd agree that we should run it to the ground, punish the guilty. As it is, we've destroyed two sources Moscow can scarcely afford to lose."

"Until they trapped her, Mills was innocent . . ."

"If she'd played by the rules and asked for help, she'd be alive . . ."

"It's not good enough . . ." Widgery shook his head in frustration.

Trosper finished his drink. "If it's revenge you want, I can't help."

"It's not right," Widgery said.

"The war is over," Trosper said. "We've got to move ahead. We can let this dog sleep."